Orville Dewey, Mary Elizabeth Dewey

Autobiography and Letters of Orville Dewey, E. D.

Orville Dewey, Mary Elizabeth Dewey

Autobiography and Letters of Orville Dewey, E. D.

ISBN/EAN: 9783337072865

Printed in Europe, USA, Canada, Australia, Japan

Cover: Foto ©Raphael Reischuk / pixelio.de

More available books at **www.hansebooks.com**

AUTOBIOGRAPHY

AND

LETTERS

OF

ORVILLE DEWEY, D.D.

Edited by his Daughter,

MARY E. DEWEY.

———◆———

BOSTON:

ROBERTS BROTHERS.

1883.

CONTENTS.

INTRODUCTORY.

IT is about twenty-five years since, at my earnest desire, my father began to write some of the memories of his own life, of the friends whom he loved, and of the noteworthy people he had known; and it is by the help of these autobiographical papers, and of selections from his letters, that I am enabled to attempt a memoir of him. I should like to remind the elder generation and inform the younger of some things in the life of a man who was once a foremost figure in the world from which he had been so long withdrawn that his death was hardly felt beyond the circle of his personal friends. It was like the fall of an aged tree in the vast forests of his native hills, when the deep thunder of the crash is heard afar, and a new opening is made towards heaven for those who stand near, but when to the general eye there is no change in the rich woodland that clothes the mountain side.

But forty years ago, when his church in New York was crowded morning and evening, and eager multitudes hung upon his lips for the very bread of life, and when he entered also with spirit and power into the social, philanthropic, and artistic life of that great city; or nearly sixty years ago, when he carried to the beautiful town and exquisite society of New Bedford an influx of spiritual life and a depth of religious thought which worked like new yeast in the well-prepared Quaker mind, — then, had he been taken away, men would have felt that a tower of strength had fallen, and those especially, who in his parish visits had felt the sustaining comfort of his singular tenderness and sympathy in affliction, and of his counsel in distress, would have mourned for him not only as for a brother, but also a chief. Now, almost all of his own generation have passed away. Here and there one remains, to listen with interest to a fresh account of persons and things once familiar; while the story will find its chief audience among those who remember Mr. Dewey[1] as among the lights of their own youth. Those also who love the study of

---

[1] My father always preferred this simple title to the more formal " Dr.," and in his own family and among his most intimate friends he was Mr. Dewey to the last. He was, of course, gratified by the complimentary intention of Harvard University in bestowing the degree of D.D. upon him in 1839, but he never felt that his acquisitions in learning entitled him to it.

human nature may follow with pleasure the development of a New England boy, with a character of great strength, simplicity, reverence, and
honesty, with scanty opportunities for culture,
and heavily handicapped in his earlier running
by both poverty and Calvinism, but possessed
from the first by the love of truth and knowledge,
and by a generous sympathy which made him
long to impart whatever treasures he obtained.
To trace the growth of such a life to a high point
of usefulness and power, to see it unspoiled by
honor and admiration, and to watch its retirement, under the pressure of nervous disease, from
active service, while never losing its concern for
the public good, its quickness of personal sympathy, nor its interest in the solution of the
mightiest problems of humanity, cannot be an
altogether unprofitable use of time to the reader,
while to the writer it is a work of consecration.
He who was at once like a son and brother to my
father, he who should have crowned a forty-years'
friendship · by the fulfilment of this pious task,
and who would have done it with a stronger
and a steadier hand than mine,—BELLOWS,—was
called first from that " fair companionship," while
still in the unbroken exercise of the varied and remarkable powers which made his life one of such

large use, blessing, and pleasure to the world.
None could make his place good to his elder
friend, whose approaching death was visibly has-
tened by grief for the loss of the constant sympathy and devotion which had faithfully cheered
his declining years.   Many and beautiful tributes
were laid upon my father's tomb by those whom
he left here.   Why should we not hope that that
of Bellows was in the form of greeting?

ST. DAVID'S, *July*, 1883.

AUTOBIOGRAPHY.

I WAS born in Sheffield, Mass., on the 28th of March, 1794. My grandparents, Stephen Dewey and Aaron Root, were among the early settlers of the town, and the houses they built — the one of brick, and the other of wood — still stand. They came from Westfield, about forty miles distant from Sheffield, on horseback, through the woods; there were no roads then.

We have always had a tradition in our family that the male branch is of Welsh origin. When I visited Wales in 1832, I remember being struck with the resemblance I saw in the girls and young women about me to my sisters, and I mentioned it when writing home. On going up to London, I became acquainted with a gentleman, who, writing a note one day to a friend of mine and speaking of me, said: " I spell the name after the Welsh fashion, — Dewi; I don't know how he spells it." On inquiring of this gentleman, — and he referred me also to biographical dictionaries, — I found that our name had an origin of unsuspected dignity, not to say sanctity, being no other than that of Saint David, the patron saint of Wales, which is shortened and changed in the speech of the common people into Dewi.[1]

Every one tries, I suppose, to penetrate as far back as he can into his childhood, back towards his infancy, towards that mysterious and shadowy line behind which lies his unremembered existence. Besides the usual life of a child in the country, — running foot-races with my brother Chandler, building brick ovens to bake apples in the side-hill opposite the house, and the steeds of willow sticks cut there, — and beyond the unvarying gentleness of my mother and the peremptory decision and playfulness at the same time of my father, — his slightest word was enough to hush the wildest tumult among us children, and yet he was usually gay and humorous in his family, — besides and beyond this, I remember nothing till the first event in my early childhood, and that was acting in a play. It was performed in the church, as part of a school exhibition. The stage was laid upon the pews, and the audience seated in the gallery. I must have been about five years old then, and I acted the part of a little son. I remember feeling, then and afterwards, very queer and shamefaced about my histrionic papa and mamma. It is striking to observe, not only how early, but how powerfully, imagination

---

[1] This was the reason why Mr. Dewey gave to the country home which he inherited from his father the name of " St. David's," by which it is known to his family and friends. — M. E. D.

is developed in our childhood. For some time after, I regarded those imaginary parents as sustaining a peculiar relation, not only to me, but to one another; I thought they were in love, if not to be married. But they never were married, nor ever thought of it, I suppose. All that drama was wrought out in the bosom of a child. It is worth noticing, too, the freedom with sacred things, of those days, approaching to the old *fêtes* and mysteries in the church. We are apt to think of the Puritan times as all rigor and strictness. And yet here, nearly sixty years ago, was a play acted in the meeting-house: the church turned into a theatre. And I remember my mother's telling me that when she was a girl her father carried her on a pillion to the raising of a church in Pittsfield; and the occasion was celebrated by a ball in the evening. Now, all dancing is proscribed by the church there as a sinful amusement.

The next thing that I remember, as an event in my childhood, was the funeral of General Ashley, one of our townsmen, who had served as colonel, I think, in the War of the Revolution. I was then in my sixth year. It was a military funeral; and the procession, for a long distance, filled the wide street. The music, the solemn march, the bier borne in the midst, the crowd!— it seemed to me as if the whole world was at a funeral. The remains of Bonaparte borne to the Invalides amidst the crowds of Paris could not,

I suppose, at a later day, have affected me like
that spectacle. I do not certainly know whether
I heard the sermon on the occasion by the pastor,
the Rev. Ephraim Judson; but at any rate it was
so represented to me that it always seems as if
I had heard it, especially the apostrophe to the
remains that rested beneath that dark pall in the
aisle. " General Ashley ! " he said, and repeated,
" General Ashley ! — he hears not."

To the recollections of my childhood this old
pastor presents a very distinct, and I may say
somewhat portentous, figure, — tall, large-limbed,
pale, ghostly almost, with slow movement and
hollow tone, with eyes dreamy, and kindly, I
believe, but spectral to me, — coming into the
house with a heavy, deliberate, and solemn step,
making me feel as if the very chairs and tables
were conscious of his presence and did him reverence; and when he stretched out his long, bony
arm and said, " Come here, child ! " I felt something as if a spiritualized ogre had invited me.
Nevertheless, he was a man, I believe, of a very
affectionate and tender nature; indeed, I afterwards came to think so; but at that time, and
up to the age of twelve, it is a strict truth that I
did not regard Mr. Judson as properly a human
being, — as a *man* at all. If he had descended
from the planet Jupiter, he could not have been
a bit more preternatural and strange to me. Indeed, I well remember the occasion when the
idea of his proper humanity first flashed upon

my mind. It was when I saw him, one day, beat the old black horse he always rode, — apparently in a passion like any other man. The old black horse — large, fat, heavy, lazy — figures in my mind almost as distinctly as its master; and if, as it came down the street, its head were turned aside towards the school-house, as indicating the rider's intent to visit us, I remember that the school was thrown into as much commotion as if an armed spectre were coming down the road. Our awe of him was extreme; yet he loved to be pleasant with us. He would say, — examining the school was always a part of his object, — " How much is five times seven?" — "Thirty-five," was the ready answer. " Well," replied the old man, " *saying* so don't *make* it so ; " a very significant challenge, which we were ill able to meet. At the close of his visit he always gave an exact and minute account of the Crucifixion, — I think always, and in the same terms. It was a mere appeal to physical sympathy, awful, but not winning. When he stood before us, and, lifting his hands almost to the ceiling, said, " And so they reared him up ! " it seemed as if he described the catastrophe of the world, not its redemption. Indeed, Mr. Judson appeared to think that anything drawn from the Bible was good, whether he made any moral application of it or not. I have heard him preach a whole sermon, giving the most precise and detailed description of the building of the Tabernacle, without one word of com-

ment, inference, or instruction.   But he was a
good and kindly man; and when, as I was going
to college at the age of eighteen, he laid his hand
upon my head, and gave me, with solemn form
and tender accent, his blessing, I felt awed and
impressed, as I imagine the Hebrew youth may
have felt under a patriarch's benediction.

With such an example and teacher of religion
before me, whose goodness I did not know, and
whose strangeness and preternatural ·character
only I felt; and indeed with all the ideas I got of
religion, whether from Sunday-keeping or cate-
chising, my early impressions on that subject
could not be happy or winning.   I remember the
time when I really feared that if I went out into
the fields to walk on Sunday, bears would come
down from the mountain and catch me.   At a
later day, but still in my childhood, I recollect a
book-pedler's coming to our house, and when he
opened his pack, that I selected from a pile of
story-books, Bunyan's " Grace Abounding to the
Chief of Sinners."   Religion had a sort of horrible attraction for me, but nothing could exceed
its gloominess.   I remember looking down from
the gallery at church upon the celebration of the
Lord's Supper, and pitying the persons engaged in
it more than any people in the world, — I thought
they were so unhappy.   I had heard of " the unpardonable sin," and well do I recollect lying in
my bed — a mere child — and having thoughts
and words injected into my mind, which I im-

agined were that sin, and shuddering, and trembling, and saying aloud, "No, no, no; I do not, — I will not." It is the grand mystery of Providence that what is divinest and most beautiful should be suffered to be so painfully, and, as it must seem at first view, so injuriously misconstrued. But what is universal, must be a law; and what is law, must be right, — must have good reasons for it. And certainly so it is. Varying as the ages vary, yet the experience of the individual is but a picture of the universal mind, — of the world's mind. The steps are the same, — ignorance, fear, superstition, implicit faith; then doubt, questioning, struggling, long and anxious reasoning; then, at the end, light, more or less, as the case may be. Can it, in the nature of things, be otherwise? The fear of death, for instance, which I had, which all children have, — can childhood escape it? Far onward and upward must be the victory over that fear. And the fear of God, and, indeed, the whole idea of religion, — must it not, in like manner, necessarily be imperfect? And are imperfection and error peculiar to our religious conceptions? What mistaken ideas has the child of a man, of his parent when correcting him, or of some distinguished stranger! They are scarcely less erroneous than his ideas of God. What mistaken notions of life, of the world, — the great, gay, garish world, all full of cloud-castles, ships laden with gold, pleasures endless and entrancing! What mistaken impressions about nature; about the material world upon which childhood has alighted, and of which it must necessarily be ignorant; about clouds and storms and tempests; and of the heavens above, sun and moon and stars! I remember well when the fable of the Happy Valley in Rasselas was a reality to me; when I thought the sun rose and set for us alone, and how I pitied the glorious orb, as it sunk behind the western mountain, to think that it must pass through a sort of Hades, through a dark underworld, to come up in the east again. It is a curious fact, that the Egyptians in the morning of the world had the same ideas. Shall I blame Providence for this? Could it be otherwise? If earthly things are so mistaken, is it strange that heavenly things are? And especially shall I call in question this order of things, — this order, whether of men's or of the world's progress, — when I see that it is not only inevitable, the necessary allotment for an experimenting and improving nature, which is human nature, but when I see too that each stage of progress has its own special advantages; that "everything is beautiful in its time;" that fears, superstitions, errors, quicken imagination and restrain passion as truly as doubts, reasonings, strugglings, strengthen the judgment, mature the moral nature, and lead to light?

I am dilating upon all this too much, perhaps. I let my pen run. Sitting down here in the blessed country home, with nothing else in particular just now to do, at the age of sixty-three, I have time and am disposed to look back into my early life and to reason upon it; and although I have nothing uncommon to relate, yet what pertains to *me* has its own interest and significance, just as if no other being had ever existed, and therefore I set down my experience and my reflections simply as they present themselves to me.

In casting back my eyes upon this earliest period of my life, there are some things which I recall, which may amuse my grandchildren, if they should ever be inclined to look over these pages, and some of which they may find curious, as things of a bygone time.

Children now know nothing of what " 'Lection" was in those days,—the annual period, that is, when the newly elected State government came in. It was in the last week in May. How eager were we boys to have the corn planted before that time ! The playing could not be had till the work was done. The sports and the entertainments were very simple. Running about the village street, hither and thither, without much aim ; stands erected for the sale of gingerbread and beer, — home-made beer, concocted of sassafras roots and wintergreen leaves, etc.; games of ball, not base-ball, as now is the fashion, yet with wickets, — this was about all, except that at the end there was always horse-racing.

Having witnessed this exciting sport in my

boyhood, without any suspicion of its being wrong, and seen it abroad in later days, in respectable company, I was led, very innocently, when I was a clergyman in New York, into what was thought a great misdemeanor. I was invited by some gentlemen, and went with them, to the races on Long Island. I met on the boat, as we were returning, a parishioner of mine, who expressed great surprise, and even a kind of horror, when I told him what I had been to see. He could not conceal that he thought it very bad that I should have been there; and I suppose it was. But that was not the worst of it. Some person had then recently heard me preach a sermon in which I said, that, in thesis, I had rather undertake to defend Infidelity than Calvinism. In extreme anger thereat, he wrote a letter to some newspaper, in which, after stating what I had said, he added, " And this clergyman was lately seen at the races!" It went far and wide, you may be sure. I saw it in newspapers from all parts of the country; yet some of my friends, while laughing at me, held it to be only a proof of my simplicity.

There were worse things than sports in our public gatherings; even street fights, — pugilistic fights, hand to hand. I have seen men thus engage, and that in bloody encounter, knocking one another down, and the fallen man stamped upon by his adversary. The people gathered round, not to interfere, but to see them fight it out.

Such a spectacle has not been witnessed in Sheffield, I think, for half a century.

But as to sports and entertainments in general, there were more of them in those days than now. We had more holidays, more games in the street, — of ball-playing, of quoits, of running, leaping, and wrestling. The militia musters, now done away with, gave many occasions for them. Every year we had one or two great squirrel-hunts, ended by a supper, paid for by the losing side, that is, by the side shooting the fewest. Almost every season we had a dancing-school. Singing-schools, too, there were every winter. There was also a small band of music in the village, and serenades were not uncommon. We boys used to give them on the flute to our favorites. But when the band came to serenade us, I shall never forget the commotion it made in the house, and the delight we had in it. We children were immediately up in a wild hurry of pleasure, and my father always went out to welcome the performers, and to bring them into the house and give them such entertainment as he could provide.

The school-days of my childhood I remember with nothing but pleasure. I must have been a dull boy, I suppose, in some respects, for I never got into scrapes, never played truant, and was never, that I can remember, punished for anything. The instruction was simple enough. Special stress was laid upon spelling, and I am inclined to think that every one of my fellow-pupils learned to spell more correctly than some gentlemen and ladies do in our days.

Our teachers were always men in winter and women in summer. I remember some of the men very well, but one of them especially. What pupil of his could ever forget Asa Day, — the most extraordinary figure that ever I saw, a perfect *chunk* of a man? He could not have been five feet high, but with thews and sinews to make up for the defect in height, and a head big enough for a giant. He might have sat for Scott's " Black Dwarf; " yet he was not ill-looking, rather handsome in the face. And I think I never saw a face that could express such energy, passion, and wrath, as his. Indeed, his whole frame was instinct with energy. I see him now, as he marched by our house in the early morning, with quick, short step, to make the school-room fire ; and a roaring one it was, in a large open fireplace; for he did everything about the school. In fact, he took possession of school, schoolhouse, and district too, for that matter, as if it were a military post; with the difference, that he was to fight, not enemies without, but within, — to beat down insubordination and enforce obedience. And his anger, when roused, was the most remarkable thing. It stands before me now, through all my life, as the one picture of a man in a fury. But if he frightened us children, he taught us too, and that thoroughly.

In general our teachers were held in great

reverence and affection. I remember especially
the pride with which I once went in a chaise, when
I was about ten, to New Marlborough, to fetch the
schoolma'am. No courtier, waiting upon a prin-
cess, could have been prouder or more respect-
ful than I was.

To turn, for a moment, to a different scene, and
to much humbler persons, that pass and repass in
the *camera obscura* of my early recollections. The
only Irishman that was in Sheffield, I think, in
those days, lived in my father's family for several
years as a hired man, — Richard; I knew him by
no other name then, and recall him by no other
now, — the tallest and best-formed "exile of
Erin" that I have ever seen; prodigiously strong,
yet always gentle in manner and speech to us
children; with the full brogue, and every way
marked in my view, and set apart from every one
around him, — "a stranger in a strange land."
The only thing besides, that I distinctly remember
of him, was the point he made every Christmas
of getting in the "Yule-log," a huge log which
he had doubtless been saving out in chopping
the wood-pile, big enough for a yoke of oxen to
draw, and which he placed with a kind of ceremony and respect in the great kitchen fireplace.
With our absurd New England Puritan ways, —
yet naturally derived from the times of the English Commonwealth, when any observance of
Christmas was made penal and punished with

imprisonment, — I am not sure that we should have known anything of Christmas, but for Richard's Yule-log.

There was another class of persons who were frequently engaged to do day's work on the farm, — that of the colored people. Some of them had been slaves here in Sheffield. They were virtually emancipated by our State Bill of Rights, passed in 1783. The first of them that sought freedom under it, and the first, it is said, that obtained it in New England, was a female slave of General Ashley, and her advocate in the case was Mr. Sedgwick, afterwards Judge Sedgwick, who was then a lawyer in Sheffield.

There were several of the men that stand out as pretty marked individualities in my memory, — Peter and Cæsar and Will and Darby; merry old fellows they seemed to be, — I see no laborers so cheerful and gay now, — and very faithful and efficient workers. Peter and his wife, Toah (so was she called), had belonged to my maternal grandfather, and were much about us, helping, or being helped, as the case might be. They both lived and died in their own cottage, pleasantly situated on the bank of Skenob Brook. They tilled their own garden, raised their own " sarse," kept their own cow; and I have heard one say that " Toah's garden had the finest damask roses in the world, and her house, and all around it, was the pink of neatness."

In taking leave of my childhood, I must say

that, so far as my experience goes, the ordinary poetic representations of the happiness of that period, as compared with after life, are not true, and I must doubt whether they ought to be true. I was as happy, I suppose, as most children. I had good health; I had companions and sports; the school was not a hardship to me, — I was always eager for it; I was never hardly dealt with by anybody; I was never once whipped in my life, that I can remember; but instead of looking back to childhood as the blissful period of my life, I find that I have been growing happier every year, up to this very time. I recollect in my youth times of moodiness and melancholy; but since I entered on the threshold of manly life, of married and parental life, all these have disappeared. I have had inward struggles enough, certainly, — struggles with doubt, with temptation, — sorrows and fears and strifes enough; but I think I have been gradually, though too slowly, gaining the victory over them. Truth, art, religion, — the true, the beautiful, the divine, — have constantly risen clearer and brighter before me; my family bonds have grown stronger, friends dearer, the world and nature fuller of goodness and beauty, and I have every day grown a happier man.

To take up again the thread of my story, I pass from childhood to my youth. My winters, up to the age of about sixteen, were given to school, — the common district-school, — and my summers, to assisting my father on the farm; after that, for a year or two, my whole time was devoted to preparing for college.   For this purpose I went first, for one year, to a school taught in Sheffield by Mr. William H. Maynard, afterwards an eminent lawyer and senator in the State of New York.   He came among us with the reputation of being a prodigy in knowledge; he was regarded as a kind of walking library; and this reputation, together with his ceaseless assiduity as a teacher, awakened among us boys an extraordinary ambition.   What we learned, and how we learned it, and how we lost it, might well be a caution to all other masters and pupils.   Besides going through Virgil and Cicero's Orations that year, and frequent composition and declamation, we were prepared, at the end of it, for the most thorough and minute examination in grammar, in Blair's Rhetoric, in the two large octavo volumes of Morse's Geography, — every fact committed to memory, every name of country, city, mountain, river, every boundary, population, length, breadth, degree of latitude, — and we could repeat, word for word, the Constitution of the United States. The consequence was, that we dropped all that load of knowledge, or rather burden upon the memory, at the very threshold of the school. Grammar I did study to some purpose that year, though never before.   I lost two years of my childhood, I think, upon that study, absurdly regarded as teaching children to speak the English language, instead of being considered as what it properly is, the philosophy of language, a science altogether beyond the reach of childhood.

Of the persons and circumstances that influenced my culture and character in youth, there are some that stand out very prominently in my recollection, and require mention in this account of myself.

My father, first of all, did all that he could for me. He sent me to college when he could ill afford it. But, what was more important as an influence, all along from my childhood it was evidently his highest desire and ambition for me that I should succeed in some professional career, I think that of a lawyer. I was fond of reading, — indeed, spent most of the evenings of my boyhood in that way, — and I soon observed that he was disposed to indulge me in my favorite pursuit. He would often send out my brothers, instead of me, upon errands or " chores," to save me from interruption. What he admired most, was eloquence; and I think he did more than Cicero's *De Oratore* to inspire me with a similar feeling. I well remember his having been to Albany once, and having heard Hamilton, and the unbounded admiration with which he spoke of him. I was but ten years old when Hamilton was stricken down; yet such was my interest in

him, and such my grief, that my schoolmates
asked me, "What is the matter?" I said,
"General Hamilton is dead." "But what is it?
Who is it?" they asked. I replied that he was a
great orator; but I believe that it was to them
much as if I had said that the elephant in a me-
nagerie had been killed. This early enthusiasm I
owed to my father. It influenced all my after
thoughts and aims, and was an impulse, though
it may have borne but little appropriate fruit.

For books to read, the old Sheffield Library
was my main resource. ,It consisted of about
two hundred volumes, — books of the good old
fashion, well printed, well bound in calf, and well
thumbed too. What a treasure was there for me!
I thought the mine could never be exhausted.
At least, it contained all that I wanted then, and
better reading, I think, than that which generally engages our youth nowadays, — the great
English classics in prose and verse, Addison and
Johnson and Milton and Shakespeare, histories,
travels, and a few novels. The most of these
books I read, some of them over and over, often
by torchlight, sitting on the floor (for we had a
rich bed of old pine-knots on the farm); and to this
library I owe more than to anything that helped
me in my boyhood. Why is it that all its volumes are scattered now? What is it that is
coming over our New England villages, that
looks like deterioration and running down? Is
our life going out of us to enrich the great West?

I remember the time when there were eminent men in Sheffield. Judge Sedgwick commenced the practice of the law here; and there were Esquire Lee, and John W. Hurlbut, and later, Charles Dewey, and a number of professional men besides, and several others who were not professional, but readers, and could quote Johnson and Pope and Shakespeare; my father himself could repeat the " Essay on Man," and whole books of the " Paradise Lost."

My model man was Charles Dewey, ten or twelve years older than myself. What attracted me to him was a singular union of strength and tenderness. Not that the last was readily or easily to be seen. There was not a bit of sunshine in it, — no commonplace amiableness. He wore no smiles upon his face. His complexion, his brow, were dark; his person, tall and spare; his bow had no suppleness in it, — it even lacked something of graceful courtesy, — rather stiff and stately; his walk was a kind of stride, very lofty, and did not say " By your leave," to the world. I remember that I very absurdly, though unconsciously, tried to imitate it. His character I do not think was a very well disciplined one at that time; he was, I believe, " a good hater," a dangerous opponent, yet withal he had immense self-command. On the whole, he was generally regarded chiefly as a man of penetrative intellect and sarcastic wit; but under all this I discerned a spirit so true, so delicate and tender, so touched with a profound and exquisite, though concealed, sensibility, that he won my admiration, respect, and affection in an equal degree. He removed early in life to practise the law in Indiana. We seldom meet; but though twenty years intervene, we meet as though we had parted but yesterday. He has been a Judge of the Supreme Court, and, I believe, the most eminent law authority in his adopted State; and he would doubtless have been sent to take part in the National Councils, but for an uncompromising sincerity and manliness in the expression of his political opinions, little calculated to win votes.

And now came the time for a distinct step forward, — a step leading into future life.

It was for some time a question in our family whether I should enter Charles Dewey's office in Sheffield as a student at law, or go to college. It was at length decided that I should go; and as Williams College was near us, and my cousin, Chester Dewey, was a professor there, that was the place chosen for me. I entered the Sophomore class in the third term, and graduated in 1814, in my twenty-first year.

Two events in my college life were of great moment to me, — the loss of sight, and the gain, if I may say so, of insight.

In my Junior year, my eyes, after an attack of measles, became so weak that I could not use them more than an hour in a day, and I was obliged to rely mainly upon others for the prosecution of my studies during the remainder of the college course. I hardly know now whether to be glad or sorry for this deprivation. But for this, I might have been a man of learning. I was certainly very fond of my studies, especially of the mathematics and chemistry. I mention it the rather, because the whole course and tendency of my mind has been in other directions. But Euclid's Geometry was the most interesting book to me in the college course; and next, Mrs. B.'s Chemistry: the first, because the intensest thinking is doubtless always the greatest possible intellectual enjoyment; and the second, because it opened to me my first glance into the wonders of nature. I remember the trembling pride with which, one day in the Junior year, I took the head of the class, while all the rest shrunk from it, to demonstrate some proposition in the last book of Euclid. At Commencement, when my class graduated, the highest part was assigned to me. " Pretty well for a blind boy," my father said, when I told him of it; it was all he said, though I knew that nothing in the world could have given him more pleasure. But if it was vanity then, or if it seem such now to mention it, I may be pardoned, perhaps, for it was the end of all vanity, effort, or pretension to be a learned man. I remember when I once told Channing of this, and said that but for the loss of sight I thought I should have devoted myself to the pursuits of learning, his

reply was, " You were made for something better." I do not know how that may be; but I think
that my deprivation, which lasted for some years,
was not altogether without benefit to myself. I was
thrown back upon my own mind, upon my own
resources, as I should never otherwise have been.
I was compelled to *think* — in such measure as I
am able — as I should not otherwise have done.
I was astonished to find how dependent I had
been upon books, not only for facts, but for the
very courses of reasoning.. To sit down solitary
and silent for hours, and to pursue a subject
through all the logical steps for myself, — to
mould the matter in my own mind without any
foreign aid, — was a new task for me. Ravignan,
the celebrated French preacher, has written a
little book on the Jesuit discipline and course of
studies, in which he says that the one or two
years of silence appointed to the pupil — absolute seclusion from society and from books too —
were the most delightful and profitable years of
his novitiate. I think I can understand how that
might be true in more ways than one. Madame
Guyon's direction for prayer — to pause upon
each petition till it is thoroughly understood and
felt — had great wisdom in it. We read too
much. For the last thirty years I have read as
much as I pleased, and probably more than was
good for me.

The disease in my eyes was in the optic nerve;
there was no external inflammation. Under the

best surgical advice I tried different methods of cure, — cupping, leeches, a thimbleful of lunar caustic on the back of the neck, applied by Dr. Warren, of Boston; and I remember spending that very evening at a party, while the caustic was burning. So hopeful was I of a cure, that the very pain was a pleasure. I said, "Bite, and welcome!" But it was all in vain. At length I met with a person whose eyes had been cured of the same disease, and who gave me this advice: "Every evening, immediately before going to bed, dash on water with your hands, from your wash-bowl, upon your closed eyes; let the water be of about the temperature of spring-water; apply it till there is some, but not severe, pain; say for half a minute; then, with a towel at hand, wipe the eyes dry before opening them, and rub the parts around smartly; after that do not read, or use your eyes in any way, or have a light in the room." I faithfully tried it, and in eight months I began to experience relief; in a year and a half I could read all day; in two years, all night. Let any one lose the use of his eyes for five years, to know what that means. Afterwards I neglected the practice, and my eyes grew weaker; resumed it, and they grew stronger.

The other event to which I have referred as occurring in my college life was of a far different character, and compared to which all this is nothing. It is lamentable that it ever should be an *event* in any human life. The sense of religion should be breathed into our childhood, into our youth, along with all its earliest and freshest inspirations; but it was not so with me. Religion had never been a delight to me before; now it became the highest. Doubtless the change in its form partook of the popular character usually attendant upon such changes at the time, but the form was not material. A new day rose upon me. It was as if another sun had risen into the sky; the heavens were indescribably brighter, and the earth fairer; and that day has gone on brightening to the present hour. I have known the other joys of life, I suppose, as much as most men; I have known art and beauty, music and gladness; I have known friendship and love and family ties; but it is certain that till we see GOD in the world — GOD in the bright and boundless universe — we never know the highest joy. It is far more than if one were translated to a world a thousand times fairer than this; for that supreme and central Light of Infinite Love and Wisdom, shining over this world and all worlds, alone can show us how noble and beautiful, how fair and glorious, they are. In saying this, I do not arrogate to myself any unusual virtue, nor forget my defects; these are not the matters now in question. Nor, least of all, do I forget the great Christian ministration of light and wisdom, of hope and help to us. But the one thing that is especially signalized in my experience is this, — the Infinite Goodness and Loveliness began to be revealed to me, and this made for me " a new heaven and a new earth."

The sense of religion comes to men under different aspects; that is, where it may be said to *come;* where it is not imbibed, as it ought to be, in early and unconscious childhood, like knowledge, like social affection, like the common wisdom of life. To some, it comes as the consoler of grief; to others, as the deliverer from terror and wrath. To me it came as filling an infinite void, as the supply of a boundless want, and ultimately as the enhancement of all joy. I had been somewhat sad and sombre in the secret moods of my mind, — read Kirke White and knew him by heart; communed with Young's " Night Thoughts," and with his prose writings also; and with all their bad taste and false ideas of religion, I think they awaken in the soul the sense of its greatness and its need. I nursed all this, something like a moody secret in my heart, with a kind of pride and sadness; I had indeed the full measure of the New England boy's reserve in my early experience, and did not care whether others understood me or not. And for a time something of all this flowed into my religion. I was among the strictest of my religious companions. I was constant to all our religious exercises, and endeavored to carry a sort of Carthusian silence into my Sundays. I even tried, absurdly enough, to pass that day without a smile upon my countenance. It was on the ascetic side only that I had any Calvinism in my religious views, for in doctrine I immediately took other ground. I maintained, among my companions, that whatever God commanded us to do or to be, that we had power to do and be. And I remember one day rather impertinently saying to a somewhat distinguished Calvinistic Doctor of Divinity: "You hold that sin is an infinite evil?" "Yes." "And that the atonement is infinite?" "Yes." "Suppose, then, that the first sinner comes to have his sins cancelled; will he not require the whole, and nothing will be left?" "Infinites! infinites!" he exclaimed; "we can't reason about infinites!"

In connection with the religious ideas and impressions of which I have been speaking, comes before me one of the most remarkable persons that I knew in my youth, Paul Dewey, — Uncle Paul, we always called him. He was my father's cousin, and married my mother's half-sister. His religion was marked by strong dissent from the prevailing views; indeed, he was commonly regarded as an infidel. But I never heard him express any disbelief of Christianity. It was against the Church construction of it, against the Orthodox creed, and the ways and methods of the religious people about him, that he was accustomed to speak, and that in no doubtful language. I was a good deal with him during the year before I went to college, for he taught me the mathematics ; and one day he said to me, " Orville, you are going to college, and you will be converted there." I said, "Uncle, how can you speak in that way to me?" "Nay," he replied, " I am perfectly serious; you will be converted, and when you are, write to me about it, for I shall believe what you say." When that happened which he predicted, — when something had taken place in my experience, of which neither he, nor I then, had any definite idea, — I wrote to him a long letter, in which I frankly and fully expressed all my feelings, and told him that what he had thus spoken of, whether idly or sincerely, had become to me the most serious reality. I learned from his family afterwards that my letter seemed to make a good deal of impression on him. He was true to what he had said; he did take my testimony into account, and from that time after, spoke with less warmth and bitterness upon such subjects. Doubtless his large sagacity saw an explanation of my experience, different from that which I then put upon it. But he saw that it was at least sincere, and respected it accordingly. Certainly it did not change his views of the religious ministrations of the Church. He declined them when they were offered to him upon his death-bed, saying plainly that he did not wish for them. He was cross with Church people even then, and said to one of them who called, as he thought obtrusively, to talk and pray with him, "Sir, I desire neither your conversation nor your prayers." All this while, it is to be remembered that he was a man, not only of

great sense, but of incorruptible integrity, of irre-
proachable habits, and of great tenderness in his
domestic relations. Whatever be the religious
judgments formed of such men, mine is one of
mingled respect and regret. It reminds me of an
anecdote related of old Dr. Bellamy, of Connecti-
cut, the celebrated Hopkinsian divine, who was
called into court to testify concerning one of his
parishioners, against whom it was sought to be
proved that he was a very irascible, violent, and
profane man ; and as this man was, in regard to
religion, what was called in those days "a great
opposer," it was expected that the Doctor's testimony would be very convincing and overwhelming. "Well," said Bellamy, " Mr. —— *is* a
rough, passionate, swearing man, — I am sorry to
say it; but I do believe," he said, hardly repress-
ing the tears that started, " that there is more
of the milk of human kindness in his heart than
in all my parish put together! "

I may observe, in passing, that I heard, in those
days, a great deal of dissent expressed from the
popular theology, beside my uncle's. I heard
it often from my father and his friends. It was
a frequent topic in our house, especially after a
sermon on the decrees, or election, or the sinner's
total inability to comply with the conditions on
which salvation was offered to him. The dislike
of these doctrines increased and spread here, till
it became a revolt of nearly half the town, I think,
against them; and thirty years ago a Liberal

society might have been built up in Sheffield, and ought to have been. I very well remember my father's coming home from the General Court,[1] of which he was a member, and expressing the warmest admiration of the preaching of Channing. The feeling, however, of hostility to the Orthodox faith, in his time, was limited to a few; but somebody in New York, who was acquainted with it, — I don't know who, — sent up some infidel books. One of them was lying about in our house, and I remember seeing my mother one day take it and put it into the fire. It was a pretty resolute act for one of the gentlest beings that I ever knew, and decisively showed where *she* stood. She did not sympathize with my father in his views of religion, but meekly, and I well remember how earnestly, she sought and humbly found the blessed way, such as was open to her mind.

As my whole view of religion was changed from indifference or aversion to a profound interest in it, a change very naturally followed in my plan for future life, that is, in my choice of a profession, — very naturally, at least then; I do not say that it would be so now. I expected to be a lawyer; and I have sometimes been inclined to regret that I was not; for courts of law always have had, and have still, a strange fascination for me, and I see now that a lawyer's or physician's life may be

[1] The Massachusetts Legislative Assembly is so called. — M. E. D.

actuated by as lofty principles, and may be as
noble and holy, as a clergyman's. But I did not
think so then. Then, I felt as if the life of a minister of religion were the only sacred, the only
religious life; as, in regard to the special objects
with which it is engaged, it is. But what especially moved me to embrace it, I will confess, was
a desire to vindicate for religion its rightful claim
and place in the world, — to roll off the cloud
and darkness that lay upon it, and to show it in
its true light. It had been dark to me; it had
been something strange and repulsive, and even
unreal, — something conjured up by fear and
superstition. I came to see it as the divinest, the
sublimest, and the loveliest reality, and I burned
with a desire that others should see it. This
" divine call " I had, whether or not it answers to
what is commonly meant by that phrase, and I
am glad that I obeyed it.

But now, how was I to prosecute this design?
how carry on the preparatory studies, when my
eyes did not permit me to read more than half
an hour a day? I hesitated and turned aside,
first to teach a school in Sheffield for a year, and
next, for another year, to try a life of business
in New York. At length, however, my desire for
my chosen profession became so irrepressible,
that I determined to enter the Theological Seminary at Andover, and to pursue my studies as
well as I could without my eyes, expecting afterwards to preach without notes.

At Andover I passed three years, attending to the course of studies as well as I was able. I gave to Hebrew the half-hour a day that I was able to study; with the Greek Testament I was familiar enough to go on with my room-mate, Cyrus Byington,[1] who since has spent his life as a missionary among the Choctaws; and for reading I was indebted to his unvarying kindness and that of my classmates and friends. Still, I was left, some hours of every day, to my own meditations. But the being obliged to think for myself upon the theological questions that daily came before

[1] Byington was a young lawyer, here in Sheffield, of good abilities and prospects, but under a strong religious impression he determined to quit the law and study theology. He was a man of ardent temperament, whose thoughts were all feelings as well, which, though less reliable as thought, were strong impulses, always directed, consecrated to good ends. A being more unselfish, more ready to sacrifice himself for others, could not easily be found. This spirit made him a missionary. When our class was about leaving Andover, the question was solemnly propounded to us by our teachers, who of us would go to the heathen? I well remember the pain and distress with which Byington examined it, — for no person could be more fondly attached to his friends and kindred, — his final decision to go, and the perfect joy he had in it after his mind was made up. He went to the Choctaw and Cherokee Indians in Florida, and, on their removal to the Arkansas reservation, accompanied them, and spent his life among them. He left, as the fruit of one part of his work, a Choctaw grammar and dictionary, and a yet better result in the improved condition of those people. Late in life, on a visit here, he told me that the converted Indians in Arkansas owned farms around him, laboring, and living as respectably as white people do. Here was that very civilization said to be impossible to the Indian.

the class, instead of reading what others had said about them, seemed to me not without its advantages.

Andover had its attractions, and not many distractions. I liked it, and I disliked it. I liked it for its opportunities for thorough study, — our teachers were earnest and thorough men, — and for the associates in study that it gave me. I could say, " For my companions' sake, peace be within thy walls." I disliked it for its monastic seclusion. Not that this was any fault of the institution, but for the first time in my life I boarded in commons; the domestic element dropped out of it, and I was persuaded, as I never had been before, of the beneficence of that ordinance that " sets the solitary in families." It was a fine situation in which to get morbid and dispirited and dyspeptic. On the last point I had some experiences that were somewhat notable to me. We were directed, of course, to take a great deal of exercise. We were very zealous about it, and sometimes walked five miles before breakfast, and that in winter mornings. It did not avail me, however; and I got leave to go out and board in a family, half a mile distant. I found that the three miles a day in going back and forth, that regular exercise, was worth more to me than all my previous and more violent efforts in that way. But I imagine that was not all. I had the misfortune to scald my foot, and was obliged for three weeks to sit perfectly still.

When I came back, Professor Stuart said to me, "Well, how is it with your dyspepsia?"—"All gone," was the reply. "But how have you lived?" for his dietetics were very strict. "Why, I have eaten pies and pickles,—and pot-hooks and trammels I might, for any harm in the matter." Here was a wonder,—no exercise and no regimen, and I was well! The conclusion I came to, was, on the whole, that cheerfulness first, and next regularity, are the best guards against the monster dyspepsia. And another conclusion was, that exercise can no more profitably be condensed than food can.

As to morbid habits of mind, to which isolated seminaries are exposed, I had also some experience. What complaints of our spiritual dulness constantly arose among us! And there was other dulness, too,—physical, moral, social. I remember, at one time, the whole college fell into a strange and unaccountable depression. The occasion was so serious that the professors called us together in the chapel to remonstrate with us; and, after talking it all over, and giving us their advice, one of them said: "The evil is so great, and relief so indispensable, that I will venture to recommend to you a particular plan. Go to your rooms; assemble some dozen or twenty in a room; form a circle, and let the first in it say 'Haw!' and the second 'Haw!' and so let it go round; and if that does n't avail, let the first again say 'Haw! haw!' and so on." We tried it, and the result may be imagined. Very astonishing it must have been to the people without, but the spell was broken.

But more serious matters claim attention in connection with Andover. I was to form some judgment upon questions in theology. I certainly was desirous of finding the Orthodox system true. But the more I studied it, the more I doubted. My doubts sprung, first, from a more critical study of the New Testament. In Professor Stuart's crucible, many a solid text evaporated, and left no residuum of proof. I was startled at the small number of texts, for instance, which his criticism left to support the doctrine of " the personality of the Holy Spirit." I remember saying to him in the class one day, when he had removed another prop, — another proof-text : " But this is one of the two or three passages that are left to establish the doctrine." His answer was : " Is not one declaration of God enough? Is it not as strong as a thousand? " It silenced, but it did not satisfy me. In the next place, I found difficulties in our theology from looking at it in a· point of view which I had not before considered, and that was the difference between *words* and *ideas*, — between the terms we used and the actual conceptions we entertained, or between the abstract thesis and the living sense of the matter. Thus with regard to the latter point, I found that the more I believed in the doctrine of literally eternal punishments, the more

I doubted it. As the living sense of it pressed more and more upon my mind, it became too awful to be endured; it darkened the day and the very world around me. At length I could not see a happy company or a gay multitude without falling into a sadness that marred and blighted everything. All joyous life, seen in the light of this doctrine, seemed to me but a horrible mockery. It is evident that John Forster's doubts sprung from the same cause. And then, I had been accustomed to use the terms "Unity" and "Trinity" as in some vague sense compatible; but when I came to consider what my actual conceptions were, I found that the Three were as distinct as any three personalities of which I could conceive. The service which Dr. Channing's celebrated sermon at the ordination of Mr. Sparks in Baltimore did me, was to make that clear to me. With such doubts, demanding further examination, I left the Seminary at Andover.

We parted, we classmates, many of us in this world never to meet again. Some went to the Sandwich Islands, one to Ceylon, one to the Choctaw Indians; most remained at home, some to hold high positions in our churches and colleges, — Wheeler, President of the Vermont University, a liberal-minded and accomplished man; Torrey, Professor in the same, a man of rare scholarship and culture; Wayland, President of Brown University, in Rhode Island, well and widely known; and Haddock, Professor in Dartmouth College, New Hampshire, and recently our *chargé d'affaires* in Portugal. Haddock, I thought, had the clearest head among us. Our relations were very friendly, — though I was a little afraid of him, — and with him I first visited his uncle, Daniel Webster, in Boston. I was struck with what Mr. Webster said of him, many years after, considering that the great statesman was speaking of a comparatively retired and studious man : " Haddock I should like to have always with me; he is full of knowledge, — of the knowledge that I want, — pure-minded, agreeable, pious," — I use his very words, — " and if I could afford it, and he would consent, I would take him to myself, to be my constant companion."

I left Andover, then, in the summer of 1819, and in a state of mind that did not permit me to be a candidate for settlement in any of the churches. I therefore accepted an invitation from the American Education Society to preach in behalf of its objects, in the churches generally, through the State, and was thus occupied for about eight months.

Some time in the spring, I think, of 1820, I went down to Gloucester to preach in the old Congregational Church, and was invited to become its pastor. I replied that I was too unsettled in my opinions to be settled anywhere. The congregation then proposed to me to come and preach a year to them, postponing the decision, both on their part and mine, to the end of it. I was very glad to accept this proposition, for a year of retired and quiet study was precisely what I wanted. I spent that year in examining the questions that had arisen in my mind, especially with regard to the Trinity. I read Emlyn's " Humble Inquiry," Yates and Wardlaw, Channing and Worcester, besides other books; but especially I made the most thorough examination I was able, of all the texts in both Testaments that appeared to bear upon the subject. The result was an undoubting rejection of the doctrine of the Trinity. The grounds for this, and other modifications of theological opinion, I need not give here; they are sufficiently stated in what I have written and published.

And here let me say that, although I had my anxieties, I had none about my personal hold upon heart-sustaining *truth*. It was emphatically a year of prayer, — if I may without presumption or indelicacy say so. Humbly and earnestly I sought to the God of wisdom and light to guide me; and I never felt for a moment that I was perilling my salvation. I had a foundation of repose, stronger than mere theology can give, deep and sure beneath me. I had indeed my anxieties. I felt as if I were putting in peril all my worldly welfare. All the props which a man builds up around him in his early studies, all the props of church relationship and religious friendship, seemed to be suddenly falling away, and I was about to take my stand on the threshold of life, alone, unsupported, and unfriended.

I soon had practical demonstration of this, not only in the coldness and the withdrawal of friends, — all natural enough, I suppose, and conscientious, no doubt, — but in the summons of the Presbytery of the city of New York, from which I had taken out my license to preach, to appear before it and answer to the charge of heresy. The summons was made in terms at war, I thought, with Christian liberty, and I refused to obey it. The terms may have been in consonance with the Presbyterian discipline, and perhaps I ought not to have refused. What I felt was, — and this, substantially, I believe, was what I said, — that, if " the Presbytery propose to examine me simply to ascertain whether my opinions admit of my standing in the Presbyterian Church, I have no objection; I neither expect nor wish to remain with it; but it appears to me to assume a right and authority over my opinions to which I cannot submit."

At the end of the year passed in Gloucester, it appeared that the congregation was about equally divided on the question of retaining me as pastor; at any rate, the circumstances did not permit me to think of it, and I went up to Boston to assist Dr. Channing in his duties as pastor of the Federal Street Church.

But I must not pass over, yet cannot comment upon, the great event of my year at Gloucester, — the greatest and happiest of my life, — my marriage.[1] It took place in Boston, on the 26th day of December, 1820, the Rev. Dr. Jarvis officiating as clergyman, my wife's family being then in attendance upon his church. As in the annals of nations it is commonly said that, while calamities and disasters crowd the page, the happy seasons are passed over in silence and have no record, so let it be here.

My going up to Boston, to be acquainted with Channing, and to preach in his church, excited in me no small expectation and anxiety. I approached both the church and the man with something of trembling. Of Channing, of his character, of his conversation, and the great impression it made upon me, as upon everybody that approached him, I have already publicly spoken, in a sermon which I delivered on my return from Europe after his death,[2] and in a letter to be inserted in Dr. Sprague's "Annals of the American Pulpit." In entering the pulpit of Dr. Channing, as his assistant for a season, I felt that I was committing myself to an altogether new ordeal. I had been educated in the Orthodox Church; I knew little or nothing about the style and way of preaching in the Unitarian churches; I knew only the pre-eminent place which Dr.

[1] To Louisa Farnham, daughter of William Farnham, of Boston. — M. E. D.

[2] This sermon, a noble, tender, and discriminating tribute to Dr. Channing, was reprinted in 1881, on the occasion of the Channing Centennial Celebration at Newport, R. I. — M. E. D.

Channing occupied, both as writer and preacher, and I naturally felt some anxiety about my reception. I will only say that it was kind beyond my expectation. After some months Dr. Channing went abroad, and I occupied his pulpit till he returned. In all, I was in his pulpit about two years. On my taking leave of it, the congregation presented me with a thousand dollars to buy a library. It was a most timely and welcome gift.

During my residence in Boston, I made my first appearance, but anonymously, in print, in an essay entitled " Hints to Unitarians." How ready this body of Christians has always been to accept sincere and honest criticism, was evinced by the reception of my adventurous essay. My gratification, it may be believed, was not small on learning that it had been quoted with approbation in the English Unitarian pulpits ; and Miss Martineau told me, when she was in this country, — then learning that I was the author, — that she, with a friend of hers, had caused it to be printed as a tract for circulation. She would say now that it was in her nonage that she did it.

The most remarkable man, next to Channing, that I became acquainted with during this residence of two years in Boston, was Jonathan Phillips. He was a merchant by profession, but inherited a large fortune, and was never, that I know, engaged much in active business. He led, when I knew him, a contemplative life, was an assiduous reader, and a deeper thinker. He had a splendid library, and spent much of his time among his books. If he had had the proper training for it, I always thought he would have made a great metaphysician. His conversation was often profound, and always original, — always drawn from the workings of his own mind, and was always occupied with great philosophical and religious themes. It was born of struggle, more, I think, than any man's I ever talked with. For he had a great moral nature, and great difficulties within, arising partly from his religious education, but yet more from the contact with actual life of a very sensitive temperament and much ill health. He had worked his way out independently from the former, and stood on firm ground; and when some of his family friends charged Channing with having drawn him away from Orthodoxy, Channing replied, "No; he has influenced me more than I have influenced him."

In London, in 1833, I met Mr. Phillips with Dr. Tuckerman, well known as the pioneer in the " Ministry to the Poor in Cities," about to take the tour on the Continent. He invited me to join them, and we travelled together on the Rhine and in Switzerland. It was on this journey that I became acquainted with the sad effect produced upon him by great and depressing indisposition. His case was very singular, and explains things in him that surprised his acquaintances very much, and, in fact, did him much wrong with them. It was a scrofulous condition of the stomach, and

when developed by taking cold, it was something
dreadful to hear him describe. The effect was to
make entirely another man of him. He who was
affluent in means and disposition became suddenly
not only depressed and melancholy, but anxious
about expenses, sharp with the courier upon that
point, and not at all agreeable as a travelling companion. But when the fit passed off, which seemed
for the time to be a kind of insanity, his spirits
rose, and his released faculties burst out in actual
splendor. He became gay; he enjoyed everything, and especially the scenery around him. I
never knew before that his æsthetic nature was
so fine. He said so many admirable things while
we were going over Switzerland, that I was sorry
afterwards that I had not noted them down at the
time, and written a sheet or two of Phillipsiana.
His countenance changed as much as his conversation, and its expression became actually beautiful. There was a miniature likeness taken of him
in London. I went to see it; and when I expressed
to the artist my warm approval of it, he said: " I
am glad to have you say that; for I wanted to
draw out all the sweetness of that man's face."[1]

One of the most distinguished persons in Dr.
Channing's congregation was Josiah Quincy, who,
during his life, occupied high positions in the
country, and of a very dissimilar character,—

[1] The point in this is that Mr. Phillips' features were of singular and almost repellent homeliness till irradiated by thought
or emotion. — M. E. D.

Member of Congress, Mayor of Boston, and President of Harvard University, — all of which posts he filled with credit and ability; always conscientious, energetic, devoted to his office, high-toned, and disinterested. He was a model of pure and unselfish citizenship, and deserves for that a statue in Boston.

When Mr. Quincy was a very old man, I asked him one day how he had come to live so long, and in such health and vigor. He answered: "For forty years I have taken no wine; and every morning, before dressing myself, I have spent a quarter of an hour in gymnastic exercises." I adopted the practice, and have found it of great benefit, both as exercise, and inuring against colds. It is really as much exercise as a mile or two of walking. President Felton said: "After that, I can let the daily exercise take care of itself, without going doggedly about it." I find that a good many studious men are doing the same thing. I asked Bryant how much time he gave, and he said, "Three quarters of an hour." After that, at least in his summer home, he is upon his feet almost as much as a cat, and about as nimbly. With his thin and wiry frame, and simple habits, he is likely to live to a greater age than anybody I know.[1]

[1] Mr. Bryant and my father were about of an age. They had known each other almost from boyhood, and their friendship had matured with time. The sudden death of the poet in 1878, from causes that seemed almost accidental, was a great and unexpected blow to the survivor, then himself in feeble health. — M. E. D.

I shall add a word about the healthfulness of these exercises, since it is partly my design in this sketch to give the fruits of my experience. It is true one cannot argue for everybody from his own case. Nevertheless, I am persuaded that this morning exercise and the inuring would greatly promote the general health. " Catching cold " is a serious item in the lives of many people. One, two, or three months of every year they have a cold. For thirty years I have bathed in cold water and taken the air-bath every morning; and in all that time, I think, I have had but three colds, and I know where and how I got these, and that they might have been avoided.

But I have wandered far from my ground, — Boston, and my first residence there. I was Dr. Channing's guest for the first month or two, and then and afterwards knew all his family, consisting of three brothers and two sisters. They were not people of wealth or show, but something much better. Henry lived in retirement in the country, not having an aptitude for business, but a sensible person in other respects. George was an auctioneer, but left business and became a very ardent missionary preacher; and Walter was a respectable physician. William was placed in easy circumstances by his marriage. Their sister Lucy, Mrs. Russel of New York, told me that she was very much amused one day by something that her brother William said to Walter. "Walter," he said, " I think we are a very prosperous family. There is Henry, — he is a very excellent man. And George, — why, George has come out a great spiritual man. And you, — you know how you are getting along. And as for me, I do what I can. I think we are a very prosperous family."

Mrs. Russel was a person of great sense, of strong, quiet thought and feeling; and some of her friends used to say that, with the same advantages and opportunities her brother had, she would have been his equal.

On a day's visit which Henry once made me in New Bedford, I remember we had a long conversation on hunting and fishing, in which he condemned them, and I defended. Pushed by his arguments, at length I said, — for I went a-fishing myself sometimes with a boat on the Acushnet; yes, and barely escaped once being carried out to sea by the ebb tide, — I said, " My fishing is not a reckless destruction of life; somebody must take fish, and bring them to us for food, and those I catch come to my table." — " Now," said he, " that is as if you said to your butcher, ' You have to slay a certain number of cattle, calves, and sheep, and turkeys, and fowls for my table; let me have the pleasure of coming and killing them myself.' "

Of Dr. Channing himself, I should, of course, have much to say here, if, as I have just said, I had not already expressed my thoughts of him in print. His conversation struck me most; more even than any of his writings ever did. He was an invalid, and kept much at home and indoors, and he talked hour after hour, day after day, and sometimes for a week, upon the same subject, without ever letting it grow distasteful or wearisome. Edward Everett said, — he had just returned from Europe, where doubtless he had seen eminent persons, — "I have never met with anybody to whom it was so interesting to listen, and so hard to talk when my turn came." There was, indeed, a grand and surprising superiority in Channing's talk, both in the topics and the treatment of them. There was no repartee in it, and not much of give and take, in any way. People used to come to him, his clerical brethren, — I remember Henry Ware and others speaking of it, — they came, listened to him, said nothing themselves, and went away. In fact, Channing talked for his own sake, generally. His topic was often that on which he was preparing to write. It was curious to see him, from time to time, as he talked, dash down a note or two on a bit of paper, and throw it into a pigeon-hole, which eventually became quite full.

It would appear from all this that Channing was not a genial person, and he was not. He was too intent upon the subjects that occupied his mind for that varied and sportive talk, that *abandon,* that sympathetic adjustment of his thoughts to the moods of people around him, which makes the *agreeable* person. His thoughts moved in solid battalions, but they carried keen weapons. It would have been better for him if he had had more variety, ease, and joyousness in society, and he felt it himself. He was not genial either in his conversation or letters. I doubt if one gay or sportive letter can be found among them all. His habitual style of address, out of his own family, was "My dear Sir," never "My dear Tom," or "My dear Phillips," scarcely, "My dear Friend." Once he says, "Dear Eliza," to Miss Cabot, who married that noble-minded man, Dr. Follen, and in them both he always felt the strongest interest. Let any one compare Channing's letters with those of Lord Jeffrey, for instance. The ease and freedom of Jeffrey's letters, their mingled sense and playfulness, but especially the hearty grasp of affection and familiarity in them, make one feel as if he were introduced into some new and more charming society. Jeffrey begins one of his letters to Tom Moore thus: "My dear Sir — damn Sir — My dear Moore." Whether there is not, among us, a certain democratic reserve in this matter, I do not know; but I suspect it. Reserve is the natural defence set up against the claims of universal equality.

In the autumn of 1823, on Dr. Channing's return to his pulpit, I went to New Bedford to preach in the Congregational Church, formerly Dr. (commonly called Pater) West's, was invited to be its pastor, and was ordained to that charge on the 17th of December, Dr. Tuckerman giving the sermon. An incident occurred at the ordination which showed me that I had fallen into a new latitude of religious thought and feeling. After the sermon, and in the silence that followed, suddenly we heard the voice of prayer from the midst of the congregation. At first we were not a little disturbed by the irregularity, and the clergymen who leaned over the pulpit to listen looked as if they would have said, " This must be put a stop to; " but the prayer, which was short, went on, so simple, so sincere, so evidently unostentatious and indeed beautiful, so in hearty sympathy with the occasion, and in desire for a blessing on it, that when it closed, all said, " Amen ! Amen ! " It was a pretty remarkable conquest over prejudice and usage, achieved by simple and self-forgetting earnestness. Indeed, it seemed to have a certain before unthought-of fitness, as a response from the congregation, which is not given in our usual ordination services. The ten years' happy, and, I hope, not unprofitable ministration on my part that followed, and of fidelity on the part of the people, were perhaps some humble fulfilment and answer to the good petitions that it offered, and to all the brotherly exhortations and supplications of that hour.

The congregation was small when I became its pastor, but it grew; a considerable number of families from the Society of Friends connected themselves with it, and it soon rose, as it continues still, to be one of the wealthiest and most liberal societies in the country.

My duties were very arduous. There was no clergyman with whom I could exchange within thirty miles;[1] relief from this quarter, therefore, was rare, not more than four or five Sundays in the year. I was most of the time in my own pulpit, sometimes for ten months in succession. In addition to this, I became a constant contributor to the " Christian Examiner," — for some years, I think as often as to every other number. It was not wise. The duties of the young clergyman are enough for him. The lawyer, the physician, advances slowly to full practice; the whole weight falls upon the clergyman's young strength at once. Mine sunk under it. I brought on a certain nervous disorder of the brain, from which I have never since been free. Of course it interfered seriously with my mental work. How many days — hundreds and hundreds — did one hour's study in the morning paralyze and prostrate me as completely as if I had been knocked on the head, and lay me, for hours after, helpless on my sofa! After the Sunday's preaching, — the effect of which upon me was perhaps singular, making my back and bones ache, and my sinews as if they had been stretched on the rack, making me

---

[1] This distance, which now seems so trifling, then involved the hire of a horse and chaise for three days, and two long days' driving through deep, sandy roads. — M. E. D.

feel as if I wanted to lie on the floor or on a hard board, — if any one knows what that means, — after all this, it would be sometimes the middle of the week, sometimes Thursday or Friday, before I could begin to work again, and prepare for the next Sunday. My professional life was a constant struggle; and yet I look back upon it, not with pain, but with pleasure.

Besides all this, subjects of great religious interest to me constantly pressed themselves upon my attention. I remember Dr. Lamson, of Dedham, a very learned and able man, asking me one day how I "found subjects to write upon;" and my answering, "I don't find subjects; they find me." I may say they pursued me. It may be owing to this that my sermons have possibly a somewhat peculiar character; what, I do not know, but I remember William Ware's saying, when my first volume of Discourses appeared, "that they were written as if nobody ever wrote sermons before," and something so they *were* written. I do not suppose there is much originality of thought in them, nor any *curiosa felicitas* of language, — I could not attend to it; it was as much as I could do to disburden myself, — but original in this they are, that they were wrought out in the bosom of my own meditation and experience. The pen was dipped in my heart, — I do know that. With burning brain and bursting tears I wrote. Little fruit, perhaps, for so much struggle; be it so, — though it could not be so to me. But so we work, — each one in his own way; and altogether something comes of it.

Early in my professional life, too, I met certain questions, which every thinking man meets sooner or later, and which were pressed upon my mind by the new element that came into our religious society. The Friends are trained up to reverence the inward light, and have the less respect for historical Christianity. The revelation in our nature, then, and the revelation in the Scriptures; the proper place of each in any just system of thought and theology; what importance is to be assigned to the primitive intuitions of right and wrong, and what to the supernaturalism, to the miracles of the New Testament, — these were the questions, and I discussed them a good deal in the pulpit, as matters very practical to many of the minds with which I was dealing. I admitted the full, nay, the supreme value of the original intuitions, of the inward light, of the teachings of the Infinite Spirit in the human soul; without them we could have no religion; without them we could not understand the New Testament at all, and Christianity would be but as light to the blind; but I maintained that Christ's teaching and living and dying were the most powerful appeal and help and guidance to the inward nature, to the original religion of the soul, that it had ever received. And I believed and maintained that this help, at once most divine and most human, was commended to the world by miraculous attestations. Not that the miracle, or the miracle-sanctioned Christianity, was intended to supersede or disparage the inward light; not that it made clearer the truth that benevolence is right, any more than it could make clearer the proposition that two and two make four; not that it lent a sanction to any intuitive truth, but that it was *the seal of a mission,* — this was what I insisted on. And certainly a being who appeared before me, living a divine life, and assuring me of God's paternal care for me and of my own immortality, would impress me far more, if there were "works" done by him "which no other man could do, which bore witness of him." And although it should appear, as in a late work on "The Progress of Religious Ideas" it has been made to appear, that in the old systems there were foreshadowings of that which I receive as the most true and divine; that the light had been shining on brighter and brighter through all ages, — that would not make it any the less credible or interesting to me, that Jesus should be the consummation of all, — the "true Light" that lighteth the steps of men; and that this Light should have come from God's especial illumination, and should be far above the common and natural light of this world's day. Nay, it would be more grateful to me to believe that all religions have had in them something supernaturally and directly from above, than that none have.

But time went on, and work went on, reason as I might; though time would have lost its light and life, and work all cheer and comfort, if I had not believed. But work grew harder; I was obliged to take longer and longer vacations, — one of them five months long at the home in Sheffield. . . . After this I went back to my work, preaching almost exclusively in my own pulpit, seldom going away, unless it was now and then for an occasional sermon.

I went over to Providence in 1832, to preach the sermon at Dr. Hall's installation as pastor of the First Church. Arrived on the evening before, some of us of the council went to a caucus, preparatory to a Presidential election, General Jackson being candidate for the Presidency and Martin Van Buren for Vice-President. Finding the speaking rather dull, after an hour or more we rose to leave, when a gentleman touched my arm and said, " Now, if you will stay, you will hear something worth waiting for." We took our seats, and saw John Whipple rising to speak. I was exceedingly grateful for the interruption of our purpose, for I never heard an address to a popular assembly so powerful; close, compact, cogent, Demosthenic in simplicity and force, — not a word misplaced, not a word too many, — and fraught with that strange power over the feelings, lent by sadness and despondency, — a state of mind, I think, most favorable to real eloquence, in which all verbiage is eschewed, and the burden upon the heart is too heavy to allow the speaker to think of himself.

Mr. Whipple was in the opposition, and his main charge against Van Buren especially, was, that it was he who had introduced into our politics the fatal principle of " the spoils to the victors," — a principle which, as the orator maintained, with prophetic sagacity, threatened ruin to the Republic.   Still there was no extravagance in his way of bringing the charge.   I remember his saying, "Does Mr. Van Buren, then, wish for the ruin of his country?   No; Cæsar never wished for the glory of Rome more than when he desired her to be laid, as a bound victim, at his feet."

We have learned since more than we knew then of the direful influence of that party cry, " The spoils to the victors."   It has made our elections scrambles for office, and our parties " rings."   Mr. Whipple portrayed the consequences which we are now feeling, and powerfully urged that his State, small though it was, should do its utmost to ward them off.   As he went on, and carried us higher and higher, I began to consider how he was to let us down.   But the skilful orator is apt to have some clinching instance or anecdote in reserve, and Mr. Whipple's close was this : —

" There sleep now, within the sound of my voice, the bones of a man who once stood up in the revolutionary battles for his country.   In one of them, he told me, when the little American army, ill armed, ill clad, and with bleeding feet, was drawn up in front of the disciplined troops of England, 'General Washington passed along our lines, and when he came before us, he stopped, and said, "I place great confidence in this Rhode Island regiment." And when I heard that,' said he, ' I clasped my musket to my breast, and said, Damn 'em ; let 'em come !' The immortal Chieftain [said the orator] is looking down upon us now ; and he says, ' I place great confidence in this Rhode Island regiment.' "

And now, on the whole, what shall I say of my life in New Bedford? It was, in the main, very happy. I thought I was doing good there; I certainly was thoroughly interested in what I was doing. I found cultivated and interesting society there. I made friends, who are such to me still. In the pastoral relation, New Bedford was, and long continued to be, the very home of my heart; it was my first love.

In 1827 I was invited to go to New York. I did not wish to go, so I expressly told the church in New York (the Second Church) ; but I consented, in order to accomplish what they thought a great good, provided my congregation in New Bedford would give their consent. They would not give it; and I remained. I believe that I should have lived and died among them, if my health had not failed.

But it failed to that degree that I could no longer do the work, and I determined to go abroad and recruit, and recover it, if possible.

This was in 1833. The Messrs. Grinnell & Co., of New York, offered me a passage back and forth in their ships, — one of the thousand kind and generous things that they were always doing, — and I sailed from New York in the "George Washington" on the 8th of June. It was like death to me to go. I can compare it to nothing else, — going, as I did, alone.

In London I consulted Sir James Clarke, who told me that the disease was in the brain, and that I must pass three or four years abroad if I would recover from it. I believe I stared at his proposition, — it seemed to me so monstrous, — for he said, in fine: "Well, you may go home in a year, and think yourself well; but if you go about your studies, you will probably bring on the same trouble again; and if you do, in all probability you will never get rid of it." Alas! it all proved true. I came home in the spring of 1834, thinking myself well. I had had no consciousness of a brain for three months before I left Europe. I went to work as usual; in one month the whole trouble was upon me again, and it became evident that I must leave New Bedford. I could write no more sermons; I had preached every sermon I had, that was worth preaching, five times over, and I could not face another repetition. I retired with my family to the home in Sheffield, and expected to pass some years at least in the quiet of my native village.

I should like to record some New Bedford names here, so precious are they to me. Miss Mary Rotch is one, — called by everybody "Aunt Mary," from mingled veneration and affection. It might seem a liberty to call her so; but it was not, in her case. She had so much dignity and strength in her character and bearing that it was impossible for any one to speak of her lightly. On our going to New Bedford, she immediately called upon us, and when she went out I could not help exclaiming, "Wife, were ever hearts taken by storm like that!" *Storm*, the word would be, according to the usage of the phrase; but it was the very contrary, — a perfect simplicity and kindliness. But she was capable, too, of righteous wrath, as I had more than one occasion afterwards to see. Indeed, I was once the object of it myself. It was sometime after I left New Bedford, that, in writing a review of the admirable Life of Blanco White by the Rev. J. H. Thom, of Liverpool, while I spoke with warm appreciation of his character, I commented with regret upon his saying, toward the close of his life, that he did not care whether he should live hereafter; and I happened to use the phrase, " He died and made no sign," without thinking of the miserable Cardinal Beaufort, to whom Shakespeare applies it. Aunt Mary immediately came down upon me with a letter of towering indignation for my intolerance. I replied to her, saying that if ever I should be so happy as to arrive at the blessed world where I believed that she and Blanco White would be, and they were not too far beyond me for me to have any communion with them, she would see that I was guilty of no such exclusiveness as she had ascribed to me. She was pacified, I think, and we went on, as good friends as ever. Her religious opinions were of the most catholic stamp, and in one respect they were peculiar. The Friends' idea of the " inward light" seemed to have become with her coincident with the idea of the Author of all light; and when speaking of the Supreme Being, she would never say " God," but "that Influence." That Influence was constantly with her; and she carried the idea so far as to believe that it prompted her daily action, and decided for her every question of duty.

Miss Eliza Rotch had come from her English home shortly before my going to New Bedford, and had brought, with her English education and sense, more than the ordinary English powers of conversation. She, like all her family, had been bred in the Friends' Society; and she came with many of them to my church. She was a most remarkable *hearer*. With her bright face, and her full, speaking eye, and interested especially, no doubt, in the new kind of ministration to which she was listening, she gave me her whole attention, — often slightly nodding her assent, unconsciously to herself and unobserved by others. She married Professor John Farrar of Harvard, an able mathematician, and one of the most genial and lovable men that ever lived.

Life, in our quiet little town, was more leisurely than it is in cities, and the consequence was an unusual development of amusing qualities. There was more fun, and I ventured sometimes to say, there was more wit, in New Bedford than there was in Boston. To be sure, we could not pretend to compare with Boston in culture and in high and fine conversation, — least of all in music, which was at a very low ebb with us. I remember being at an Oratorio in one of our churches, where the trump of Judgment was represented by a horn not much louder than a penny-whistle, blown in an obscure corner of the building!

Charles H. Warren was the prince of humorists among us, and would have been so anywhere. Channing said to me one day, " I want to see your friend Warren; I want to see him as you do." I could not help replying, " That you never will; I should as soon expect to hear a man laugh in a cathedral." I never knew a man quite so full of the power to entertain others in conversation as he was. Lemuel Williams, his brother lawyer, had perhaps a subtler wit. But the way Warren would go on, for a whole evening, letting off *bon-mots*, repartees, and puns, made one think of a magazine of pyrotechnics. Yet he was a man of serious thought and fine intellectual powers. He was an able lawyer, and, placed upon the bench at an uncommonly early age, he sustained himself with honor. I used to lament that he would not study more, — that he gave himself up so much to desultory reading; but he had no ambition. Yet, after all, I believe that the physical organization has more to do with every man's career than is commonly suspected. His was very delicate, his complexion fair, and his face, indeed, was fine and expressive in a rare degree. The sanguine-bilious, I think, is the temperament for deep intellectual power, — like Daniel Webster's. It lends not only strength, but protection, to the workings of the mind within. It is not too sensitive to surrounding impressions. Concentration is force. Long, deep, undisturbed thinking, alone can bring out great results. I have been accustomed to criticise my own temperament in this respect, — too easily drawn aside from study by circumstances, persons, or things around me, external interests or trifles, the wants and feelings of others, or their sports, a playing child or a crowing cock. My mind, such as it is, has had to struggle with this outward tendency, — too much feeling and sentiment, and too little patient thinking, — and I believe that I should have accomplished a great deal more if I had had, not the sanguine alone, but the sanguine-bilious temperament.

Manasseh Kempton had it. He was the deacon of my church. I used to think that nobody knew, or at least fairly appreciated, him as I did. Under that heavy brow, and phlegmatic aspect,

and reserved bearing, there was an amount of fire
and passion and thought, and sometimes in conversation an eloquence, which showed me that,
with proper advantages, he would have made a
great man.

James Arnold was a person too remarkable to
be passed over in this account of the New Bedford
men. With great wealth, with the most beautiful situation in the town, and, yet more, with the
aid of his wife, — never mentioned or remembered
but to be admired, — his house was the acceptable
resort of strangers, more than any other among
us. Mr. Arnold was not only a man of unshaken
integrity, but of strong thought; and if a liberal
education had given him powers of utterance, —
the habit of marshalling his thoughts, equal to
the powers of his mind, — he would have been
known as one of the remarkable men in the
State.

One other figure rises to my recollection,
which seems hardly to belong to the modern
world, and that is Dr. Whittredge of Tiverton.
In his religious faith he belonged to us, and occasionally came over to attend our church. I
used, from time to time, to pay him visits of a
day or two, — always made pleasant by the placid
and gentle presence of his wife, and by the brisk
and eager conversation of the old gentleman.
He was acquainted in his earlier days with my
predecessor, of twenty-five years previous date,
Dr. West, himself a remarkable man in his day,

and almost equally so, both for his eccentricity and his sense. An eccentric clergyman, by the by, is rarely seen now; but in former times it was a character as common as now it is rare. The commanding position of the clergy — the freedom they felt to say and do what they pleased — brought that trait out in high relief. The great democratic pressure has passed like a roller over society: everybody is afraid of everybody; everybody wants something, — office, appointment, business, position, — and he is to receive it, not from a high patron, but from the common vote or opinion.

Dr. West's eccentricity arose from absorption into his own thoughts, and forgetfulness of everything around him. He would pray in the family in the evening till everybody went to sleep, and in the morning till the breakfast was spoiled. He would preach upon some Scripture passage till some one went and moved his mark forward. He once paid a visit to the Governor in Boston, and, having got drenched in the rain, was supplied with a suit of his host's, which unconsciously, he wore home, and arrayed in which, he appeared in his pulpit on Sunday morning. At the same time he was a man of strong and independent thought. I have read a " Reply " of his to Edwards on the Will, in which the subject was ably discussed, but without the needful logical coherence, perhaps, to make its mark in the debate.

The conversations of West with his friend, Dr. Whittredge, as the latter told me, ran constantly into theological questions, — upon which they differed. West was a frequent visitor at Tiverton, and, when the debate drew on towards midnight, Whittredge was obliged to say, " Well, I can't sit here talking with you all night; for I must sleep, that I may go and see my patients to-morrow." He was vexed, he said, that he should thus 'seem to "cry quarter" in the controversy again and again, and he resolved that the next time he met West, *he* would not stop, be they where they might. It so happened that their next meeting was at the head of Acushnet River, three miles above New Bedford, where Whittredge was visiting his patients, and West his parishioners. This done, they set out towards evening to walk to New Bedford. Whittredge throwing the bridle-rein over his arm, they walked on slowly, every now and then turning aside into some crook of the fence, — the horse meantime getting his advantage in a bit of green grass, — and thus they talked and walked, and walked and talked, till the day broke !

But the most remarkable thing about my venerable parishioner remains to be mentioned. Dr. Whittredge was an alchemist. He had a furnace, in a little building separate from his house, where he kept a fire for forty years, till he was more than eighty, — visiting it every night, of summer and winter alike, to be sure of keeping it alive;

and melting down, as his family said, many a good guinea, and all to find the philosopher's stone, — the mysterious metal that should turn all to gold. From delicacy I never alluded to the subject with him, — I am sorry now that I did not. And he never adverted to it with me but once, and that was in a way which showed that he had no mean or selfish aims in his patient and mysterious search; and, indeed, no one could doubt that he was a most benevolent and kind-hearted man. The occasion was this: He had been to our church one day, — indeed, it was his last attendance, — and as we came down from the pulpit, where he always sat, the better to hear me, and as we were walking slowly through the broad aisle, he laid his hand upon my shoulder, and said, " Ah, sir, this is the true doctrine ! But it wants money, — it wants money, sir, to spread it, and *I hope it will have it before long.*"

While in Europe I had kept a journal, and I now published it under the title of " The Old World and the New," and about the same time, I forget which was first, a volume of sermons entitled, " Discourses on Various Subjects." The *idea* of my book of travels, I think, was a good one, — to survey the Old World from the experience of the New, and the New from the observation of the Old; but it was so ill carried out that what I mainly proposed to myself on my second visit to Europe, ten years after, was to fulfil, as far as I could, my original design. But my health did not allow of it. I made many notes, but brought nothing into shape for publication. I still believe that America has much to teach to Europe, especially in the energy, development, and progress lent to a people by the working of the *free principle;* and that Europe has much to teach to America, in the value of order, routine, thorough discipline, thorough education, division of labor, economy of means, adjustment of the means to living, etc. As to my first volume of sermons, — if any one would see his thoughts laid out in a winding-sheet, let them be laid before him in printer's proofs; that which had been to me alive and glowing, and had had at least the life of earnest utterance, now, through this weary looking over of proof-sheets, seemed dead and shrouded for the grave. It did not seem to me possible that anybody would find it alive. I have hardly ever had a sadder feeling than that with which I dismissed this volume from my hands.

At the time of my retirement to Sheffield, the Second Congregational Church in New York, which had formerly invited me to its pulpit, was without a pastor, and I was asked to go down there and preach. I could preach, though I could not write; my sermons, with their five ear-marks upon them in New Bedford, would be new in another pulpit, and I consented. I was soon invited to take charge of the church, but declined it. It was even proposed to me to be established simply as preacher, and to be relieved from parochial visiting; but as the congregation was small, and could not support a pastor beside me, I declined that also. But I went on preaching, and after about a year, feeling myself stronger, I consented to be settled in the church with full charge, and was installed on the 8th November, 1835, Dr. Walker preaching the sermon.

The church was on the corner of Mercer and Prince Streets; a bad situation, inasmuch as it was on a corner, that is, it was noisy, and the annoyance became so great that I seriously thought more than once of proposing to the congregation to sell and build elsewhere. On other accounts the church was always very pleasant to me. It was of moderate size, holding seven or eight hundred people, and became in the course of a year or two quite full. The stairs to the galleries went up on the inside, giving it, I know not what, — a kind of comfortable and domestic air, very social and agreeable; and last, not least, it was easy to speak in. This last consideration, I am convinced, is of more importance, and is so in more ways, than is commonly supposed. A place hard to speak in is apt to create, especially in the young preacher just forming his habits, a hard and unnatural manner of speaking. More than one young preacher have I known, who began with good natural tones, in the course of a year or two, to fall into a loud, pulpit monotone, or to bring out all his cadences with a jerk, or with a disagreeable stress of voice, — *to be heard.* One must be heard, — that is the first requisite, — and to have one and another come out of church Sunday after Sunday, and touch your elbow, and say, " Sir, I could n't *hear* you; I was interested in what I could hear, but just at the point of greatest interest, half of the time, I lost your cadence," is more than any man can bear for a long time, and so he resorts to loud tones and monotonous cadences, and he is obliged to think, much of the time, more of the mere dry fact of being heard, than of the themes that should pour themselves out in full unfolding ease and freedom. I have fought through my whole professional life against this criticism, striving to keep some freedom and nature in my speech, though I have made every effort consistent with that to be heard. I have not always succeeded; but I have tried, and have always been grateful — a considerable virtue, especially when the hearer was himself a little deaf — to every one who admonished me. This is really a matter that seriously concerns the very religion that we preach. Everybody knows what the *preaching tone* is; it can be distinguished the moment it is heard, outside of any church, school-house, or barn where it is uplifted; but few consider, I believe, of what immense disservice it is to the great cause we have at heart. Preaching is the principal ministration of religion, and if it be hard and unnatural, the very idea of religion is likely to be hard and unnatural, — far away from the every-day life and affections of men. Stamp upon music a character as hard, technical, unnatural as most preaching has, and would men be won by it? I do not say that what I have mentioned is the sole cause of the " preaching tone;" false ideas of religion have, doubtless, even more to do with it. But still it is of such importance that I think no church interior should be built without especial — nay, without sole — reference to the end for which it is built, namely, *to speak in.* Let what can be done for the architecture of the exterior building; but let not an interior be made with recesses and projections and pillars and domes, only to please the eye, while it is to hurt the edification of successive generations, for two or for ten centuries. No ornamentation can compensate for that injury. The science of acoustics is as yet but little understood; all that we seem to know thus far is that the plain, un-adorned parallelogram is the best form. And even if we must stick to that, I had rather have it than a church half ruined by architectural devices. Our Protestant churches are built, not for ceremonies and spectacles and processions, but for prayer and preaching. And the fitness of means to ends — that first law of architecture — is sacrificed by a church interior made more to be looked at than to be heard in.

But to return: we were not long to occupy the pleasant little church in Mercer Street, — pleasant memories I hope there are of it to others besides myself. On Sunday morning, the 26th November, 1837, it was burned to the ground. Nothing was saved but my library, which was flung out of the vestry window, and the pulpit Bible, which I have, — a present from the trustees.

The congregation immediately took a hall for temporary worship in the Stuyvesant Institute, and directed its thoughts to the building of a new church. Much discussion there was as to the style and the locality of the new structure, and at length it was determined to build in a semi-Gothic style, on Broadway. I was not myself in favor of Broadway, it being the great city thoroughfare, and ground very expensive; but it was thought best to build there. It was contended that a propagandist church should occupy a conspicuous situation, and perhaps that view has been borne out by the result. One parishioner, I remember, had an odd, or at least an old-fashioned, idea about the matter. " Sir," said he, "you don't understand our feeling about Broadway. Sir, there is but one Broadway in the world." It is now becoming a street of shops and hotels, and is fast losing its old fashionable prestige.

The building was completed in something more than a year, and on the 2d May, 1839, it was dedicated, under the name of the Church of the Messiah. The burning of our sanctuary had proved to be our upbuilding; the position of the Stuyvesant Institute on Broadway, and the plan of free seats, had increased our numbers, and we entered the new church with a congregation one third larger than that with which we left the old. The building had cost about $90,000, and it was a critical moment to us all, but to me especially, when the pews came to be sold. It may be judged what was my relief from anxiety when word was brought me, two hours after the auction was opened, that $70,000 worth of pews were taken.

It was a strong desire with me that the church should have some permanent name. I did not want that it should be called my church, and then by the name of my successor, and so on; but that it should be known by some fixed designation, and so pass down, gathering about it the sacred associations of years and ages to come. I believe that it was the first instance in our Unitarian body of solemnly dedicating a church by some sacred name.

Another wish of mine was to enter the new church with the Liturgy of King's Chapel in Boston for our form of service. The subject was repeatedly discussed in meetings of the congregation; but although it became evident that there would be a majority in favor of it, yet as these did not demand it, and there was a considerable minority strongly opposed to it, we judged that there was not a state of feeling among us that would justify the introduction of what so essentially required unanimity and heartiness as a new form of worship. And I am now glad that it was not introduced. For while I am as much satisfied as ever of the great utility of a Liturgy, I have become equally convinced that original, spontaneous prayer is likely to open the preacher's heart, or to stir up the gift in him in a way very important to his own ministration and to the edification of his people. The best service, I think, should consist of both.

And I cannot help believing that a church service will yet be arranged which will be an improvement upon all existing ones, Roman Catholic, Church of England, or any other. If in the highest ranges of human attainment there is to be an advancement of age beyond age, surely there. is to be a progress in the spirit and language of prayer. From some forming hand and heart, by the united aid of consecrated genius, wisdom, and piety, something is to come greater than we have yet seen. No Homeric poem or vision of Dante is so grand as that will be. What is the highest idea of God, — excluding superstition, anthropomorphism, and vague impersonality alike, — what is the fit and true utterance of the deepest and divinest heart to God, — this, I must think, may well occupy the sublimest meditations of human intellect and devotion. Not that the entire Liturgy, however, should be the product of any one man's thought. I would have in a Liturgy some of the time-hallowed prayers, some of the Litanies that have echoed in the ear of all the ages from the early Christian time. The churches of Rome and England and Germany have some of these; and in a service-book, supposed to be compiled by the Chevalier Bunsen, there are others, — prayers of Basil and of Jerome and Augustine, and of the old German time. There are beautiful things in them, — especially in the old German prayers there is something very filial, free, and touching; but they would want a great deal of expurgation, and I believe that better prayers are uttered to-day than were ever heard before; and it is from uttered, not written prayers, if I could do so by the aid of a stenographer or of a perfect memory, that I would draw contributions to a book of devotion. What would I not give for some prayers of Channing or of Henry Ware! — some that I have heard by their own firesides, — or of Dr. Gardiner Spring, or of Dr. Payson of Portland, that I heard in church many years ago, — for the very words that fell from their lips! I do not believe that the right prayers were ever *composed*, or ever will be.

After the dedication of our church I went on with my duties for three years, and then again broke down in health, able indeed, that is, with physical strength, to preach, but not able to write sermons. The congregation increased; many of its members became communicants; in the last year before I went abroad once more, the church was crowded; in the evening especially, the aisles as well as pews were sometimes filled.

It was this fulness of the attendance in the evening that reconciled me to a second service; especially it was that many strangers came, to whom I had no other opportunity to declare my views of religion. For I judge that, for any given congregation, one service of worship, and of meditation such as the sermon is designed to awaken, is enough for one day. In the "Christian Examiner," — two or three years after this, I think it was, — I published an article on this subject, in which I maintained that there was too much preaching, — too much preaching for the preacher, and too much preaching for the people. It was received with great surprise and little favor, I believe, at the time; but since then not a few persons, both of the clergy and laity, have expressed to me their entire agreement with it. What I said, and say, is that one sermon, one discourse of solemn meditation, designed to make a distinct and abiding impression upon the heart and life, is all that anybody should preach or hear in one day, and that the other part of Sunday should be used for conference or Sunday-school, or instructive lecture, or something with a character and purpose different from the morning meditation, — something to instruct the people in the history, or evidences, or theory, or scriptural exposition of our religion. Indeed, I did this myself as often as I was able, though it tried the religious prejudices of some of my people, and my own too, about what a sermon should be. I discussed the morals of trade, political morality, civic duty, — that of voters, jurymen, etc., — social questions, peace and war, and the problem of the human life and condition. Some portions of these last were incorporated into the course of Lowell Lectures on this subject, which I afterwards published. And it is high time to take this matter into serious consideration; for in all churches where the hearing of two or three sermons on Sunday is not held to be a positive religious duty, the second service is falling away into a thin and spectral shadow of public worship, discouraging to the attendants upon it, and dishonoring to religion itself.

The pastor of a large congregation in the city of New York has no sinecure. The sermons to be written, the parochial visiting, — once a year, at least, to each family, and weekly or daily to the sick and afflicted, — my walks commonly extended to from four to seven miles a day, — the calls of the poor and distressed, laboring under every kind of difficulty, the charities to be distributed, — I was in part the almoner of the congregation, — the public meetings, the committees to be attended, the constantly widening circle of social relations and engagements, the pressure, in fine, of all sorts of claims upon time and thought, — all this made a very laborious life for me. Yet it was pleasant, and very interesting. I thought when I

first went to the great city, — when I first found
myself among those busy throngs, none of whom
knew me, — beside those ranges of houses, none of
which had any association for me, — that I should
never feel at home in New York. But it became
very home-like to me. The walls became familiar
to my eye; the pavement grew soft to my foot.
I built me a house, that first requisite for feeling
at home. I chanced to see a spot that I fancied:
it was in Mercer Street, between Waverley Place
and Eighth Street, just in the centre of everything,
a step from Broadway and my church, just out of
the noise of everything; there we passed many
happy days. I have been quite a builder of
houses in my life. I built one in New Bedford.
My study had the loveliest outlook upon Buz-
zard's Bay and the Elizabeth Islands, — I shall
never have such a study again. Oh, the joy of
that sea view! When I came to it again, after a
vacation's absence, it moved me like the sight of
an old friend. And I have built about the old
home in Sheffield, till it is almost a new erection.

But to return to New York: I was very happy
there. I had a congregation, I believe, that was
interested in me. I made friends that were and
are dear to me. When I first went to New York,
I was elected a member of the Artists' Club, or
Club of the Twenty-one, as it was called; by what
good fortune or favor I know not, for I was the
first clergyman that had ever been a member of
it. It consisted of artists and other gentlemen,

—an equal number of each. Cole and Durand and Ingham and Inman and Chapman and Bryant and Verplanck and Charles Hoffman were in it when I first became acquainted with it; and younger artists have been brought into it since, Gray and Huntingdon and Kensett, and other non-professional gentlemen interested in art, and the meetings have been always pleasant. It was a kind of heart's home to me while I lived in New York, and I always resort to it now when I go there, sure of welcome and kindly greeting.[1]

Then, again, I had in William Ware, the pastor of the First Church, a friend and fellow-laborer, than whom, if I were to seek the world over, I could not find one more to my liking. Our friendship was as intimate as I ever had with any man, and our constant intercourse, — to enter his house as freely as my own, — his coming to mine was as a sunbeam, as cheering and undisturbing, — I thought I could not get along without it. But I was obliged to do so. He had often talked of resigning his situation, and I had obtained from him a promise that he would never do it without consulting me. Great was my surprise, then, to learn, one day while in the country, that he had sent in his resignation. My first word to him on going to town was, "What is this? You have broken your promise." "I did not consult even

---

[1] The well-known Century Club of New York is the modern development of what was first known as the Sketch Club, or the XXI. — M. E. D.

my father or my brothers," was his reply. I could say nothing. The truth was, that things had come to that pass in his mind that the case was beyond consultation. He considered himself as having made a fatal mistake in his choice of a profession. I have some very touching letters from him, in which he dwells upon it as his " mistake for a life." His nature was essentially artistic; he would have made a fine painter. He could have worked between silent walls. He could write admirably, as all the world knows; I need only mention "Zenobia" and "Aurelian" and " Probus." But there was a certain delicacy and shrinking in his nature that made it difficult for him to pour himself out freely in the presence of an audience. And yet a congregation, consisting in part of some of the most cultivated persons in New York, held him, as preacher and pastor, in an esteem and affection that any man might have envied.

.   .   .   .

And to repair the circle of my happy social relations, broken by Ware's departure, came Bellows to fill his place. I gave him the right hand of fellowship at his ordination; and I remember saying in it, that I would not have believed it possible for me to welcome anybody to the place of his predecessor with the pleasure with which I welcomed *him*. The augury of that hour has been fulfilled in most delightful intercourse with one of the noblest and most generous men I ever knew. With a singularly clear insight and penetration into the deepest things of our spiritual nature, with an earnestness and fearlessness breaking through all technical rules and theories, with a buoyancy and cheerfulness that nothing can dampen, with a fitness and readiness for all occasions, his power as a preacher and his pleasantness as a companion have made him one of the most marked men of his day.

As to my general intercourse with society, whether in New York or elsewhere, I have always felt that its freedom lay under disagreeable restrictions, if not under a lay-interdict; and when travelling as a stranger I have always chosen not to be known as a clergyman, and commonly was not. I once had a curious and striking illustration of the feeling about clergymen to which I am alluding. I was invited by Mr. Prescott Hall, the eminent lawyer, to meet the Kent Club at his house, — a law club then just formed. As I arrived a little before the company, I said to him: " Mr. Hall, I am sorry you have formed this kind of club, — a club exclusively of lawyers. In Boston they have one of long standing, consisting of four professions, and four members of each, that is, of lawyers, doctors, clergymen, and merchants." —" To tell you the truth," he answered, " I don't like the clergy." I said that I could conceive of reasons, but I should like to hear him state them. —" Why," said he, " they come over me; they don't put themselves on a level with me; they talk *ex cathedra.*" I was obliged to bow my head in acquiescence; but I did say, " I think I know a class of clergymen of whom that is not true; and, besides, if I could bring all the clergy of this city into clubs of the Boston description, I believe those habits would be broken up in a single year."

There were two men who came to our church whose coming seemed to be by chance, but was of great interest to me, for I valued them greatly. They were Peter Cooper and Joseph Curtis. Neither of them, then, belonged to any religious society, or regularly attended upon any church. They happened to be walking down Broadway one Sunday evening as the congregation were entering Stuyvesant Hall, where we then temporarily worshipped, and they said, " Let us go in here, and see what *this* is." When they came out, as they both told me, they said to one another, " This is the place for us." And they immediately connected themselves with the congregation, to be among its most valued members.

Peter Cooper was even then meditating that plan of a grand Educational Institute which he afterwards carried out. He was engaged in a large and successful business, and his one idea — which he often discussed with me — was to obtain the means of building that Institute. A man of the gentlest nature and the simplest habits; yet his religious nature was his most remarkable quality. It seemed to breathe through his life as fresh and tender as if it were in some holy retreat, instead of a life of business. Mr. Cooper has become a distinguished man, much engaged in public affairs, and much in society. I have seen him but little of late years; but I trust he has not lost that which is worth more than all the distinctions and riches in the world.

Joseph Curtis was a man much less known generally, and yet, in one respect, much more, — and that was in the sphere of the public schools. He did more, I think, than any man to bring up the free schools of New York to such a point as compelled our Boston visitors to confess that they were not a whit inferior to their own. And his were voluntary and unpaid services, though his means were always moderate. He neither had, nor made, nor cared to make, a fortune.- He cared for the schools as for nothing else; and there is no wiser or nobler care. For more than twenty years he spent half of his time in the schools, walking among them with such intelligent and gentle oversight as to win universal confidence and affection, so that he was commonly called, by teachers and pupils, " Father Curtis."

At the same time, his hand and heart were open to every call of charity. I remember once making him umpire between me and Horace Greeley, the only time that I ever met the latter in company. He was saying, after his fashion in the " Tribune,"— he was from nature and training a Democrat, and had no natural right ever to be in the Whig party, — he was saying that the miseries of the poor in New York were all owing to the rich; when I said, " Mr. Greeley, here sits Mr. Joseph Curtis, who has walked the streets of New York for more years than you and I have been here, and I propose that we listen to him." He could not refuse to make the appeal, and so I put a series of questions upon the point to Mr. Curtis. The answers did not please Mr. Greeley. He broke in once or twice, saying, " Am not I to have a chance to speak?" But I persisted and said, " Nay, but we have agreed to listen to Mr. Curtis." The upshot was, that, in his opinion, the miseries of the poor in New York were not owing to the rich, but mainly to themselves; that there was ordinarily remunerative labor enough for them; and that, but in exceptional cases of sickness and especial misfortune, those who fell into utter destitution and beggary came to that pass through their idleness, their recklessness, or their vices. That was always my opinion. They besieged our door from morning till night, and I was obliged to help them, to look after them, to go to their houses; my family was worn out with these offices. But I looked upon beggary as, in all ordinary cases, *prima facie* evidence that there was something wrong behind it.

The great evil and mischief lay in indiscriminate charity. Many were the walks we took to avoid this, and often with little satisfaction. I have walked across the whole breadth of the city, on a winter's day, to find a man dressed better than I was, — with blue broadcloth and metal buttons and new boots, — and just sitting down to a very comfortable dinner. The wife was rather taken aback by my entrance, — it was she who had come to me, — and the man, of course, must say something for himself, and this it was: He " had fallen behind of late, in consequence of not receiving his rents from England. He was the owner of two houses in Sheffield." — " Well," I said, " if that is so, you are better off than I am; " and I took a not very courteous leave of them.

To give help in a better way, an Employment Society was formed in our church to cut out and prepare garments for poor women to sew, and be paid for it. A salesroom was opened in Amity Street, to sell the articles made up, at a trifling addition to their cost. The ladies of the congregation were in attendance at the church, in a large ante-room, to prepare the garments and give them out, and a hundred or more poor women came every Thursday to bring their work and receive more; and they have been coming to this day. It was thought an excellent plan, and was adopted by other churches. The ladies of All Souls joined in it, and the institution is now transferred to that church.

One day, in the winter I think of 1837, I heard of an association of gentlemen formed to investigate this terrible subject of mendicity in our city, and to find some way of methodizing our chari-tics and protecting them from abuse. I went down immediately to Robert Minturn, who, I was told, took a leading part in this movement, and told him that I had come post-haste to inquire what he and his friends were doing, for that nothing in our city life pressed upon my mind like this. I used, indeed, to feel at times — and Bellows had the same feeling — as if I would fain fling up my regular professional duties, and plunge into this great sea of city pauperism and misery.

Mr. Minturn told me that he, with four or five others, had taken up this subject; that, for more than a year past, they had met together one evening in the week to confer with one another upon it; that they had opened a correspondence with all our great cities, and with some in Europe; and sometimes had sent out agents to inquire into the methods that had been adopted to stem these enormous city evils. Mr. Minturn wished me to join them, and I expected to be formally invited to do so; but I was not, nor to a great public meeting called soon after, under their auspices. I suppose there was no personal feeling against me, — only an Orthodox one. Well, no matter. It was a noble enterprise, better than any sectarianism ever suggested, and worthy of record, especially considering its spontaneity, labor, and expense.

Their plan, when matured, was this: to district the city; to appoint one person in each district to receive all applications for aid; to sell tickets of various values, which we could buy and give the applicant at our doors, to be taken to the agent, who would render the needed help, according to his judgment.   Of course the beggars did not like it.   I found that, half the time, they would not take the tickets.   It would give them some trouble, but the special trouble, doubtless, with the reckless and dishonest among them, was that it would prevent them from availing themselves of the aid of twenty families, all acting in ignorance of what each was doing.

.   .   .   .

Jonathan Goodhue was a man whom nobody that knew him can ever forget.   Tall and fine-looking in person, simple and earnest in manners, with such a warmth in his accost that to shake hands with him was to feel happier for it all the day after.   I remember passing down Wall Street one day when old Robert Lenox was standing by his side.   After one of those warm greetings, I passed on, and Mr. Lenox said, "Who is that?" — "Mr. Dewey, a clergyman of a church in the city." — "Of which church?" said Mr. Lenox. — "Of the Unitarian church." — "The Lord have mercy upon him!" said the old man. It was a good prayer, and I have no doubt it was kindly made.

Alas! what I am writing is a necrology: they are all gone of whom I speak.   George Curtis, too; he died before I left the Church of the Messiah, — died in his prime.   George William Curtis is his son, well known as one of our most graceful writers and eloquent men: something hereditary in that, for his father had one of the clearest heads I knew, and a gifted tongue, though he was too modest to be a great talker. He could make a good speech, and once he made one that was more effective than I could have wished. The question was about electing Thomas Starr King to be my colleague. The congregation was immensely taken with him; but Mr. Curtis opposed on the ground that King was a Universalist, and he carried everything before him. He said, as it was reported to me, " I was born a Unitarian; I have lived a Unitarian; and, if God please, I mean to die a Unitarian ! " He had the old-fashioned, and indeed well-founded, dislike of Universalism. But all that is changed now, — was changing then; for the Universalists have given up their preaching of *no* retribution hereafter. They are in other respects, also, Unitarians, and the two bodies affiliate and are friends.

Moses Grinnell was a marked man in New York. A successful and popular merchant, his generosity was ample as his means; and I have known him in circumstances that required a higher generosity than that of giving money, and he stood the test perfectly. His mind, too, grew with his rise in the world. He was sent to Congress, and his acquaintance from that time with many distinguished men gave a new turn to his thoughts and a higher tone to his character and conversation. At his house, where I was often a guest, I used to meet Washington Irving, whose niece he married. Of course everybody knows of Washington Irving; but there are one or two anecdotes, of which I doubt whether they appear in his biography, and which I am tempted to relate. He told me that he once went to a theatre in London to hear some music. (They use theatres in London as music-halls, and I went to one myself, once, to hear Paganini, and enjoyed an evening that I can never forget. His one string — for he broke all the others — was a heart-string.) Mr. Irving said that on entering the theatre he found in the pit only three or four English gentleman, who had evidently come early, as he had, to find a good place. Accordingly, he took his seat near them, when one of them rather loftily said, "That seat is engaged, sir." He got up and took a seat a little farther off, when they said, "That, too, is engaged." Again he meekly rose, and took another place. Pretty soon one of the party said, "Do you remember Washington Irving's description of a band of music?" (It is indeed a most amusing caricature. One of the performers had blown his visnomy to a point. Another blew as if he were blowing his whole estate, real and personal, through his instrument. I quote from memory.) Mr. Irving said they went over with the whole description, with much entertainment and laughter. They little knew that they had thrust aside the author of their pleasure, who sat there, like the great Caliph, *incognito*, and they would have paid him homage enough if they had known him.

Mrs. S. told me that one evening he strolled up to their piazza, — they lived near to one another in the country, — and fell into one of those easy and unpremeditated talks, in which, to be sure, he was always most pleasant, when he said, among other things, " Don't be anxious about the education of your daughters: they will do very well; don't teach them so many things, — teach them one thing." — " What is that, Mr. Irving? " she asked. — " Teach them," he said, " to be easily pleased."

Bryant, too, everybody knows of. Now he is chiefly known as poet; but when I went to New York people thought most about him as editor of the " Evening Post," and that with little enough complacency in the circles where I moved. How many a fight I had for him with my Whig friends! For he was my parishioner, and it was known that we were much together. The " Evening Post " was a thorn in their sides, and every now and then, when some keen editorial appeared in it, they used to say, " There! what do you say of that ? " I always said the same thing : " Whether you and I like what he says or not, whether we think it fair or not, of one thing be sure, — he is a man of perfect integrity; he is so almost to a fault, if that be possible, regarding neither feelings nor friendships, nor anything else, when justice and truth are in question."

Speaking of Bryant brings to mind Audubon, the celebrated naturalist. I became acquainted with him through his family's attending our church, and one day proposed to Mr. Bryant to go with me to see him. Seating himself before the poet, Audubon quietly said, "You are our flower," — a very pretty compliment, I thought, from a man of the woods.

I happened to fall in with Mr. Audubon one day in the cars going to Philadelphia, when he was setting out, I think, on his last great tour across the American wilderness. He described to me his outfit, to be assumed when he arrived at the point of departure, a suit of dressed deerskin, his *only* apparel. In this he was to thread the forest and swim the rivers; with his rifle, of course, and powder and shot; a tin case to hold his drawing-paper and pencils, and a blanket. Meat, the produce of the chase, was to be his only food, and the earth his bed, for two or three months. I said, shrinking from such hardship, " I could n't stand that." — " If you were to go with me," he replied, " I would bring you out on the other side a new man." He broke down under it, however, rather prematurely; for in that condition I saw him once more, — his health and faculties shattered, — near the end of his life.

But to return,—turning and returning upon one's self must be the course of an autobiography, — my health having a second time completely failed, I determined again to go abroad; and to make the measure of relief more complete, I determined to go for two years, and to take my family with me. The sea was a horror to me, but beyond it lay pleasant lands that I wanted to look upon once more, galleries of art by which I wished to sit down and study at my leisure, and, above all, *rest:* I wanted to be where no one could call on me to preach or lecture, to do this or do that.

We sailed for Havre in October, 1841, passed the winter in Paris, the summer following in Switzerland, the next winter in Italy, and, returning through Germany, spent two months in England, and came home in August, 1843.

While in Geneva I was induced for my health to make trial of the " water-cure," and first to try what they call the " Arve bath." The *campagne* at Champel, where we were passing the summer, is washed for half a mile by the Arve. In hot August days I walked slowly by the river-bank, with cloak on, till a moderate perspiration was induced, then jumped in,—and out as quick! for the river, though it had run sixty miles from its source, seemed as cold as when it left the glacier of the Arveiron at Chamouni. Experiencing no ill effect, however, I determined to try the regular water-cure, and for this purpose, in

our travel through Switzerland, stopped at Meyringen in the Vale of Hasli. I was " packed," —
bundled up in bed blankets every morning at daybreak, went through the consequent furnace of heat and drench of perspiration for two or three hours, — then was taken by a servant on his back, me and my wrappages, the whole bundle, and carried down to the great bath, only 6° of Réaumur above ice (45° Fahrenheit), plunged in, got out again in no deliberate way, was pushed under a shower-bath of the same glacier water, fought my way out of that, at arm's end with the attendant, when he enveloped me in warm, dry sheets, and made me comfortable in one minute. It was of no use, however. My brain grew more nervous, the doctor agreed that it did not suit me, and shortly I gave it up.

At Rome we were introduced with a small American party to the Pope, Gregory XVI. It was just after the Carnival and just before Lent. The old man expressed his pleasure that the people had enjoyed themselves in Carnival, " But now," said he, " I suppose a great many of them will find themselves out of health in Lent, and will want indulgences." I could not help thinking how much that last was like a Puritan divine.

What a life is life in Rome ! — not common, not like any other, but as if the pressure of stupendous and crowding histories were upon every day. A presence haunts you that is more than all you see. We Americans, with some invited guests, celebrated Washington's birthday by a dinner. In a speech I said, " I was asked the other day, what struck me most in Rome, and I answered, — ' To think that this is Rome ! ' " Lucien Bonaparte, who sat opposite me at table, bowed his head with emphasis, as if he said, " That is true." He was entitled to know what great historic memories are ; and those of his family, criticise them as we may, — and I am not one of their admirers, — do not, perhaps, fall below much of the Roman imperial grandeur.

On coming to England from the Continent, among many things to admire, there were two things we were especially thankful for, — comfort and hospitality. We had not been in London half a day before I had rented a furnished house, and we were established in it. That is, the owner, occupying the basement, gave us the parlors above and ample sleeping-rooms, and the use of her servants, — we defraying the expense of our table, — for so much a month. We took possession of our apartments an hour after we had engaged them, and had nothing to do but order our dinner and walk out ; and all this for less, I think, than it would have cost us to live at a good boarding-house in Broadway.

· · · · · · · ·

We visited various parts of England, — Warwick, Kenilworth, Oxford, Birmingham, and Liverpool, and made acquaintance with persons whom to know was worth going far, and whom to remember has been a constant pleasure ever since.

Well, we came back in August, 1843, in the steamer " Hibernia." What a joy to return home! We landed in Boston. The railroad across Massachusetts had been completed during our absence, and brought us to Sheffield in six or seven hours; it had always been a weary journey before, of three days by coach, or a week with our own horse. A few days' rest, and then six or eight hours more took us to New York, where we found the water fountains opened; the Croton had been brought in that summer. Did it not seem all very fit and festal to us? For we had come home!

My health, however, was only partially reestablished, and the recruiting which had got lasted me for constant service in my church but three years more. The winter of 1846-47 I passed in Washington, serving the little church there. In the spring I returned to New York, struggled on with my duties in the church for another year; in the spring of 1848 sold my house, and retired to the Sheffield home, continuing to preach occasionally in New York for a number of months longer, when, early in 1849, my connection with the Church of the Messiah was finally dissolved. I would willingly have remained with it on condition of discharging a partial service, with a colleague to assist me: it was the only chance I saw

of continuing in my profession. The congregation, at my instance, had sought for a colleague,
both during my absence in Europe and in the
later years of my continuance with it, but had
failed, — there appearing to be some singular
reluctance in our young preachers to enter
into that relation, — and there seemed nothing for
the church to do but to inaugurate a new
ministration.

It was in this crisis of my worldly affairs, so
trying to a clergyman who is dependent on his
salary, that I experienced the benefit of a rule
that early in life I prescribed to myself; and that
was, always to lay up for a future day some portion of my annual income. I insisted upon it
that, with as much foresight as the ant or the bee,
I might be allowed without question so to use
the salary appointed to me as to make some
provision for the winter-day of life, or for the
spring that would come after, and might be to
others bleak and cold and desolate without it.
So often have I witnessed this, that I am most
heartily thankful that, on leaving New York, I was
not reduced to utter destitution, and that with
some moderate exertion I am able to provide for
our modest wants. At the same time I do not
feel obliged to conceal the conviction, and never
did, that the service of religion in our churches
meets with no just remuneration. One may suffer
martyrdom and not complain; but I do not think
one is bound to say that it is a reasonable or
pleasant thing.

Another thing I will be so frank as to say on leaving New York, and that is, that it was a great moral relief to me to lay down the burden of the parochial charge. I regretted to leave New York; I could have wished to live and die among the friends I had there; I should make it my plan now to spend my winters there, if I could afford it: but that particular relation to society, — no man, it seems to me, can heartily enter into it without feeling it to weigh heavily upon him. Sympathy with affliction is the trial-point of the clergyman's office. In the natural and ordinary relations of life every man has enough of it. But to take into one's heart, more or less, the personal and domestic sorrows of two or three hundred families, is a burden which no man who has not borne it can conceive of. I sometimes doubt whether it was ever meant that any man, or at least any profession of men, should bear it; whether the general ministrations of the pulpit to affliction should not suffice, leaving the application to the hearer in this case as in other cases; whether the clergyman's relations to distress and suffering should not be like every other man's, — general with his acquaintance, intimate with his friends; whether, if there were nothing conventional or customary about this matter, most families would not prefer to be left to themselves, without a professional call from their minister. Suppose that there were no rule with regard to it; that the clergyman, like every other man, went where his feelings carried him, or his relations warranted; that it was no more expected of him, as a matter of course, to call upon a bereaved family, than of any other of their acquaintance, — would not that be a better state of things? I am sure I should prefer it, if I were a parishioner. When, indeed, the minister of religion wishes to turn to wise account the suffering of sickness or of bereavement, let him choose the proper time: reflection best comes after; it is not in the midst of groans and agonies, of sobs and lamentations, that deep religious impressions are usually made.

I have a suspicion withal, that there is something semi-barbaric in these immediate and urgent ministrations to affliction, — something of the Indian or Oriental fashion, — or something derived from the elder time, when the priest was wise and the people rude. For ignorant people, who have no resources nor reflections of their own, such ministrations may be proper and needful now. I may be in the wrong about all this. Perhaps I ought to suspect it. There is more that is hereditary in us all, I suppose, than we know. My father never could bear the sight of sickness or distress: it made him faint. There is a firmness, doubtless, that is better than this; but I have it not. Very likely I am wrong. My friend Putnam[1] lately tried to convince me of it, in a conversation we had; maintaining that the

---

[1] Rev. George Putnam, D. D., of Roxbury, Mass. — M. E. D.

parochial relation ought not to be, and need not be, that burden upon the mind which I found it. And I really feel bound on such a point, rather than myself, to trust him, one of the most finely balanced natures I ever knew. Why, then, do I say all these things? Because, in giving an account of myself, I suppose I ought to say and confess what a jumble of *pros* and *cons* I am. Heaven knows I have tried hard to keep right; and if I am not as full as I can hold of one-sided and erratic opinions, I think it some praise. . . . I do strive to keep in my mind a whole rounded circle of truth and opinion. It would be pleasant to let every mental tendency run its length; but I could not do so. It may be pride or narrowness; but I *must* keep on some terms with *myself.* I cannot find my understanding falling into contradiction with the judgments it formed last month or last year, without suspecting not only that there was something wrong then, but that there is something wrong now, to be resisted. That "there is a mean in things" is held, I believe, to be but a mean apothegm now-a-days; but I do not hold it to be such. All my life I have endeavored to hold a balance against the swayings of my mind to the one side and the other of every question. I suppose this appears in my course, such as it has been, in religion, in politics, on the subject of slavery, of peace, of temperance, etc. It may appear to be dulness or tameness or time-serving or cowardice or folly, but I simply do not believe it to be either.

But to return: we were now once more in Sheffield, and I was without employment, — a condition always most irksome to me. Hard work, I am persuaded, is the highest pleasure in the world, and, from the day when I was in college, vacations have always proved to me the most tedious times in my life.

I determined, therefore, to pursue some study as far as I could, and my subject, — the choice of years before, — was the philosophy of history and humanity. While thus engaged, I received an invitation from Mr. John A. Lowell, trustee of the Lowell Institute, to deliver one of its annual popular courses of lectures in Boston. This immediately gave a direction to my thoughts, and by the winter of 1850-51 I was prepared to write the lectures, which I ventured to denominate, "Lectures on the Problem of Human Destiny," and I gave them in the autumn of 1851. My reason for adopting such a title I gave in the first lecture, and I might add that, with my qualifications, I was ashamed to put at the head of my humble work such great words as " Philosophy of History and Humanity," — the title of Herder's celebrated treatise. The truth was, I had, or thought I had, something to say upon the philosophy of the human condition, — upon the end for man, and upon the only way in which it could be achieved, — upon the terrible problem of sin and suffering in this world, — and I tried to say it. I so far succeeded with my audience in Boston, that, either from report of that, or from the intrinsic interest of the subject, I was invited to repeat the lectures in various parts of the country; and during the four or five years following I repeated them fifteen times, — in New Bedford, New York, Brooklyn, Washington, Baltimore, St. Louis, Louisville, Madison, Cincinnati, Nashville, Sheffield, Worcester, Charleston, S. C., New Orleans, and Savannah in part, and the second time also, I gave them, by Mr. Lowell's request, in the Boston Institute. At the same time, I was not idle as a preacher, having preached every Sunday in the places where I lectured, besides serving the church in Washington two long winters. I also wrote another course of lectures for the Lowell Institute, on the " Education of the Human Race," and repeated it in several places.

At the time that I was invited to Washington, I received, in February, 1851, a document from the Government, which took me so much by surprise that I supposed it must be a mistake. It was no other than a commission as chaplain in the Navy. I wrote to a gentleman in Washington, asking him to make inquiry for me, and ascertain what it meant. He replied that there was no mistake about it, and that it was intended for me. I then concluded, as there was a Navy Yard in Washington, and as the President, Mr.

Fillmore, attended the church to which I was invited, that he intended by the appointment to help both the church and me, and I accepted it. On going to Washington I found that there was a chaplain already connected with the Navy Yard, and on his retirement some months later, and my offering to perform any duties required there, being answered that there was really nothing to be done, I resigned the commission.

Life in Washington was not agreeable to me, and yet I felt a singular attachment to the people there. This mixture of repulsion and attraction I could not understand at the time, or rather, — as is usually the case with our experience while pássing, — did not try to; but walking those streets two or three years later, when experience had become history, I could read it. In London or Paris the presence of the government is hardly felt; the action of public affairs is merged and lost in the life of a great city; but in Washington it is the one, all-absorbing business of the place. Now, whether it be pride or sympathy, one does not enjoy a great movement of things going on around him in which he has no part, and the thoughts and aims of a retired and studious man, especially, sever him from the views and interests of public men. But, on the other hand, this very pressure of an all-surrounding public life brings private men closer together. There they stand, while the tides of successive Administrations sweep by them, and their relation be-

comes constantly more interesting from the fluc-
tuation of everything else.   It is really curious to
see how the private and resident society of Washington breathes freer, and prepares to enjoy itself
when Congress is about to rise and leave it to
itself.

Among the remarkable persons with whom I
became acquainted in Washington, at this or a
former time, was John C. Calhoun.   I had with
him three interviews of considerable length, and
I remember each of them, the more distinctly
from the remarkable habit he had of talking
upon *subjects*, — not upon the general occur-
rences of the day, but upon some particular
topic.   The first two were at an earlier period
than that to which this part of my narrative re-
lates; it was when he was Vice-President of the
United States, under the administration of John
Quincy Adams.   I went to his room in the Capi-
tol to present my letter of introduction; it was
just before the assembling of the Senate, arfd I
said, of course, that I would not intrude upon his
time at that moment, and was about to withdraw;
but he kindly detained me, saying, "No: it will
be twenty minutes before I go to the Senate; sit
down."   And then, in two minutes, I found him
talking upon a purely literary point, — I am sure
I do not know how he got to it; but it was this,
that the first or second book of every author, so
he maintained, was always his best.   He cited a

number of instances in support of his position. I do not remember what they were; but it occurred to me in reflecting upon it afterwards, that, in purely literary composition, there were some reasons why it might be true. An author writes his first books with the greatest care; he naturally puts into them his best and most original thoughts, which he cannot use again; and if he succeeds, and gains reputation, he is liable to grow both careless. and confident, — to think that the things which people admire are his peculiarities, and not his general merits, and so to fall into mannerism and repetition. I remember Mrs. George Lee, of Boston, a sagacious woman, saying to me one day, when I told her I was going to write a second sermon on a certain subject, — she had praised the first, — " I have observed that the second sermon, on any subject, is never so good as the first; even Channing's are not."

Mr. Calhoun, on my leaving him, invited me to pass the evening with him at his house in Georgetown. I went, expecting to meet company, but found myself alone with him, and then the subject of conversation was the advantage and necessity of an Opposition in Government. He was himself then, of course, in the Opposition, and he was very candid: he said he did not question the motives of the Administration, while he felt bound to oppose it. I was struck with his candor, — a thing I did not look for in a political opponent, — but especially with what he said about the benefit of an Opposition; both were rather new to me.

My third interview with him was at a later period, when his discourse turned upon this question: What is the greatest thing that a man can do? His answer was characteristic of the statesman. "It is," he said, "to speak the true and saving word in a great national emergency. For it implies," he continued, "the fullest knowledge of the past, the largest comprehension of the present, and the clearest foresight of the future." He might have added, to complete the idea, that this word was sometimes to be spoken when it involved the greatest peril to the position and prospects of the speaker. But how much moral considerations were apt to be present to his mind, I do not know. He was mostly known — so we of the North thought — as an impracticable reasoner. Miss Martineau said, "He was like a cast-iron man on a railroad."

I was introduced to Mr. Adams, but saw him little, and heard him less, as I will relate. Mr. Reed, of Barnstable, introduced me, — "Father Reed," as they used to call him, from his having been longer a member of Congress than any other man in the House, — and I said to him, as we were entering the White House, "Now tell Mr. Adams who I am and where from ; for I think he must be puzzled what to talk about, with so many strangers coming to him." Well, I was introduced accordingly, and Mr. Reed retired. I was offered a seat, and took it. I was a young man, and felt that it did not become me to open a conversation. And there we sat, five minutes, without a word being spoken by either of us! I rose, took my leave, and went away, I don't know whether more angered or astonished. I once, by the by, visited his father, old John Adams, then living in retirement at Quincy. Mr. Josiah Quincy took me to see him. *He* was not silent, but talked, I remember, full ten minutes — for we did not interrupt him — about Machiavel, and in language so well chosen that I thought it might have been printed.

But the most interesting person, as statesman, that I saw in Washington, was Thomas Corwin, of Ohio, commonly called Tom Corwin. This was at a later period.

Circumstances, or the chances of conversation, sometimes lead to acquaintance and friendship, which years of ordinary intercourse fail to bring about. It happened, the first time I saw Mr. Corwin, that some observation I made upon political morality seemed to strike him as a new thought; I suppose it was a topic seldom touched upon in Washington society. It led to a good deal of conversation, then and afterwards; and I must say that a more high-principled and religiously minded statesman I have never met with than Mr. Corwin.

When he was preparing to deliver his celebrated speech in the Senate against the war with Mexico, he told me what he was going to say, and asked me if I thought he could say it and not be politically ruined by it. I answered that I did not know; but that I would say it if it did ruin me.

The day came for his speech, and I never saw the Senate Chamber so densely packed as it was to hear him. He told me that he should not speak more than half an hour; but he did speak three hours, not only against the Mexican war, but against the system of slavery, in the bitterest language. His friends in Ohio told me, years after, that it did ruin him. But for that, they said, he would have been President of the United States.

Thackeray came to Washington while I was there. He gave his course of lectures on the "English Humorists of the Eighteenth Century." His style, especially in his earlier writings, had one quality which the critics did not seem to notice; it was not conventional, but spun out of the brain. With the power of thought to take hold of the mind, and a rich, deep, melodious voice, he contrived, without one gesture, or any apparent emotion in his delivery, to charm away an hour as pleasantly as I have ever felt it in a lecture. What he told me of his way of composing confirms me in my criticism on his style. He did not dash his pen on paper, like Walter Scott, and write off twenty pages without stopping, but, dictating to an amanuensis, — a plan which leaves the brain to work undisturbed by the pen-labor, — dictating from his chair, and often from his bed, he gave out sentence by sentence, slowly, as they were moulded in his mind.

Thackeray was sensitive about public opinion; no writer, I imagine, was ever otherwise. I remember, one morning, he was sitting in our parlor, when letters from the mail came in. They were received with some eagerness, of course, and he said, "You seem to be pleased to have letters; *I* am not." — "No?" we said. — "No. I have had letters from England this morning, and they tell me that 'Henry Esmond' is not liked."

This led to some conversation on novels and novel-writing, and I ventured to say: "How is it that not one of the English novelists has ever drawn any high or adequate character of the clergyman? Walter Scott never gave us anything beyond the respectable official. Goldsmith's Dr. Primrose is a good man, the best we have in your English fiction, but odd and amusing rather than otherwise. Then Dickens has given us Chadband and Stiggins, and you Charles Honeyman. Can you not conceive," I went on to say, "that a man, without any chance of worldly profit, for a bare stipend, giving his life to promote what you must know are the highest interests of mankind, is engaged in a noble calling, worthy of being nobly described? Or have you no examples in England to draw from?"

This last sentence touched him, and I meant it should.

With considerable excitement he said, "I delivered a lecture the other evening in your church in New York, for the Employment Society; would you let me read to you a passage from it?" Of course I said I should be very glad to hear it, and added, "I thank you for doing that." — "I don't know why you should thank me," he said; "it cost me but an hour's reading, and I got $1,500 for them. I thought I was the party obliged. But I did tell them they should have a dozen shirts made up for me, and they did it." He then went and brought his lecture, and read the passage, which told of a curate's taking him to visit a poor family in London, where he witnessed a scene of distress and of disinterestedness very striking and beautiful to see. It was a very touching description, and Thackeray nearly broke down in reading it.

A part of the winter of 1856-57 I passed with my family at Charleston, S. C. I went to preach in Dr. Gilman's pulpit, and to lecture. I had been there the spring before, and made very agreeable acquaintance with the people. My reception, both in public and in private, was as kindly and hospitable as I could desire. I was much interested in society there, and strongly attached to it. But in August following, in an address under our Old Elm-tree in Sheffield,

I made some observations upon the threatened extension of the slave-system, that dashed nearly all my agreeable relations with Charleston. I am not a person to regard such a breach with indifference: it pained me deeply. My only comfort was, that what I said was honestly said; that no honorable man can desire to be respected or loved through ignorance of his character or opinions; and that the ground then recently taken at the South — that the institution of human slavery is intrinsically right, just, and good — seems to me to involve such a wrong to humanity, such evil to the South, and such peril to the Union of the States, that it was a proper occasion for speaking earnestly and decidedly.

I was altogether unprepared for the treatment I received. One year before, I had been in the great Charleston Club, when the question of the perpetuity of the slave-system was discussed; when, indeed, an elaborate essay was read by one of the members, in which the ground was taken, that the dark cloud would sink away to the southwest, to Central America perhaps, from whence the slave population would find an exodus across the water to Africa; and of twenty members present, seventeen agreed with the essayist.

And I take occasion here to say, that this position of the seventeen was mainly satisfactory to me. I would, indeed, have had the South go farther. I would have had it take in hand the business of putting an end to slavery, by laws providing for its gradual abolition, and by preparing the slaves for it; but I did not believe then, and do not now,[1] that immediate emancipation was theoretically the best plan. It was forced upon us by the exigencies of the war. And, independently of that, such was the infatuation of the Southern mind on the subject that there seemed to be no prospect of its ever being brought to take that view of it which was prevailing through the civilized and Christian world. But if it had taken that view, and had gone about the business of preparing for emancipation, I think the general public sentiment would have been satisfied; and I believe the result would have been better for the slaves, and better for the country. To be sure, things are working better perhaps now than could have been expected, and it may turn out that instant emancipation was the best thing. But the results of great social changes do not immediately reveal themselves. We are feeling, for instance, the pressure and peril of the free system in government more than we did fifty years ago, and may have to feel and fear it more than we do now. The freedmen are, at present, upon their good behavior, and are acting under the influence of a previous condition. But when I look to the future, and see them rising to wealth, culture, and refinement, and, as human beings, entitled to consideration as much as any other,

---

[1] The date of this passage must be in or about 1863.—M. E. D.

and yet forbidden intermarriage with the whites, as they should be for physiological reasons, — when, in fine, they see that they have *not* any fair and just position in American society and government, — they may be sorry that they were not gradually emancipated, and colonized to their own native country; and for ourselves — for our own country — the seeds may be sowing, in the dark bosom of the future, which may spring up in civil wars more terrible than ever were seen before.

Such speculations and opinions, I am sensible, would meet with no favor among us now. The espousal of the slave-man's cause among our Northern people is so humane and hearty that they can stop nowhere, for any consideration of expediency, in doing him justice, after all his wrongs; and I honor their *feeling*, go to what lengths it will. Nevertheless, I put down these my thoughts, for my children to understand, regard them as they may.

But what it is in my style or manner of writing that has called forth such a hard feeling towards me, from extremists both North and South, upon this slavery question, I cannot understand. In every instance in which I have spoken of it, I have been drawn out by a sense of duty, — there certainly was no pleasure in it. I have never assailed the motives of any man or party; I have spoken in no feeling of unkindness to anybody; there can have been no bitterness in my speech.

And yet something, I suppose, there must have been in my way of expressing myself, to offend. It may have been a fault, it may have been a merit for aught I know; for truly I do not know what it was.

After all, how little does any man know of his own personality, — of his personality in action. He may study himself; he may find out what his faculties, what his traits of character are, in the abstract as it were; but what they are in action, in movement, — how they appear to others, — he cannot know. The eye that looks around upon a landscape sees everything but itself. It is just as a man may look in the glass and see himself there every day; but he sees only the framework, only the " still life " in his face; he does not see it in the free play of expression, — in the strong workings of thought and feeling. I was one day sitting with Robert Walsh in Paris, and there was a large mirror behind him. Suddenly he said, " Ah, what a vain fellow you are ! " — " How so? " I asked. — " Why," said he, " you are not looking at me as you talk, but you are looking at yourself in the glass." — " It is a fact ! " I exclaimed, " I never saw myself talking before, — never saw the play of my own features in conversation." Had the *mind* a glass thus to look in, it would see things, see wonders, it knows nothing of now. It might see worse things, it might see better things, than it expected.

And yet I have been endeavoring in these pages

to give some account of myself, while, after all, I am obliged to say that it is little more than a *post mortem* examination. If I had been dealing with the living subject, I suppose I could not have dealt so freely with myself. The last thing which I ever thought of doing is this which I have now done. Autobiographies are often pleasant reading; but I confess that I have always had a kind of prejudice against them. They have seemed to me to imply something of vanity, or a want of dignified reserve. The apology lies, perhaps, in the writer's ignorance, after all, of his own and very self. He has only told the *story* of a life. He has not come much nearer to himself than statistics come to the life of a people.

All that I know is, that I have lived a life mainly happy in its experience, not merely according to the average, not merely *as things go* in this world, but far more than that; which I should be willing to live again for the happiness that has blessed it, yet more for the interests which have animated it, and which has always been growing happier from the beginning. I have lived a life mainly fortunate in its circumstances both of early nurture and active pursuit; marred by no vice, — I do not remember even ever to have told a lie, — stained by no dishonor; laborious, but enjoying labor, especially in the sphere to which my life has been devoted; suffering from no pressing want, though moderate in means, and successful in every way, as much as I had any

right or reason to expect. I have been happy
(the word is weak to express it) in my domestic
relations, happy in the dearest and holiest friendships, and happy in the respect of society. And
I have had a happiness (I dread the appearance
of *profession* in saying it) in things divinest, in
religion, in God, — in associating with him all the
beauty of nature and the blessedness of life,
beyond all other possible joy. And, therefore,
notwithstanding all that I have suffered, notwithstanding all the pain and weariness and anxiety
and sorrow that necessarily enter into life, and
the inward errings that are worse than all, I would
end my record with a devout thanksgiving to the
great Author of my being. For more and more
am I unwilling to make my gratitude to him what
is commonly called " a thanksgiving for mercies,"
— for any benefits or blessings that are peculiar to
myself, or my friends, or indeed to any man.
Instead of this, I would have it to be gratitude
for *all* that belongs to my life and being, — for
joy and sorrow, for health and sickness, for success and disappointment, for virtue and for temptation, for life and death; because I believe that
all is meant for good.

Something of what I here say seems to require
another word or two to be added, and perhaps it
is not unmeet for me to subjoin, as the conclusion
of the whole matter, my theory and view and
summing up of what life is; for on it, to my
apprehension, the virtue and happiness of life

mainly repose. It revealed itself dimly in my earlier, it has become clearer to me in my later, years; and the best legacy, as I conceive, that I could leave to my children would be this view of life.

I know that we are not, all the while, thinking of any theory of life. So neither are we all the while thinking of the laws of nature; the attraction of gravitation, for instance. But unless there were some ultimate reference to laws, both material and moral, our minds would lose their balance and security. If I believed that the hill by my side, or the house I live in, were liable any moment to be unseated and hurled through the air by centrifugal force, I should be ill at ease. And if I believed that the world was made by a malignant Power, or that the fortunes of men were the sport of a doubtful conflict between good and evil deities or principles, my life, like that of the ancients, would be filled with superstitions and painful fears. The foundation of all rational human tranquillity, cheerfulness, and courage, whether we are distinctly conscious of it or not, lies in the ultimate conviction, that God is good, — that his providence, his order of things in the world, is good; and theology, in the largest sense of the term, is as vital to us as the air we breathe.

If, then, I thought that this world were a castoff, or a wrecked and ruined, world; if I thought that the human generations had come out from the dark eclipse of some pre-existent state, or from the dark shadow of Adam's fall, broken, blighted, accursed, propense to all evil, and disabled for all good; and if, in consequence, I believed that unnumbered millions of ignorant heathens, and thousands around me, — children but a day old in their conscious moral probation, and men, untaught, nay, ill-taught, misled and blind, — were doomed, as the result of this life-experiment, to intense, to unending, to infinite pain and anguish, — most certainly I should be miserable in such a state, and nothing could make life tolerable to me. Most of all should I detest myself, if the idea that *I* was to escape that doom could assuage and soothe in my breast the bitter pain of all generous humanity and sympathy for the woes and horrors of such a widespread and overwhelming catastrophe.

What, then, do I say and think? I say, and I maintain, that the constitution of the world is good, and that the constitution of human nature is good; that the laws of nature and the laws of life are ordained for good. I believe that man was made and destined by his Creator ultimately to be an adoring, holy, and happy being; that his spiritual and physical constitution was designed to lead to that end; but that end, it is manifest from the very nature of the case, can be attained only by a free struggle; and this free struggle, with its mingled success and failure, is the very story of the world. A sublime story it is, therefore. The life of men and nations has not been a floundering on through useless disorder and confusion, trial and strife, war and bloodshed; but it has been a struggling onward to an end.

This, I believe, has been the story of the world from the beginning. Before the Christian, before the Hebrew, system appeared, there was religion, worship, faith, morality, in the world, and however erring, yet always improving from age to age. Those systems are great steps in the human progress; but they are not the only steps. Moses is venerable to me. The name of Jesus is " above every name; " but my reverence for him does not require me to lose all interest in Confucius and Zoroaster, in Socrates and Plato.

In short, the world is a school; men are pupils in this school; God is its builder and ordainer. And he has raised up for its instruction sages and seers, teachers and guides; ay, martyred lives, and sacrificial toils and tears and blood, have been poured out for it. The greatest teaching, the greatest life, the most affecting, heart-regenerating sacrifice, was that of the Christ. From him I have a clearer guidance, and a more encouraging reliance upon the help and mercy of God, than from all else. I do not say the only reliance, but the greatest.

This school of life I regard as the infant-school of eternity. The pupils, I believe, will go on forever learning. There is solemn retribution in this system, — the future must forever answer for the past; I would not have it otherwise. I must fight the battle, if I would win the prize; and for all failure, for all cowardice, for all turning aside after ease and indulgence in preference to virtue and sanctity, I must suffer; I would not have it otherwise. There is help divine offered to me, there is encouragement wise and gracious; I welcome it. There is a blessed hereafter opened to prayer and penitence and faith; I lift my hopes to that immortal life. This view of the system of things spreads for me a new light over the heavens and the earth. It is a foundation of peace and strength and happiness more to be valued, in my account, than the title-deed of all the world.

LETTERS.

THE foregoing pages, selected from many written at intervals between 1857 and 1870, tell nearly all of their writer's story which it can be of interest to the public to know; and although I have been tempted here and there to add some explanatory remarks, I have thought it best on the whole to leave them in their original and sometimes abrupt simplicity. The author did not intend them for publication, but for his family alone; and in sharing a part with a larger audience than he contemplated, we count upon a measure of that responsive sympathy with which we ourselves read frequently between the lines, and enter into his meaning without many words.

But there is one point I cannot leave untouched. There is one subject on which some of those who nevertheless honor him have scarcely understood his position.

Twenty-five years ago slavery was a question upon which feeling was not only strong, but roused, stung, and goaded to a height of passion where all argument was swept away by the common emotion as futile, if not base. My father, thinking the system hateful in itself and productive of nearly unmingled evil, held nevertheless that, like all great and established wrongs, it must be met with wise and patient counsel; and that in the highest interest of the slave, of the white race, of the country, and of constitutional liberty, its abolition must be gradual. To the uncompromising Abolitionists such views were intolerable; and by some of those who demanded immediate emancipation, even at the cost of the Union and all that its destruction involved, it was said that he was influenced by a mean spirit of expediency and a base truckling to the rank and wealth which sustained this insult to humanity.

They little knew him. The man who at twenty-five had torn himself from the associations and friendships of his youth, and, moved solely by love of truth, had imperilled all his worldly hopes by joining himself to a small religious body, despised and hated as heretics by most of those whom he had been trained to love and respect, was not the man at fifty to blench from the expression of any honest conviction; and, to sum up all in one word, he held his views upon this subject, as upon all others, bravely and honestly, and stated them clearly and positively, when he felt it his duty to speak, although evasion or silence would have been the more comfortable alternative. " I doubt," says Mr. Chadwick,[1] " if Garrison or Parker had a keener sense than his of the enormity of human slavery. Before the first Abolitionist Society had been organized, he was one of the organizers of a committee for the discussion and advancement of emancipation. I have read all of his principal writings upon slavery, and it would be hard to find more terrible indictments of its wickedness. He stated its defence in terms that Foote and Yancey might have made their own, only to sweep it all away with the 'blazing ubiquity' that the negro was a man and an immortal soul. Yet when the miserable days of fugitive-slave rendition were upon us, he was with Gannett in the sad conviction that the law must be obeyed. We could not see it then; but we can see to-day that it was possible for men as good and true as any men alive to take this stand. And nothing else brings out the nobleness of Dewey into such bold relief as the fact, that the immeasurable torrent of abuse that greeted his expressed opinion did not in any least degree avail to make him one of the pro-slavery faction. The concession of 1850 was one which he would not have made, and it must be the last. Welcome to him the iron flail of war, whose tribulation saved the immortal wheat of justice and purged away the chaff of wrong to perish in unquenchable fire!"

His feelings retained their early sensitiveness

---

[1] The Rev. John W. Chadwick, of Brooklyn, N. Y., in a sermon preached after Dr. Dewey's death.

in a somewhat remarkable degree. In a letter written when he was near seventy he says, —

"I do believe there never was a man into whose manhood and later life so much of his foolish boyhood flowed as into mine. I am as anxious to go home, I shall be all the way to-morrow as eager and restless, and all the while thinking of the end of my journey, as if I were a boy going from school, or a young lover six weeks after his wedding-day. Shall I ever learn to be an old man?"

But it was this very simplicity and tenderness that gave such a charm to his personal intercourse. His emotions, like his thoughts, had a plain directness about them which assured you of their honesty. With a profound love of justice, he had an eminently judicial mind, and could not be content without viewing a subject from every side, and casting light upon all its points. The light was simple sunshine, — clear, untinged by artificial mixtures; the views were direct and straightforward, with no subtle slants of odd or recondite position; and in his feelings, also, there was the same large and natural simplicity. You felt the ground-swell of humanity in them, and it was this breadth and genuineness which laid the foundation of his power as a preacher, making him strike unerringly those master chords that are common and universal in every audience. Gifts of oratory he had, both natural and acquired, — a full, melodious voice, so sympathetic in modulation and so attuned to

reverence that I have heard more than one person say that his first few words in the pulpit did
more towards lifting them to a truly religious
frame of mind than the whole service from any
other lips, — a fine dramatic power, enough to
have given him distinction as an actor, had that
been the profession of his choice, — a striking
dignity of presence, and an easy and appropriate
gesticulation. But these, as well as his strong
common sense, that balance-wheel of character,
were brought into the service of his earnest convictions. What he had to say, he put into the
simplest form ; and if his love of art and beauty,
and his imaginative faculty, gave wealth and orna-
ment to his style, he never sacrificed a particle of
direct force for any rhetorical advantage. His
function in life — he felt it to his inmost soul —
was to present to human hearts and minds the
essential verities of their existence in such a manner that they could not choose but believe in them.
His strength was in his reverent perception of the
majesty of Right as accordant with the Divine and
Eternal Will; his power over men was in the
sublimity of his appeal to an answering faith in
themselves.

He was greatest as a preacher, and it is as a
preacher that he will be best remembered by the
public. The printed page, though far inferior to
the fervid eloquence of the same words when
spoken, will corroborate by its beauty, its pathos,
and its logical force, the traditions that still linger

of his deep impressiveness in the pulpit. In making the following selections from his letters, I have been influenced by the desire to let them show him in his daily and familiar life, with the easy gayety and love of humor which was as natural to him as the deep and solemn meditations which absorbed the larger part of his mind. They are very far from elaborate compositions, being rather relaxations from labor, and he thought very slightly of them himself; yet I think they will present the real man as nothing but such careless and conversational writing can.

No letters of his boyhood have been preserved, and very few of his youth. This, to Dr. Channing, was probably written at Plymouth, while there on an exchange of pulpits, soon after his ordination at New Bedford: —

To Rev. William Ellery Channing, D.D.

PLYMOUTH, *Dec.* 27, 1823.

DEAR SIR, — I was scarcely disappointed at your not coming to my ordination, and indeed I have felt all along that, if you could not preach, I had much rather see you at a more quiet and leisurely time. I thank you for the hope you have given me of this in the suggestion you made to Mr. Tuckerman. When the warm season comes, I pray you to give Mrs. Dewey and me the pleasure of trying what we can do to promote your comfort and health, and of enjoying your society for a week.

Our ordination was indeed very pleasant, and our prospects are becoming every day more encouraging. The services of that occasion were attended with the most gratifying and useful impression. Our friend, Mr. Tuckerman, preached more powerfully, and produced a greater effect, than I had supposed he ever did. I must remind you, however, that his sermon, like every good sermon, had its day when it was delivered. We cannot print the pathos, nor you read the fervor, with which it was spoken.

I have had no opportunity to express to you the very peculiar and high gratification with which I have received the late expression of the liberality and kindness of your society, nor can it be necessary.[1] I cannot fail to add, however, that the pleasure is greatly enhanced by the knowledge that I owe the occasion of it to your suggestion.

I hope to visit Boston this winter, or early in the spring. I often feel as if I had a burden of questions which I wish to propose to you for conversation. The want of this resource and satisfaction is one of the principal reasons that make me regret my distance from Boston. I shall always remember the weeks I spent with you, two years ago, with more interest than I shall ever feel it proper to express to you. It is one of my most joyful hopes of heaven, that such intercourse shall be renewed, and exalted and perpetuated forever.

To the Same.

NEW BEDFORD, *Sept.* 21, 1824 (?).

DEAR SIR, — I thank you for your letter and invitation. . . . The result of your going to Boston is what I

---

[1] See p. 50.

feared, and it seems too nearly settled that nothing will give you health, but a different mind, or a different mode of life. Quintilian advises the orator to retire before he is spent, and says that he can still advance the object of his more active and laborious pursuits by conversing, by publishing, and by teaching others, youths, to follow in his steps. I do not quote this advice to recommend it, if it were proper for me to recommend anything. But I have often revolved the courses that might preserve your life, and make it at once happy to yourself and useful to us, for many years to come. I cannot admit any plan that would dismiss you altogether from the pulpit, nor do I believe that any such could favor your happiness or your health. But could you not limit yourself to preaching, say ten times in a year (*provided one of them be in New Bedford*)? and will you permit me to ask, nor question my modesty in doing so, if you could not spend a part of the year in a leisurely preparation of something for the press? I fear that your MSS., and I mean your sermons now, would suffer by any other revisal and publication than your own. With regard to the last suggestion of Quintilian's, I have supposed that it has been fairly before you ; but perhaps I have already said more than becomes me. If so, I am confident at least that I deserve your pardon for my good intentions ; and with these, I am, dear sir, most truly as well as

Respectfully your friend,

O. Dewey.

I am tempted to introduce here a sketch of my father as he appeared in those early days, written by Rev. W. H. Channing, for the London "Enquirer" of April 13, 1882 : —

"It so happened then to me, while a youth of twelve or fifteen years in training at the Boston Latin School for Harvard University, that Dr. Dewey became a familiar guest in my mother's hospitable house. He was at this period the temporary minister of Federal Street Church, while Dr. Channing was seeking to renew his wasted energies, for better work, in Europe. And on Mondays — after his exhausting outpourings of Sunday — he was wont to 'drop in, while passing,' to talk over the themes of his discourse, or for friendly interchange of thought and sympathy. A special attraction was that the Misses Cabot, the elder of whom became a few years later Mrs. Charles Follen (both of whom will be remembered by English friends), made a common home with my mother; and the radiant intelligence, glowing enthusiasm, hearty affectionateness, and genial merriment of these bright-witted sisters charmed him. Sometimes they probed with penetrating questions the mystical metaphysics of the preceding day's sermon. Then, deeply stirred, and all on fire with truths dawning on his vision, he would rise from his chair and slowly pace the room, in a half soliloquy, half rejoinder. At these times of high-wrought emotion his aspect was commanding. His head was rounded like a dome, and he bore it erect, as if its weight was a burden; his eyes, blue-gray in tint, were gentle, while gleaming with inner light; the nostrils were outspread, as if breathing in mountain-top air; and the mobile lips, the lower of which protruded, apparently measured his deliberately accented words as if they were coins stamped in the mint. It was intense delight for a boy to listen to these luminous self-unfoldings, embodied in rhythmic speech. They moved me more profoundly even than the suppressed feeling of his awe-struck prayers, or the fluent fervor of his pulpit addresses ; for they raised the veil, and admitted one into his Holy of holies. At other times, literary or artistic themes, the newest poem, novel, picture, concert, came up for discussion ; and as these ladies were verse-writers, essayists, critics, and lovers of beauty in all forms, the conversations called out the rich genius and complex tendencies and aptitudes of Dr. Dewey in stimulating suggestions, which were refreshing as spring breezes. His mind gave hospitable welcome to each new fact disclosed by science, to all generous hopes for human refinement and ennobling ideals, while his discernment was keen to detect false sentiment or flashy sophisms. Again, some startling event would bring conventional customs and maxims to the judgment-bar of pure Christian ethics, when his moral indignation blazed forth with impartial equity against all degrading views of human nature, debasing prejudices, and distrust of national progress, — sparing no tyrant, however wealthy or high in station ; pleading for the downcast, however lowly ; hoping for the fallen, however scorned. Thanks to this clear-sighted moralist, he gave me, in his own example, a standard of generous Optimism too sun-bright ever to be eclipsed. Let it not be inferred from these hasty outlines, however, that Dr. Dewey was habitually grave, or intent on serious topics solely, in social intercourse. So far from this, he continually startled one by his swift transitions from solemn discourse to humorous descriptions of persons, places, experiences. And as the Misses Cabot and my mother alike regarded healthful laughter, cheery sallies, and childlike gayety as a wise relief for overwrought brains or high-strung sensibilities, our fireside sparkled with brilliant repartees and scintillating mirth. It is pleasantly remembered that, in such by-play, Dr. Dewey, while often satirical, and prone to good-tempered banter, was never cynical, and was intolerant of personal gossip or the intrusion of-mean slander. And to close the chapter of boyhood's acquaintance, it is gratefully recalled how cordially sympathetic this earnest apostle was with my youthful studies, trials, aspirations. All recollections, indeed, of my uncle's curate — whom, as is well-known, he wished to become his colleague — are charming; and before my matriculation at Harvard, one of my most trusted religious guides was Orville Dewey."

The Wares, both Henry and William, were among my father's dearest friends at this time, and the intimacy was interrupted only by death.

To Rev. Henry Ware.

NEW BEDFORD, *Feb.* 2, 1824.

MY DEAR FRIEND, —

. . . .

There is a great cause committed to us, — not that of a party, but that of principles. A contest as important as that of the Reformation is to pass here, and I trust, — though with trembling, — I trust in God that it is to be maintained with a better spirit. I cannot help feeling that generations as boundless as shall spread from the Atlantic to the Pacific shores wait for the result. The importance of everything that is doing for the improvement of this country is fast swelling to infinitude. These, dear sir, are some of my dreams, I fear I must call them, rather than waking thoughts. It seems to me not a little to know the age and country we live in. I think, and think, and think that something must be done, and often

I feel, and feel, and feel that I do nothing. What *can* we do to make ourselves and others aware of our Christian duties and of the signs of this time?

There is one comfort, — Unitarianism will succeed just as far as it is worthy of it, — and there are some forms of practical Unitarianism that ought not to meet with any favor in the world. If the whole mass becomes of this character, let it go down, till another wave of providence shall bring it up again.

But enough of this preaching: you think of all these things, and a thousand more, better than I can say them. I turn to your letter. Elder H., for whom you ask, is a very good man, — very friendly to me; but he is a terrible fanatic. He has Unitarian revivals that might match with any of them. It is a curious fact that the *Christians*, as they call themselves, Unitarian as they are, form the most extravagant, fiery, fanatical sect in this country.

.   .   .   .

Mrs. Dewey desires very friendly regards to Mrs. Ware, of whose continued illness we are concerned to hear. Let my kind remembrance be joined with my wife's, and believe me very truly,

Your friend and brother,

ORVILLE DEWEY.

To the Same.

NEW BEDFORD, *Feb.* 14, 1824.

MY DEAR FRIEND, — I cannot repress the inclination to offer you my sympathy.[1] I have often thought with

---

[1] Mrs. Ware died in the interval between those two letters. She was the daughter of Dr. Benjamin Waterhouse, of Cambridge, Mass. In 1827 Mr. Ware was again married to Miss Mary Lovell Pickard.

pain of what was coming upon you ; and I fear, though long threatening, it has come at last with a weight which you could hardly have anticipated. May God sustain and comfort you ! You are supported, I well know, while you are afflicted, in every recollection of what you have lost. Surely the greatness of your trial argues the kindness of Heaven, for it proves the greatness of the blessing you have enjoyed.

But, my dear sir, I will not urge upon you words which are but words, and touch not the terrible reality that occupies your mind. You want not the poor and cold sayings of one who knows not — who cannot know — what you suffer. You need not the aids of reflection from me. But you need what, in common with your friends, I would invoke for you, — the aid, the consolation that is divine. God grant it to you, — all that affection can ask, — all that affliction can need, — prays

Your friend and brother,

O. Dewey.

To Dr. Channing.

New Bedford, *Oct.* 16, 1827.

My Dear and Revered Friend, — Excuse me for calling you so ; may the formalities and the English reserves excuse me too.

I have had two letters from New York, one from Mr. Sewall, and the other from Mr. Ware, which are so pressing as really to give me some trouble. Do say something to me on this subject, if you have anything to say. There certainly are many reasons, and strong as numerous, why I should not at present leave New Bedford, — why I should not take such a post. I cannot say I am made to doubt what I ought to do ; but I have a fear lest

I should not do right, lest I should love my ease too well, lest it should be said to me in the other world, " A great opportunity, a glorious field was opened to you, and you did not improve it," — lest, in other words, I should not act upon considerations sufficiently high, comprehensive, and disinterested, — fit, in short, for contemplation from the future world as well as from the present.

I do not write asking you to reply ; for I do not suppose you have anything to say which you would not have suggested when I was with you. Indeed, I believe I write, as much as for anything, because I want to communicate with you about something, and this is uppermost in my mind.

Present my affectionate regards to Mrs. Channing and the children, and to Miss Gibbs.

Yours most affectionately,

O. Dewey.

To Rev. Henry Ware.

New Bedford, *March* 29, 1829.

My Dear Friend, — I cannot let you go off without my blessing. I did not know of your purpose till last evening, or I should not have left myself to write to you in the haste of a few minutes snatched on Sunday evening, to say nothing of the aching nerves and the palsied hand that usually come along with it. By the by, I have a good mind to desire you to propose a year's exchange [for me] to somebody in England. If you meet with a man who is neither too good nor too bad, suppose you suggest it to him, — not as from me, however.

I should think that a man, in going to England, would feel the evil of belonging to a sect, unless that sect embraced all the good and wise and gifted,— which can be said of no sect. The sectarianism of sects, however, is the bad thing. These are necessary; that is not necessary, but to human weakness. But fie upon discoursing to a man who is just stepping on shipboard ! May it bear you safely ! May it tread the mountain wave " as a steed that knows its rider," and is conscious of *what* it bears from us ! My heart will go with you in a double sense ; for I want to see England, — I want to see Italy, and the Alps, and the south of France. I don't know whether you intend to do all this ; and I am very certain not to do any of it. I know that yours will not be a travelled heart, any more than Goldsmith's. Let me lay in my claim for as many of its kind thoughts as belong to me. But yet more, let me assure you, as the exigency demands, that for every one you have thus to render, I have five to give in return.

I believe you will not be sorry, at this time, that my lines and words are few and far between ; for your leisure cannot serve to read many.

Mrs. D. desires her best wishes to you. We do not know whether Mrs. Ware goes with you, but hope she does.

I took my pen feeling as if I had not a word to say, but — God bless you ! and that I say with all my heart. Write me from abroad if you can, but make no exertion to do so.   Yours as ever,

O. DEWEY.

To the Same.

NEW BEDFORD, *Sept.* 14, 1830.

DEAR WARE, — I write down the good old compellation here, not because I have anything in particular to say

to you, but just to assure myself in the agreeable conviction that you are again within sixty miles of me. When
you get a little quiet, when matters have taken some form
with you, when you have seen some hundreds of people,
and answered some thousands of questions, then take
your pen for the space of ten minutes, and tell me of
your "whereabouts," and how your strength and spirits
hold out, and what is the prospect.

I hope you will not disappoint me of the visit this
autumn, for I want to talk the sun down and the stars up
with you. I suppose you have tales enough for "a
thousand and one nights." You have made friends here,
moreover, even in Rome, — some by hearsay, and others
who will be here probably in a fortnight or three weeks.
And *Mrs.* Ware has admirers here. Think of that, sir !
that while Mr. W. is spoken of only with a kind of reverence, the lady carries off all the charms and fascinations
of epithet. But alas ! such is the hard fate of us of the
wiser sex. There are other senses than Saint Paul's in
which we may say, " Where I am weak, there am I
strong."

Pray excuse the levity (specific) of this letter, on two
grounds, — first, that I am very heavy, and should sink
in any other vessel ; and, secondly, that I cannot take in
any of the weighty matters, because I have no room for
them.

Mrs. Dewey joins me in the regards to you and Mrs.
Ware, with which I am, Most truly yours,

O. DEWEY.

In less than three years from this time the
nervous suffering from overwork became so intense that Mr. Dewey was advised to go abroad

to obtain the absolute rest from labor that was impossible here.

To Miss Catherine M. Sedgwick.

SHEFFIELD, *May 2*, 1833.

MY DEAR FRIEND, — I am about to go abroad. I have made up my mind to that huge, half pleasurable, half painful undertaking ; or shall I say, rather, that both the pleasure and the pain come by wholes, and not by halves? The latter I feel as a domestic man, for I must go alone ; the former I feel as a civilized man. Civilized, I say, for who that has the lowest measure of educated intelligence and sensibility can expect to tread all the classic lands of the world, Greece only excepted, without a thrill of delight?

If you should think that I had written thus much as claiming your sympathy in what so much interests me, and if you should think this without accusing me of pre-sumption, I should be tempted, were I assured of the fact, to stop here, and to leave the matter on a footing so gratifying to my feelings. But I must not venture to take so considerable a risk, and must therefore hasten to tell you that what I have said is only a vestibule to some-thing further.

Nor is the vestibule at all too large or imposing for the object, as I conceive it, to which it is to open the way ; for I am about to ask through you, if you will consent and condescend to be the medium, a very considerable favor of a very distinguished man. Among many letters of introduction which I have received, it so happens, as they say in Parliament, that I can obtain none to certain persons that I want to see quite as much as any others in Europe.　None of our Boston gentlemen that I can find are acquainted with Professor Wilson, or Miss Ferrier, the author of " Inheritance," or Thomas Moore, or Campbell, or Bulwer.　The " Noctes Ambrosianæ," with other things, have made me a great admirer of Wilson ; and Miss Ferriers (I don't know whether her name ends with *s* or not) I had rather see than any woman in Europe.　She comes nearer to Sir Walter, I think, than any writer of fiction abroad, and in depth of religious sentiment goes very far beyond him.　Now, I presume that Washington Irving is acquainted with all these individuals ; and what I venture to ask is, whether, through your intervention, letters can be obtained from him to any of them, and especially to the two first.

Now I must make you comprehend how little I wish you to go out of your way, or to put any constraint on yourself in the matter.　I have none of the passion for seeing celebrated men, merely as such.　Those whose writings have interested me, I do, of course, wish to see ; but I am to be too hasty a traveller to make it a great object to see them, or to go very much out of my way for it.　Above all, if you have the least reluctance to ask this of Mr. Irving, you must allow me to impose it as a condition of my request that you will not do it ; or if Mr. Irving is reluctant to give the letters, do not undertake to tell me so with any circumlocution, for I understand all about the delicacy of these Transatlantic connections.　I only fear that the very length of this letter will convey to you an undue impression of the importance which I give to the subject of it.　Pray construe it not so, but set it down as one of the involuntary consequences of the pleasure I have in conversing with you.　Very truly your friend,　　　　　　　　　　　　　　　　ORVILLE DEWEY.

The letters, and every other advantage that the kindness of friends could provide, were given him, and the mingled anticipations with which he entered on his year of solitary exile were all fulfilled. His enjoyment in the wonders of nature and of art, in society, and in the charm of historical and romantic association which is the peculiar pleasure to an American of travel in the Old World, was very great, and the relief to his brain from the weekly pressure of original production gave him ease for the present and hope for the future. But the year was darkened for him by the death of his youngest sister, who had been married the previous summer to Mr. Andrew L. Russell, of Plymouth, and of his wife's brother, John Hay Farnham, of Indiana; and when he returned home, three months' work convinced him that arduous and prolonged mental labor was henceforth impossible for him. With deep disappointment and sorrow, he resigned his charge at New Bedford, and left the place and people which had been and always remained very dear to him.

Few are left of those who heard his first preaching there. One of his sisters says: "To me, brought up on the Orthodoxy of Berkshire, it was like a revelation, and I think it was much the same to the Quakers. Those views of life and human nature and its responsibilities that are common now, were new then, and the effect produced upon us all was most thrilling and solemn; and when, service over, we passed out of the church, I remember there were very few words spoken, — a contrast to the custom nowadays of chatting and laughing at the door." I have heard others speak of the overwhelming pathos of his manner, and I asked the Rev. Dr. Morison, who came to New Bedford as a young man during the last years of our stay there, to put some of his personal remembrances on paper. In a note from him, dated 10th January, 1883, he says: " I have not forgotten my promise to send you some little account of your father's preaching in New Bedford. He was so great a man, uttering himself in his preaching, the sources of his power lay so deep, his words came to us so vitally connected with the most subtle and effective forces of the moral and spiritual universe, that I can no more describe him than I could a June day, in all its glory and beauty and its boundless resources of joy and life, to one who had never known it."

The following pages, which Dr. Morison was nevertheless kind enough to send, have touching value and beauty : —

" More than half a century ago, in March, 1832, I went to New Bedford, and, for nearly a year, was a constant attendant at Mr. Dewey's church. During that year he preached most of the sermons contained in the first volume that he published. As we read them, they are among the ablest and most impressive sermons in the language. But when read now they give only a slight idea of what they were as they came to us then, all glowing and alive with the emotions of the preacher. When he walked through the church to the pulpit, his head swaying backward and forward as if too heavily freighted, his whole bearing was that of one weighed down by the thoughts in which he was absorbed and the solemn message which he had come to deliver. ·The old prophetic ' burden of the Lord ' had evidently been laid upon him. Some hymn marked by its depth of religious feeling was read. This was followed by a prayer, which was not the spontaneous, easy outflowing of calmly reverential feelings, but the labored utterance of a soul overawed and overburdened by emotions too strong for utterance. There was sometimes an appearance almost of distress in this exercise, so utterly inadequate, as it seemed to him, were any words of his to express what lay deepest in his mind, when thus brought face to face with God. ' I do not shrink,' he said, ' from speaking to man.' But, except in his rarest and best moments, he was oppressed by a sense of the poverty of any language of thanksgiving or supplication that he could use in his intercourse with God.

" His manner in preaching was marked by great depth and strength of feeling, but always subdued. He spoke on great subjects. He entered profoundly into them, and treated them with extraordinary intellectual ability and clearness. They who were seeking for light found it in his preaching. But more than any intellectual precision or clearness of thought was to be gained from him in his treatment of the momentous questions which present themselves, sooner or later, to every thoughtful mind. Behind these questions, more important than any one or all of them intellectually considered, was the realm of thought, emotion, aspiration, out of which religious ideas are formed, and in which the highest faculties of our nature are to find their appropriate nourishment and exercise. He spoke to us as one who belonged to this higher world. The realm in which he lived, and which seemed never absent from his mind, impressed itself as he spoke, and gave a deeper solemnity and attractiveness to his words than could be given by any specific and clearly-defined ideas. A sense of mystery and awe pervaded his teachings, and infused into his utterances a sentiment of divine sacredness and authority. He preached as I never, before or since, have heard any one else, on human nature, on retribution, on the power of kindness, on life and death, in their relations to man and to what is divine. He stood before us compassed about by a religious atmosphere which penetrated his inmost nature, and gave its tone and coloring to all he said. For he spoke as one who saw rising visibly before him the issues of life and of death.

"He was gifted with a rare dramatic talent. But it was a gift, not an art, and showed itself in voice and gesture as by the natural impulse of a great nature profoundly moved, and in its extremest manifestations so subdued as to leave the impression of a vast underlying reserved force. His action, so full of meaning and so effective, was no studied or superficial movement of hand and voice, but the action of the whole man, body and soul, all powerfully quickened and moved from within by the living thoughts and emotions to which he was giving utterance.

"I have heard many of the greatest orators of our time. But, with the exception of Daniel Webster and Dr. Channing in their highest moments, Mr. Dewey was the most eloquent man among them all, and that not once or twice, on great occasions, but Sunday after Sunday, forenoon and afternoon, for months together.

" Some allowance should perhaps be made for the state of mind and the period of life in which I heard him. I had just come from college, where the intellect had been cultivated in advance of the moral and religious faculties. The equilibrium which belongs to a perfectly healthy and harmonious nature was disturbed, and, as a necessary consequence of this unbalanced and distempered condition, there was a deep inward unrest, and a craving for something, — the greatest of all, — which had not yet been attained. Mr. Dewey's preaching came in just at this critical time, and it was to me the opening into a new world. The hymn, the prayer, the Scripture reading, usually brought me into a reverent and plastic state of mind, ready to receive and be moulded by the deepest and loftiest Christian truths. From the beginning to the end of the sermon I was under the spell which he had thrown over me, and unconscious of everything else. Very seldom during my life, and then only for a few minutes at a time, has any one, by his eloquence, exercised this absorbing and commanding influence over me. Once or twice in hearing Dr. Channing I felt as I suppose the prophet may have felt when he heard ' the still small voice,' at which ' he wrapped his face in his mantle,' and listened as to the voice of God. A few such experiences I have had with other men ; but with Mr. Dewey more than with all others. And when the benediction was pronounced, I wished to go away and be by myself in the new world of spiritual ideas and emotions into which I had been drawn. Those were to me great experiences, inwrought into the inmost fibres of my nature, and always associated in my mind with Mr. Dewey's preaching.

" Nor were these experiences peculiar to any one person. The audience as a whole were affected in a similar manner. A deep solemnity pervaded the place. There was not merely silence, but the spell of absorbed attention that makes itself felt, and spreads itself as by a general sympathy through a congregation profoundly moved by great thoughts filled out and made alive by deep and uplifting emotions. The exercises in the church were often followed by lasting convictions. The Sunday's sermon was the topic, not of curious discussion. or indiscriminate eulogy, but of serious conversation among the young, who looked forward to the coming Sunday as offering privileges which it would be a misfortune to lose. The services of the church were remembered and anticipated as the most interesting and important event of the week.

" I shall never cease to think with gratitude of Mr. Dewey's preaching. In common with other great preachers of our denomination, — Dr. Channing, for example, Dr. Nichols, and Dr. Walker, — he spoke as one standing within the all-encompassing and divine presence. He awakened in us a sense of that august and indefinable influence from which all that is holiest and best must come. He brought us into communication with that Light of life. He showed us how our lives, our thoughts, and even our every-day acts, may be sanctified and inspired by it, as every plant and tree is not only illuminated by the sun but vitally associated with it.

" If, in the light of later experience, I were to criticise

the preaching I then heard, I should say that it was too intense. The writing and the delivery of such sermons subjected the preacher to too severe a strain both of body and mind. No man could go on preaching in that way, from month to month, without breaking down in health. And it may be questioned whether a mind acting under so high a pressure is in the best condition to take just views, to preserve its proper equipoise, or to impart wise and healthful instruction. The stimulus given may be too strong for the best activity of those who receive it. They whose sensitive natures are most deeply affected by such an example may, under its influence, unconsciously form an ideal of intellectual attainments too exacting, and therefore to them a source of weakness rather than of strength.

" The danger lies in these directions. But Mr. Dewey's breadth of apprehension, his steadfast loyalty and devotion to the truth, the judicial impartiality with which he examined the whole field before making up his mind, saved him from one-sided or ill-balanced conclusions. And the intense action of all the faculties not only enables a man of extraordinary intellectual powers to impress his thought on others and infuse his very soul into theirs; but it also, as we see in the best work of Channing, Dewey, and Emerson, opens to them realms of thought which otherwise might never have been reached, and gives to them glimpses of a divine love and splendor never granted to a less earnest and passionate devotion."

In the autumn of 1835 Mr. Dewey was settled over the Second Unitarian Church in New York, trusting to his stock of already written discourses to save him from a stress of intellectual labor too severe for his suffering brain, which was never again to allow him uninterrupted activity in study. When his life-work is viewed, it should always be remembered under what difficulties it was carried on. It was work that taxed every faculty to the uttermost, while the physical organ of thought had been so strained by over-exertion at the beginning of his professional career, owing to a general ignorance of the bodily laws even greater then than it is now, that the use of it during the rest of his life was like that which a man has of a sprained foot; causing pain in the present exercise, and threatening far worse consequences, if the effort is continued. Fortunately, his health in all other respects was excellent, and his spirits and courage seldom flagged. I remember him as lying much on the sofa in those days, and liking to have his head "scratched" by the hour together, with a sharp-pointed comb, to relieve by external irritation the distressing sensations, which he compared to those made, sometimes by a tightening ring, sometimes by a leaden cap, and sometimes (but this was in later life) by a dull boring instrument. Yet he was the centre of the family life, and of its merriment as well; and his strong social instincts and lively animal spirits made him full of animation and vivacity in society, although he was soon tired, and with a nervous restlessness undoubtedly the effect of disease, never wanted to stay long in any company.

He preached a sermon after the great fire in New York, in December, 1835, which drew forth the following letter from Mr. Henry Ware: —

Cambridge, *Jan.* 15, 1836.

Dear Friend, — I must acknowledge your sermon, — you made me most happy by it. It was so true, so right, so strongly and movingly put; it was the word that ought to be said, the word in season. My feeling was: God Almighty be praised for sending that man there to speak to that great and mighty city, and to interpret to it his providence. You cannot but feel gratitude in being appointed to be such an instrument; and I trust that you are to be used much and long, and for great good. Keep yourself well and strong; look on yourself as having a message and a mission, and live for nothing else but to perform it.

I happen to have found out, very accidentally, what is always the most secret of undiscoverable secrets, — that you are asked to preach the Dudleian Lecture. Do not let anything hinder you. We want you: you must come; do not hesitate; and, *mind*, I speak first, to have you come and house it with me while you are in Cambridge. Pray, deny me not.

Shall I tell you? Your sermon made me cry so that I could not finish reading it, but was obliged to lay it down. Not from its pathos, — but from a stronger, higher, deeper, holier something which it stirred up. I am almost afraid for you when I think what a responsibility lies on you for the use of such powers. May He that gave them give you grace with them! Love to you and yours, and all peace be with you. Yours ever,

H. Ware, Jr.

In the same year he addressed a letter to Emerson, who, as a cousin of his wife, was well known to him from the first. The familiarity of the opening recalls what he said in writing of him many years after: "Waldo, we always called him in those days, though now all adjuncts have dropped away from the shining name of Emerson."

To Ralph Waldo Emerson.

BOSTON, *May* 15, 1836.

DEAR WALDO, — I felt much disappointed when, on going to Hancock Place the third time, I found that you had gone to Concord ; for I was drawn to you as by a kind of spell. I wanted to see you, though it seemed to me that I could not speak to you one word. I can do no more now, — I am dumb with amazement and sorrow ;[1] and yet I must write to you, were it only to drop a tear on the page I send. Your poor mother ! I did not know she had come with you. Miss Hoar[2] I do not know, and will intrude no message ; but I think of her more than many messages could express. My dear friend, I am as much concerned for you as for any one. God give you strength to comfort others ! Alas ! we all make too much of death. Like a vase of crystal that fair form was shattered, — in a moment shattered ! Can such an event be the catastrophe we make it ?

---

[1] This letter was called forth by the sudden death of Charles Chauncey Emerson, a younger brother of Ralph Waldo Emerson, and one of the noblest young men of America.

[2] Miss Hoar was betrothed to Charles Emerson.

I preached to-day at Chauncey Place.[1] I will copy a passage. (I have not space to give the connection.)

"There stood once where now I stand, a father, — I knew him not, but to some of you he was known, — who, ere his children were trained up for life, was called to leave them, but whose fair example and fervent prayer visited them, and dwelt among them, and helped, with much kindly nurture, to form them to learning, virtue, honor, and to present them to the world a goodly band of brothers. And say not, because one and another has fallen on the threshold of life, — fallen amidst the brightest visions and most brilliant promises of youth, — that it is all in vain ; that parental toils and cares and prayers are all in vain. There is another life, where every exalted power trained here shall find expansion, improvement, and felicity. [Those sons of the morning, who stand for a moment upon the verge of this earthly horizon amidst the first splendors of day, and then vanish away into heaven, as if translated, not deceased, seem to teach us, almost by a sensible manifestation, how short is the step and how natural is the passage from earth to heaven.[2]] They almost open heaven to us, and they help our languid efforts to reach it, by the most powerful of all earthly aids, — the memory of admired and loved virtues. Yes, the mingled sorrow and affection which have swelled many hearts among us within the last week, tell me that the excellence we have lost has not lived in vain. Precious memory of early

---

[1] The church formerly ministered to by the Rev. William Emerson, the father of these rare sons.

[2] This letter is taken from a copy, not the original ; and the meaning of the brackets is uncertain. Probably, however, the passage which they enclose is a quotation.

virtue and piety ! and such memories, and more than one such, there are among you. Hold these bright companions ever dear, my young friends ; embalm their memory in the fragrant breath of your love ; follow them with the generous emulation of virtue ; let the seal which death has set upon excellence stamp it with a character of new sanctity and authority ; let not virtue die and friendship mourn in vain ! "

Remember me with most affectionate sympathy to your mother, and Aunt Mary, and to Dr. Ripley.

With my kind regards to your wife, I am, dear Waldo, in love and prayer, yours,

O. DEWEY.

Everybody mourns with you. Dr. Channing said yesterday, " I think Massachusetts could not have met with a greater loss than of that young man."

Mr. Emerson's letter in reply is beautiful in itself, and has the added interest attaching now to every word of his : —

CONCORD, *May* 23, 1836.

MY DEAR SIR, — I received the last week your kind letter, and the copy of your affectionate notice of Charles at Chauncey Place. I remember how little while ago you consoled us by your sympathy at Edward's departure, — a kind, elevating letter, which I have never acknowledged. I feel as if it was kind, even compassionate, to remember me now that these my claims to remembrance are gone.

Charles's mind was healthy, and had opened steadily (with a growth that never ceased from month to month) under favorable circumstances. His critical eye was so acute, his rest on himself so absolute, and his power of illustrating his thought by an endless procession of fine images so excellent, that his conversation came to be depended on at home as daily bread, and made a very large part of the value of life to me. His standard of action was heroic, — I believe he never had even temptations to anything mean or gross. With great value for the opinion of plain men, whose habits of life precluded compliment and made their verdict unquestionable, he held perhaps at too low a rate the praise of fashionable people, — so that he steadily withdrew from display, and I felt as if nobody knew my treasure. Meantime, like Aaron, " he could speak well." He had every gift for public debate, and I thought we had an orator in training for the necessities of the country, who should deserve the name and the rewards of eloquence. But it has pleased God not to use him here. The Commonwealth, if it be a loser, knows it not ; but I feel as if bereaved of so much of my sight and hearing.

His judgment of men, his views of society, of politics, of religion, of books, of manners, were so original and wise and progressive, that I feel — of course nobody can think as I do — as if an oracle were silent.

I am very sorry that I cannot see you, — did not when we were both in Boston. My mother and brother rejoice in your success in New York, and I with them. They have had their part in the benefit. I hear nothing of the aching head, and hope it does not ache. . . . Cannot I see you in Concord during some of your Boston visits? I will lay by every curious book or letter that I can think might interest you. My cousin Louisa, I know, would be glad to see this old town, and the old man at the parsonage whilst he is yet alive. My mother joins me in sending love to her.

Yours affectionately,

R. WALDO EMERSON.

Mr. Dewey's mind was too logical in its methods for entire intellectual sympathy with Mr. Emerson; but that he thoroughly appreciated his spiritual insight is shown by the following passage from a manuscript sermon on Law, preached 13th August, 1868, on the occasion of the earthquake of that year in South America: —

"But the law[1] does stand fast. Nothing ever did, ever shall, ever can escape it. Take any essence-drop or particle of evil into your heart and life, and you shall pay for it in the loss, if not of gold or of honor, yet of the finest sense and the finest enjoyment of all things divinest, most beautiful and most blessed in your being. I know of no writer among us who has emphasized this fact, this law, more sharply than Waldo Emerson, and I commend his pages to you in this view. Freed from all conventionalism, whether religious or Scriptural, though he has left the ranks of our faith, yet he has gone, better than any of us, to the very depth of things in this matter."

To Rev. William Ware.

NEW YORK, *Nov.* 7, 1836.

MY DEAR WARE, — Shall I brood over my regrets in secret, or shall I tell you of them? I sometimes do not care whether any human being knows what is passing in

[1] Of retribution.

me ; and then again my feelings are all up in arms for sympathy, as if they would take it by storm. I declare I have a good deal of liking for that other, — that sullenness, or sadness, or what you will; it is calmer and more independent. So I shall say nothing, only that I miss you even more than I expected.[1] Never, in all this great city, will a face come through my door that I shall like to see better than yours, — I doubt if so well.

The next nearest thing to you is Furness's book: Have you got it? Is it not charming? It is a book of beauty and life. Spots there are upon it, — they say there are upon the sun. Certes, there are tendencies to naturalism in Furness's mind which I do not like, — do not think the *true* philosophy ; but it is full of beauty, and hath much wisdom in it too.

I write on the gallop. My dinner is coming in three minutes, and a wagon is coming after that to carry me to Berkshire, that is, by steamboat to Hudson as usual. But I am going to send this, though it be worth nothing but to get a letter from you.

If letters, like dreams, came from the multitude of business, I should write of nothing but that tragedy *extempore*, — for I am sure it was got up in a minute, — the argument whereof was your running away. It positively is the staple of conversation. And I think it is rather hard upon me, too. *I* am here ; but that seems to go for nothing. All their talk is of your going away, — *running* away, I say, — desertion, — and help yourself if you can. . . .

My love to Henry Ware, and the love of me and mine to you and yours.   Yours ever,

O. DEWEY.

<hr>

[1] See p. 86.

To the Same.

NEW YORK, *Dec.* 1, 1836.

MY DEAR SIR WILLIAM, — For a prince you are in letter-writing, and you can call me Lord Orville, for I have a birthright claim to that title.[1] Excuse this capricole of my pen; it has been drawing hard enough at a sermon all the morning, and can't help cutting a caper when it is let out. You won't get the due return for your good long letter this time, nor ever, I think. I am taking comfort in the good long letters that are going with mine, and of whose sending by this conveyance I am the cause.

This conveyance is Miss Searle; and if you and Mrs. Ware don't cultivate her, or let her cultivate you, your folly will be inconceivable.

Mrs. Jameson I have missed two or three chances of seeing, — very bright sometimes, and very foolish others; but who shall resist such intoxicating draughts as have for some years been offered to her! She set off for Canada yesterday, going for her husband, since he could n't or would n't come for her.

Ingham has just finished one of the most exquisite portraits of Miss Sedgwick that eye ever saw. Did you see anything of it before you went?

Furness ['s book] is selling much, and I hear nothing but admiration, save the usual quaver in the song about the part on miracles. Apropos, . . . I think that the explication of the miracles must be a moot and not a test point, and I would not break with the

---

[1] He was named after Lord Orville, the hero of Miss Burney's "Evelina," which his mother had read with delight shortly before his birth.

"Christian Examiner" upon it; and yet I think the heterodox opinions of Ripley should have come into it in the shape of a letter, and not of a review. It is rather absurd to say "We" with such confidence, and that for opinions in conflict with the whole course of the "Examiner" and the known opinions of almost all its supporters. . . .

Yours forever and a day,
ORVILLE DEWEY.

To the Same.

NEW YORK, *Jan.* 2, 1837.

. . . A WEEK ago to-day I sat down at my desk, spread before me a sheet of paper, grasped my pen energetically, and had almost committed myself for a letter to you, when suddenly it occurred to me that Mrs. Schuyler was in Boston, and would have told you just what it was my special design to write ; that is, all about the congregation of the faithful in Chambers Street. Well, I suppose she has ; but I shall have my say. The congregation has certainly not improved, as you seem, in your preposterous modesty, to suppose, but suffered by your leaving it. The attendance, I should think, is about the same. . . . But I am afraid that the society is gradually losing strength.

. . . .

I have been preaching some Sunday-evening sermons to the merchants. Have n't you heard of them? And if you have n't, do you pretend that Brookline is a place? Take my word, Sir, that it is not to be found on the map of the world, — not known either to the ancients or the moderns. You are not in existence, Sir, take my word for it, if you have not heard of these crowded, listening, etc. assemblies at the Mercer Street Church. Well, really, I have seen a packed audience there, and even the galleries pretty well filled. I have thoughts of publishing the discourses (only three, more than an hour long, however), and if I could only write three more, I would; but my brain got into a pretty bad condition by the third week, and I don't know whether I can go on at present.

To the Same.

NEW YORK, *March* 27, 1837.

MY DEAR WARE, — I should like to know what you mean by not letting me hear from you these three months. Do you not know that you are in my debt for a letter at least twenty lines long, which it took me three minutes to write ? And three minutes and twenty lines, in this Babel, are equal to one hour and two sheets in Brookline. Do you not know that everybody is saying, " When have you heard from Mr. Ware ? " Do you not know that ugly and choking weeds will spring up on the desolation you have made here if you do not scatter some flower-seeds upon it ? Consider and tremble. Or, respect this and repent, as the Chinese say.

Well, Dr. Follen is to be here for a twelvemonth, and we shall not get you back again, — ohime !

.   .   .   .

Dr. Follen has quite filled the church at some evening lectures on Unitarianism. Good ! and everything about him is good, but that he comes after you.

To the Same.

NEW YORK, *July* 10, 1837.

MY DEAR WARE, — I can scarcely moderate my expressions to the tone of wisdom in telling you how much pleasure I have had in reading your book, — how much I am delighted with you and for you. There is no person to whom I would more gladly have had the honor fall of writing the "Letters from Palmyra." And it *is* a distinction that places your name among the highest in our — good-for-nothing — literature, as the Martineau considers it. By the bye, you need n't think you are a-going to stand at the head of everything, as she will have it. Have not I written a book too, to say nothing of the names less known of Channing, Irving, Bryant, etc. ? And, by the bye, again, speaking of the Martineau, she is a woman of one idea, — takes one view, that is, and knows nothing of qualification, — and hence is opinionated and confident to a degree that I think I never saw equalled. Julia, Fausta, nay, Zenobia, for me, rather. How beautifully have you shown them up ! And Gracchus and Longinus as nobly. What things is literature doing to gratify ambition, — things beyond its proudest hope ! How little thought Zenobia that her character, two thousand years after she lived, would be illustrated by the genius of a clime that she dreamed not of !

.   .   .   .

My love and congratulations to your wife ; my love and envy to you.

O. DEWEY.

To the Same.

NEW YORK, *May* 13, 1838.

MY DEAR WARE, — Brother Pierpont has preached finely for me this morning, and is to do so again this evening ; and for this I find myself indirectly indebted to you. But you are one of those to whom I can't feel much obligation — for the love I bear you.

I wrote to you three weeks ago. I hope Mrs. Ware is patient and sustained. Of you I expect it. But, O heaven ! what a world of thought does it take even to look on calamity !

Your name is abroad in the world as it should be. I rejoice. Pierpont is now sitting by me, reading the London and Westminster article on "Zenobia, or the Fall of Palmyra." I am glad you have altered the title. We are looking for the sequel.

The next letter describes some of the difficulties of a journey from Berkshire to New York forty years ago. The route by Hartford was probably chosen instead of the ordinary one by Hudson, to take advantage of the new railroad between that city and New Haven.

To his Wife.

NEW YORK, *Friday, February* 5, 1841.

I PRAY you to admire my style of writing February. I began to write July, but the truth is, I nearly lost my wits on my journey. Twelve or thirteen mortal hours in getting to Hartford.[1] After two or three hours, called

---

[1] Fifty miles.

up, just when the sleep had become so profound that on being waked I could not, for some seconds, settle it on what hemisphere, continent, country, or spot of the creation I was, nor why I was there at all. Then whisked away in the dark to the science-lighted domes of New Haven, but did n't see them — for why? I was asleep as I went through to the wharf. From the wharf, pitched into the steamboat, not having the points of compass, nor the time of day, nor the zenith and nadir of my own person. After two previous months of quiet, the whirl-about made me feel very

> " like an ocean weed uptorn
> And loose along the world of waters borne."

If not a foundered weed, a very dumfoundered one at least.

To Rev. William Ware.

SHEFFIELD, *Feb.* 15, 1841.

How glad I am you wrote to me, my dear W. ! Is n't that a queer beginning? But there are people who say that everything natural is beautiful, and I am sure that first line was as natural as the gushing out of a fountain ; for the very sight of your handwriting was as a sunbeam in a winter's day. By the bye, speaking of sunbeams, they certainly do wonders in winter weather. Have you ever seen such blue depths, or depths of blue, in the mountains, that it seemed as if the very azure of the sky had fallen and lodged in their clefts and leafless trees? Yesterday I was looking towards our barn roofs covered with snow, — and you know they are but six rods off, — and so deep was the color that I thought for the moment it was the blue of the distant horizon.

Our friend Catherine Sedgwick, writing to me a day or two ago, speaks in raptures of it. She says it is like the haze over Soracte or Capri.

So you see my paragraph has led me from winter to summer. Summer is gone to New York a week since. No doubt it will produce beautiful flowers in due time, many of them culled from far distant lands, but most of them native, I ween. Foreign seeds, you know, can do nothing without a good soil. In truth, I am looking with great interest for Catherine Sedgwick's book.

.   .   .   .

"Hard work to write." Yes, terribly hard it has been for me these two years past; but when I am vigorous, I like it. However, the pen is ever, doubtless, a manacle to the thought; draws it out, if you please, but makes a dragging business of it. By the bye, is your laziness making an apology for not finishing "Scenes in Judea"? Hear a compliment of my mother's for your encouragement. "I should think the man that could write the ' Letters from Palmyra,' — anything so beautiful and so powerful too " (her very words), — "could write anything."

I am delighted to hear of Mr. Farrar's being better. Give my love to them, and tell him I know of nothing in the world I could hear with more pleasure than of his improvement. What a beautiful, gentle, precious spirit he is !

Yes, I grant you all about Cambridge ; and if I don't go abroad, perhaps we will come and live with you a year or two. Something I must do ; I get no better.

I can't guess your plaguy charade. I never thought of one a minute before, and I have ruminated upon yours an hour.

Oh that you were my colleague, or I yours, as you please !

With our love to your wife and children,

I am as ever,

ORVILLE DEWEY.

To Dr. Channing.

NEW YORK, *Sept.* 30, 1841.

MY DEAR SIR, — I cannot go away for two years without taking leave of you. I wish I could do so by going to see you. But my decision to go is not more than three weeks old, and the intervening time has been overwhelmed with cares. Among other things, I have been occupied with printing a volume of sermons. I feel as if it were a foolish thing to confess, but I imagined that I had something to say about " human life " (that is my subject), though I warrant you will find it little enough. But then, you are accustomed to say so much better things than the rest of us, that you ought to distrust your judgment.

I sail for Havre on the 8th October with my family.

.   .   .   .

I am extremely glad to learn from Mrs. G. that your health is so good, and that you pass some time every day with your pen in hand. The world, I believe, is to want for its guidance more powerful writing, during twenty years to come, than it has ever wanted before, or will again, and I hope you will be able to do your part. Perhaps this is speaking more oracularly than becomes my ignorance ; but it does appear to me that the civilized world is on the eve of a change and a progress, putting all past data at fault, and outstripping all present imagination. What questions are to arise and to be

hotly agitated about human rights, social position, lawful
government, and the laws that are to press man down
or to help him up? What Brownsons and Lamennais'
and Strauss' are to come upon the stage, and to be con-
fronted with sober and earnest reasoning?

But I did not think to put my slender finger into such
great matters, but only to say adieu ! If you would write
me while abroad, you know it would give me great
pleasure.

With my most kind and affectionate regards to Mrs.
Channing, and my very heart's good wishes and felicita-
tions to M., I am as ever,

Very truly your friend,

ORVILLE DEWEY.

To Rev. William Ware.

PARIS, *Dec.* 25, 1841.

MY DEAR FELLOW,— You see how I begin ; truth is,
I feel more like writing a love-letter to you than a letter
about affairs, or matters, or things ; for have you not
been my fellow more than anybody else has been?
Have we not lived and labored together, have I not been
in your house as if it were my own, and have you not
come into my study many a time and oft, as little dis-
turbing my thought, and seeming as much to belong
there, as any sunbeam that glided into it? And
furthermore, is not this anniversary time not only a fellowship season for all Christian souls, but especially a
reminder to those who have walked to the house of God
in company?

Still, however, it is of affairs that I have felt pressed
to write you ever since I left home, — indeed, ever
since I received your letter from Montreal. I have felt

that I ought at least to tell you that I see no prospect of doing anything that you desire of me. When I shall be able to address myself to any considerable task again, I know not. At present I am lying quite *perdu*. I have lost all faculty, but to read French histories, memoirs, novels, periodicals, etc., and to run after this great show-world of Paris, — Louvre, gallery, opera, what not. I am longing to get behind these visible curtains, and to know the spirit, character, manner of being, of this French people. At present all is problem to me. No Sunday, literally no cessation of labor, no sanctity of domestic ties with multitudes, no honesty or truth (it is commonly reported), but courtesy, kindness, it seems, and a sort of conventional fidelity, — for instance, no stealing ; a million of people here, but without either manufactures or commerce on a great scale ; *petit* manufacture, *petit* trade, *petit* ménage, *petit* prudence unexampled, and the grandest tableaux of royal magnificence in public works and public grounds to be seen in the world ; the *rez-au-chaussée* (ground floor) of Paris, a shop ; all the stories above, *to be let ;* a million of people, and nobody at *home*, in our American sense of the word ; an infinite *boutiquerie*, an infinite *bonbonnerie*, an infinite stir and movement, and no deep *moral* impulse that I can see ; a strange *mélange* of the most shallow levity in society, the most atrocious license in literature, and the most savage liberalism in politics, — on the whole, what sort of people is it?

Hé bien ! — to come down from my high horse before I break my neck, — here we are, at honest housekeeping ; for we hope to pay the bills. Hope to pay, did I say? We pay as we go ; that is the only way here ; no stores, no larder, no bins, no garners, — the shops of

Paris are all this to every family. Our greatest good-fortune here is in having the Walshes for our next-door neighbors; and who should I find in Mrs. W. but a very loving cousin and hearty admirer of yours? She wishes to write a P. S. in my letter, and I am so happy to come to you in such good company, as well as to enhance the value of my letter with something better than I can write, that I very gladly give the space to her. I am only sorry and ashamed that it is so little. And so, with all our love to you all,

I am as ever yours,

ORVILLE DEWEY.

To the Same.

CHAMPEL, NEAR GENEVA, *July* 18, 1842.

MY DEAR FELLOW AND FRIEND, — At the hour of midnight, with the moon shining in at my open window, the sound of the rushing Arve in my ears, — around me, a fine table of land a hundred feet above the stream that washes its base, and covered with a hundred noble chestnuts, and laid out with beautiful walks, — thus "being and situate," I take in hand this abominable steel pen to write you. Envy me not, William Ware ! Let no man, that is well, envy him that is sick. If I were "*lying* and being and situate," as the deeds have it, and as I *ought* to have it, I should think myself an object of envy, that is, supposing I thought at all. No ; in this charmèd land, and in every land where I go, I bear a burden of diseased nerves which I might well exchange for the privilege of living on the Isle of Shoals, could I but have the constitution of some of its *pêchereux* (by contraction, pesky) inhabitants.

. . . There has come a new day, and I have got a new

pen. Last night I was too much awake; I got up from my bed and wrote in my dressing-gown; to-day I am too much asleep. But *allons*, and see what will come of it.

This morning we walked into Geneva to church, the air so clear that it seemed as if we could count every tile on the houses. The chimneys are crowned with a forest of tin pipes, twisted in every direction to carry off smoke. At dusky eve, in a superstitious time, a man, coming suddenly upon the town, might think that an army of goblins had just alighted upon its roofs. . . . What stupendous things do ages accumulate upon every spot where they have passed! Every time we go into town we pass by the very place where Servetus was burned. And Geneva is old enough to have seen Julius Cæsar!

. . . Here 's another new day, William; and I wish I were a new man. But the heavens are bright, and the air so clear that I can define every man's patch of vine-yard and farm on the Jura, ten miles off; every fissure and seam on Salève, two miles back of us; and through a gap in the Salève, I do not doubt, were I to go out on the grounds, I could see the top of Mont Blanc. And yet lay one or two ounces' weight on a man's brain, and a tackle, standing on the Jura, Salève, and Mont Blanc together, can't lift him up. You see, I am resolved you shan't envy me. However, not to be too lugubrious, I *am* improving; that is, the paroxysms of this trouble are less severe, though I am far from being relieved of the burden.

But it is time I turn to your letter, which I received here with Henry's, on the 12th June. Thank him, for I cannot write you both now. Much news he gave me; ·

but how much that was distressing, and that concerning himself most of all. What *is* to become of our churches? And what is *he* to do? It relieves me very much to hear that Gannett's case is no worse. My love and sympathy to him when you see him. Is he not one of our noblest and most disinterested, as well as ablest men, — nay, as an extemporaneous speaker, unrivalled among us? . . .

To Miss Catherine M. Sedgwick.

CHAMPEL, NEAR GENEVA, *July* 13, 1842.

MY DEAR FRIEND, — The public prints have doubtless relieved me from what I should consider a most painful duty, — that of announcing to you the death of your friend Sismondi! He died on the 25th of last month. I saw Mme. Sismondi yesterday, and she desired me to tell you particularly that she must defer writing to you some little time; that she did not feel that she *could* write now, especially in a way to give you any comfort. She thought it was better that I should announce it to you, not seeming to be aware that the death of her husband is one of the events that the newspapers soon carry through the world. Indeed, the modesty of Sismondi and his wife is one of the things in them that has most struck me. Mme. S. said yesterday, in speaking of the commencement of your friendship, that " Sismondi was so grateful to her for finding him out." And Sismondi, when I saw him on my arrival, in expressing to me his regret and concern that it was so long since he had heard from you, said he knew that you had many letters to write, etc.; as if that. could be the reason why you did not write to *him !* Well, there is more modesty in the world than we think, I verily believe.

. . . Speaking of her husband, Mme. S. said : "Of his acquisitions and powers, I say nothing ; but it was *such* a heart, — there never *was* such a heart ! "

I ought to add, while speaking of Mme. S., since we owe it all to you, that her reception of us was the kindest possible. She brought us all, children and all, to her house immediately to pass an evening, and indeed took all our hearts by storm, — if that can be said of a creature so gentle and modest. . . .

I wrote the foregoing this morning. At dinner-time your letter of June 12 came, which, with several others, has so turned my head, that I don't know whether it is morning or afternoon. We are conscious, " at each remove," of dragging " the lengthening chain," but we do not know exactly how heavy or how strong it is, till some one lays a hand on the other end. The lightest pressure there ! — you know how it is when some one steps on the end of a long string which a boy draws after him. God bless you ! — it was in my heart to say no less, — for thinking it is a long time. . . . We read and walk and talk and laugh, and sometimes sigh. Switzerland has no remedy against that. Of myself I have nothing to say that is worth the saying. I am improving somewhat, but I am suffering much and almost continually, and as yet I recover no energy for work.

To Rev. Henry W. Bellows.

Florence, Italy, *Nov.* 24, 1842.

. . . It is now a fortnight or more since the overwhelming news came to us of the death of Channing. During this time my mind has been passing through steps of gradual approximation to the reality, but never did it

find, or else voluntarily interpose, so many barriers between itself and reality as in this most deplorable event.
There are losses which I should more acutely feel than
the loss of Channing ; because friendship with him lacked,
I imagine, in all who enjoyed it, those little familiarities,
those fonder leanings, which leave us, as it were, bewil-
dered and utterly prostrate when the beloved object is
gone. But there is here a sense of general and irrepa-
rable loss, such as the people of a realm might be supposed to feel when its cherished head is suddenly taken
away. For I suppose that no person sustained so many
and such vital relations to the whole republic of thought,
to the whole realm of moral feeling among us, as this, our
venerated teacher and friend. To call him " that great
and good man," does not meet the feeling we have about
him. Familiar to almost nobody, he was near to everybody. His very personality seems to have been half
lost in the sense of general benefit. He was one of
those great gifts of God, like sunlight or the beauty of
nature, which we scarcely know how to live without,
or in the loss of which, at least, life is sadly changed, and
the world itself is mournfully bereft.

But a letter affords no scope for such a theme ; and
besides, painful as it is to pass to common topics, they
claim their dues. Life, ay, common life, must go on as
it ever did, and nothing shall tear that infinite web of
mystery in which it walks enveloped. Ours, however,
in these days, is rather a shaded life. Absence from
home, a strange land, a land, too, that sits in mourning
over the great relics of the past, — all this tends to make
it so. More material still is what passes within the micro-
cosm, and I am not yet well. Not that I am worse, for
I am continually better. But — but, in short, not to

speak too gravely, if a man feels as if one of the snakes
of Medusa's head were certainly in his brain, — I have
seen a horrible picture of the Medusa to-day by Leo-
nardo da Vinci, — he cannot be very happy, you know.
And if those around him be of such as " bear one another's burdens," then you see how the general consequence follows.

But let me not make the picture too dark, for the sake
of truth and gratitude. Pleasantly situated we are, in
this fair Florence. which grows fairer to my eye the more
I see it. Our rooms look to the south, and down from
a balcony upon a garden full of orange-trees, and roses
and chrysanthemums in full bloom. . . . Then we have
reading and music in-doors, and churches and palaces
and galleries out-doors. And such galleries ! they grow
upon me daily; the more ordinary paintings, or those
that seemed such at first, reveal something new on
every new perusal. It is great reading with such walls
for pages. Still there is a longing, almost a sick pining,
for home at times. . . .

To Rev. William Ware.

NEW YORK, *Sept.* 26, 1843.

MY DEAR FRIEND, — Why have I not written to you,
before? Every day for the last three weeks I have
thought of it. I have been with you in thought, and
with *him*, your dear brother, — my dear friend ! [1] If he
could have known me and conversed with me, I could
not have refrained from making the journey to see him.
How easy his converse ever was, how natural, how sen-

[1] Rev. Henry Ware, D.D.

sible and humorous by turns, but especially so unforced that for me it always had a charm by itself. The words seemed to drop from our lips almost without our will, and yet with nobody could I get through so much conversation in so little time. Neither of us seemed to want much explanation from the other; I think we understood one another well.

Where is he *now?* With whom talks he now? Perhaps with Channing and Greenwood! Oh! are not the best of us gone; and all in one year! Was there ever such a year?

My dear William Ware, we must hold on to the ties of life as we may, and especially to such as unite you and me. But are you not getting a strange feeling of nonchalance about everything, — life, death, and the time of death, what matters it? I rather think it is natural for the love of life to grow stronger as we advance in life; and yet it is so terribly shaken by the experience of life, and one is so burdened at times by the all-surrounding and overwhelming mystery and darkness, that one is willing to escape any way and on any terms.

I have your few kind words. I hope I shall have such oftener than *once* or *twice* a year. I will try to take care of myself, and to live. . . .

To the Same.

NEW YORK, *Oct.* 17, 1844.

MY DEAR WARE, — I ought not — I must not — I cannot — I *dare* not, — at least not at present. When the present stress is over, I may feel better. The fact is, at present I am scarcely fit to take care of my parish, and it would be madness to take upon myself any new burden. See there! a fine fellow I should be to have charge of the " Examiner," who have written *present* three times in as many lines! However, I am writing now in terrible haste, on the spur of an instant determination; for I must and will put this thing off from my mind. I have kept it there for a fortnight. I have wished to do this. First, because you wished it;—secondly, because others wish it; and, thirdly, I had a leaning to it. In case of a colleagueship, and that must come, I might be glad of it. Bellows, too, would help me, — would take charge with me, — and that may be, if the thing is open by and by, but not now; I must not think of it any more now. I have not slept a wink all night for thinking of this and other things.

.   .   .   .

All this, my dear fellow, is somewhat confidential. I do not wish to be considered a good-for-nothing. Perhaps I shall rally. I was doing very well when I left the Continent. England overwhelmed me with engagements, and so it is here. With our love to your love and the children,

Yours as ever,

ORVILLE DEWEY.

To the Same.

NEW YORK, *Jan.* 6, 1845.

MY DEAR FRIEND, — I shall make no due return for your good long letter; I have none of the Lamb-ent light which plays around your pen wherewith to illuminate my page, and indeed am in these days, I am sorry to say, something more dark than usual. However, if wishes be such good things as you ingeniously represent,

I judge that attempts are worth something. Ergo, Q. S., which means *quod sequitur;* it can hardly be a *non sequitur*, if nothing follows.

.   .   .   .

There ! I have just touched all the points of your letter, I think. I have sent my light comment-stone skittering over your full smooth lake.

Well, I see you on the bank of your literal lake, your beautiful Menotomy, — beautiful as Windermere, only not so big ; and I see the spring coming to cover that bank with verdure, and I long for both ; that is, for spring and you. I always long for you, and for spring, I think I long for it more than I ever did It must be that I am growing old. Shall we ever meet, my friend, if not by Menotomy, by those fountains where Christ leads his flock in the immortal clime, and rejoin our beloved Henry, and Greenwood, and Channing? I am not sad, but my thoughts this winter are far more of death than of life. Ought one to part with his friends so? No ; happy New Year to you. Hail the expected years, and the years of eternity ! God bless you.

As ever,

ORVILLE DEWEY.

To the Same.

SHEFFIELD, *Aug.* 18, 1845.

MY DEAR FRIEND, — . . . The whole previous page is to no purpose but to let you know that I have thought about you incessantly ; for you know that I have a sympathy not only with your heart, but with your head, if that be again, as I suppose it is, the seat of your trouble. Heads certainly can bear a great deal. Mine has ; and

I am now reading the work, in six volumes, of a man who was out of his head for years from hard study; and yet these volumes are full of thought, full of minute and endless explications on the greatest of subjects. It is the work of Auguste Comte on the " Philosophie Positive," essentially an attempt at a philosophic appreciation of the whole course of human thought and history. With an awfully involved style, with a great over-valuation of his own labor, he seems to me to have done a great deal. I have met with nothing on the philosophy of history to compare with it, *as philosophy*, though I have read Vico and Herder.

.   .   .   .

I shall not be easy till I know something about your health and plans. My vacation is nearly ended. I go down to New York the 1st of September. . . .

As ever yours,

ORVILLE DEWEY.

To Rev. Henry W. Bellows.

SHEFFIELD, *Aug.* 25, 1845.

DEAR BELLOWS, — I thought to answer you in your own vein, but I am made very serious just now by reading the first five chapters of Matthew. How many things to think of! Does no doubt arise concerning those introductory chapters? And then what heart-penetrating, what tremendous teaching is that of the Sermon on the Mount!

In fact, though jests have flown pretty freely about the house, and hearty laughter is likely to be where the Deweys muster in much strength, yet I have had a pretty serious vacation. I set for my *stent*, to read the

New Testament, or the Gospels at least, in Greek, and to master the great work of Auguste Comte, and to write one or two sermons. With the philosopher I have spent the most time. Morning after morning, with none to annoy or make me afraid, I have gone out on the green grass under the trees, and, seated in the bosom of the world, I have striven with the great problem of the world. The account looks fanciful, perhaps, but the matter is not so; for amidst this solitude and silence, and this infinitude which nature opens to me as the city never does, I find the most serious and terrible business of my existence. I do not mean terrible in a bad sense; I have courage and faith, but I can gain no approach towards philosophical apathy.

.   .   .   .

We are well, and expect to· go down on Wednesday next, and we too begin to feel a longing for New York and you. With our love to E.

As ever,

ORVILLE DEWEY.

To Mrs. Ephraim Peabody.

NEW YORK, *Oct.* 24, 1845.

MY DEAR MRS. PEABODY, — Do not regret that you have let us have your husband a few days. He has done us much good; unless I am to put in the opposite scale his having stolen away the hearts of my children.

If you had heard him last evening, I think you would have been satisfied, though wives are hard to please. It was a majestical and touching ministration; I have never felt anything from the pulpit to be more so. The hearty, honest, terrible tears it wrung from me were

such as I have given to no sermon this many a day, —
I think, never.

I hope you are better ; and with all other good wishes,
I am,   Yours very truly,

ORVILLE DEWEY.

To Rev. William Ware.

NEW YORK, *Jan.* 27, 1846.

MY DEAR FRIEND, — This week is a little breathing-
time, the first I have allowed myself for five months ;
and my old pile of sermons shows such a sprinkling of
new ones as it has not in any equal time these ten years.
Sometimes I have thought I might get my head strong
and clear again, and good as anybody's ; but this last
week has brought me to a stand, and made me think of
that monitory prediction of yours when I came home, two
years ago. . . . To be sure, I do not usually think of any
retreat that will separate me entirely from New York.   I
have expected to live and die in connection with this
church ; but I have had a feeling this winter as if a new
voice might be better for them ; and any way it may
be better for them to have one man than two ; that is,
myself and a colleague.   Somewhere, indeed, I expect to
preach as long as I can do anything, for I suppose this
is my vocation, if I have any, poorly as it is discharged.
Poorly ; alas ! how does this eternal ideal fly before us,
and leave us ever restless and unsatisfied !   How much
Henry felt it ! more, indeed, than I had thought, well as
I knew his humility.   And indeed I cannot help thinking that he did not sufficiently distinguish between outward and inward defect.   I can very well understand
how, in any right mind, the latter should give deep pain.
But for Henry Ware to charge himself with indolence

and idleness, — with not doing enough ! Why, he was ever doing more than his health would bear. The Memoir, I hardly need say, is read here with deep interest. Tell your brother, with my regards and thanks to him, that it appears to me a perfect biography in this, — that it placed me in the very presence of my friend, and made me feel, all the while I was reading it, as if he were with me. I laid it down, however, I may confess to you, with one sad feeling beyond that of the general loss ; and that was that nowhere throughout was there one recognition of the friendship that bound me and Henry Ware together. It is nobody's fault, unless it be mine. And I am led sometimes to query whether there be not something strange about me in my friendly relations ; some apparent repulsion, or some want of visible kindliness. One thing I do know ; that we are all crushed down under this great wheel of modern life and labor, and friendships seem to have but poor chance of culture and expression.

To pass on ; with regard to our New York churches, we have, more visible activity this winter than usual. I hold a weekly evening meeting in the library of our church ; Mr. Bellows also. Our Sunday school is re-organized, being divided into two, and the numbers are more than doubled ; and we have formed a Unitarian Association for the State of New York, with headquarters in the hall over the entrance to the Church of the Divine Unity.

To the Same.

NEW YORK, *May* 4, 1846.

MY DEAR — not " rugged and dangerous," but gentle and good-natured, — I foresee a biography (far be the day when it shall be required !) in which it is not difficult to anticipate a passage running somewhat as follows : —

"He seemed to possess every attribute of genius but self-reliance. From this cause, doubtless, he failed to some extent of what he might otherwise have accomplished. He himself thought that the choice of his profession was the fatal mistake of his life ; and perhaps he might have found a more congenial sphere. But it may be doubted whether his self-distrust might not have prevented him from putting. forth his full strength, or rather, perhaps, from giving full play to his mind in any walk of literature or art. Even in those beautiful Oriental and Roman fictions there is a certain staidness, a measured step, from which he never departs. Even in some of those chapters of ' Zenobia,' which a critic of the day pronounced to be 'absolute inspiration,' the light glows through the smooth and polished sentences as through the crevices of plated armor. In fact, it was only in his familiar letters that his genius seemed to break out into perfect freedom. In these he approached the letters of Charles Lamb nearer than any writer of his day.

"There is a curious and really amusing specimen of his modesty in a letter of his to a friend of the name of Dewey, — if we read the name rightly in his somewhat illegible manuscripts. This Dewey, it seems, had published some sermons, or volumes of sermons, we know not which, — for they are long since swept down beneath the flood of time to that oblivion to which many cart-loads of such things are worthily destined, — and the author of ' Zenobia ' really addresses this forgotten preacher as his superior in strength, in power, and, it would seem, even in the felicities of style. We hope

---

the good man had too much sense, or humility at least, to have his head turned by such inexplicable fatuity."

Now I will thank you to preserve this letter among your papers, that the biographer may light upon some evidence of "the good man's" sanity.

. . . I do not think I shall go to the great May meetings in Boston. I am afraid I am not made for them. It wants a man, at any rate, with all his faculties about him, ready and apt and in full vigor; and mine are not, — certainly not now-a-days, if they ever are. The condition of my brain at present makes quiet necessary to me. Every exertion is now something too much.

I have addressed the trustees of the church to-day, to express my conviction to them that, by next autumn, some material change must be made. By that time all my sermons will be preached to death, and I shall have no power to make new ones. The church must determine whether it will relinquish my services entirely, or have them one quarter or one third of the time.

The thought of having soon to be done with time and life has almost oppressed me for the year past, so constantly has it been with me. And indeed I have felt that there may be too much of this for the vigor, not to say the needful buoyancy, of life. Earth is our school, our sphere; and I more than doubt whether the anchorite's dreaming of heaven, or the spirit of the "Saints' Rest," is the true spiritual condition. I have long wanted to review Baxter's work, in this and other views.

With my love to your wife and children, — I mean, by your leave, your wife especially, — I am, as ever,

　　　　　　　　Yours,

　　　　　　　　　　ORVILLE DEWEY.

To the Same.

NEW YORK, *July* 10, 1846.

MY DEAR FRIEND, — If from this awful heat (90° in my study) where I am busy, I were not going to an equally awful country heat where I shall be lazy, I would put off writing a few days. . . . My principal — no, I won't say that — my most painful business is hunting up sermons fit to be preached. The game grows scarce, and my greatest vexation is that every now and then, when I think I have got a fox or a beaver, it turns out to be a woodchuck or a muskrat.

From the tenor of some of our late letters, I believe we should be thought to belong to the " Mutual Admiration Society." I deny that of us both, though appearances are rather against us. I will have done, at any rate, for your last has quite knocked me down, or rather so outrageously set me up, as I was never before.

With regard to my plans, I myself prefer four months in the pulpit here, and that was what I proposed ; but something had been said by me about three months in a different connection, and the congregation, I am told, thought that in naming three they were conforming precisely to my wishes. But that will be arranged satisfactorily. I am to go out of town, of course ; I cannot live here upon a quarter or third of a salary. I have something of my own, this house and a little more, — twelve thousand dollars, perhaps, in all ; so far I have carried out the plan you speak of. I have had reasons more than most others for attending to the means, for I am the only surviving male member of my family. I have had the satisfaction of doing something for them all along, and shall have that of leaving to my mother and sisters a house to cover them, and forty acres of land. . . .

Yours as ever, only more than ever,

Orville Dewey.

To Rev. Henry W. Bellows.

Washington, *Nov.* 2, 1846.

My Dear Bellows, — Suppose I take my pen and write just what comes into my head. Did you expect things coming from anywhere else, I would like to know? It 's a pretty serious condition, however. Conceive — I am to write in total forgetfulness that I am a Dr., and without any fear before my eyes of having it printed in a biography. Bah ! if anybody ever did write letters that never *could* be printed anywhere, I am that person. What the reason is precisely, I do not know, but I always fancied it was because I had no time and no superfluous energies to throw away upon letters, any more than upon conundrums. And I have fancied, too, that when the blessed leisure days should come in the quiet country, — not only the *otium cum dignitate,* but the silence and the meditation, — that then I should pour myself out in letters. But the time has n't come yet. Consider that my leisure as yet extends to only about (I 've pulled out my watch to see) three hours and twenty minutes. It is now Monday, 11 : 20 A.M., and we did not arrive here till Saturday evening.

. . . .

Let me hear from you as soon as ten thousand things will let you. You will easily see that there is no good reason why I have written this letter but this, — that I have left the greater part of my heart in New York, and naturally turn back to find it. Remind your three houses of the stock they have in it, bad as it is; and, to be most sadly serious, remember my very affectionate regards to Mrs. Kirkland, and give my love to the ——s and ——s, and believe me,

Ever your friend,

ORVILLE DEWEY.

To the Same.

WASHINGTON, *Dec.* 10, 1846.

... FOR am I not through the one third of the second of the five months, and am I not very glad of it? And yet I am very glad I came away. You have no idea how I am relieved, and I shall not go back empty-handed. But the relief I feel admonishes me never to return to the full charge. How little do people know or conceive what it is! One case, like what I fear Mrs. ——'s is, of slow decline, — one such case weighs upon the mind and heart for months. If you could go and make the call, without any sad anticipation or afterthought; but you cannot. And then, when it is not one case that draws upon your sympathies, but several, and you are made the confidant of many sorrows besides, and you are anxious for many minds; and when, moreover, your studies are not of the habitudes of bees, and the length of butterflies' wings, but wasting thoughts of human souls in sorrow and peril, and your Sundays rack your sinews with pain, — I declare I wonder that men live through it at all.

To the Same.

WASHINGTON, *Feb.* 7, 1847.

MY DEAR BELLOWS, — I consider it a mercy to you to put some interval between my letters; indeed, I do not know how you write any, ever; besides, I feel all the while as if some of your burdens were to be laid at the door of my delinquencies. . . . Indeed, I rejoice in you always. I never hear of you but to hear good of you; and it is often that I hear. . . .

As to the sermons I have been writing here, I consider your suggestion that you might read since you will not hear them such an enormous compliment, such a reckless piece of goodness, that all your duties in regard to them are fully discharged in the bare proposition. And I am not going to have you canonized and sent down to all ages as the most suffering saint in the nineteenth century, for having read twelve of Dewey's manuscript sermons. I have preached one of them this evening, and it made so much impression (upon *me*) that I was quite taken by surprise. The title is " Nature." . . . Last week I wrote the most considerable lucubration of the winter, on the darkest problem in the philosophy of life and history, "the ministry of error and evil in the world," to wit, Polytheism, Despotism, War, and Slavery. . . . Always my poor mind and heart are struggling with one subject, and that is the great world-question.

You speak of my opportunities here. Perhaps I have not improved them very well. I am not very enterprising in the social relations, and half of the winter I have not cared for Washington, nor anything else but what was passing in my own mind. . . . I have met some admirable persons here, of those I did not know before. Crittenden and Corwin and Judge McLean have interested me most; men they seem to me of as fine and beautiful natures as one can well meet. I have had two interviews with Calhoun that interested me much;

and the other evening I met Soulé, the Louisiana senator, and had a long conversation with him, chiefly about
slavery, — a very remarkable person. There is no face
in the Senate, besides Webster's, so lashed up with the
strong lines of intellect; and his smile shines out as
brightly and beautifully from the dark cloud of his
features.

To his Daughter Mary.

NEW YORK, *May* 23, 1847.

DEAR MOLLY, — I thought M. E. D. made you m-a-d;
but you shall have it hereafter, if it makes you " demni-
tion " mad; no appreciation of my delicacy in leaving
out the E, — which stands for error, egotism, eggnog,
epsom-salts, and every erroneous entity extant. Yes,
the E, — have it, with all its compounds. The fact is,
I suppose, that when people retire up into the country,
they grow monstrous avaricious, and exact everything
that belongs to them; lay up their best clothes and go
slip-shod. I 'm preparing for that condition, mentally
and bodily. You see I begin to slip already in language.
Your mother is trying to persuade me to buy a dressing-
gown. A dressing-gown! when I don't expect to dress
at all. As if a beggar who never expects to dine were
to buy a service of plate, or a starving man should have
his picture taken, and give a hundred dollars for famine
in effigy. I *have* ordered a suit of summer clothes, to
be sure, because I feel very thin, and expect to feel very
light some five weeks hence. I shall get some cigars by
the same token, because all things with me are vanishing
into smoke. And if thin clothes can't live, can't be dis-
tended, filled out, and look respectable, upon smoke, let
'em die, and be crushed before the moth.

Monday morning. These tantrums, dear Molly, were
— what? cut up? — last night after preaching, and mortal tired I was too. I do not know how it is, but it
seems to me that every sermon I take now, every poor,
little, innocent sermon comes bouncing out in the pulpit
like a Brobdingnag.

To Rev. William Ware.

SHEFFIELD, *Aug.* 22, 1847.

DEAR FRIEND, — I don't like Commencements. I
hate travelling. And just now I hate my pen so much
that I can scarce muster patience to tell you so.

.   .   .   .

I have been reading Prescott's " Peru." What a fine
accomplishment there is about it ! And yet there is
something wanting to me in the moral nerve. History
should teach men how to estimate characters. It should
be a teacher of morals. And I think it should make us
shudder at the names of Cortez and Pizarro. But Prescott's does not. He seems to have a kind of sympathy
with these inhuman and perfidious adventurers, as if they
were his heroes. It is too bad to talk of them as the
soldiers of Christ. If it were said of the Devil, they
would have better fitted the character.

Monday morning. The shadows of the lilac fall upon
my page, checkered with the .slant rays of the morning
light ; there is a slope of green grass under the window ;
there is quiet all around ; I wish you were here. My
love to your wife and children.

Yours as ever,

ORVILLE DEWEY.

To the Same.

SHEFFIELD, *Sept.* 30, 1847.

MY DEAR FRIEND, — I should have answered your letter of the 6th before, but sermons have been in hand for the first and second Sundays of October in New York, and my hand is commonly too weary, when engaged in such tasks, to turn to anything else.

I sent the late edition of my — *things* (works, they call 'em) to the Harvard College Library, and if you will take the second volume, you will see, in a sermon "On the Slavery Question," how entirely I agree with you that this is the great trial question of the country. And I think it will press upon the country this coming winter as it never has before. It certainly will if the Californias are ceded to us, and the Wilmot Proviso is brought before Congress, not for hypothetical, but for practical, actual decision. If it should be, I entertain the most painful apprehensions for the result. We have lost a host by the death of Silas Wright. A sagacious politician said to a friend of mine the other day, "It is a special providence, for it has saved us from a dissolution of the Union." His opinion was that Silas Wright, if he had lived, would have been President; and you know that he would have taken his stand on the Proviso.

The judgment of the individual to whom I have just referred presents the true issue. It is *Policy* against *Right*. I suppose there is not a man in New England who does not wish for the extinction of Slavery. I suppose there is hardly a man at the North who does not feel that the system is wrong, that it ought to be abolished, and must eventually be abolished; and that the only question about its abolition is a question of time.

But here is the peril,—that a good many persons in Congress and out of Congress will falter in their conviction before the determined stand of the South,—the determination, that is to say, to break off from the Union rather than submit to the Wilmot Proviso. And I do most seriously fear, for my part, that they would hold to that determination. But I am prepared, for myself, to say that, rather than yield the national sanction to this huge and monstrous wrong, I would take the risk of any consequences whatever. I reason for the nation as I would for myself. I say, rather than tell a lie, I would die. I cannot deliberately do wrong, and I cannot consent that my people shall. I would rather consent to the dismemberment of my right hand than to lay it in solemn mockery on the altar of injustice. As I have said in the sermon to which I have referred you, suppose that we were called upon to legalize polygamy or no marriage in California ; would we do it? Certainly we would not, though all the Southern States should threaten to break off from us for our refusal, and should actually do it. I asked a similar question with regard to legalizing theft, in my sermon on the Annexation of Texas ; and one of the stanchest opposers of the Wilmot Proviso once told me that that was the hardest instance he had ever been called upon to answer.

But though he felt the force of the moral parallel, still policy was carrying it with him over the right ; or rather I should say, perhaps, that he resolved the right of the matter into temporary expediency. He did not mean to cross the line of conscience, but he thought it should sway to this great emergency.

This, I say, is the great peril ; and he who would raise up this nation to the height of this great argument, must

lift it to the determination to do no wrong, — must lift it
high enough, in fact, to see that the right is the only
true policy.

Who shall do it? You exhort me to write. I shall
do so as I am able, and see occasion, as I *have* done.
I shall scarcely refrain, I suppose, from writing this winter. But alas! I am broken in health, and am totally
unable fairly and fully to grapple with any great subject.
I have more than I can well, or, I fear, safely do to meet
the ordinary calls of my pulpit.

In fact I am a good deal discouraged about my ability
to do good in any way, unless it be by quiet study, and
such fruits as may come of it. I have encountered so
much misconstruction within a year past, or rather have
come to the knowledge of so much, that I am seriously
tempted, at times, to retire from the pulpit, from the
church, from the open field of controversy in every form,
and to spend the remainder of my days in studies, which,
if they last long enough, may produce a book or two that
will not subject me to that sort of personal inquisition
which I find has beset me hitherto.

You may be surprised at my saying this, and may ask
if I have not had as much honor and praise as I deserve.
I do not deny it. But still there is, unless I am mistaken, a sort of question about me as a professional person, — about my professional sanctity, or strictness, or
peculiarity, that moves my indignation, I must say, but
(what is more serious) that makes me doubt whether,
as a clergyman, I am doing any good that is proportion-
ate to my endeavors, and inclines me to retreat from this
ground altogether. How, for instance, if I have any
desirable place in one denomination, could the " Christian World " venture to say that I had done more hurt

by my observation about teetotalism in my Washington discourse than all the grog-shops in the land! How could a clerical brother of mine seriously propose, as if he spoke the sense of many, to have me admonished about my habits of living, — of eating, he said, but perhaps he meant drinking, too, — *my habits*, who am a remarkably simple and small eater; and, as to wine, do not taste it one day in twenty! Yet this person actually attributed my ill-health to luxurious living. I live as I list; I feast as other men feast, when I *am* at a feast, which is very rarely; I laugh as other men laugh; I *will not have* any clerical peculiarity in my manners; and if this cannot be understood, I will retire from the profession, for I will be a man more than a minister. I came into the profession from the simplest possible impulse, — from a religious impulse; I have spoken in it as I would, — with earnestness, if nothing else, — and I cannot throw away this earnestness upon a distrusting community. Besides, I confess that I am peculiarly sensitive to personal wrong. I do not suppose that this blackguardism of the Abolition press would have found anywhere a more sensitive subject than I am. It fills me with horror, — as if I had been struck with a blow, and beaten into the mire and dust in the very street.

I must have some great faults, — that is my conclusion, — and such faults, perhaps, as unfit me for doing much good. I open my heart to you. God bless you and yours.

Your assured friend,

ORVILLE DEWEY.

To Mrs. David Lane.

SHEFFIELD, *Oct.* 19, 1847.

MY DEAR FRIEND, — I cannot feel easy without knowing how little C. is getting along. I pray you to take your pen, if you are not too busy, or she too ill, and tell me how she is.

And now, having *my* pen in hand, I could and should go on and write a letter to you, were it not that all ingenuity, fancy, liberty of writing, is put to a complete nonplus by the uncertainty in what state of mind my writing will find *you.* I must not write merrily, I would not write sadly. I hope all is well, I fear all is not, and I know not how to blend the two moods, though an apostle *has* said, "As sorrowful, yet always rejoicing." But apostolic states of mind somehow seem to me too great to enter into letters, and there is nothing to me more surprising than to find in biography — Foster's, for instance — long letters occupied with the profoundest questions in religion. If I were not habitually engaged in the contemplation of such subjects, if I had not another and appropriate vehicle for them, and if they did not always seem to me too vast for a sheet or two of paper, I suppose that *my* letters, too, might be wise and weighty. As it is, they are always mere relaxations, or mere chippings and parings from the greater themes, at the most. So you see that neither you nor the public lose anything by my being a negligent and reluctant letter-writer.

Well, I shall make a serious letter, if I do not mind, about nothing, and so doubly disprove all I have been saying. I trust C. is getting well, but I am always anxious about that fever. Pray write a word to relieve my solicitude, which my wife shares with me, as in the affectionate regard with which I am,

Ever yours,

ORVILLE DEWEY.

Our kind remembrances to Mr. Lane. We are busy, as city people cannot conceive of, in getting the indoors and outdoors to rights.

To Rev. Henry W. Bellows.

SHEFFIELD, *Nov.* 26, 1847.

MY DEAR FRIEND, — I have thought much of what you said the other morning; and though I expect to see you again in a fortnight, I cannot let the interval pass without a few words. The new interest in your mind, as far as it is spiritual, and the new measures you propose to adopt in your church, so far as I understand them, have my entire sympathy. But I demur to your manner of stating the speculative grounds of this change in your feeling and view. Certainly my mind is, and has been for a long time, running in a direction contrary to your present leanings. I cannot think that human nature is so low and helpless as you seem to think, nor that the Gospel is so entirely the one and exclusive remedy. And yet I agree, too, with much (in its practical bearing) of what you say, in the direction that your mind is taking. I have often insisted in the pulpit that the people do not yet understand Christianity; its spiritual nature, however, rather than its positive facts, its simple love and disinterestedness rather than its supernaturalism, were to me the points where they have failed. . . . I fully admit, too, the need of progress in our denomination, but I do not believe in any grand new era to be introduced into its history by the views you urge, or any other views. All good progress must be gradual. If there is a revolution in your mind, does it follow that that must be the measure for others, for your brethren, for the denomination, in past or present time?

Your sympathies are wide; the tendency to outward action is strong in you; your generous nature opens the doors of your mind to light from every quarter; need is, to carry on a strong discriminating work in a mind like yours. With your nature, so utterly opposed to everything sluggish and narrow, you have need of a large and well-considered philosophy, "looking before and after," and settling all things in their right places, and questioning every new-coming thought with singular caution, lest it push you from your propriety or consistency. In truth, you quite mistake me when you say that I have not studied your mind. I have watched its workings with the greatest interest, often with admiration, and sometimes — may I say? — with anxiety. There was a time when I greatly feared that you would go the lengths of Parker. The turn in your mind to what I deem healthier views took place about the time I went abroad; and the relief your letters gave me while I was in Europe, you can hardly have suspected. Now, it seems to me, you are liable to go to the opposite extreme. The truth is, your intellectual insight seems to me greater than your breadth of view, your penetration greater than your comprehension; and the consequence has been a course of thought, as I believe you are aware, somewhat zigzag.

Have I not thought of you, my dear fellow? I guess I have; and among other things I have so thought of you that I now entirely confide in the magnanimity of your mind to receive with candor all this, and more if I should say it, — saying it, as I do, in the truest love and cherishing of you.

My love to E. and all the phalanstery.

As ever, yours,
ORVILLE DEWEY.

P. S. I read this letter to my wife last evening, and I told her of your criticism on the sermon at Providence. She made the very rejoinder that I made to you, — "The power to cast one's self on the great Christian resource, to put one's self in relation with God the Father and with spiritual help, is the very power which he denies to human nature, and the very thing that Mr. H. contended for." Nor yet do I like your mode of statement, for Christianity does not represent itself to me as a sort of Noah's Ark, and human nature as in stormy waters, — to be saved if it can get its foot on that plank, and not otherwise. I prefer my figure of the shower specially sent on the feeble and half-withered plant. All the divines of every school have always said that there is light enough in nature, if with true docility and love men would follow it. Christ came to shed more light on our path, not the only light; to lift up the lame man, not to create limbs for him or to be limbs for him.

And I confess, too, that I do not like another aspect in the state of your mind; and that is, that your newly awakened zeal should fasten, as it seems to do, upon the *positive* facts and the supernaturalism of Christianity. Not, as I think, that I undervalue them. I do not know of any rational and thinking man that lays more stress on them in their place than I do. But certainly there is something beyond to which they point; and that is, the deep spiritualism of the Gospel, the deep heart's repose and sufficiency in things divine and infinite. If your mind had fastened upon this as the newly found treasure in the Gospel, I should have been better satisfied. I am writing very frankly to you, as you are wont to write to me (and I believe that you and I can bear these terms, and bless them too), and therefore I will add that my greatest distrust of your spiritual nature turns to this very point : whether you have, in the same measure as you have other things, that deep heart's rest, that quiet, profound, all-sufficing satisfaction in the infinite resource, in the all-embosoming love of the All-Good, in silent and solitary communion with God, settling and sinking the soul, as into the still waters and the ocean depths. Your nature runs to social communions, to visible movements, to outwardness, in short, more than to the central depths within. The defects in your preaching, which I have heard pointed out by the discerning, are the want of consistency, — of one six months with another six months, — and the want of spiritual depth and vitality ; of that calm, deep tone of. thought and feeling that goes to the depths of the heart.

God knows that I do very humbly attempt to criticise another's religion and preaching, being inexpressibly concerned about the defects of my own. And, dear friend, I speak to you as modestly as I do frankly. I may be wrong, or I may be only partly right. But in this crisis I think that I ought to say plainly what I feel and fear. I cannot bear, for every reason, — for your sake and for the sake of the church, in which, for your age, you are rooting yourself so deeply, — that you should make any misstep on the ground upon which you seem to be entering.

To Rev. William Ware.

SHEFFIELD, Dec. 6, 1847.

MY DEAR WARE, — I think my pen will run on, with such words to start from, though it have spent itself on the weary "Sermons." This is Monday morning, and I am not quite ready in mind to begin on a new one. The readiness, with me, is nine tenths of the battle. I never, or almost never, write a sermon unless it be upon a subject that I *want* to write upon. I never cast about for a subject; I do not find the theme, but the theme finds me. Last week I departed from my way, and did not make good progress. The text, "What shall it profit a man?" struck upon my heart as I sat down on Monday morning, and I wrote it at the head of my usual seven sheets of white paper, and went on. But the awfulness of the text impressed me all the while with the sense of failure, and though the sermon was finished, I mainly felt at the end that I had lost my week.

One thing I find in my preaching, more and more, and that is that the simplest things become more and more weighty to me, so that a sermon does not require to be anything remarkable to interest me deeply. Everything that I say in the pulpit, I think, is taking stronger and stronger hold upon me, and that which might have been dull in my utterance ten years ago, is not so now. I say this to you, because it has some bearing on one of the matters discussed in our last letters; that is, whether I should leave the pulpit. If I leave it, it will be with a fresher life in it, I think, than has stirred in me at any previous part of my course. And certainly I have long believed that it was my vocation to *preach*, above all things, — more than to visit parishioners, though I always visit every one of them once a year, — more than to write, though you say I have written to some purpose (and your opinion is a great comfort to me). Certainly, then, I shall not retire from the pulpit, but upon the maturest reflection and for what shall seem to be the weightiest reasons. And I did not mean that the things I referred to should be *prima facie* reasons for retirement ; but the question with me was whether my unprofessional way of thinking and acting were not so misconstrued as to lessen my power to do good ; whether the good I do is in any proportion to the strength I lay out.

But enough of myself, when I am much more concerned about you. I see plainly enough how intense is your desire to go to Rome. I see how all your culture and taste and feeling urge you to go, and yet more what a reason in many ways your health supplies. And I declare the author of Zenobia and Probus and Julian ought to go to Rome ! There is a fitness in it, and I trust it will come to pass. But you should not go alone. Every one wants company in such a tour, — that I know full well ; but your health demands it. You must not be subject to sudden seizures in a strange city, — a stranger, alone. Your family never will consent to it, and I think never ought to. Do give up that idea entirely, — of going alone. Have patience. There will be somebody to go with next spring, or next summer. I would that I could go with you where you go, and lodge with you where you lodge. But somebody will go. Something better will turn up, at any rate, than to go alone. There are young men every year who want to go abroad in quest of art and beauty and culture, and to whom your company would be invaluable. I do not forget the difficulty about expense. But there are those who, like you, would be glad to go directly by Marseilles or Leghorn. It is quite true that *movement* is the mischief with the purse. *Abiding* in Rome or Florence, you can live for a dollar a day. A room, or two rooms (parlor and little sleeping-room), say near the Piazza di Spagna, or the Propaganda just by, can be hired, with bed, etc., all to be kept in order, for three or four pauls (thirty or forty cents, you know) a day. And you can breakfast at a *café* any time you fancy, while wandering about, for two pauls, and dine at a *trattoria* for from two to four pauls. I have more than once dined on a bowl of soup and bread and butter for two pauls. I hate heavy dinners. In Rome, one should always take a room in which the sun lies. "Where the sun comes, the doctor does n't," they say there. But you won't go before I come and see you and talk it all over with you. Don't fail to let me know if you set seriously about it, for I shall certainly come. The truth is, *Mrs. Ware should go with you.* It is true the women are very *precious* when it comes to casting them up in a bill of expense, as in all things else. Does not that last clause save me, madam? And, madam dear, I want to talk with *you* about this project of William's, as much as I want to hear what he says.

About the war, dear Gulielmus, and slavery, and almost everything else under heaven, I verily believe I think just as you do; so I need not write. And my hand is very tired. With ten thousand blessings on you,

Yours ever,

ORVILLE DEWEY.

To his Daughter Mary.

SHEFFIELD, *July* 13, 1848.

DEAR MOLLY, — You 're an awful *miss* when you 're not here; what will you be, then, when you descend upon us from the heights of Lenox, — from the schools of wisdom, from fiction and fine writing, from tragedy and comedy, from mountain mirrors reflecting all-surrounding beauty, down to plain, prosaic still-life in Sheffield? I look with anxiety and terror for the time; and, to keep you within the sphere of familiarity as much as possible, I think it best to write sometimes; and, to adopt the converse of the Western man's calling his bill " William," I call my William, bill, — my Mary, Molly, thereby softening, mollifying (as I may say) the case as much as possible.

One thing I must desire of you. You are on an experiment.[1] Now be honest. Don't bring any " sneeshin " down here to throw dust in our poor, simple eyes in the valley. Much as ever we can see anything for fogs. Mind ye, *I* shall be sharp, though. If you fall into any of those practices, I shall say you brought the trick from Lenox. You may say " I-ketch-you " as much as you please, but you won't ketch *me.*

To Rev. Henry W. Bellows.

SHEFFIELD, *Dec.* 19, 1848.

MY DEAR BELLOWS, — Now shall I heap coals of fire on your head. You ought to have written to me forty days ago. Your letter bears date of yesterday. I

---

[1] To try whether the air of Lenox, on the hills, would have any effect in averting an annual attack of hay-fever.

received it this afternoon. I am replying this evening.
How does your brain-pan feel, with this coal upon it?
" How has it happened that there has been no communication?" Why, it has happened from your being the
most unapprehensive mortal that ever lived, or from your
having your wits whirled out of you by that everlasting
New York tornado. As to letters, I wrote the two last,
though the latter was a bit of one. As to the circumstances, my withdrawal from your society was involuntary, and painful to me. You should have written at
once to your *emeritus* coadjutor, your senior friend. I
have been half vexed with you, my people quite.

There ! I love you too much not to say all that. But
I am not an exacting or punctilious person, and that is
one reason why we have got along so well together ; as
well as that you are one whom nobody can know without taking a plaguy kindness and respect for, and can't
help it. And all that you say about our past relation and
intercourse I heartily reciprocate, excepting that which
does you less than justice, and me more. As to deep
talks, I really believe there is no chance for them in
Gotham. And this reminds me that my wife has just
been in my study to desire me to send a most earnest
invitation to you and E. to come up here this winter and
pass a few days with us. It will be easier than you may
think at first. The New York and New Haven Railroad
will be open in a few days, and then you can be here in
seven or eight hours from your own door. Do think of
it, — and more than think of it.

To the Same.

AREN'T you a pretty fellow, — worse than Procrustes,
— to go about the world, measuring people's talent and

promise by their noses? . . . Why, man, Claude Lorraine and Boccaccio and Burke had "small noses;" and Kosciusko and George Buchanan had theirs turned up, and could n't help it. It reminds me of what a woman of our town said, who had married a very heinous-looking blacksmith. Some companions of our " smithess " saw him coming along in the street one day, and unwittingly exclaimed, " What dreadful-looking man is that?" " That's my husband," said the wife, " and God made him."

To the Same.

SHEFFIELD, *Jan.* 2, 1849.

MY DEAR BELLOWS, — Your letter came on New Year's Day, and helped to some of those cachinnations usually thought to belong to such a time; though for my part I can never find set times particularly happy or even interesting, — partly, I believe, from a certain obstinacy of disposition that does not like to do what is set down for it.

As to church matters, I said nothing to you when I was down last, because I knew nothing. That is, I had no hint of what the congregation was about to do, — no idea of anything in my connection with the church that needed to be spoken of. I was indeed thinking, for some weeks before I went down, of saying to the congregation, that unless they thought my services very important to them, I should rather they would dispense with them, and my mind was just in an even balance about the matter. But one is always influenced by the feeling around him, — at least I am, — and when I found that every one who spoke with me about my coming again seemed to depend upon it, and to be much interested in it, I determined to say nothing about withdrawing. My reasons for wishing to retire were, that I was working hard — hard for me — to prepare sermons which, as my engagement in my view was temporary, might be of no further use to me; and that if I were to enter upon a new course of life, the sooner I did so the better.

And here I may as well dispose of what you and others say and urge with regard to my continuance in the profession. To your question whether I have not sermons enough to last me for five years in some new place, I answer, No, not enough for two. And if I had, I tell you that I cannot enter into these affecting and soul-exhausting relations again and again, any more than I could be married three or four times. The great trial of our calling is the wrenching, the agonizing, of sympathy with affliction; and there is another trying thing which I have thought of much of late, and that is the essential moral incongruity of such relations, and especially with strangers. I almost feel as if nobody but an intimate friend had any business in a house of deep affliction. In a congregation ever so familiar there is trial enough of this kind. If my friend is sick or dying, I go to his bedside of course, but it is as a friend, — to say a word or many words as the case may be; to look what I cannot say; to do what I can. But to come there, or to come to the desolate mourner, in an official capacity, — there is something in this which is in painful conflict with my ideas of the simple relations of man with man. Now all this difficulty is greatly increased when one enters upon a new ministration in a congregation of strangers. Therefore on every account I must say, no more pastoral relations for me. I cannot take up into my heart another heap of human chance and change and sorrow. Do you not see it? Why, what takes place in New Bedford now moves me a hundred times more than all else that is in the world. And so it will always be with all that befalls my brethren in the Church of the Messiah.

As to the world's need of help, I regard it doubtless as you do ; and I am willing and desirous to help it from the pulpit as far as I am able. But I cannot hold that sort of irregular connection with the pulpit called " supplying " ; nor can I go out on distant missionary enterprises, — to Cincinnati, Mobile, or New Orleans. The first would yield me no support ; and as to the last, I must live in my family. Besides, there is sphere enough with the pen ; and study may do the world as much good as action. And there is no doubt what direction my studies must take. Why, I have written out within a week — written incontinently in my commonplace book, my pen *would* run on — a thesis on Pantheism nearly as long as a sermon. And as to preaching, what ground have I to think that mine is of any particular importance? Not that I mean to affect any humility which I do not feel. I profess that I have quite a good opinion of myself as a preacher. Seriously, I think I have one or two rather remarkable qualifications for preaching, — a sense of reality in the matter of the vitality of the thing, and then an edge of feeling (so it seems to me) which takes off the technical and commonplace character from discourse. Oh ! if I could add, a full sense of the divineness of the thing, I should say all. Yet something of this, too, I hope ; and I hope to grow in this as I hope to live, and do not dread to die. But though *I* think all this, with all due modesty, it does not follow that others do ; and the evidence seems to be rather against it, does it not?

As ever, yours,

ORVILLE DEWEY.

In connection with this letter, and with his own frank but moderate estimate of his gift as a preacher, it is interesting to read the following extract from a paper in his memory, read before the annual meeting of the American Unitarian Association by Rev. Dr. Briggs, May 30, 1882:

"I remember well the way in which he seemed to me to be a power in the pulpit. He was the first man who made the pulpit seem to me as a throne. When he stood in it, I recognized him as king. I remember how eager I was to walk in from the Theological School at Cambridge to hear him when there was an opportunity to do so in any of the pulpits of Boston. I remember walking with my classmate, Nathaniel Hall, — when the matter of the expense of a passage was of great concern to me, — to Providence, where Mr. Dewey was to preach at the installation of Dr. Hall. My Brother Hall was not drawn there simply for the sake of his brother's installation, I, not from the fact that Providence was the home of my boyhood ; but both of us, more than by anything else, by our eager desire to hear this preacher where he might give us a manifestation of his power. And, as he spoke from the text, ' I have preached righteousness in the great congregation,' we felt that we were well repaid for all our efforts to come and listen to him.

~" I have heard of some one who heard him preach from the text on dividing the sheep from the goats, and as he came away, he said, ' I felt as if I were standing before the judgment-seat.'   I remember hearing him preach from the text, ' Thou art the man,' and I felt that that word was addressed to me as directly as it was by the prophet to the king.   His was a power scarcely known to the men of this later generation.

"It would be difficult, I think, to analyze his character and mind, and to say just in what his power consisted. He did not have the reasoning power that distinguished Dr. Walker; he did not have the poetic gift that gave such a charm to the sermons of Ephraim Peabody; he did not have that peculiarity of speech which made the sermons of Dr. Putnam so effective upon the congregation, and yet he was the peer of any one of them.   It was, I think, because the truth had possession of his whole being when he spoke.   It was because he always had a high ideal of the pulpit, and was striving to come up to it, and because he went to the pulpit with that preparation which alone makes any preaching effective, and which will make it mighty forever."

To Rev. Henry W. Bellows.

SHEFFIELD, *Feb.* 26, 1849.

MY DEAR BELLOWS, — I came from Albany to-day at noon, and have had but this afternoon to reflect upon your letter.   But I see that you ought to have an answer immediately; and my reply to your proposition to me grows out of such decided considerations, that they seem to me to require no longer deliberation.   I see that you desire my help, and I am very sorry that I cannot offer it to you; but consider.   You ask of me what, with my habits of thought and methods of working, would be equal to writing one sermon in a fortnight.   I would *rather* do this than to write four or even three columns for the "Inquirer," considering, especially, that I must find such a variety of topics, and must furnish the tale of brick every week. I have always been obliged to work irregularly, when I could; and this weekly task-work would allow no indulgence to such poor habits of study. Besides, this task would occupy my whole mind; that is, such shattered mind as I have at present to give to anything; I could do nothing else, — nothing to supply my lack of means to live upon. I could better take the "Christian Examiner;" it would cost me much less labor, and it would give me the necessary addition to my income, provided I could find some nook at the eastward where I could live as cheaply as I can here.

I think the case must be as plain to your mind as it is to mine. If I were to occupy any place in your army, it would be in the flying artillery; these solid columns will never do for me. Why, I can't remember the time when I have written twenty-five sermons in a year, and that, I insist, is the amount of labor you desire of me. You may think that I overrate it, and you speak of my writing from "the level of my mind." The highest level is low enough, and this I say in sad sincerity. In fact, if nothing offers itself for me to do that I can do, I think that I shall let the said mind lie as fallow ground for a while, hoping that, through God's blessing, leisure and leisurely studies may give strength for some good work by and by. How to live, in the mean time, is the question; but I can live poor, and must, if necessary, trench upon my principal. But if I am driven to this resort, I will make thorough work of it; I will bind myself to no duty, professional, literary, or journalistic; if a book, or a little course of lectures, or any other little thing comes out from under my hands at the end of one, two, or three years, let it; but I will do nothing upon compulsion, though the things to do be as thick as blackberries. There's my profession of — duty! I have worked hard, however imperfectly. I have worked in weariness, in tribulation, and to the very edge of peril; and I believe that the high Taskmaster, to whom I thus refer with humble and solemn awe, will pardon me some repose, if circumstances beyond my control assign it to me for my lot.

As to the "Inquirer," in times past, you should remember that in what I said of it that was disparaging, I excepted your part in it. That certainly has not lacked interest, whatever else it has lacked. You have, I think, some remarkable qualifications for the proposed enterprise; and if you could give your whole mind and life to it, I should augur more favorably of such a monarchy than of the proposed oligarchy. You are a live man; you have a quick apprehension of what is going on about you; you have insight, generosity, breadth of view. And yet, if I were fully to state what I mean by this last qualification, I should say it is breadth rather than comprehension. You see a great way on one side of a subject, rather than all round. *This* requires a great deal of quiet, silent study, and where you are going to find space for it, I do not see, look all round as I may, or may pretend to. What I shall most fear about the "Inquirer" is, that it will give an uncertain sound; and this danger will be increased by the number of minds brought into it. Associate editors ought to live near to each other, and to compare notes. How do you know that Mr. C. will not cross Mr. O.'s track, or both of them Mr. Bellows, even if Mr. Bellows do not cross his own? You say you will put your own stamp upon the paper,

of course. But your stamp has been rather indefinite
as yet. "Shaper and Leader," say you? Suggester and
Pioneer, rather, is my thought of your function. This
is pretty plain talk; but, confound you, you can bear it.
And I can bear to say it, because I love — because I
like you, and because I think of you as highly, I guess,
as you ought to think of yourself. After all, I do expect
a strong, free, living journal from you, and the men of
your age, or thereabouts, who are united with you.

You say that I do not understand a "certain spirit of
expectation and seeking" in these men. Perhaps not;
it is vaguely stated, and I cannot tell. One of these
days you will spread it out and I shall see. I *have* ideas
of progress, with which my thoughts are often wrestling,
and I shall be glad to have them made more just, ex-
panded, and earnest. With love to all,

Yours ever,
ORVILLE DEWEY.

To Rev. William Ware.

SHEFFIELD, *May* 25, 1849.

MY DEARLY BELOVED AND LONGED FOR, — I can't have
you go to New York and not come here; and my special
intent in writing now is to show you how little out of
your way it is to return to Cambridge by Berkshire, and
how little more expense it is. I trust that Mrs. Ware is
to be with you.

.   .   .   .

There! it's a short argument, but a long conclusion
shall follow, — a week long of talk and pleasure, which
shall be as good as forty weeks long, by the heart's
measurement.

.   .   .   .

Alas! these college prayers! If I *had* anything to do with them, it would be upon the plan of remodelling them entirely. I would have them but once in a day, at a convenient hour, say eight or nine o'clock in the morning. I would have leave to do what my heart might prompt in the great hours of adoration. Reading the Scriptures with a word of comment, sometimes, or a word uttered as the spirit moved, without reading; or instead, a matin hymn or old Gregorian chant, solemn orisons, free breathings of veneration and joy; sometimes the reading of a prayer of the Episcopal Church, or of the venerable olden time, — always a bringing down of the great sentiment of devotion into young life, to be its guidance and strength, — this should be college prayers. . . .

To Rev. Henry W. Bellows.

SHEFFIELD, *Feb.* 11, 1850.

MY DEAR FRIEND, — In the first place, La Bruyère was the name of the French satirist that I could not remember the other day. In the second place, I have a letter from Mr. Lowell, inviting me to deliver the second course of lectures, and the time fixed upon is the winter after next; I can't be prepared by next winter. As to the title, I think, after all, Herder's is the best: " Philosophy of Humanity," or I should as lief say, " On the Problem of Evil in the World." You said of me once in some critique, I believe, that I always seemed to write as in the presence of objectors. I shall be very likely to do so now. Well, here is work for me for two years ahead, if I have life and health, and work that I like above all other. In the third place, I don't think I shall do much for the " Inquirer." My name has really no business on the first page ; in fact, I never thought of its standing there as a fixture. I supposed you would say for once in your opening that such and such persons would help you. With my habits of writing, I am better able to write long articles than short ones ; and the "Christian Examiner" pays more than you, and I am obliged to regard that consideration. I must have three or four hundred dollars a year beyond my income, or sell stock, — a terrible alternative. In the fourth place, every man is right in his own eyes ; I am a man : therefore I am right in my eyes. I am very unprofessional ; that is, in regard to the etiquette and custom of the profession. I am so ; and in regard to the professional mannerism and spirit of routine, I am very much afraid of it. But I do not think that many persons have ever enjoyed the religious services of our profession more than I have ; the spiritual communion, which is its special function, and that, not through sermons alone, but in sacraments, in baptisms, in fireside conference with darkened and troubled minds, has long been to me a matter of the profoundest interest and satisfaction. It is the one reigning thought of my life now to see and to show how the Infinite Wisdom and Loveliness shine through this universe of forms. To this will I devote myself ; nay, am devoted, whether I will or not. This will I pursue, and will preach it. I will preach it in the Lowell Lectures. Shall I be wrong if I give up other preaching for the time? You think so. Perhaps you are right. Any way, it is not a matter of much importance, I suppose. There is a great deal too much of preaching, such as it is. The world is in danger of being preached out of all hearty and spontaneous religion. What would you think, if the love of parents and children were made the subject of a weekly lecture in the family, and of such lecture as the ordinary preaching is? Oh ! if a Saint Chrysostom, or even a Saint Cesarius, or a Robert Hall could come along and speak to us once in half a year, they would leave, perhaps, a deeper imprint than this perpetual and petrifying drop-dropping of the sanctuary.

By the bye, read those extracts from the sermons of Saint Cesarius, in the sixteenth lecture of Guizot on French civilization, and see if they are not worth inserting in the " Inquirer." The picture which Guizot gives in that and the following lecture, of Christianity struggling in the bosom of all-surrounding wrong, cruelty, and sensualism, is very beautiful. It is one of the indications of the raging ultraism of the time, that the calm wisdom and piety of such a man as Guizot should be so little appreciated.

When I read such writers as this, I am rather frightened at my undertaking ; but I believe there is a great deal to be said to the *people* that is not beyond me, and I shall modestly do what I can. I began yesterday to study Hegel's " Philosophy of History," and though I can read but a few pages a day, I believe I shall master it ; and after one gets through with his theory, I imagine, in looking at his topics ahead, that I shall find matters that are intelligible and practical. I am, as ever,

Yours,

ORVILLE DEWEY.

To William Cullen Bryant, Esq.

SHEFFIELD, *Feb.* 25, 1850.

MY DEAR BRYANT, — You will remember, perhaps, our conversation when you were last up here, about our Club of the XXI. You know my attachment to it. The loss of those pleasant meetings is indeed one of the things I most regret in leaving the city. I cannot bear to forfeit my place in that good company. In this feeling I am about to make a proposition which I beg you will present for me, and that you will, as my advocate, try to explain and show that it is not so enormous as at first it may seem. I pray, then, my dear Magnus,[1] that you will turn your poetical genius to account by describing the beautiful ride up the valley of the Housatonic, and this our beautiful Berkshire, and will put in the statistical fact that it is but six hours and a half from New York to Sheffield,[2] and then will request the Club to meet at my house some day in the coming summer. I name Wednesday, the 19th of June. I propose that the proper Club-meeting be on the evening of that day. The next day I propose that we shall spend among the mountains, — seeing Bash-pish, and, if possible, the Salisbury Lakes. And I will thank you, as my faithful solicitor, that, if you are obliged of your knowledge to confess to the fact of my very humble housekeeping, you will also courageously maintain that with the aid of my friends I can make our brethren as comfortable as people expect to be on a frolicking bout, and that I can easily get good country wagons to take them on a jaunt among the mountains. You will tell me, I hope, how my proposition is received ; and by received, I do not mean any vote or resolution, but whether the gentlemen seem to think it would be a pleasant thing.

And when you write, tell me whether you or Mrs. Bryant chance to know of any person who would like to

---

[1] Mr. Dewey was wont to call his friend "our Magnus Apollo."
[2] Now lessened to five hours.

come up here this summer and teach French in my sister's school an hour or two a day for a moderate compensation. It must be a French person, — one that can speak the language. Her school is increasing, and she must have more help.

With mine and all our kindest regards to Mrs. Bryant and Julia and Fanny, I am, as ever,

Yours truly,

ORVILLE DEWEY.

Tell Mrs. Bryant we depend on her at the Club.

To his Daughter Mary.

SHEFFIELD, *March* 4, 1850.

. . . As I suppose you are tormented with the question, " What 's your father doing in Sheffield? " you may tell them that I have taken to lecturing the people, and that I give a second lecture to-morrow evening, and mean to give a third. Forbye reading Hegel every morning, and what do you think he said this morning? Why, that he had read of a government of women, " ein Weiberstaat," in Africa, where they killed all the men in the first place, and then all the male children, and finally destined all that should be born to the same fate. And what do you think your mother said when I told her of these atrocities? Even this: " That shows what bad creatures the men must have been." And that 's all I get when trying to enlighten her upon the wickedness of her sex.

And I 'm just getting through with Guizot's four volumes, too. Oh, a very magnificent, calm, and beautiful course of lectures! You must read them. It 's the best French history, so far as it goes.

To Rev. Henry W. Bellows.

SHEFFIELD, *March* 6, 1850.

. . . To my poor apprehension this is an awful crisis, especially if pushed in the way the Northern *doctrinaires* desire. I feel it so from what I saw of Southern feeling in Washington the winter I passed there. I fear disunion, and no mortal line can sound the depth of that calamity. I sometimes think that it would be well if we could wear around this last, terrible, black headland by sounding, and trimming sails, rather than attempt to sail by compass and quadrant. Do not mistake my figure. I am no moral trimmer, and that you know. Conscience must be obeyed. But conscience does not forbid that we should treat the Southern people with great consideration. What we must do, we may do in the spirit of love, and not of wrath or scorn. Oh, what a mystery of Providence, that this terrible· burden — I had almost said millstone — should ever have been hung around the neck of this Confederation !

To William Cullen Bryant, Esq.

SHEFFIELD, *June* 7, 1850.

MY DEAR SIR, — You should n't have lived in New York, and you should n't have been master of the French language, and you should n't have been Mr. Bryant, and, in fact, you should n't have been at all, if you expected to escape all sorts of trouble in this world ! Since all these conditions pertain to you, see the inference, which, stated in the most skilfully inoffensive way I am able, stands or runs thus : —

[Here followed a request that Mr. Bryant would make

some inquiries concerning a French teacher who had applied, and the letter continued :]

Now, in fine, if you don't see that all this letter is strictly logical, — an inference from the premises at the beginning, — I am sorry for you ; and if you do see it, I am sorry for you. So you are pitied at any rate.

The 19th draws nigh. If any of the Club are with you and Mrs. Bryant in coming up, do not any of you be so deluded as to listen to any invitation to dine at Kent, but come right along, hollow and merry, and — I don't say I promise you a dinner, but what will suffice for *natur,* anyhow. Art, to be sure, is out of the question, as it is when I subscribe myself, and ourselves, to you and Mrs. Bryant, with affectionate regard,

Yours truly,
ORVILLE DEWEY.

To Rev. William Ware.

SHEFFIELD, *Oct.* 13, 1850.

"THAT's what I will," I said, as I took up your letter just now, to read it again, thinking you had desired me to write *immediately.* " How affectionate !" thinks I to myself; " that must have been a good letter that I wrote him last; I really think some of my letters must be pretty good ones, after all; I hate conceit, — I really believe my tendency is the other way, — but, hang it ! who knows but I may turn out, upon *myself,* a fine letter after all? But at any rate Ware loves me, does n't he? He wants me to write a few lines, at least, very soon. It 's evident he would be pleased to have me, — 'pleased'? as the Laird of Ellangowan said of the king's commission, — ' good honest gentle-

man, he can't be more pleased than I am !'"   But oh !
the slips of those who are shodden with vanity ! I read
on, thinking it was a nicè letter of yours, — feeling
something startled, to be sure, at the compellation, as if
you were *mesmerisé*, and had got an insight (—— calls
me bambino half of the time) — looking at your mood
reverential as a droll jest, — vexed at first, but then
reconciled, about the book and the lecturing, — charmed
and grateful beyond measure at what you say about your
health, — when ! at last !! I fell upon your request:
"Now give me one brief epistle *between this and our
seeing you.*" !!! BETWEEN ! what a word ! what a hiatus !
what a gulf ! Down into it tumbled pride, vanity, pleasure, everything. Well, great occasions call out virtue.
As I emerged, as I came up, I came up a hero ; the
vanities of this world were all struck off from me in my
fall, and I came up a *hero ;* for I determined I *would*
write to you *immediately.* There ! beat that if you can !
I give you a chance, — one chance, — I *don't ask* you
to write at all.

          .   .   .   .

What is it you call my study now-a-days, — "terrible
moral metaphysics"? You may well say "weighed
down" with them. I was never in my life before quite
so modest as I am now. Not that I have n't enough to
say, and all my faculties leap to the task ; but all the
while there looms up before me an ideal of what such a
course of lectures might be, that I fear I shall never
reach up to, no, nor one twentieth part of the way
to it. . . .

To Mrs. David Lane.

SHEFFIELD, *Jan.* 25, 1851.

MY DEAR FRIEND, — You *won't* come, and I *will* write to you! See the difference. See how I return good for evil!

I say, you won't come; for I have a letter from Mrs. Curtis, from which it is evident *she* will not, and so I suppose that laudable conspiracy falls to the ground. However, we shall *sort o'* look for you all the week. But you won't come. I know it to my fingers' ends. Cradled in luxury, wrapped in comfort, enervated by city indulgences, sophisticated by fashionable society — well, I won't finish the essay; but you won't come.

Ah! speaking of fashionable society, — that reminds me, — you ask a question, and say, "Answer me." Well, then, — society we must have; and all the question I should have to ask about it would be whether it pleased me, — not whether everybody in it pleased me, but whether its general tone did not offend me, and then, whether I could find persons in it with whose minds I could have grateful and good intercourse. If I could, I don't think the word "fashion," or the word "world," would scare me. As to the time given to it, and the time to be reserved for weightier matters, that is, to be sure, very material. But the chief thing is a *reigning spirit* in our life, gained from communion with the highest thoughts and themes, which consecrates all time, and subordinates all events and circumstances, and hallows all intercourse, and turns the dust of life into golden treasures.

I have no thoughts of going to New York or anywhere

else at present.   I finished my eighth lecture yesterday. This is my poor ·service to the world in these days, — since you insist that I have relations to the world.

I reciprocate Mr. Lane's kind wishes, and am, as ever,

Yours, with no danger of forgetting,

ORVILLE DEWEY.

To Rev. William Ware.

SHEFFIELD, *July* 3, 1851.

DEAR GWYLLYM (is n't that Welsh for William?) — I don't know whether your letter with nothing in it, and the postage paid on the contents, is on the way to me; but I am writing to all my friends, to celebrate the Independence-day of friendship and to help the revenue, and not to write to you would be lese-majesty to love and law.

Is it not a distinct mark higher up on the scale of civilization, — this cheap postage? The easier transmission of produce is accounted such a mark, — much more the easier transmission of thought.

Transmission, indeed! When I had got so far, I was called away to direct Mr. P. about the sink. And do you know what directing a man is, in the country? Why, it is to do half the work yourself, and to take all the responsibility. And, in consequence of Mr. P., you won't get a bit better letter than you proposed to send.

Where 's your book? What are you doing? What do you think of your Miss Martineau now? Is n't the Seven Gables a subtile matter, both in thought and style?

Have n't I said the truth about the much preaching? Some of the clergy, I perceive, say with heat that preaching is not cold and dull. Better let the laity testify.

There is Mr. P. again.

Yours ever,

ORVILLE DEWEY.

To Rev. Henry W. Bellows.

WASHINGTON, *Dec.* 11, 1851.

. . . HAVE you seen the " great Hungarian "? Great indeed, and in a way we seem not to have thought of. Is n't there a story somewhere of a man uncaging, as he thought, a spaniel, and finding it to be a lion? We thought we had released and were bringing over a simple, harmless, inoffensive, heart-broken emigrant, who would be glad to *settle*, and find rest, and behold, we have upon our hands a world-disturbing propagandist, a loud pleader for justice and freedom, who does not want to settle, but to fight ; who will not rest upon his country's wrongs, nor let anybody else if he can help it ; who does not care for processions nor entertainments, but wants help. Kossuth has doubtless made a great mistake in taking his position here ; it is the mistake of a word-maker and of a relier on words, and he has not mended the matter by defining. But I declare he is infinitely more respectable in my eyes than if he had come in the character in which we expected him, — as the *protégé* and beneficiary of our people, who was to settle down among us and be comfortable.

To Rev. William Ware.

WASHINGTON, *Jan.* 3, 1852.

. . . I MUST fool a little, else I shan't know I am writing to *you*. And really I must break out somewhere, life is such a solemn abstraction in Washington to a clergyman. What has he to do, but what's solemn? The gayety passes him by; the politics pass him by. Nobody wants him; nobody holds him by the button but some desperate, dilapidated philanthropist. People say, while turning a corner, " How do you do, Doctor?" which is very much as if they said, "How do you do, Abstraction?" I live in a "lone conspicuity," preach in a vacuum, and call, with much ado, to find nobody. "What doest thou here, Elijah?" one might say to a prophet in this wilderness.

What a curious fellow you are! calm as a philosopher, usually, wise as a judge, possessed in full measure of the very Ware moderation and wisdom, and yet every now and then taking some tremendous lurch — against England or for Kossuth! I go far enough, — go a good way, please to observe, — but to go to war, that would I not, if I could help it. Fighting won't prepare men for voting. Peaceful progress, I believe, is the only thing that can carry on the world to a fitness for self-government. I have no idea that the Hungarians are fit for it. See what France has done with her free constitution! Oh! was there ever such a solemn farce, before Heaven, as that voting, — those congratulations to the Usurper-President, and his replies?

To Rev. Henry W. Bellows.

WASHINGTON, *March* 7, 1852.

. . . I HAVE seen a good deal of Ole Bull here within a week or two. I admire his grand and simple, reverent and affectionate Norwegian nature very much. He has come out here now with views connected with the wel-

fare of his countrymen ; I do not yet precisely understand them. Is it not remarkable that he and Jenny
Lind should have this noble nationality so beating at
their very hearts?

To the Same.

I DON'T see but you must insert these articles in the
" Inquirer " as " Communications." Some of them will
have things in them that cannot possibly be delivered as
*W*egotisms. Don't be stiff about the matter. I tell you
there is no other way ; and indeed I think it no harm,
but an advantage, to diversify the form, and leave out
the solemn and juridical *Wego* sometimes, for the more
sprightly and " sniptious " Ego.

To his Daughter Mary.

WASHINGTON, *May*, 1852.

DEAREST MOLLY, — To be sure, how could you? And,
indeed, what did you for? Oh ! for little K.'s sake.
Well, anything for little K.'s sake. Indeed, it's the duty
of parents to sacrifice themselves for their children. It's
the final cause of parents to mind the children. Poor
little puss ! We shall feel relieved when we hear she is
in New York, and safe under the sisterly wing. I am
afraid she is getting too big for nestling. How I want
to see the good little comfort ! *Is* she little? Tell us
how she looks and does.

Yesterday, beside preaching a sermon more than half
new, and attending a funeral (out of the society), I read
skimmingly more than half Nichol's " Architecture of the
Heavens." I laid aside the book overwhelmed. What
shall we do? What shall we think? Far from our

Milky Way, — there they lie, other universes, — nebulæ resolved by Rosse's telescope into stars, starry realms, numerous, seemingly innumerable, and as vast as our system ; and yet from some of them it takes the light thirty — sixty thousand years to come to us : nay, twenty millions, Nichol suggests, I know not on what grounds. And yet in the minutest details such perfection ! A million of perfectly formed creatures in a drop of water ! I do not doubt that it is this overwhelming immensity of things that leads some minds to find a sort of relief, as it were, in the idea of an Infinite Impersonal Force working in all things. But it is a child's thought. Nay, does not the very fact that my mind can take in so vast a range of things lead me better to conceive of what the Infinite Mind can do? An ant's mind, if it had one, might find it just as hard to conceive of me.

. . . .

With love to you two miserable creatures, away from your parents,

Thine ever,

ORVILLE DEWEY.

To the Same.

[Undated.]

What have I not written to you about, you cross thing? Oh ! Kossuth. Well, then, here is an immensely interesting person, whom we invited over here to settle, and who is much more likely to *un*settle *us*. How far would you *have* him unsettle us? To the extent of carrying us into a war with Russia, or of banding us, with all liberal governments, in a war with the despotic governments, so that Europe should be turned into a caldron of blood for years to come, millions of people sacrificed, unutterable miseries inflicted, the present frame of society torn in pieces ; and, when all is done, the human race no better off, — *worse* off? You say, no. Well, anything short of that I am willing Kossuth should accomplish. Any expression of *opinion* that he can get here, from the people or the government, asserting the rights of nations and the wrong of oppression, let him have, — let all the world have it. *Moral* influence, gradually changing the world, is what *I* want. But Kossuth and the Liberals of Europe want to bring on that great *war of opinion*, which, I fear, will come only too soon. I fear that Kossuth has fairly broached the question of intervention here, and that in two years it will enter the ballot box. I fear these tendencies to universal overthrow that are now revealing themselves all over the civilized world.

Kossuth is a man all enthusiasm and eloquence, but not a man, I judge, of deep practical sagacity. A sort of Hamlet, he seems to me, — graceful, delicate, thoughtful, meditative, moral, noble-minded ; and I should not wonder if he was now feeling something of Hamlet's burden : —

> " The time is out of joint : oh, cursed spite,
> That ever I was born to set it right ! "

A lady, who saw him two days ago, told me that so sad a face she never saw ; it haunted her.

It was on his return to his Berkshire home, after this winter in Washington, that the next merry little letter, describing his renewed acquaintance with his country neighbors, was sent to me. The custom of ringing the church bell at noon and at nine in the evening had not then been relinquished, although it has since died out.

To his Daughter Mary.

SHEFFIELD, *July* 23, 1852.

DEAR MOLLY, — Dr. K. and H. called upon us the very evening after we arrived ! Mrs. K. as usual. Mrs. B. is on a visit to her friends ; the children with their grandmother. . . . Mr. D. does n't raise any tobacco this summer. I saw Mr. P. lying flat on his back yesterday, — not floored, however, but high and dry on Mr. McIntyre's counter. Mr. M. has succeeded Doten, Root, and Mansfield. These three gentlemen have all flung themselves upon the paper-mill, hardly able to supply the Sheffield authors. Mr. Austin continues to announce the solemn procession of the hours. Mr. Swift is building an observatory to see 'em as they pass. There are thoughts of engaging me to note 'em down, as I have nothing else to do.

I am particularly at leisure, having demitted all care of the farm to Mr. Charles, and committed all the income thereof to him, down to the smallest hen's-egg.

Your mother is always doing something, and always growing handsomer and lovelier, so that I told her yesterday I should certainly call her a sa-int, if she was n't always a do-int !

I have nothing to tell of myself; no stitches or aches to commemorate, being quite free and whole in soul and body, and, freely and wholly

Your loving father,

ORVILLE DEWEY.

To Rev. Henry W. Bellows.

SHEFFIELD, *July* 24, 1852.

MY DEAR BELLOWS, — Amidst all this lovely quiet, and the beautiful outlooks on every side to the horizon, my thoughts seem ever to mingle with the universe; they bear me beyond the horizon of life, and your reflections, therefore, fall as a touching strain upon the tenor of mine. Experience, life, man, seem to me ever higher and more awful; and though there is constantly intervening the crushing thought of what a poor thing I am, and my life is, and I am sometimes disheartened and tempted to be reckless, and to say, "It's no matter what this ephemeral being, this passing dust and wind, shall come to," — yet ever, like the little eddying whirlwinds that I see in the street before me, this dusty breath of life struggles upward. I am very sad and glorious by turns; and sometimes, when mortality is heavy and hope is weak, I take refuge in simple resignation, and say: "Thou Infinite Goodness! I can desire nothing better than that thy will be done. But oh! give me to live forever! — eternal rises that prayer. Give me to look upon thy glory and thy glorious creatures forever!" What an awful anomaly in our being were it, if that prayer were to be denied! And what would the memory of friends be, so sweet and solemn now, — what would it be, but as the taper which the angel of death extinguishes in this earthly quagmire?

After you went away, I read more carefully the splendid article on the " Ethics of Christendom ; " [1] and I confess that my whole moral being shrinks from the position

---

[1] From the " Westminster Review," vol. lvii. p. 182, or, in the American edition, p. 98.

of the writer (which brings down the majesty of the Gospel almost to the level of Millerism), that Jesus supposed the end of the world to be at hand, and that he should come in the clouds of heaven, and be seated with his disciples on airy thrones, to judge the nations. No; the false *double ethics* of the pulpit, which I have labored, though less successfully, all my life to expose, has its origin, I believe, in later superstition, and not in the teachings of Christ. The passages referred to by the writer, I conceive to be more imaginative, and less formalistic and logical, than he supposes.

To the Same.

WASHINGTON, *Dec.* 28, 1852.

MY DEAR BELLOWS, — I will wish you all a happy New York, (ahem! you see how naturally and affectionately my pen turns out the old beloved name!) — a happy New Year. After all, it isn't so bad; a happy New Year and a happy New York must be very near neighbors with you. I sometimes wish they could have continued to be so with me, for those I have learnt to live with most easily and happily are generally in New York. Our beloved artists, the goodly Club, were a host to me by themselves. I wish I could be a host to them sometimes.

Well, heigho! (pretty ejaculation to come into a New Year's greeting — but they come everywhere!) Heigho! I say submissively — things meet and match us, perhaps, better than we mean. I am *not* a *clergy*man — perhaps was never meant for one. I question our position more and more. We are not fairly thrown into the field of life. We do not fairly take the free and unobstructed pressure of all surrounding society. We are hedged around with artificial barriers, built up by superstitious reverence and false respect. We are cased in peculiarity. We meet and mingle with trouble and sorrow, — enough of them, too much, — but our treatment of them gets hackneyed, worn, weary, and reluctant. We grapple with the world's strife and trial, but it is in armor. Our excision from the world's pleasure and free intercourse, I doubt, is not good for us. We are a sort of moral eunuchs.

To his Daughter Mary.

WASHINGTON, *June* 19, 1853.

THOUGH it is very hot,
Though bladed corn faint in the noontide ray,
And thermomèters stand at ninety-three,
And fingers feel like sticks of sealing-wax,
Yet I will write thee.

This evening I saw Professor Henry, who said he saw you at the Century Club last Wednesday evening; that he did not speak to you, but that you seemed to be enjoying yourself. I felt like shaking hands with him on the occasion, but restrained myself. But where *are* you, child, this blessed minute? . . . I would have you to know that it is a merit to write to somebody who is nowhere. Why in thunder don't you write to *me?* If I were nobody, I am somewhere. I hope you are enjoying yourself, but I can't think you can, *conscientiously*, without telling me of it.

.   .   .   .

My love to the Bryants. I hope it may greet the Grand Panjandrum himself. Tell Mrs. C. I should write to her, but I have too much regard for her to think of such a thing with the themometer at 93°, and that it is as much as I can do to keep cool at any time, when I think of her.

To Mrs. David Lane.

SHEFFIELD, *Sept.* 2, 1853.

MY DEAR FRIEND, — Do you remember when we were walking once in Weston, that we saw the carpenter putting sheets of tarred paper under the clapboarding of a house? I want you to ask your father if he thinks that a good plan; if he knows of any ill effect, as, for instance, there being a smell of tar about the house, or the tar's running down between the clapboards. If he thinks well of it (that is question first) ; question second is, What kind of paper is used? and question third, Is it simply boiled tar into which the paper is dipped? I state *précisement,* and number the queries, because *nobody ever yet answered all* the questions of a letter. I hope in your reply you will achieve a distinction that will send down your name to future times. . . .

To the Same.

Sept. 9, 1853.

YOU have achieved immortal honor ; the answers, Numbers 1, 2, and 3, are most satisfactory. I have thoughts of sending your letter to the Crystal Palace. I am much obliged to your father, and I will avail myself of his kindness, if I should find it necessary, next year, when I may be building an addition here.

I am sorry things don't go smoothly with ——— ; but I *guess* nothing ever *did* go on without some hitches, that is, on this earth. It is curious, by the bye, how we go on blindly, imagining that things go smoothly with many people around us, — with *some* at least, — with some Wellington, or Webster, or Astor, when the truth is, they *never* do with anybody. To take our inevitable part with imperfection, in ourselves, in others, in things, — to take our part, I say, in this discipline of imperfection, without surprise or impatience or discouragement, as a part of the fixed order of things, and no more to be wondered at or quarrelled with than drought or frost or flood, — this is a wisdom beyond the most of us, farther off from us, I believe, than any other. Ahem! when you told me of those rocks in the foundation of the house, you did not expect this "sermon in stones." . . .

To William Cullen Bryant.

SHEFFIELD, *May* 13, 1854.

DEAR EDITOR, — Are we to have fastened upon us this nuisance that is spreading itself among all the newspapers, — I mean the abominable *smell* caused by the sizing or something else in the manufacture? For a long time it was the "Christian Register" alone that had it, and I used to throw it out of the window to air. Now I perceive the same thing in other papers, and at length it has reached the "Post." Somebody is manufacturing a villanous article for the paper-makers! (I state the fact with an awful and portentous generality.) But do you not perceive what the nuisance is? It is a stink, sir. I am obliged to sit on the windward side of the paper while I read its interesting contents, and to wash my hands afterwards — immediately.

But, to change the subject, — yes, *toto cælo*, — for I turn to something as fragrant as a bed of roses, — will not you and Mrs. Bryant come to see us in June? *Do.* It is a long time since I have sat on a green bank with you, or anywhere else. I want some of your company, and talk, and wisdom. The first Lowell Lecture I wrote was after a talk with you here, three or four years ago. Come, I pray, and give me an impulse for another course. Bring Julia, too. I will give her my little green room.

I shall be down in New York on business a fortnight hence, and shall see you, and see if we can't fix upon a time.

With all our loves to you all,

Yours as ever,

ORVILLE DEWEY.

Mr. Dewey's father died at the very beginning of his son's career, in 1821, and early in 1855 he lost also his mother from her honored place at his fireside. He was, nevertheless, obliged to leave home in March, to fulfil an engagement made the previous autumn to lecture in Charleston, S. C.

To his Daughter Mary.

CHARLESTON, *March* 16, 1855.

I HAVE been trying four hours to sleep. No dervise ever turned round more times at a bout, than I have turned over in these four hours. I dined out to-day, at Judge King's, and afterwards we went to the celebrated Club; and, whether it is that I was seven consecutive hours in company, or that I drank a cup of coffee,—

> The reason why, I cannot tell,
> But this I know full well,

that here I am, at three o'clock in the morning, venting
my rage on you.

.   .   .   .

It would do your heart good to see the generous and
delighted interest which the G.'s and D.'s, and indeed
many more, take in the phenomenon of the lectures.
The truth is, that their attention to the matter, *and* the
intelligence of the people, *and* the merits of the lecturer,
must be combined to account for such an unprecedented
and beautiful audience, — larger, and much more select,
they say, than even Thackeray's. I 'll send you a newspaper slip or two, if I can lay my hand upon them,
upon the last lecture, which, assembled (the audience, I
mean), under a clouded sky, and in face of a threatening
thunder-gust, was a greater wonder, some one said, than
any I undertook to explain.

Bah! what stuff to write! But all this is such an
agreeable surprise to me, and will, I think, give me so
much better a reward for this weary journey and absence
than I expected, that you must sympathize what you
can with my dotage.

.   .   .   .

As to the "Corruptions of Christianity," dear, if you
don't find enough of them about you, — and you may
not, as you live with your mother mostly, — you will
find them in the library somewhere. There were, I
think, two editions, one in one volume, and another in
two. There are a hundred in the world.

The Club mentioned in this letter was that of
which my father wrote in his Reminiscences : —

" This Charleston Club, then, I think, forty years old,
was one of the most remarkable, and in some respects

the most improving, that I have ever known. An essay
was read at every meeting, and made the subject of discussion. One evening at Dr. Gilman's was read for
the essay a eulogy upon Napoleon III. It was written
con amore, and was really quite sentimental in its admiration, — going back to his very boyhood, his love of his
mother, and what not. I could not help touching the
elbow of the gentleman sitting next me and saying,
'Are n't we a pretty set of fellows to be listening to
such stuff as this?' He showed that he thought as I
did. When the reading was finished, Judge King, who
presided, turned to me and asked for my opinion of the
essay. I was 'considerably struck up,' to be the first
person asked, and confessed to some embarrassment.
I was a stranger among them, I said, and did not know
but my views might differ entirely from theirs. I was
not accustomed to think myself illiberal, or behind the
progress of opinion, and I knew that this man, Louis
Napoleon, had his admirers, and perhaps an increasing
number of them; but if I must speak, — and then I
blurted it out, — I must say that it was with inward
wrath and indignation that I had listened to the essay,
from beginning to end. There was a marked sensation
all round the circle; but I defended my opinion, and, to
my astonishment, all but two agreed with me."

The following winter he was invited to repeat
his lectures in Charleston, and passed some time
there, accompanied by his family. In March,
1856, he went with Mrs. Dewey to New Orleans,
and, returning to Charleston at the end of April,
went home in June.

To his Daughters.

ON BOARD THE " HENRY KING," ON THE
ALABAMA RIVER, *March* 18, 1856.

. . . SUCH charming things cars are ! No dirt, — no
sp—tt—g, oh ! no, — and such nice places for sleeping !
Not a long, monotonous, merely animal sleep, but intellectual, a kind of perpetual solving of geometric problems, as, for instance, — given, a human body ; how
many angles is it capable of forming in fifteen minutes?
or how many more than a crab in the same time? And
then, no crying children, — not a bit of *that*, — singing
cherubs, innocently piping, — cheering the dull hours
with dulcet sounds.

.   .   .   .

I write in the saloon, on this jarring boat, that shakes
my hand and wits alike. We are getting on very pros-
perously. Your mother bears the journey well. This
boat is very comfortable — *for a boat;* a good large
state-room, and positively the neatest public table I have
seen in all the South.

There ! that 'll do, — or must do. I thought wife
would do the writing, but I have "got my leg over the
harrow," and Mause would be as hard to stop.

To Mrs. David Lane.

NEW ORLEANS, *March* 29, 1856.

DEAR FRIEND, — Yesterday I was sixty-two years old.
After lecturing in the evening right earnestly on " The
Body and Soul," I came home very tired, and sat down
with a cigar, and passed an hour among the scenes of
the olden time. I thought of my father, when, a boy, I
used to walk with him to the fields. Something way-

ward he was, perhaps, in his moods, but prevailingly bright and cheerful, — fond of a joke, — strong in sense and purpose, and warm in affection, — steady to his plans, but somewhat impulsive and impatient in execution. Where is he *now?* How often do I ask! Shall I see him again? How shall I find him after thirty, forty years passed in the unseen realm? And of my mother you will not doubt I thought, and called up the scenes of her life : in the mid-way of it, when she was so patient, and often weary in the care of us all, and often feeble in health; and then in the later days, the declining years, so tranquil, so gentle, so loving, — a perfect sunshine of love and gentleness was her presence.

But come we to this St. Charles Hotel, where we have been now for a week, as removed as possible from the holy and quiet dreamland of past days. Incessant hubbub and hurly-burly are the only words that can describe it, — seven hundred guests, one thousand people under one roof. What a larder! what a cellar! what water-tanks, pah! filled from the Mississippi, clarified for the table with alum. People that we have known cast up at all corners, and many that we have not call upon us, — good, kind, sensible people. I don't see but New Orleans is to be let into my human world.

You see how I blot, — I 'm nervous, — I can't write at a marble table. Very well, however, and wife mainly so. Three weeks more here, and then back to Savannah, where I am to give four lectures. Then to Charleston, to stay till about the 25th May.

The lectures go here very fairly, — six hundred to hear. They call it a very large audience for lectures in New Orleans. . . . With our love to all your household,

Yours ever,

ORVILLE DEWEY.

The Same.

SHEFFIELD, *Aug.* 10, 1856.

DEAR FRIEND, — My time and thoughts have been a good deal occupied of late by the illness and death of Mr. Charles Sedgwick. The funeral was on last Tuesday, and Mr. Bellows was present, making the prayer, while I read passages, and said some words proper for the time. They were hearty words, you may be sure; for in some admirable respects Charles Sedgwick has scarcely left his equal in the world. His sunny nature shone into every crack and crevice around him, and the poor man and the stranger and whosoever was in trouble or need felt that he had in him an adviser and friend. The Irish were especially drawn to him, and they made request to bear his body to the grave, that is, to Stockbridge, six miles. And partly they did so. . . . It was a tremendous rain-storm, but the procession was very long.

But I must turn away from this sad affliction to us all, — it will be long before I shall turn my thought from it, — for the world is passing on; it will soon pass by my grave and the graves of us all. I do not wonder that this sweeping tide bears our thoughts much into the coming world, — mine, I sometimes think, too much.

But we have to fight our battle, perform our duties, while one and another drops around us; and one of the things that engages me just now, is to prepare a discourse to be delivered under our Elm Tree on the 21st.

The Elm Tree Association, before which the address just alluded to was made, was a Village Improvement Society, of which my father was one of the founders, and which took its name from an immense tree, one of the finest in Massachusetts, standing near the house of his maternal grandfather. To smooth and adorn the ground around the Great Elm, and make it the scene of a yearly summer festival for the whole town, was the first object of the Society, extending afterwards to planting trees, grading walks, etc., through the whole neighborhood; and it was one of the earlier impulses to that refinement of taste which has made of Sheffield one of the prettiest villages in the country. With its fine avenue of elms, planted nearly forty years ago, its gardens and well-shaven turf, it shows what care and a prevailing love of beauty and order will do for a place where there is very little wealth. It was about this time that my father planted in an angle of the main street the Seven Pines, which now make, as it were, an evergreen chapel to his memory, and with the proceeds of some lectures that he gave in the town, set out a number of deciduous trees around the Academy, many of which are still living, though the building they were intended to shade is gone.

The Elm Tree Association, however, from one cause and another, was short-lived; but

"It lived to light a steadier flame"

in the Laurel Hill Association, of Stockbridge, which, taking the idea from the Sheffield plan, continues to develop it in a very beautiful and admirable manner.

The address at the gathering in 1856 was chiefly occupied with a review of the history of the town, and with the thoughts appropriate to the place of meeting; and at the close the speaker took occasion to explain to his townspeople his ideas upon the national crisis of the day, and the changed aspect that had been given to the slavery question by the fresh determination of the South to maintain the excellence of the system and to force it upon the acceptance of the North in the new States then forming. Against this he made earnest and solemn protest, with a full expression of his opinion as to the innate wrong to the blacks, and the destructive effects on the whites, of slavery; but at the same time he spoke with large and kindly consideration for the Southerners. After doing justice to the care and kindness of many of them for their slaves, he said, in close: —

"I have listened also to what Southern apologists have said in another view, — that this burden of slavery was none of their choosing; that it was entailed upon them; that they cannot immediately emancipate their people; that they are not qualified to take care of themselves; that this state of things must be submitted to for a while, till remedial laws and other remedial means shall bring relief. And so long as they said *that*, I gave them my sympathy. But when they say, 'Spread this system, — spread it far and wide,' I cannot go another step with them. And it is not *I* that has changed, but *they*. When they say, 'Spread it, — spread it over

Kansas and Nebraska, spread it over the far West, annex Mexico, annex Cuba, annex Central America, make slavery a national institution, make the compact of the Constitution carry it into all Territories, cover it with the national ægis, set it up as part of our great republican profession, stamp on our flag and our shield and our scutcheon the emblem of human slavery,' I say, — no — never — God forbid ! "

It seems strange now that so temperate and candid a speech should have raised a storm of anger when read in Charleston. But the sore place was too tender for even the friendliest touch, and of all those who had greeted him there so cordially the winter before, but two or three maintained and strengthened their relations with him after this summer. It was one of many trials to which his breadth of view exposed him.

To Rev. Henry W. Bellows, D.D.

SHEFFIELD, Aug. 11, 1856.

MY DEAR BELLOWS, — I do not complain of your letter; but what if it should turn out that I cannot agree with you? What if my opinions, when *properly understood*, should displease many persons? Is it the first time that honest opinions have been proscribed, or the expression of them thought " unfortunate "?

I appreciate all the kindness of your letter, and your care for my reputation; but you are not to be told that there is something higher than reputation.

You write with the usual anti-slavery assurance that your opinion is the correct one. It is natural; it is the first-blush, the impromptu view of the matter. But whether there is not a juster view, coming out of that same deliberateness and impartiality that you accuse me of, — whether there is not, in fact, a broader humanity and a broader politics than yours or that of your party, is the question.

I don't like the tendencies of your mind (I don't say *heart*) on this question ; your willingness to bring the whole grand future of this country to the edge of the present crisis ; your idea of this crisis as a second Revolution, and of the cause of liberty as equally involved ; your thinking it so fatal to be classed with Tories, or with ——, ——, and ——, and your regret that I should have gone down South to lecture. It all looks to me narrow.

I may address the public on this subject. But if I do, I shan't do it mainly for my own sake ; at any rate, I shall write to you when I get leisure.

With love to E.,

Yours ever,

ORVILLE DEWEY.

To Rev. Ephraim Peabody, D.D.

SHEFFIELD, *Nov.* 10, 1856.

MY DEAR PEABODY, — I have written you several imaginary letters since I saw you, and now I 'm determined (before I go to Baltimore to lecture, which is next week) that I will write you a real one. I desired H. T. to inquire and let me know how you are, and she writes that you are very much the same as when I was in Boston, — riding out in the morning, and passing, I fear, the same sad and weary afternoons. I wish I were near you this winter, that is, if I could help you at all through those heavy hours.

I am writing a lecture on " Unconscious Education ; " for I want to add one to the Baltimore course. And is not a great deal of our education unconscious and mysterious? *You* do not know, perhaps, all that this long sickness and weariness and prostration are doing for you. I always think that the future scene will open to us the wonders of this as we never see them here.

Heine says that a man is n't worth anything till he has suffered ; or something like that. I am a great coward about it ; and I imagine sometimes that deeper trial might make something of me.

My dear friend, if I may call you so, I write to little purpose, perhaps, but out of great sympathy and affection for you. I do not know of a human being for whom I have a more perfect esteem than for you. And in that love I often commend you, with a passing prayer, or sigh sometimes, to the all-loving Father. We believe in Him. Let us "believe the love that God hath to us."

With all our affectionate regards to your wife and girls and to you,

Yours ever,

ORVILLE DEWEY.

Within a few weeks the pure and lofty spirit to whom these words were addressed was called hence, and the following letter was written : —

SHEFFIELD, *Dec.* 17, 1856.

MY DEAR MRS. PEABODY, — Do you not know why I dread to write to you, and yet why I cannot help it? Since last I spoke to you, such an event has passed, that I tremble to go over the abyss and speak to you again. But you and your children stand, bereft and stricken, on the shore, as it were, of a new and strange world, — for strange must be the world to you where that husband and father is not, — and I would fain express the sympathy which I feel for you, and my family with me. Yet not with many words, but more fitly in silence, should I do it. And this letter is but as if I came and sat by you, and only said, " God help you," or knelt with you and said, "God help us all ; " for we are all bereaved in your bereavement.

True, life passes on visibly with us as usual ; but every now and then the thought of you and *him* comes over me, and I exclaim and pray at once, in wonder and sorrow.

But the everlasting succession of things moves on, and we all take our place in it — now, to mourn the lost, and now, ourselves to be mourned — till all is finished. It is an Infinite Will that ordains it, and our part is to bow in humble awe and trust.

I had a letter once, from a most lovely woman, announcing to me the death of her husband, a worthless person ; and she spoke of it with no more interest than if a log had rolled from the river-bank and floated down the stream. What do you think of that, — with affections, venerations, loves, sympathies, swelling around you like a tide?

I know that among all these there is an unvisited loneliness which nothing can reach. May God's peace and presence be there !

· I could not write before, being from home. I do not *write* anything now, but to say to you and your dear children, " God comfort you ! "

From your friend,

ORVILLE DEWEY.

To his Daughter Mary.

BALTIMORE, *Nov.* 24, 1856.

DEAREST MOLLY, — I must send you a line, though somehow I can't make my table write yet. I have just been out to walk in the loveliest morning, and yet my nerves are ajar, and I can't guide my pen. I preached very hard last evening. I don't know but these people are all crazy, but they make me feel repaid. The church was full, as I never saw it before. The lecture Saturday evening was crowded. So I go.

I am reading Dr. Kane's book. Six pages could give all the actual knowledge it contains; but that fearful conflict of men with the most terrible powers of nature, and so bravely sustained, makes the story like tragedy; and I read on and on, the same thing over and over, and don't skip a page. But Mrs. —— has just been in, and sat down and opened her widowed heart to me, and I see that life itself is often a more solemn tragedy than voyaging in the Arctic Seas. Nay, I think the deacon himself, when he accepted that challenge (how oddly it sounds !), must have felt himself to be in a more tragic strait than " Smith's Strait," or any other that Kane was in.

Your letters came Saturday evening, and were, by that time, an indispensable comfort. . . .

This will be with you before the Thanksgiving dinner. Bless it, and you all, prayeth, giving thanks with and for you,

Your

ORVILLE DEWEY.

Mr. Dewey had been asked repeatedly, since his retirement from New York, to take charge of Church Green, in Boston, a pulpit left vacant by the death of Dr. Young; and he consented to go there in the beginning of 1858, with the understanding that he should preach but once on a Sunday. He had an idea of a second service, which should be more useful to the people and less exhausting to the minister than the ordinary afternoon service, which very few attended, and those only from a sense of duty. · He had written for this purpose a series of " Instructions," as he called them, on the 104th Psalm. Each was about an hour long, and they were, in short, simple lectures on religious subjects. To use his own words, " This was not preaching, and was attended with none of the exhaustion that follows the morning service. Many people have no idea, nor even suspicion, of the difference between praying and preaching for an hour, with the whole mind and heart poured into it, and any ordinary public speaking for an hour. They seem to think that in either case it is *vox et preterea nihil,* and the more voice the more exhaustion; but the truth is, the more the *feelings* are enlisted in any way, the more exhaustion, and the difference is the greatest possible."

To William Cullen Bryant, Esq.

BOSTON, *Sept.* 7, 1858.

DEAR BRYANT, — You have got home. If you pronounce the charm-word four times after the dramatic (I mean the *true* dramatic) fashion, all is told. It makes me think of what Mrs. Kemble told us the other day. In a play where she acted the mistress, and her lover was shot, — or was supposed to be, but was reprieved, and came rushing to her arms, — instead of repeating a long and pretty speech which was set down for her, the *dramatic passion* made her exclaim: "ALIVE! ALIVE! *alive!* alive!"

Well, you are such a nomadic cosmopolitan, that I won't answer for *you;* but I will be bound it is so with Mrs. Bryant, and I guess Julia too. How you all are, and how she is especially, is the question in all our hearts; and without waiting for forty things to be done, all working you like forty-power presses, pray write us three words and tell us.

. . . I hope that some time in the winter I shall get a sight of you. You and the Club would make my measure full. And yet Boston is great.

To Mrs. David Lane.

BOSTON, *Sept.* 20, 1858.

MY DEAR FRIEND, — Dr. Jackson is fast turning me into a vegetable, —*homo multi-cotyledonous* is the species. My head is a cabbage — brain, cauliflower; my eyes are two beans, with a short cucumber between them, for a nose; my heart is a squash (very soft); my lungs — cut a watermelon in two, lengthwise, and you have them;

my legs are cornstalks, and my feet, pota*toes*. I eat nothing but these things, and I am fast becoming nothing else. I am potatoes and corn and cucumber and cabbage, — like the chameleon, that takes the color of the thing it lives on. Dr. Jackson will have a great deal to answer for to the world. Had n't you better come into town and see about it? Perhaps you can arrest the process. . . .

I declare I think it is too bad to send such a poor dish to you as this, and especially in your loneliness; but it is all Dr. Jackson's fault.

Think of mosquito-bars in Boston! They must be very trying things — to the mosquitoes. You see they don't know what to make of it; and very likely their legs and wings get caught sometimes in the " decussated, reticulated interstices," as Dr. Johnson calls them. At any rate, from their noise, they evidently consider themselves as the most ill-treated and unfortunate outcasts upon earth. Paganini wrote the " Carnival of Venice." I wonder somebody does n't write the no-carnival of the mosquitoes.

To the Same.

Boston, *Dec.* 30, 1858.

Dear my Friend, — I cannot let the season of happy wishes pass by without sending mine to you and yours. But you must begin to gather up patience for your venerable friend, for the happy anniversaries somehow begin to gather shadows around them; they are both reminders and admonishers.

Nevertheless, it is noteworthy that the " Happy New Year!" is never sounded out in the minor key; always it has a ring of joyousness and hope in it. Read that little piece of Fanny Kemble's, on the 179th page, — the " Answer to a Question." I send you the volume [1] by this mail. Ah ! what a clear sense and touching sensibility and bracing moral tone there is, running through the whole volume ! But I was going to say that that little piece tells you what I would write better than I can write it. We all send " Merry Christmas " and " Happy New Year " to you all, in a heap ; that is, a heap of us to a heap of you, and a *heap* of good wishes.

.   .   .   .

My poor head is rather improving, but it is n't worth much yet, as you plainly see. Nevertheless, in the other and sound part of me I am,

As ever, your friend,

ORVILLE DEWEY.

To his Sister, Miss F. Dewey.

[Date missing. About 1859.]

So you remember the old New Bedford times pleasantly, — and I do. And I remember my whole lifetime in the same way. And even if it had been less pleasant, if there had been many more and greater calamities in it, still I hold on to that bottom-ground of all thanksgiving, even this, that God has placed in us an immortal spark, which through storm and cloud and darkness may grow brighter, and in the world beyond may shine as the stars forever. I heard Father Taylor last Sunday afternoon. Towards the close he spoke of his health as uncertain and liable to fail ; " But," said he, " I have felt a little more of immortality come down into me to-day, and as if I should live awhile longer here."

[1] Mrs. Kemble's Poems.

To Mrs. David Lane.

BOSTON, Saturday evening [probably *Oct.*, 1859].

DEAR MY FRIEND, — I imagine you are all so cast down, forlorn, and desolate at my leaving you, and especially

> " At the close of the day, when the hamlet is still,
>   And mortals the sweets of forgetfulness prove,
> When naught but the torrent is heard on the hill,
>   And naught but the nightingale's song in the grove,"

that I ought to write a word to fill the void. I *should* have said, on coming away, like that interesting child who had plagued everybody's life out of them, " I 'll come again ! ".

Bah ! you never asked me ; or only in such a sort that I was obliged to decline. *Am* I such a stupid visitor? Did I not play at bagatelle with L.? Did I not read eloquently out of Carlyle to you and C.? Did I not talk wisdom to you by the yard? Did I not let drop crumbs of philosophy by the wayside of our talk, continually? Above all, am I not the veriest *woman*, at heart, that you ever saw? Why, I had like to have choked upon " Sartor Resartus." I wonder if you saw it. But, ahem ! — a great swallow a man must have, to gulp down the " Everlasting Yea." And a great swallow implies a great stomach. And a great stomach implies a great brain, unless a man 's a fool. " If not, why not ? " as Captain Bunsby says ; " therefore."

Oh, what a mad argument to prove a man sane, — and good company besides ! Well, I *am* mad, and expect to be so, — at least I think I have a right to be so, in the proportion of one hour to twenty-four, being so rational the rest of the time. I think it 's but a reasonable allowance.

You will judge that this is my mad hour to-day, and it *is;* nevertheless, I am, soberly,

Your friend,

ORVILLE DEWEY.

In the winter of 1859 he writes to the same friend upon New York City politics with a passionate vivacity that old New Yorkers will sadly appreciate.

" I took up the paper this morning that announced Fernando Wood's election by two thousand plurality. If you had seen the way in which I brought down my hand upon the table, — minding neither muscle nor mahogany, — you would know how people at a distance, especially if they have ever lived in New York, feel about it.   I hope he will pay you well.   I wish he would take out some of your rich, stupid, arms-folding, purse-clutching millionnaires into Washington Square and flay them alive.   Something of the sort must be done, before our infatuated city upper classes will come to their senses."

To his Sister, Miss F. Dewey.

SHEFFIELD, *Oct.* 5, 1859.

I HAVE got past worrying about things, myself.   I see all these movements, this way and that way, as a part of that great oscillation in which the world has been swinging, to and fro, from the beginning, and *always advancing*.   These are the natural developments of the freed mind of the world; and whoever lives now, and yet more, whoever shall live through this century, must take this large and calm philosophy to his heart, or he will find himself cast upon the troubled waters without rudder or compass. Daniel Webster, one day at Marshfield, when his cattle came around him to take an ear of corn each from his hand, said to Peter Harvey, who was by, as he stood looking at them, " Peter, this is better company than Senators." So I am tempted to turn from all the religious wranglings and extravagances of the time, to nature and to the solid and unquestioned truths of religion. I sometimes doubt whether I will ever read another word of the ultraists and the one-sided men. They will do their work, and it will all come to good in the long run ; but it is not necessary that I should watch it or care for it. I did, indeed, print a political sermon four months ago, and I said a few words in the " Register " last week (which I will send you), but I am not the man to be heard in these days. *I can't take a side. . . .*

Yours as always,

Orville Dewey.

To William Cullen Bryant, Esq.

Sheffield, *May* 7, 1860.

Well, did I address you as a poet, Ap Magnus ; for none but a poet or a Welshman could write such a reply. Do you know I am Welsh? So was Elizabeth Tudor ; so is Fanny Kemble, and other good fellows.

Well, I take your poetry as if it were just as good as prose. But you don't consider, my dear fellow, that if we make our visit when I go down to preach for Bellows, that I can't preach for your Orthodox friend. . . .

Oh, ay, I quite agree with you about leaving the world-mêlée to others. For my part, I feel as if I were dead and buried long ago. You said, awhile ago, that you did n't so well like to work as you once did. Sensible, that. I feel the same, in my bones — or brains. There it is, you always *say*, what I *think;* except sometimes, when you scathe the opponents, — for I am tender-hearted. I don't like to have people made to feel so "bad." Seriously, I wonder that some of you editors are not beaten to death every month. Ours is a much-enduring society. I could enlarge, but I have n't time; for I must go and set out some trees — for posterity.

With our love to your wife and all,

Yours ever,

ORVILLE DEWEY.

To Mrs. David Lane.

BOSTON, *Dec.* 11, 1860.

DEAREST FRIEND (for I think friends draw closer to one another in troublous times), — Indeed I am sad and troubled, under the most favorable view that can be taken of our affairs; for though all this should blow over, as I prevailingly believe and hope it will, yet the crisis has brought out such a feeling at the South as we shall not easily forget or forgive. To be sure, as the irritation of an arraigned conscience, we may partly over-look it, as we do the irritation of a blamed child, — as an arraigned, and, I add, not quite easy conscience; for surely conscious virtue is calmer than the South is, to-day. I know that other things are mixed up with this feeling of the South; but if it felt that its moral position was high and honorable and unimpeachable before the world, it would not fly out into this outrageous passion. If the ground it stood upon in former days were held now, it might be calm, as it was then; but ever since the day when it changed its mind, — ever since it has as-sumed that the slave system is right and good and admirable, and ought to be perpetual, — it has been growing more and more passionate. Well, we must be patient with them. For my part, I am frightened at the condition to which their folly is bringing them. It is terrible to think that the distrust and fear of their slaves is spreading itself all over the South country. To be sure, they, in their unreasonableness, blame us for it. They might as well accuse England; they might as well accuse all the civilized world. For the conviction that slavery is wrong, that it ought not to be advocated, but to be condemned, and *ultimately* removed from the world, — this conviction is one of the inevitable developments of modern Christian thought and sentiment. It is not we that are responsible for the rise and spread of this sentiment: it is the civilized world; it is humanity itself.

And now what is it that the South asks of us as the condition of union with it? Why, that we shall say and *vote* that we so much approve of the slave-system, that we are willing, not merely that it should exist untouched by us, — that is not the question, — but that it should be taken to our bosom as a cherished national institution.

I hope we shall firmly but mildly refuse to say it. It is the only honorable or dignified or conscientious position for us of the North. But, do you see the result of these municipal elections in Massachusetts? That does not look like firmness. There may be flinching. But so it is, under the great Providence, that the world *wears* around questions which it cannot sharply meet.

These matters take precedence of all others now-a-days, or else my first word would have been to say how glad we were to hear that C. is well again. . . .

Yours as ever,

ORVILLE DEWEY.

To his Daughter Mary.

Boston, *Feb.* 10, 1861.

Happily for my peace of mind, I have been over to
the post-office this evening and got your letter. For my
one want has been to know how that tremendous Thursday afternoon and night took you; that is, whether it
took you off the ground, or the roof off the house.
Here, it did not unroof any houses, but it blew over a
carryall in Beacon Street; and when Dr. J. went out,
like a good Samaritan, to help the people, it did not
respect his virtue at all, but blew *him* over. Blew him
over the fence, it was said; at any rate, landed him on
his face, which was much bruised, and dislocated his
shoulder. So you see I could not tell what pranks the
same wind might play around the corners of certain
houses or barns afar off.

Was there ever anything like the swing of the weather?
Now it is warm here again, and ready to rain. Agassiz
told me that the change in Cambridge, on Thursday,
was 71° in ten hours. In Boston it was 60°, being 10°
or 11° colder in Cambridge.

I see Agassiz often of late at Peirce's Lowell Lectures
on "the Mathematics in the Cosmos." The object is
to show that the same ideas, principles, relations, which
the mathematician has wrought out from his own mind,
are found in the system of nature, indicating an iden-
tity of thought. You see of what immense interest the
discussion is. But Peirce's delivery of his thoughts is
very lame and imperfect (extemporaneous). Two lectures ago, as I sat by Agassiz, I said at the close, " Well,
I feel obliged to apologize to myself for being here."

A. Why?

D. Because I don't understand half of it.

A. No? I am surprised. I do.

D. Well, that is because you are learned. (Thinking with myself, however, why does he? For he knows no more of the mathematics than I do. But I went on.)

D. Well, my apology is this : Peirce is like nature, — vast, obscure, mysterious, — great bowlders of thought, of which I can hardly get hold ; dark abysses, into which I cannot see ; but, nevertheless, flashes of light here and there, and for these I come.

A. Why, yes, I understand him. Just now, when he drew that curious diagram to illustrate a certain principle, I saw it clearly, for I know the same thing in organic nature.

D. Aha ! the Mathematics in the Cosmos !

Was it not striking? Here are the Mathematics (Peirce), and Natural Science (Agassiz), and they easily understand each other, because the lecturer's principle is true.

The three or four years which Mr. Dewey spent in Boston with his family were full of enjoyment to him; but in December, 1861, he withdrew finally to Sheffield, which he never left again for more than a few weeks or months at a time.

To Rev. Henry W. Bellows, D.D.

SHEFFIELD, *July* 26, 1861.

MY DEAR BELLOWS, — God bless you for what you and your Sanitary Commission are doing for our people in the camps ! It goes to my heart to be sitting here in quiet and comfort, these lovely summer days, while they are braving and enduring so much. And so, though of silver and gold I have not much, I send my mite ($20), to help, the little that I can, the voluntary contribution for your purposes.

Last Monday night was the bitterest time we have had yet.[1] Some, even in this quiet village, did not sleep a wink. Confound sensation newspapers and newspaper correspondents! That fellow who writes to the —— is enough to drive one mad. The "Evening Post" is the wisest paper. But it is too bad that that rabble of civilians and teamsters should have brought this apparent disgrace upon us.

We have an immense amount of inexperience, and of rash, opinionated thinking to deal with; but we shall get over it all.

If you are staying in New York, I wish you could run up and take a little breathing-time with us. Come any time; we have always a bed for you.

We are all well, and all unite in love to you and E.

Yours ever,

ORVILLE DEWEY.

To Miss Catherine M. Sedgwick.

SHEFFIELD, *Feb.* 5, 1862.

MY FRIEND, — I must report myself to *you*. I must have you sympathize with my life, or — I will not say I shall drown myself in the Housatonic, but I shall feel as if the old river had dried up, and forsaken its bed.

I do not know how to set about telling you how happy I am in the old home. I feel as if I had arrived after a long voyage, or were reposing after a day's

---

[1] Alluding to the battle and rout of Bull Run, July 21, 1861.

work that had been forty years long. Indeed, it is forty-two years last autumn since I left Andover and began to preach. And I have never before had any cessation of work but what I regarded as temporary. Indeed, I have never before had the means to retire upon. And although it is but a modest competence, — $1,500 a year, — yet I am most devoutly thankful to Heaven that I have it, and that I am not turned out, like an old horse upon the common. To be sure, I should be glad to be able to live nearer to the centres of society ; but you can hardly imagine what comfort and satisfaction I feel in having enough to live upon, instead of the utter poverty which I might well have feared would be, and which so often is, the end of a clergyman's life.[1]

This house of ours is very pleasant, — you would think so if you were in it, — all doors open, as in summer, a summer temperature from the furnace, day and night, moderate wood-fires in the parlor and library, cheering to the eye, and making of the chimneys excellent ventilators, and the air pure ; and this summer house seated down amidst surrounding cold, and boundless fields of snow, — it seems a miracle of comfort.

And then, this surrounding splendor and beauty, — the valley, and the hills and mountains around, — the soft-falling snow, the starry crystals descending through the still air, — the lights and shadows of morning and evening, — this wondrous meteorology of winter — but you know all about it. Really, I think some days that winter is more beautiful than summer. Certainly I would not have it left out of my year. . . . "Aha ! all is rose-colored to *him !*" Well, nay, but it is literally

---

[1] He had just received a legacy of $5,000 from Miss Eliza Townsend, of Boston.

so. The white hill opposite, looking like a huge snow-
bank, only that it is checkered with strips and patches
of wood, dark as Indian-ink, *is* stained of that color
every clear afternoon, and rises up at sundown into a
bank of roseate or purple bloom all along above the
horizon.

6th. I did n't get through last evening. No wonder,
with so much heavy stuff to carry. Did I ever write
such a stupid letter before? Well, do not say anything
about it, but quickly cover it over with the mantle of
one of your charming epistles. It is not often that one
has a chance to show so much Christian generosity.
Besides, consider that I do not altogether despair of
myself. I am reviving; and you don't know what a
letter I may write you one of these days, if you toll me
along.

In the autumn his only son enlisted for nine
months in the 49th Massachusetts Regiment.

To his Daughters.

SHEFFIELD, *Oct.* 13, 1862.

MY DEAR GIRLS, — Charles has enlisted. It was at a
war-meeting at the town-hall last evening. You have
known his feelings, and perhaps will not be surprised.
I did not expect it, and must confess I was very much
shaken in spirit by it. But, arriving through some sleep-
less hours at a calmer mood, I do not know that it is
any greater sacrifice than we as a family ought to make.

Although it will throw a great deal of care upon me,
and there is all this extra work to do, yet, that excepted,
perhaps he could not go at any better time than now.

It is for the winter, and nine months is a fitter term for a family man, circumstanced as he is, than three years ; and this enlistment precludes all liability to future draft. This is in the key of prudence ; but I do think that men with young families dependent upon them should be the last to go. And yet I had rather have in C. the patriotic spirit that impels him, than all the prudence in the world.

To the Same.

Oct. 16, 1862.

C. is steadily and calmly putting all things into order that he can. . . . He came in the morning after he had enlisted, and said to me with a bright, vigorous, and satisfied expression of countenance, "Well, you see what I have done." I believe some people have been very much stirred and moved by his decision. It is said to have given an impulse to the recruiting, and the quota, I am told, is now about full, and there will be no drafting here.

.   .   .   .

Thinking of these things, — thinking of all possible good or ill to come, your mother and I go about, from hour to hour, sometimes very much weighed down, and sometimes more hopeful and cheerful ; and poor J., with the tears ready to come at every turn, is yet going on very bravely and well. . . . Cassidy is to look after barn-yard, etc., for the winter.

But all this is nothing. Good heaven ! do people know, does the world know, what we are doing, when we freely send our sons from peaceful and happy homes to meet what camp-life, and reconnoissances, and battles may bring to them and us ? God help and pity us !

To Mrs. David Lane.

SHEFFIELD, *Dec.* 19, 1862.

DEAR FRIEND, — I wrote to Mrs. Curtis [1] last Saturday, before I knew what had befallen her, and in that letter sent a message to you, to know of your whereabouts, provided you were still in town. I don't expect an answer from her now, of course, though I have written her since; but thinking that you are probably in New York, I write.

I had hoped to hear from you before now. Through this heavy winter cloud I think friendly rays should shine, if possible, to warm and cheer it. It is, indeed, an awful winter. I will not say dismal; my heart is too high for that. But public affairs, and my private share in them, together, make a dread picture in my mind, as if I were gazing upon the passing of mighty floods, that may sweep away thousands of dwellings, and mine with them. And though I lift my thoughts to Heaven, there are times when I dare not trust myself to pray aloud; the burden is too great for words. It is singular, but you will understand it, — I think there was never a time when there was less visible devotion in my life than now, when my whole being is resolved into meditations, and strugglings of faith, and communings with the supreme and holy will of God.

I am writing, my friend, very solemnly for a letter; but never mind that, for we are obliged to take into our terrible questioning now what is always most trying in the problem of life, — the results of human imperfec-

---

[1] Mrs. George Curtis, of New York, whose son, Joseph Bridgham Curtis, lieutenant-colonel, commanding a Rhode Island regiment, had just fallen at Fredericksburg, Va.

tion, human incompetence, brought into the most immediate connection with our own interests and affections.
See what it is for our friend Mrs. Curtis to reflect that
her son was slain in that seemingly reckless assault upon
the intrenchments at Fredericksburg, or for me that
my son may be sent off in rotten transports that may
founder amidst the Southern seas.

But do I therefore spend my time in complainings
and reproaches, and almost the arraigning of Providence? No. I know that the governing powers are
trying to do the best they can. The fact is, a charge is
devolved upon them almost beyond human ability to
sustain. Neither Russia nor Austria nor France, I believe, ever had a million of soldiers in the field, to clothe,
to equip, to feed, to pay, and to direct. We have them,
— we, a peaceful people, suddenly, with no military experience, and there *must* be mistakes, delays, failures.
What then? Shall we give up the cause of justice, of
lawful government, of civilization, and of the unborn
ages, and do nothing? If we will not, — if we will not
yield up lawful sovereignty to mad revolt, then must we
put what power, faculty, skill, we have, to the work, and
amidst all our sacrifices and sorrows bow to the awful
will of God.

Have you seen Mrs. Curtis? In her son there was a
singular union of loveliness and manliness, of gentleness
and courage, and, high over all, perfect self-abnegation.
A mother could not well lose in a son more than she
has lost. I hope she does not dwell on the seeming
untowardness of the event, or that she can take it into a
larger philosophy than that of the New York press. . . .

To the Same.

SHEFFIELD, *July* 26, 1863.

YOUR sympathy, my friend, for us and Charles, is very comforting to me. Yes, we have heard from him since the surrender of Port Hudson. He wrote to us on the 9th, full of joy, and glorying over the event; but, poor fellow, he had only time to wash in the conquered Mississippi, before his regiment was ordered down to Fort Donaldsonville, and took part in a fight there on the 13th; and we have private advices from Baton Rouge that the brigade (Augur's) is sent down towards Brashear City. . . . Now, when we shall hear of C. I do not venture to anticipate, but whenever we do get any news, that is, any good news, you shall have it.

If these horrid New York riots had not lifted up a black and frightful cloud between us and the glorious events in Pennsylvania and the Southwest, we should have burst out into illuminations and cannon-firings all over the North. But the good time is coming! We shall be ready when Sumter is taken. I hardly know of anything that would stir the Northern heart like that.

I have not seen Mrs. Kemble's book yet. Have you read Calvert's "Gentleman"? It is charming. And "The Tropics," too. And here is Draper's book upon the "Intellectual Development of Europe" on my table. I augur much from the first dozen pages.

With kind remembrances to Mr. Lane, and love to the girls,

Yours as ever,

ORVILLE DEWEY.

To Rev. Henry W. Bellows, D.D.

SHEFFIELD, *Aug.* 15, 1863.

MY DEAR BELLOWS, — Such a frolic breeze has not fallen upon these inland waters this good while. Complain of heat ! Why, it is as good as champagne to you. Well, I shan't hesitate to write to you, for fear of adding to your overwhelming burdens. A pretty picture your letter is, of a man overwhelmed by burdens ! And weigh a hundred and eighty ! I can't believe it. Why, I never have weighed more than a hundred and seventy-six. Maybe you are an inch or two taller ; and brains, I have often observed, weigh heavy ; but yours at the top must be like a glass of soda-water ! Nature did a great thing for you, when it placed that buoyant fountain within you. I have often thought so.

But let me tell you, my dear fellow, that with all the stupendous share you have had in the burdens of this awful time, you have not known, and without knowing can never conceive, of what has weighed upon me for the last nine months. . . . I thank you most heartily for your sympathy with C. After all, my satisfaction in what he has done is not so great as in what his letters, all along, show him to be. . . .

Always and affectionately your friend,

ORVILLE DEWEY.

To Mr. and Mrs. Lindsey.

SHEFFIELD, *Nov.* 28, 1863.

MY DEAR FRIENDS, — I received your letter, dated 20 September, two days ago. I am very sorry to see that you are laboring under the mistaken impression that I have lost my son in the war. Something you misapprehended in ——'s letter. You seem to suppose that it was Charles who used that striking language, " Is old Massachusetts dead? It is sweet to die for our country !" No; it was Lieutenant-Colonel O'Brien, who fell immediately afterwards. Charles was one of the storming party under O'Brien. He stepped forward at that call, for they had all hesitated a moment, as the call was unexpected; it came upon them suddenly. He behaved as well as if he had fallen; but, thank God, he is preserved to us, and is among us in health, in these Thanksgiving days. All were around my table day before yesterday, — three children, with their mother, and three grandchildren.

To Mrs. David Lane.

SHEFFIELD, *Dec.* 29, 1863.

DEAR FRIEND, — Our life goes on as usual, though those drop from it that made a part of it. We strangely accustom ourselves to everything, — to war and bloodshed, to sickness and pain, to the death of friends ; and that which was a bitter sorrow at first, sinks into a quiet sadness. And *this* not constant, but arising as occasions or trains of thought call it forth. Life is like a procession, in which heavy footsteps and gay equipages, and heat and dust, and struggle and laughter, and music and discord, mingle together. We move on with it all, and our moods partake of it all, and only the breaking asunder of the *natural* bonds and habitudes of living together (except it be of some especial heart-tie) makes affliction very deep and abiding, or sends us away from the great throng to sit and weep alone. Of friends, I think I have suffered more from the loss of the living than of the dead.

I do not know but you will think that all this is very little like me. It certainly less belongs to the sad occasion that has suggested it than to any similar one that has ever occurred to me. I shall miss E. S. from my path more than any friend that has ever gone away from it into the unknown realm.

Oh! the unknown realm! Will the time ever come, when men will look into it, or have it, at least, as plainly spread before them as to the telescopic view is the landscape of the moon? I believe that I have as much faith in the future life as others, — perhaps more than most men, — but I am one of those who long for actual vision, who would

> "*See* the Canaan that they love,
> With unbeclouded eyes."

But now what I have been saying reasserts its claim. The great procession moves on, — past the solemn bier, past holy graves. You are in it, and in these days your life is crowded with cares and engagements. . . . I wish I could do something for the Great Fair;[1] but I am exhausted of all my means.

. . . With my love to all around you, I am, as ever,

Yours affectionately,

ORVILLE DEWEY.

---

[1] The Great Fair, held in New York for the benefit of the Sanitary Commission, and of which Mrs. Lane was the chief manager and inspiring power.

To Rev. Henry W. Bellows, D.D.

SHEFFIELD, *Dec.* 31, 1863.

. . . AH! heaven, — what *is* rash or wise, short-sighted or far-seeing, too fast or too slow, upon the profound and terrible question, "What is to be done with slavery?" You have been saying something about it, and I rather think, if I could see it, that I should very much agree with you. Bryant and I had some correspondence about it a year ago, and I said to him: "If you expect this matter to be all settled up in any brief way, if you think that the social *status* of four millions of people is to be successfully placed on entirely new ground in five years, all historical experience is against you."

However, the real and practical question now is, How ought the Government to proceed? Upon what terms should it consent to receive back and recognize the Rebel States? I confess that I am sometimes tempted to go with a rush on this subject, — since so fair an opportunity is given to destroy the monster, — and to make it the very business and object of the war to sweep it out of existence. But that *will* be the end; and for the way, things will work out their own issues. And in the mean time I do not see that anything could be better than the cautious and tentative manner in which the President is proceeding.

One thing certainly has shaken my old convictions about the feasibility of immediate emancipation, and that is the experiment of emancipated labor on the Mississippi and about Port Royal. But the severest trial of emancipation, as of democracy, — that is, of freeing black men as of freeing white men, — may not be found at the start, but long after.

To the Same.

SHEFFIELD, *Feb.* 12, 1864.

REVEREND AND DEARLY BELOVED, THOU AND THY PEO-
PLE, — We are so much indebted to you all for our four
pleasant days in the great city, that I think we ought to
write a letter to you. We feel as if we had come out of
the great waters; the currents of city life run so strong,
that it seems to us as if we had been at sea; so many
tall galleys are there, and such mighty freights are upon
the waves, and the captains and the very sailors are so
thoroughly alive, that — that — how shall I end the
sentence? Why, thus, if you please, — that it seems to
me as if I ought to be there six months of the year, and
that somebody ought to want me to do something that
would bring me there. But somebody, — who is that?
Why, nobody. You can't see him; you can't find him;
Micawber never caught him, though he was hunting for
him all his life, — always hoped the creature would turn
up, though he never did.

Well, I 'm content. I am more, I am thankful. I
have had, all my life, the greatest blessing of life, — *leave
to work* on the highest themes and tasks, and I am not
turned out, at the end, on to the bare common of the
world, to starve. I have a family, priceless to me. I
have many dear and good friends, and above all I have
learned to draw nigh to a Friendship which embraces
the universe in its love and care, if one may speak so
of That which is almost too awful for mortal word. . . .

But leaving myself, and turning to you, — what a
monstrous person you are! a prodigy of labor, and a
prodigy in some other ways that I could point out. I
always thought that the elastic spring in your nature was

one of the finest I ever knew, but I did not know that it was quite so strong. You, too, know of a faith that can remove mountains.

The Great Fair is one mountain. I hope you will get the " raffles " question amicably settled. There is the same tempest in the Sheffield teapot; for we have a fair on the 22d, and they have determined here that they won't have raffles.

. . . .

What made you think that I " dread public prayers "? Did I say anything to you about it? If I did, I should not have used exactly the word "dread." The truth is, that state of the mind which is commonly called prayer becomes more and more easy, or at least inevitable to me ; but the action has become so stupendous and awful to me, that I more and more desire the privacy in it of my own thoughts. . " Prayers," — " saying one's prayers," grows distasteful to me, and a Liturgy is less and less satisfying. Communion is the word I like better.

But I have touched too large a theme. With our love to E. and your lovely children, let me be,

Always your friend,

ORVILLE DEWEY.

To Miss Catherine M. Sedgwick.

SHEFFIELD, *Feb.* 22, 1864.

DEAR FRIEND, — You are not well; I know you are not, or you would have written to me; and indeed they told me so when I was in New York the other day. I wrote you a good (?) long letter about New Year's, which " the human race running upon our errands" (as Carlyle says) has delivered to you, unless in the confusion of these war times it has let said letter drop out of its pocket. That many-membered body, according to this account of it, has a good deal to do with us; and, do you know, I find great help by merging myself in the human race. It has taken a vast deal of worry to wash and brush it into neatness, and to train it to order, virtue, and sanctity; why should I not have my share in the worry and weariness and trouble? Many have been sick and suffering, — all mankind more or less; why should not I be? All the human generations have passed away from the world: Walter Scott died; Prescott died; Charles Dewey, of Indiana, died; E. S. has died; who am I, that I should ask to remain?

E.'s passing away was very grand and noble, — so cheerful, so natural, — so full of intelligence and fuller of trust, — this earthly land to her but a part of the Great Country that lies beyond. She left such an im-pression upon her family and friends, that they hardly yet mourn her loss as they will; they feel as if she were still of them and with them. . . .

All my people love you, as does

Your friend,

ORVILLE DEWEY.

To William Cullen Bryant, Esq.

SHEFFIELD, *May* 1, 1864.

THANK your magnificence! Perhaps I ought to say your misericordia, for Charles says you wrote to him that you knew I should n't have those grapes unless you sent them to me. And I am afraid it 's true; for I have had such poor success in my poor grape-culture, that I had about given up in despair.

Nathless, I have had these set out, according to the best of my judgment, in the best place I could find in the open garden, and I will have a trellis or something for them to run upon ; and then they may do as they have a mind to.

I have delayed to acknowledge the receipt of the grape-roots, — Charles is n't to blame, I told him I would write, — because I waited för the cider to come, that wife and I might overwhelm you with a joint letter of thanks, laudation, and praise. But I can wait no longer. That is, the cider does n't come, and I begin to think it is a myth. Poets, you know, deal in such. They imagine, they idealize, nay, it is said they *create;* and if *we* were poets, I suppose we should before now have as good as *drank* some of that Long Island champagne.

Speaking of poets reminds me that I did n't tell you how charmed I was with those translations from the Odyssey ; the blank verse is so simple, clear, and ex-quisite, — so I think.

To Miss Catherine M. Sedgwick.

SHEFFIELD, *May* 5, 1864.

MY DEAR FRIEND, — Dear B. did you no wrong, and me much right, in giving me to read a letter of yours to her, written more than a month ago, which impressed me more and did me more good than any letter I have read this long time. It was that in which you spoke of Mr. Choate. It was evidently written with effort and with interruptions, — it was not like your finished, though unstudied letters, of which I have in my garner a goodly sheaf ; but oh ! my friend, take me into your realm, your frame of mind, your company, wherever it shall be. The silent tide is bearing us on. May it never part, but temporarily, my humble craft from your lovely sail, which seems to gather all things sweet and balmy — affections, friendships, kindnesses, touches and traits of humanity, hues and fragrances of nature, blessings of providence and beatitudes of life — into its perfumed bosom.

You will think I have taken something from Choate. What a strange, Oriental, enchanted style he has! What gleams of far-off ideas, flashes from the sky, essences from Arabia, seem unconsciously to drop into it! I have been reading him, in consequence of what you wrote. It is strange that with all his seeking for perfection in this kind he did not succeed better. But it would seem that his affluent and mysterious genius could not be brought to walk in the regular paces. He was certainly a very extraordinary person. I understand better his generosity, candor, amiableness, playfulness. I understand what you mean by the resemblance between him and your brother Charles. With constant love of us all, Yours ever,

ORVILLE DEWEY.

To Mrs. David Lane.

SHEFFIELD, *Sept.* 3, 1864.

DEAR FRIEND, — . . . Mrs. —— reported you very much occupied with documents, papers, letters, and what not, on matters connected with the Sanitary. I should like to have you recognize that there are other people who need to be healed and helped besides soldiers ; and that there are other interests beside public ones to be looked after. Are not all interests *individual* interests in

the " last analysis," as the philosophers say? But I am
afraid you don't believe in analysis at all. Generality,
combination, is everything with you. One part of the
human race is rolled up into a great bundle of sickness,
wounds, and misery; and the other is nothing but a
benevolent blanket to be wrapped round it. And if any
one thread — *videlicet* I — should claim to have any
separate existence or any little tender feeling by itself,
immediately the manager of the Great Sanitary Fair
says, " Hush! lie down! *you* are nothing but a part of
the blanket."

But a truce to nonsense. Since writing the foregoing,
the news has come from Atlanta. Oh! if Grant could
do the same thing to Lee's army, not only would the
Rebellion be broken, but the Copperhead party would
be scattered to the winds!

.   .   .   .

Do you read anything this summer but reports from
Borrioboola Gha? The best book I have read —
Ticknor's "Prescott," Alger's "Future Life," Furness's
"Veil Partly Lifted," etc., notwithstanding — is De
Tocqueville's "Ancient Régime and the Revolution." . . .
Your old friend,

ORVILLE DEWEY.

To the Same.

Nov. 9, 1864.

CHARMING! I will be as bad as I can. Talk about
being "useful to the world"! If the people that do the
most good, or get it to be done, — same thing, — are to
be sought for, are n't they the wicked ones? Where had
been the philanthropists, heroes, martyrs, but for them?

Where had been Clarkson and Wilberforce, but for the slave-catchers? Where Howard, but for cruel sailors? Where Brace, but for naughty boys? Where our noble President of the Sanitary, but for the wicked Rebels? And how should I ever have known that Mrs. Lane was capable of such a fine and eloquent indignation, if, instead of being a bad boy, "neglecting the opportunities" thrown in my way, I had been just a good sort of middle-aged man, "in the prime of life," doing as I ought? Really, there ought to be a society got up to make bad people, — they are so useful!

I heard a man say of Bellows, the other day in the cars, "He is a noble man!" And it was an Orthodox, formerly a member and elder of Dr. Spring's church. And what do you think he said to *me?* "Don't you remember me?" — "No." — "Don't you remember when you were a young man, in Dodge & Sayre's book-store, that Jasper Corning and I set up a Sunday-school for colored people in Henry Street, and that you taught in it for several months? And a good teacher you were, too." Not a bit of it. Oh, dear me! I hope there are some other good things which I have done in the world that I don't remember.

"A grand sermon," you heard last Sunday, hey? And then went to the "Century" Rooms, to see the decorations of the Bryant Festival! It seems to me that was rather a queer thing to do, after sermon! You will have to write a letter to me immediately, to relieve my anxieties about your religious education. Was the text, " And they rose up early on the morrow and offered burnt sacrifices and brought peace offerings ; and the people sat down to eat and to drink, and rose up to play "? See the same, Exodus xxxii. 6.

There! I am not in deep waters, you see, but skimming on the surface, except when I subscribe myself your abused, scolded, but

Faithful friend,

ORVILLE DEWEY.

My wife and people send their love and dire indignation to you.

To Miss Catherine M. Sedgwick.

SHEFFIELD, *Dec.* 12, 1864.

. . . IT is not pleasant to think upon death. It would not be pleasant to any company of friends to think that the hour for parting was near. Death is a solemn and painful dispensation. I will have no hallucination about it. I "*wait* the great teacher, Death." I do not welcome it. It is a solemn change. It is a dread change to natures like ours. I do not believe that the Great Disposer meant that we should approach it with a smile, with an air of triumph, — with any other than feelings of lowly submission and trust. I do not want to die. I never knew anybody that did, except when bitter pain or great and irremediable unhappiness made the release welcome.

And yet, I would not remain forever in this world. And thus, like the Apostle, "I am in a strait betwixt two." And I believe that it is better to depart; but it is a kind of reluctant conclusion. It may be even cheerful; but it does not make it easy for me to tear myself from all the blessed ties of life. I submit to God's awful will; but it is with a struggle of emotions, that is itself painful and trying, — that tasks all the fortitude and faith of which I am capable.

Will you tell me that our Christian masters and martyrs spoke of a "victory" over death? Yes, but is victory all joy? Ah, what a painful thing is every victory of our arms in these bloody battles, though we desire it !

Do you feel that I am not writing to you in the high Christian strain? Perhaps not. But I confess I am accustomed to bring all that is taught me — all that is said in exceptional circumstances like those of the apostles — into some adjustment with a natural, necessary, and universal experience. Besides, Jesus himself did not approach death with a song of triumph upon his lips. What a union, in him, of sorrow and trust ! No defying of pain, no boasting of calmness or strength, no braving of martyrdom, — not half so fine and grand, to a worldly and superficial view, as many a martyr's death ! But oh, what a blending in him of everything that makes perfection, — of pain and patience, of trial and trust !

But I am writing too long a letter for you to read.

.   .   .   .

K. just came into my study, and says, " Do give my love." I answer, " I give all our love always." So I do now ; and with the kindest regards to all around you, I am, as ever,

Most affectionately your friend,

ORVILLE DEWEY.

To William Cullen Bryant, Esq.

SHEFFIELD, *Jan.* 7, 1865.

THANKS for a beautiful record of a beautiful festival [1] to a beautiful — but enough of this. You must have

[1] At the "Century," New York, Nov. 5, 1864, in honor of Mr. Bryant's seventieth birthday.

had a surfeit. 'T was all right and due, but it must have been a hard thing to bear, — to be so praised to your very face. . . . Your reply was admirable, — simple, modest, quiet, graceful, — in short, I don't see how it could be better. For the rest, I think our cousin Waldo chiselled out the nicest bit of praise that was done on the occasion.

To Rev. Henry W. Bellows, D.D.

SHEFFIELD, *Feb.* 24, 1865.

MY DEAR FRIEND, — I was intending to write to you ten days ago, and should have done so before now, but my mind has been engrossed with a great anxiety and sorrow ; my grandson and namesake was taken with a fever, which went to the brain, and he died last Monday evening. I cannot tell you — you could hardly believe what an affliction it has been to me. He was five years old, a lovely boy, and, I think, of singular promise, — of a fine organization, more than beautiful, and with a mind inquiring into the causes and reasons of things, such as I have rarely seen. . . . We meant to educate this boy ; I hoped that he would bear up my name. God's will be done !

It was of the coming Convention that I was going to write to you ; but now, just now, I have no heart for it. But I feel great interest in the movement. Would that it were possible to organize the Unitarian Church of America, — to take this great cause out of the hands of speculative dispute, and to put it on the basis of a working institution. To find a ground of union out of which may spring boundless freedom of thought, — is it impossible? I should like to see a church which could embrace and embody all sects.

To his Daughter Mary.

SHEFFIELD, *April* 11, 1865.

. . . BUT I feel as if it were profane to speak of common things in these blessed days. Did you observe what the papers say about the manner in which they received the Great News yesterday in New York,[1] — not with any loud ebullition of joy, but rather with a kind of religious silence and a gratitude too deep for utterance? And I see that they propose to celebrate, not with fireworks and firing of cannon, but with an illumination, — the silent shining out of joy from every house. Last evening the locomotive of the freight train expressed itself in a singular way. Not shutting its whistle when it left the station, it went singing all down through the valley. For my part, I feel a solemn joy, as if I had escaped some great peril, only that it is multiplied by being that of millions.

To Rev. Henry W. Bellows, D.D.

SHEFFIELD, *April* 15, 1865.

MY DEAR FRIEND, — We used to think that life in our country, under our simple republican régime and peaceful order, was tame and uneventful; given over to quiet comfort and prosaic prosperity; never startled by anything more notable than a railroad disaster or a steamer burnt at sea. Events that were typified by the sun turning to darkness and the moon to blood, and stars falling from heaven, — distress of nations with perplexity of men's hearts, failing them for fear, — all this seemed to belong to some far-off country and time.

---

[1] The surrender of the Rebel army.

But it has come to us. God wills that we should know all that any nation has known, of whatever disciplines men to awe and virtue. The bloody mark upon the lintel, for ten thousands of first-born slain, — the anxiety and agony of the struggle for national existence, — the tax-gatherer taking one fourth part of our livelihood, and a deranged currency nearly one half of the remainder, — four years of the most frightful war known in history, — and then, at the very moment when our hearts were tremulous with the joy of victory, and every beating pulse was growing stiller and calmer in the blessed hope of peace, *then* the shock of the intelligence that Lincoln and Seward, our great names borne up on the swelling tide of the nation's gratulation and hope, have fallen, in the same hour, under the stroke of the assassin, — these are the awful visitations of God!

. . . As I slowly awake to the dreadful truth, the question that presses upon me — that presses upon the national heart — is, what is to become of us? If the reins of power were to fall into competent hands, we could take courage. But when, in any view, we were about to be cast upon a troubled sea, requiring the most skilful and trusted pilots, what are we to do without them?

Monday morning, 17*th.* Why should I send you this, — partly founded on mistake, for later telegrams lead us to hope that Mr. Seward will survive, — and reading, too, more like a sermon than a letter? But my thoughts could run upon nothing else but these terrible things; and, sitting at my desk, I let my pen run, not merely dash down things on the paper, as would have been more natural.

But for these all-absorbing horrors, I should have

written you somewhat about the Convention. It was certainly a grand success. I regretted only one thing, and that was that the young men went away grieved and sad.

. . . I think, too, that what they asked was reasonable. That is, if both wings were to fly together, and bear on the body, no language should have been retained in the Preamble which both parties could not agree to.

But no more now. Love to your wife and A.

Yours ever,

ORVILLE DEWEY.

To Mrs. David Lane.

SHEFFIELD, *May* 19, 1865.

BE it known to you, my objurgatory friend, that I have finished a sermon this very evening, — a sermon of reasonings, in part, upon this very matter on which you speak; that is, the difference of opinion in the Convention.

" Prove all things; hold fast that which is good." Radicalism and Conservatism. The Convention took the ground that both, as they exist in our body, could work together; it accepted large contributions in money from both sides, and it is not necessary to decide which side is right, in order to see that a statement of faith should have been adopted in which both could agree. I was glad, for my part, to find that the conservative party was so strong. I distrust the radical more than I do the conservative tendencies in our church; still I hope we are too just, not to say liberal, to hold that mere strength can warrant us in doing any wrong to the weaker party.

To be sure, if I thought, as I suppose —— and ——
and —— do, that the radical ground was fatal to Christianity, I should oppose it in the strongest way. But the
Convention did not assume that position. On the contrary, it said, " Let us co-operate ; let us put our money
together, and work together as brethren." Then we
should not have forced a measure through to the sore
hurt and pain of either party.

As to the main question between them, — how Jesus is
to be regarded, whether simply as the loftiest imper-
sonation of wisdom and goodness, or as having a commission and power to save beyond that and different
from it, — one may not be sure. But of this I am sure,
that he who takes upon his heart the living impression
of that divinest life and love *is* saved in the noblest
sense. And I do not see but there is as much of this
salvation in those young men as in those who repel and
rebuke them.

There ! let that sheet go by itself. Alas ! the question
with me is not which of them is right, but whether *I*
am right, — and that in something far more vital than
opinion. It does seem as if one who has lived as long
as I have, *ought* to have overcome all his spiritual foes ;
but I do not find it so. I feel sometimes as if I were
only struggling harder and harder with all the trying
questions, both speculative and spiritual, that press upon
our mortal frame and fate.

To Miss Catherine M. Sedgwick.

SHEFFIELD, *Dec.* 31, 1865.

. . . . I AM talking of myself, when I am thinking more
of you, and how it is with you in these winter days, the

last of the year. I hope that they do not find you oppressed with weakness or suffering; and if they do not, I am sure that your spirit is alert and happy, and that the bright snow-fields and the lovely meteor of beauty that hangs in the air in such a morning as this was, are as charming to you as they ever were. It is a delight to your friends to know that all things lovely are, if possible, more lovely to you than ever. Are there not bright rays shining through our souls, — streaming from the Infinite Light, — that make us feel that they are made to grow brighter and brighter forever? Ah! our confidence in immortality must be *this feeling*, and never a thing to be reasoned out by any logical processes.

Jan. 1, 1866. I have stepped, you see, from the old year to the new. I wish all the good wishes to you, and take them from you in return as surely as if you uttered them.

This year is to be momentous to us, if for no other reason, that K. is to be married. And we are to be no more together much, perhaps, in this world. It is an inconceivable wrench in my existence. This marrying is the cruellest thing; and it is a perfect wonder and mystery of Providence that parents give in to it as they do.

To Rev. Henry W. Bellows, D.D.

SHEFFIELD, *Feb.* 20, 1866.

MY DEAR FRIEND, — I wonder if you can understand how happy I am in my nook, — you who have so much of another sort of happiness, but not this, (no *nook* for *you !*) with my winter's task done, " with none to hurt nor destroy," that is, my time, " in all the holy

mountain," that is, the Taghkonic. Dear old Taghkonic,
— quiet, happy valley, — blessed, undisturbed fireside, —
what contrast could be greater than New York to all
this !

"Ahem ! not so fast, my friend," say you ; " other
places are blessed and happy besides valleys and mountains." Yes, I know. And I confess my late experience inclines me to think that, for the mind's health and
sharpening, cities are desirable places to be in, for a part
of the year, notwithstanding all the notwithstandings.
Of course, strong and collected thought works free and
clear everywhere, or tends that way ; but it did seem to
me that the whirl of the great maelstrom left but few
people in a condition to think, or to form well-considered
opinions, or to meditate much upon anything. Yes, I
know it, —

"The mind is its own place,"

(nothing was ever better said), and it may be fretted and
frittered away to nothing in country quiet, and it may
be strong and calm and full in the city throng.

.   .   .   .

And more and more do I feel that this nature of mine
is the deep ground-warrant for faith in God and immortality. Everywhere in the creation there is a proportion
between means and ends, — between all natures and
their destinies. And can it be that my soul, which, in
its few days' unfolding, is already stretching out its hands
to God and to eternity, and which has all its being and
welfare wrapped up in those sublime verities, is made
to strive and sigh for them in vain, to stretch out its
hands to — nothing ?

This day rises upon us fair and beautiful, — the precursor, I believe, of endless days. If not, I would say with Job, "Let it be darkness; let not God regard it from above, neither let the light shine upon it; for darkness and the shadow of death stain it." But what a different staining was upon it this morning! As I looked out upon the mountain just before sunrise, it showed like a mountain-rose blossoming up out of the earth, — covered all over with the deepest rose-color. . . .

Ever your friend,

ORVILLE DEWEY.

To the Same.

SHEFFIELD, *March* 12, 1866.

MY DEAR FRIEND, — I should like to know whether you propose, from your own pen, to provide me with all my reading. Look which way I will, — towards the "Inquirer," the "Monthly," or the "Examiner," — and H. W. B. is coming at me with an article, and sometimes with both hands full. You must write like a horse in full gallop. And yet you don't seem to. Those articles in the "Examiner," and the letter in the "Inquirer," seem to be thoroughly well considered; the breadth of view in them, the penetration, the candor and fairness, the sound judgment, please me exceedingly. Only one thing I questioned; and that is, putting the plea for universal suffrage on the ground that it is education for the people. One might ask if it were well to put a ship in the hands of the crew because it would be a good school for them. And looking at our popular elections, one may doubt whether they *are* a good school. I should be inclined to say that if the people could consent that only property holders who could read

and write should vote, it would be better.   But they will
not consent; we are on the popular tide, and suffrage
must be universal, and the freedmen eventually must
and will have the franchise.

But with the general strain of your writing I agree
entirely.   What you say of the exceptional character of
the Southern treason is true, and it has not been so distinctly nor so well said before.   I had thought the same
myself, and, of course, you must be right !   Yet we must
take care lest the concession go too far.   Treason must
forever be branded as the greatest of crimes.   It aims
not to murder a man, but a people.   And as to opinion
and conscience, I suppose all traitors have an opinion
and a conscience.

I have read this time the whole of the " Examiner,"
which I seldom do.   It is all very good and satisfactory.
Osgood's article on Robertson is excellent; it appre-
ciates him and his time.   One laments that his mind had
so hard a lot; but every real man must, in one way or
another, fight a great battle. . . . Especially I feel indebted to Abbot's article.   Truly he says, that the great
question of the coming days is, — theism, or atheism?
Not whether Jesus is our Master, the chief among men,
but whether the God in whom Jesus believed really
exists; and, by consequence, whether the immortality
which lay open to his vision is but a dream of weary
and burdened humanity?   Herbert Spencer believes in
no such God and Father, and his religion, which he
vaunts so much, is but a hard and cold abstraction.   On
other subjects he is a great writer; and in his volume of
essays there is not one which is not marked with strong
and original thought.   It is a prodigious intellect, certainly, and struggling hard with the greatest questions.

May it find its way out to light ! Thus far its light is, to my thinking, the profoundest darkness.

With our house's love to your house,

Yours ever,

ORVILLE DEWEY.

To Miss Catherine M. Sedgwick.

SHEFFIELD, *March* 28, 1866.

MY DEAR FRIEND, — To-day I am seventy-two years old. If I write to any one to-day, it must be to some one whose friendship is nearly as old as myself. Looking about me, I find no such one but you. Fifty years I have known you. Fifty years ago, and more, I saw you in your father's house; and charming as you were to my sight then, you have never — youth's loveliness set at defiance — been less so since. Forty years I think I have. known you well. Thirty years we have been *friends;* and that word needs no epithet nor superlative to make it precious.

This morning I called my wife to come and sit down by me, saying, " I will read you an old man's Idyl." And I read that in the March number of the " Atlantic." I believe Holmes wrote it; but whoever did, it is beautiful, and more than that it was to us — for it was true.

The greatest disappointment that I meet in old age is that I am not so good as I expected to be, nor so wise. I am ashamed to say that I was never so dissatisfied with myself as I am now. It seems as if it could not be a right state of things. My ideal of old age has been something very different. And yet seventy years is still within the infancy of the immortal life and progress. Why should it not say with the Apostle, " Not as though

I had attained, neither were already perfect." I *can*
say with him, *in some respects*, "I have fought a good
fight." I have fought through early false impressions of
religion. I have fought through many life problems. I
have fought, in these later years, through Mansel and
Herbert Spencer, as hard a battle as I have ever had.
But I have come, through all, to the most rooted conviction of the Infinite Rectitude and Goodness. Nothing,
I think, can ever shake me from this, — that *all is well*,
and *shall be forever*, whatever becomes of me. . . .

Ever your friend,

ORVILLE DEWEY.

To Mrs. David Lane.

SHEFFIELD, *July* 9, 1866.

DEAR FRIEND, — I am *étonné*, as the French have it ;
at least Molière and Corneille — whom I have been reading by and large of late, having read all the *new* things
I could get hold of — are continually having their personages *étonnéd*. Or, I feel like Dominie Sampson, and
say, "Pro-di-gi-ous !" Not as he said it to Meg Merri-
lies, but rather to Miss Julia Mannering, when he was
confounded with her vivacity. What ! two letters to my
one ! I do believe you are going to be literary.

And then, — was ever seen such an ambitious woman ! Reading Mill, and going to read Herbert Spencer !
And I suppose Kant will come next. But bravo ! I say.
I am very much pleased with you. And don't say, "I
wish, — but what 's the use !" You are through with
the great absorbing mother's cares, and can undertake
studies, and I believe there is no study so worthy of our
attention as our literature. I confess that I have come

to a somewhat new thought of this matter of late. What
is there on the earth upon which we stand, — what is
there that offers to help us, to lift and build us up, that
can compare with the productions of the greatest minds
which are gathered up in our literature? Whether we
would study human nature or the Nature Divine, —
whether we would study religion, science, nature in the
world around us, in the life within us, — these are the
lights that shine upon our path. For those who have
time to read, it seems a deplorable mistake not to turn
their thoughts distinctly to what the greatest minds have
said; that is, upon as many subjects as they can compass.

If I were to undertake anything in the way of education, I would set up in New York an Institute of
English Literature. I do not know but —— might do
something of the kind, — have a house and receive
classes that should come once or twice in a week and
read in the mean time under her direction, and teach
them by reading to them, by commenting, talking, point-
ing out and opening up to them the best things in the
best authors, the poets, the essayists, the historians, the
fiction-writers, and thus making them acquainted with
the finest productions of the English mind; and, what is
better, inspiring them with an enthusiasm and taste for
pursuing, for reading such things, instead of sensation
novels and such stuff.

Molière and Corneille have struck me much on *this*
reading, — the first with the tenuity of his thought, the
slender thread on which he weaves his entertaining and
life-like drama, making it to live through the ages simply by sticking to nature, making his personages speak
so naturally; and the second, with the real dramatic

grandeur of his genius. I feel that I have never done justice to Corneille before, I have been so dissatisfied with the formal rhyme, the want of the natural dramatic play of language in his work, the stilted rhetoric. And when I heard Rachel in the Cid, I thought, by the rapid, undramatic way in which she hurried through his declamations, while, in a few exclamatory bursts, she swept everything before her, that she justified my criticism. But this was the misfortune of Corneille; he walked in shackles imposed by the taste of his time. Yet it was a lofty stride. I am particularly struck with his grand moral ideals. I wish I had a good life of him. He must have been a good man. Like Beethoven and Michael Angelo, he does not seem to have liked flattery, court, or ceremony. But I guess that is the case with most men of the higher genius. . . .

As ever,
ORVILLE DEWEY.

To Miss Catherine M. Sedgwick.

SHEFFIELD, *Aug.* 27, 1866.

MY DEAR FRIEND, — It is some time since I have written to you, and I am almost afraid you are glad of it, not having to answer. You must acknowledge, however, that I have always offered you the easiest terms of exchange; two for one, three, four, anything you liked. . . . I have been lately with Mr. Bryant, in his great affliction, staying with my sisters, who occupy one of his cottages, but spending all the time I could with him. It was very sad, — talking upon many things as we did, and much upon those things that were pressing upon his mind, for he felt that he was losing his chief earthly treasure. His wife was that to him, by her simplicity, her simple truthfulness, her perfect sincerity and heart-earnestness, latterly of a very religious character, and by her good judgment also ; he told me that he always consulted her upon everything he published, and found that her opinion was always confirmed by that of the public, that is, as to the relative merit of his writings. He was bound to her the more, because his ties of close affection with others are so very few. Sometimes he could not repress his tears in our talking ; and they told me that in the morning, when he went to her bedside, he often sat weeping, saying, "You have been suffering all night, and I have been sleeping." In the last days she longed to depart, and often said to him, "You must let me go ; I want to go." And so she went, peacefully to her rest.

We have had a very pleasant visit from Mr. R. . . . His visits are always a great pleasure to us, both for the talk we have, and the music. It is really a great thing to know anything as he knows music. As I listened to him last evening, I could not help feeling that I knew nothing as he knows that, and thinking that if there are infant schools in the next world, I should certainly be put into one of them.

.   .   .   .

I hope the weather will allow you to sit often on the piazza in the coming month. It is what we have not been able to do in the present month at all, — by a fire, rather, in the parlor, half the time.

. . . With our affectionate remembrances to those around you, hold me to be, as ever,

Yours,

ORVILLE DEWEY.

To his Daughter Mary.

St. David's, *Oct.* 28, 1866.

Dearest Molly, — I have the pleasure to be seated
at my desk to write to you, in my new gown and slip-
pers, and with my new sermon, finished, before me. A
"combination and a form," indeed, but I say no more.
"But how *is* the sermon?" you'll say. Why, as inimita-
ble as the writer. But really, I think it is worth something. I did think, indeed, when I took my pen, that
I could write a stronger argument for immortality than I
ever saw, that is, in any one sermon or thesis. And
if I have failed entirely, and shall come to think so, as is
very likely, it will be no worse, doubtless, than my pre-
sumption deserved. You and K., who are satisfied with
your spiritual instincts, would think it no better, probably, than a belt of sand to bolster up a mountain.
Well, every one must help himself as he can. This
meditation certainly has strengthened my own faith in
the immortal life.

I should like to go to church with you this morning,
where you are probably going; but the places are very
few where I should want to go. More and more do all
public services dissatisfy me, — all devout *utterances*, my
own included. Communion with the Highest, with the
Unseen and Unspeakable, seems to me to consist of
breathings, not words, and requires a freedom of all
thoughts and feelings, — of awe and wonder, of adoration and thanksgiving, of meditations and of stirrings of
the deeps within us, such as can with difficulty be brought
into a regular prayer.

To the Same.

Nov. 21, 1866.

THE last "Register" has a sermon in it of Abbot's upon the Syracuse Conference, which I thought so excellent, that I told the editor it was itself worth a quarter's payment. Your mother admires it, too. Though she has no sympathy, as you well know, with Abbot's Left-Wing views, her righteous nature warmly takes part with his argument. The fact is, the Conference is wrong. If it expects the young men to act with it, it should adopt a platform on which they can conscientiously and comfortably stand. The conduct of the majority, in my opinion, is inconsistent and ungenerous. Either take ground upon which all can stand, — and I think there is such ground, — or else say to the ultra-liberals, "We cannot consent that any part of our common means shall be used for the spread of your views, influence, and preaching, and we must part."

To Rev. Henry W. Bellows, D.D.

ST. DAVID'S, *March* 20, 1867.

COME up here, my anxious friend, and I'll read my Concio to you; for it is written, as I preferred to do, before the warm and cold, wet and dry *meslin* of April weather comes, which always breaks me up in my studies. I will read it to you, and I rather think you will like it. . . . But do not make yourself uneasy. There will be nothing in the address of what you call "a defection to the radical side," simply because, in opinion, I cannot take that ground. I do not and cannot give up the miraculous element in Christianity. But I embrace our whole denomination in my·sympathies. and do not think our differences so important as you do. That religion has its roots in our nature, if that is radicalism, I strongly hold and always have. And in its development and culture I have never given that exclusive place to Christianity that many do. I confess that I always disliked and resisted the utterances of the extreme conservatives on this point, more than those of their opponents. So you see that M. was mainly right. And certainly I think the minority in the Conference has had hard measure from the majority; and I liked Abbot's sermon as much as you heard I did.

Yours ever,

ORVILLE DEWEY.

To Mrs. David Lane.

ST. DAVID'S, *April* 14, 1867.

DEAR FRIEND, — Why should I write to you about the things you speak of in your letter which crossed mine? How vain to attempt to discuss such matters on note-paper!

But, without discussing, I will tell you, in few words, what I think.

The vitality of the Christian religion lies deeper than the miraculous element in it. The miraculous is but an attestation to that. *That* is authority to me. The authority of God is more clearly and unquestionably revealed to me, than in anything else, in the inborn spiritual convictions of my nature, without which, indeed, I could not understand Christianity, nor anything else religious. These convictions accord with the deepest truths of Christianity, else I could not receive it. Jesus has strengthened, elevated, and purified these natural convictions in such a way, — by such teachings, by such a life, by such an unparalleled beauty of character, — that I believe God has breathed a grace into his soul that he never has [given] in the same measure and perfection to any other. Effects must have causes, and such an effect seems to me fairly to indicate such a cause.

But there are those who cannot take this view; who look upon the gospel as simply the best exposition of natural religion ever given, without any other breath of inspiration upon the record than such as was breathed upon the pages of Plato or Epictetus. Now, if they went further, and disowned the very spirit of Jesus, rejected the very essence of the gospel, certainly they would not be Christians. But this they do *not;* on the contrary, they reverently and heartily accept it, and seek to frame their lives upon this model. Am I to hold such persons as outcasts from the Christian fold, to refuse them my sympathy, to accord them only my " pity "? Certainly, I can take no such ground.

The peculiarities of certain individuals — the " cold abstractions " of one, and the rash utterances of another — have nothing essentially to do with the case ; nor has the hurt they may be thought to do to our Unitarian cause anything to do with the essential truth of things. Nor do I know that extreme Radicalism does us any more harm than extreme Conservatism. I belong to neither extreme ; and my business is, without regard to public cause or private reputation, to keep, as far as I can, my own mind right.

The fact is, you are so conservative on every subject, — society, politics, medicine, religion, — that it is very difficult for you to do justice to the radical side. • But consider that such men as Martineau, Bartol, Stebbins,

Ames, and Abbot are mainly on that side, and that it will not do to cast about scornful or pitying words concerning such. As to ———, I give him up to you, for I don't like his writing any better than you do.

I think the great Exposition which you are soon to see may give you a liberalizing hint. There, the industry of all nations will be exhibited. All are bent, honestly and earnestly, upon one point, — the development of the human energies in that direction. And it will infer nothing against their good character, or their titles to sympathy and respect, that they differ more or less with regard to the modes and means of arriving at the end.

Well, you will go before I come to New York. God bless and keep you, and bring you safely back !

Ever your friend,

ORVILLE DEWEY.

There are some passages in an unpublished sermon, preached by my father at Church Green, in 1858, which I will quote presently, as illustrative of the same tone of thought shown in these letters. His clinging to the miraculous element in the life of Jesus, while refusing to base any positive authority upon it, is equally characteristic of him, arising from the caution, at once reverent and intellectual, which made him extremely slow to remove any belief, consecrated by time and affection, till it was proved false and dangerous, and from his thorough conviction that every man stands or falls by so much of the Infinite Light and Love as he is able to receive directly into his being. He was conservative by feeling, and radical by thought, and the two wrought in him a grand charity of judgment, far above what is ordinarily called toleration.

These are the extracts referred to : —

" Society as truly as nature, nay, as truly as the holy church, is a grand organism for human culture. I say emphatically, — as truly as the holy church ; for we are prone to take a narrow view of man's spiritual growth, and to imagine that there is nothing to help it, out of the pale of Christianity. We make a sectarism of our Christian system, even as the Jews did of the Hebrew, though ours was designed to break down all such narrow bounds ; so that I should not wonder if some one said to me, — ' Are you preaching the Christian religion when you thus speak of nature and society ? ' And I answer, ' No ; I am speaking of a religion elder than the Christian.' . . .

" 'There was a righteousness, then, before and beside the Christian. Am I to be told that Socrates and Plato, ánd Marcus Antoninus and Boethius, had no right culture, no religion, no rectitude ? and they were cast upon the bosom of nature and of society for their instruction, and of that ' light which lighteth every man that cometh into the world.' "

To his Daughter Mary.

ST. DAVID'S, *Sept.* 10, 1867.

. . . THINK of my having read the whole of Voltaire's " Henriade " last week ! But think especially of eminent French critics, and Marmontel among them (in the preface), praising it to the stars, saying that some of the passages are superior to Homer and Virgil ! However, it is really better than I expected, and I read on, partly from curiosity and partly for the history. The French would have been very glad to find it an epic worthy of the name, for they have n't one. Voltaire frankly confesses that the French have not a genius for great poetry, — too much in love, he says, with exactness and elegance.

I have — read — through — " Very Hard Cash ; " and very hard it is to read. Reade has some pretty remarkable powers, — powers of description and of characterization ; but the moment he touches the social relations, and should be dramatic, he is struck with total incapacity. Indeed, what one novelist has been perfect in dialogue, making each person say just what he should and nothing else, but glorious Sir Walter?

To the Same.

SHEFFIELD, *Sept.* 20, 1867.

DEAR MARY, — "Live and learn." Next time, if it ever come, I shall put up peaches in a little box by themselves. But the fact is, peaches can't travel, unless they are plucked so early as nearly to spoil them of all their " *deliciarum*," — which we are enjoying in those we eat here. And Bryant with us, — fruity fellow that he is ! — I am glad we have some good fruit to give him. Yesterday we had a very good cantelope, and pears are on hand all the while. I am sorry that I could not get the pears to you just in eating condition, and the Hurlbut apples too ; but they 'll all come right.

Yes, fruity, — that 's what Bryant is ; but rather of the quality of dried fruits, — not juicy, still less gushing, but with a good deal of concentrated essence in him (rather "frosty, but kindly"), exuding often in little bits of poetical quotations, fitly brought in from everywhere, and of which there seems to be no end in his memory.

. . . .

The woods are beginning to show lovely bits of color, but the great burden of leaves remains untouched. Bryant and I walked out to the Pine Grove, and on to Sugar-Maple Hill. Your mother admires him for his much walking; but *I* insist that he is possessed and driven about by a demon. . . . By the bye, just keep that "article" for me; I have no other copy. Bryant commended it, and said he thought the argument against the . Incomprehensible's being totally unintelligible, was new.

To his Daughter, Mrs. C.

St. David's, *July* 22, 1868.

Dear Kate, — I am going to have no more to do with the weather. You need n't expostulate with me. It's no use talking. My mind is made up. You may tell M. so. It will be hardest for her to believe it. She has partaken with me in that infirmity of noble minds, — a desire to look through the haze of this mundane atmospheric environment, and predict the future. But, alas! there is an infirmity of vision; we see through a glass darkly. We can't see through a millstone. The firmament has been very like that, for some days, — all compact with clouds. We thought something was grinding for us. "Now it is coming!" we said last evening. But no. It was no go, — or no come, rather. And this morning, at the breakfast table, sitting up

there, clothed, and in my right mind, I said to my
sister, "I am not a-going to predict about the weather
any more!"

Ask my dear M., pray her, to try to come up to the
height of that great resolution. I know the difficulty, —
the strain to which it will put all her faculties; but ask
her, implore her, to *try*.

To his Daughters, then living in London Terrace, New York.

1868.

St. David's sends a challenge to all the Terrace birds.

Show us a bird that sings in the night. *We* have a
nightingale, — a bird that has sung, for two evenings past,
between ten and twelve, as gayly as the nightingales of
Champel. It is the cat-bird, the same that comes flying
and pecking at our windows. What has come over the
little creature? I suppose the season of nest-building
and incubation is one of great excitement, — the bird's
honeymoon. And then, the full moon shining down,
and the nights warm as summer, and thoughts of the
nice new house and the pretty eggs, and the chicks that
are coming, — it could not contain itself.

Well, as I sit in my porch and look at the birds, they
seem to me a revelation, as beautiful, if not so profound,
as the Apocalypse. What but Goodness could have
made a creature at once so beautiful and so happy?
Mansel and Spencer may talk about the incomprehensi-
bility of the First Cause; I say, here is *manifestation*.
The little *Turdus felivox*, — oho! ye ignorant children,
that is he of the cat, — it sits on the bough, ten feet
from me, and sings and trills and whistles, and sends

out little jets of music, little voluntaries, as if it were freely and irrepressibly singing a lovely hymn.

.   .   .   .

This morning there is the slightest little drizzle, a mere tentative experimenting towards rain, no more, — I keep to facts. Well, all the township is saying, no doubt, "Now it is coming!" Catch me a-doing so! I *was* left to say, in an unguarded moment, "If C. had mowed his meadow two or three days ago, he would have got it all in dry." I feel a little guilty. I am afraid that incautious observation was the *nuance* of the shadow of an intimation of an opinion, bearing the faintest adumbration of a prediction. I am sorry for it. I am very sorry. I ought to have kept my lips shut. I ought to have put sealing-wax upon them the moment I got up. I won't, — I won't speak one word again.

Yours, wet or dry,

O. D

To William Cullen Bryant, Esq.

ST. DAVID'S, *July* 27, 1868.

FRIEND BRYANT, — I am a Quaker. I have just joined the sect. Thee won't believe it, because thee will think I lack the calmness and staidness that fit me for it. But I am a Quaker of the Isaac T. Hopper sort; though, alas! here the resemblance fails also, for I do no good. Dear me! I wish sometimes that I could have been one of the one-sided men; it is so easy to run in one groove! and it 's all the fashion in these days. But, avaunt expediency! Let me stick to my principles, and be a rounded mediocrity, pelted on every hand, and pleasing nobody.　By the bye, Mrs. Gibbons [1] has just señt me a fine medallion of her father, beautifully mounted.　It is a remarkable face, for its massive strength and the fun that is lurking in it.　Hopper might have been a great man in any other walk, — the statesman's, the lawyer's ; he *was*, in his own.

. . . I want to say something, through the " Post," of the abominable nuisance of the railroad whistle.　I wrote once while you were gone, and Nordhoff (how do you spell him ?) did n't publish my letter, but only introduced some of it in a paragraph of his own.　If I write again, I shall want your *imprimatur*.　This horrible shriek, which tears all our nerves to pieces, and the nerves of all the land, except Cummington and such lovely retirements, is altogether unnecessary ; a lower tone would answer just as well.　It *does* on the Hudson River Road.

To his Daughters.

ST. DAVID'S, *Oct.* 15, 1868.

. . . YOUR letter came yesterday, and was very satisfactory in the upshot ; that is, you got there.　But, pest on railroad cars l they are mere torture-chambers, with the additional chance, as Johnson said of the ship, of being land-wrecked.　Some people like 'em, though. And there are dangers everywhere.　The other day — a high windy day — a party went to the mountain, and had like to have been blown off from the top.　But they said it was beautiful.　I don't doubt, if the whole bunch had been tumbled over and rolled down to the bottom, they would all have jumped up, exclaiming, " Beautiful !

---

[1] Mrs. James Gibbons of New York, daughter of Isaac T. Hopper.

beautiful!" People so like to have it thought they have had a good time. One day they went up and all got as wet as mountain — no, as marsh — rats; and that was the most "lovely time" they have had this summer.

. . . .

Girls, I have a toothache to-day! It's easier now, or I should not be writing. But pain, what a thing it is! The king of all misery, I think, is pain. It is a part of you, and does n't lie outside; a thing to be met and mastered with healthy faculties. You can't fight with it, as you can with poverty, bankruptcy, mosquitoes, a smoky chimney, and the like. I can't be thankful enough that I have had, through my life, so little pain. What I shall do with it, if it comes, I don't know. Perhaps I need it for what Heine speaks of; that is, to make me "a man." I am afraid I am a chicken-hearted fellow. But I cannot help thinking that different constitutions take that visitation very differently.

To Rev. Henry W. Bellows, D.D.

St. David's, *Jan.* 18, 1869.

My Dear Friend, —. . . It is the audible, the uttered prayer, to which I feel myself unequal. The awfulness of prayer to me inclines me more and more to make it silent, speechless. It is so overwhelming, that I am losing all fluency, all free utterance. What it is fit for a creature to say to the Infinite One — to that uncomprehended Infinitude of Being — makes me hesitate. My mind addressing a fellow mind is easy; and yet addressing the highest mind in the world would cause me anxiety. I should feel that my thoughts were too poor to express to him. But my mind addressing itself, its thought and feeling, to the Infinite, *Infinite* Mind, — I faint beneath it. It is higher than heaven; what can I do? I am often moved to say with Abraham, "Lo! now I, who am but dust, have taken upon me to speak unto God. Oh! let not the Lord be angry, and I will speak." And indeed, so much *praying*, — this *imploring* the love and care of the Infinite Providence and Love, of which the universe is the boundless and perpetual evolution, — can that be right and fit? I often recall what Mrs. Dwight, of Stockbridge, said of the public devotions of old Dr. West, — one of the most saintly beings I ever knew, — that she had observed that they consisted less and less of prayers, and more and more of thanksgivings.

Last evening my wife read to us your article on the Mission of America. It is a grand, full stream of thought, and original, too, and ought to have a wider flow than through the pages of the "Examiner." It ought to be read not by two thousand, but by two million persons. I wish there were a popular organ, like the "Ledger" (in circulation), for the diffusion of the best thoughts, where the best minds among us could speak *of* the country *to* the country, for never was there a people that more needed to be wisely spoken to. And you are especially fitted to speak to it. Your conservative position in our Unitarian body, however it may fare among *us*, would help you with the people.

As to your position, I don't know but I am as conservative as you are. That is, I don't know but I believe in the miracles as much as you do. The difference between us is, that I do not feel the miraculous to be so essential a part of Christianity. Yet I see and feel the force of what you say about it. And the argument is put in that article of yours with great weight and power. For myself, I cannot help feeling that at length the authority of Jesus will be established on clearer, higher, more indisputable and impregnable grounds than any historic, miraculous facts.

To William Cullen Bryant, Esq.

ST. DAVID'S, *Jan.* 26, 1869.

. . . I AM thankful, every day of my life, that I have my own roof over me, and can keep it from crumbling to the ground.   Do not be proud, Sir, when you read this, nor look down from your lordliness, — of owning a dozen houses, and three of them your own to live in, — down, I say, upon my humble gratitude.   Can it be, by the bye, that Cicero had fourteen villas?   I am sure Middleton says so.   I should think they must have been fourteen of what Buckminster, in a sermon, called " bundles of cares and heaps of vexations."

. . . I read a letter of Cicero's to his friend Valerius, this morning, in which he urges him to come and see him, saying that he wants to have a pleasant time with him, — *tecum jocari*, — and says, " When you come this way, don't go down to your Apulia," — to wit, Cummington.   *Nam si illo veneris, tanquam Ulysses, cognosces tuorum neminem.*   Now don't quote Homer to me when you answer, for I am nearly overwhelmed with my own learning.

I wish you could have seen the world here for the last three weeks.   Never was such a splendid winter season. I think it 's something great and inspiring to see the whole broad, bright, white, crystal world, and the whole horizon round, instead of looking upon ,brick houses. But you will say, the human horizon widens in cities. Yes; but if there are six bright points in it you are fortunate, while here, the whole horizon round is sapphire and purple and gold.

Well, peace be with you wherever you are, and with your house. My wife and Mary send love to you all, as I do, [who] am, as ever.

Yours faithfully,

ORVILLE DEWEY.

To his Daughters.

ST. DAVID'S, *Feb.* 23, 1869.

. . . . WE are going on very nicely, neither sick nor sad. Our winter evening readings have been very fortunate this season. First, "Lord Jeffrey's Life and Letters," and now, "Draper's Intellectual Development in Europe." I had read it before, but it is a greater book than I had thought. I must say that I had rather pass my evenings as we do, — some writing, some reading, then a quiet game, and then at my desk again, — than to take the chances of society, in town or country. If I can get you to think as I do, we shall pass a happy life here. Heaven grant that I may not fall into a life of pain! With our good spirits, as they now are, we every day fall into a quantity of dramatic capers that are enough to make a cat laugh, — no *bigger* animal.

Hoping you may have as much folly, — for what saith Paley? "He that is not a fool sometimes, is always one," — and wishing you all merry, I am as ever,

Your loving father,

ORVILLE DEWEY.

Nothing can be imagined more peaceful than the retirement of Sheffield. Removed from the main lines of traffic and travel, even now that a railroad passes through it, the village remains, as it has been for a hundred and fifty years, the quiet centre of the quiet farms spread for four or five miles about it. The Housatonic wanders at its own sweet and lazy will among the meadows, turning and returning upon itself till it has loitered twenty miles in crossing the eight-mile township, but never turning a mill or offering encouragement to any industry but that of the muskrats who burrow in its banks, or the kingfishers who break its glassy surface in pursuit of their prey. No busy factories are there; no rattle of machinery or feverish activity of commerce disturbs the general placidity; and the still valley lies between its enclosing hills as if it were, indeed, that happy Abyssinian vale my father fancied it in his childhood.

The people share the calm of the landscape. Like many New England towns where neither water-power nor large capital offers opportunity for manufactures, and where farming brings but slow returns, the village has been gradually drained of the greater part of its active and enterprising younger population, and is chiefly occupied by retired and quiet persons who maintain a very gentle stir of social life, save for a month or two in summer, when the streets brighten with the influx of guests from abroad.

It must have been very different seventy years ago. Instead of three slenderly attended churches, divided by infinitesimal differences of creed, and larger variations of government and discipline, all the people then were accustomed to meet in one well-filled church; and the minister, a life resident, swayed church and congregation with large and unquestioned rule. There were several doctors with their trains of students, and lawyers of county celebrity, each with young men studying under his direction; and all these made the nucleus of a society that was both gay and thoughtful, and that received a strong impulse to self-development from the isolated condition of a small village in those days. Railroads and telegraphs have changed all this, and scarcely a hamlet is now so lonely as not to feel the great tides of the world's life sweep daily through it, bringing polish and general information with them, but washing away much of the racy individuality and concentrated mental action which formerly made the pith of its being. Sheffield has gained in external beauty and refinement year by year, but, judging from tradition, has lost in intellectual force. There is more light reading and less hard reading, much more acquaintance with newspapers and magazines, and less knowledge of great poets, than in my father's youth; but his love for his birthplace remained unchanged, and his eyes and his heart drank repose from its peaceful and familiar beauty.

To William Cullen Bryant, Esq.

St. David's, *Oct.* 6, 1869.

Dear Bryant, the bountiful, — You are something like grapes yourself. By the bye, it 's no matter what you call me ; "my dear Doctor " is well enough, if you can't do better ; only "my dear Sir " I do hate, between good old friends such as we are, as much as Walter Scott did. But, as I was saying, you are like grapes yourself, — fair, round, self-contained, hanging gracefully upon the life-vine, still full of sap ; shining under the covert of leaves, but more clearly seen, now that the frosts of age are descending, and causing them to fall away ; while I am more like — but I have so poor an opinion of myself, that I won't tell you what. This is no affected self-depreciation. I can't learn to be old, but am as full of passion, impatience, foolishness, blind reachings after wisdom, as ever. Instance : I am angry with the expressman because he did not bring the grapes to-day ; angry with the telegraph because it did not bring a despatch to tell how a sick boy was, under *nine* hours. . . .

Here I am, Thursday morning, on a second sheet, waiting for the grapes. What else, in the mean time, shall I entertain you with ? The flood ! It has been prodigious, the highest known for many years ; water, water all around, from beside the road here to the opposite hill. It is curious to see men running like rats from the deluge, up to their knees in water, on returning from a common walk (fact, happened to the S——s), trying to drive home one way and could n't, — going round to a bridge and finding that swept away, — dams torn down and mills toppled over, and half the "sure and firm-set earth " turned into water-courses and flood-trash. . . .

The afternoon train has arrived, and no grapes. Very angry.

The faithless express, you see, is a great plague to you as well as me ; for not only does it not bring me the grapes, but is the cause of your having this long dawdling letter. Why don't you show up its iniquities? What is a " Post " made and set up for, if not, among other things, to bear *affiches* testifying to the people of their wickedness? The express is the most slovenly agent and the most irresponsible tyrant in the country. What it brings is perhaps ruined by delay, — plants, for instance. No help. " Pay," it says to the station-master, " or we don't leave it." Oh, if I had the gift and grace to send articles to the " Post," from time to time, upon abuses !

Friday. No grapes. More angry.

Saturday. No grapes. I 'm furious.

This last was the record of the afternoon ; but in the evening, at half-past nine, they were sent down from the station, — and in remarkably good order, considering, and in quantity quite astonishing. The basket seemed like the conjurer's hat, out of which comes a half-bushel of flowers, oranges, and what not. We are all very much obliged to you ; and, judging from the appearance of the six heaped-up plates, I am sure, when we come to eat them, that every tooth will *testify*, if it does not speak.

To the Same.

St. David's, Feb. 28, 1870.

My Dear Bryant, — The volume has not come, but the kindness has, and I will acknowledge the one without waiting for the other; especially as it is not a case where one feels it expedient to give thanks for a book before he has read it. We all know the quality of this, from passages of the work printed in advance. It will be *the* translation into English of the Iliad, I think, though not professing to be learned in translations of Homer, still less in the original.

I read your preface in the " Post." Nothing could be better, unless it is your speech at the Williams dinner, which *was* better, and better than any occasional speech you have given, *me judice.*

Great changes are projected in Sheffield, — you will have to come and see them and us, — a widening of the village on the east, towards the meadow and pine knoll, and — what *do* you think? — a railroad to the top of Taghkonic ! 'T is even so — proposed. An eastern company has bought the Egremont Hotel, and the land along the foot of the mountain down as far as Spurr's (a mile), and they talk seriously of a railroad. So the Taghkonic is to be made a watering-place, if the thing is feasible, in quite another sense than that in which it has long sent its streams and cast its lonely shadows upon our valley.

We are having winter at last, and our ice-houses filled with the best of ice, and the prospect is fair for the wood-piles. The books you sent are turning to great account with us. In that and in every way I am obliged to you ; and am, as ever,

Yours truly,

ORVILLE DEWEY.

To Mrs. David Lane.

ST. DAVID'S, *Dec.* 20, 1870.

DEAR FRIEND, — I think I must take you into council, — not to sit upon the case, nor to get up a procession, nor to have the bells rung, if we win ; but just to sympathize, so far as mid-life vigor can, with an aged couple, who have lived together half a century, and would much rather live it over again than not to have lived it at all ; who have lived in that wonderful connection, which binds and blends two wills into one ; who do not say that *no* differences or difficulties have disturbed them, — an attainment beyond human reach, — but who have grown in the esteem and love of each other to this day (at least one of them has) ; one of whom finds his mate more beautiful than when he married her, though the other's condition, in that respect, does n't admit of more or less, being a condition of obstinate mediocrity ; and who, both of them, look with mingled wonder and gratitude to their approaching Golden Wedding Day.

So you can look upon us with pleasure, on the day after Christmas, and think of us as surrounded by all our children and grandchildren. And that is all we shall make, except in our thoughts, of our great anniversary.

Adieu. I shall not descend in this letter to meaner themes, but with our love to you all, am ever,

Your friend,

ORVILLE DEWEY.

From a Note-Book.

April 13, 1871.

FATHER TAYLOR, of Boston, has just died, — a very remarkable person. He was a sailor, and more than forty years ago he came from before the mast into the pulpit. He brought with him, I suppose, something of the roughness of his calling ; for I remember hearing of his preaching in the neighborhood of New Bedford when I first went there, and of his inveighing against paid preachers as wretched hirelings, " rocked upon five feather-beds to hell." This, I was told, was meant for me, as I had just been settled upon the highest salary ever paid in those parts. In after years I became acquainted with him, and a very pleasant and cordial acquaintance it was. His preaching improved in every way as he went on ; the pulpit proved the best of rhetorical schools for him, and he became one of the most powerful and impressive preachers in the country. He was one of nature's orators, and one of the rarest. It was said of him that he showed what Demosthenes meant by " action." The whole man, body and soul, was not only *in* action, but was *an* action concentrated into speech. His strongly built frame, — every limb, muscle, and fibre, — his whole being, spoke.

Waldo Emerson took me to his chapel the first time I ever heard him preach. As we went along, speaking of his pathos, he said, " You 'll have to guard yourself to keep from crying." So warned, I thought myself safe enough. But I was taken down at the very beginning of the service. The prayers of the congregation were asked by the family of a young man, — a sailor, who had been destroyed by a shark on the coast of Africa. In the prayer, the scene was touchingly depicted, — how the poor youth went down to bathe in the summer sea, thoughtless, unconscious of any danger, when he was seized by the terrible monster that lay in wait for him. And then the preacher prayed that none of *us*, going down into the summer sea of pleasure, might sink into the jaws of destruction that were opened beneath. I think the prayer left no dry eyes.

Father Taylor was a man of large, warm-hearted liberality. He was a Methodist; but no sect could hold him. He often came to our Unitarian meetings and spoke in them. In addressing one of our autumnal conventions in New York, I recollect his congratulating us on our freedom from all trammels of prescription, creed, and church order, and exhorting us to a corresponding wide and generous activity in the cause of religion. He was always ready with an illustration, and for his purpose used this : " We have just had a visit in Boston," he said, " from an Indian chief and some of his people. They were invited to the house of Mr. Abbot Lawrence. As Mr. Lawrence received them in his splendid parlor, the chief, looking around upon it, said,, — 'It is very good; it is beautiful;· but I — I walk large ; I go through the woods and hunting-grounds one day, and I rise up in the morning and go through them the next, — I walk large.' Brethren," said the speaker, " walk large."

Taylor's great heart was not chilled by bigotry ; neither was it by theology, nor by philosophy. His prayer was the breathing of a child's heart to an infinitely loving father ; it was strangely free and confiding. I remember being in one of the early morning prayer-meetings of an anniversary week in Boston, and Taylor was there. As I rose to offer a prayer, I spoke a few words upon the kind of approach which we might make to the Infinite Being. Something like this I said, — that as we were taught to believe that we were made in the image of God, and were his children, emanations from the Infinite Perfection, partakers of the divine nature; as the Infinite One had sent forth a portion of His own nature to dwell in these forms of frail mortality and imperfection, and no darkness, no sorrow, nor erring of ours could reach to Him; might we not think, — God knows, I said, that I would be guilty of no irreverence or presumption, — but might we not think that with infinite consideration and pity he looks down upon us struggling with our load; upon our weakness and trouble, upon our penitence and aspiration?

As the congregation was retiring, and I was passing in the aisle, I saw Father Taylor sitting by the pulpit, and he beckoned me aside. "Brother Dewey," he said, in his emphatic way, "did you ever know any one to say what you have been saying this morning?" — "Why," I replied, "does not every one say it?" — "No," he answered; "I have talked with a thousand ministers, and no one of them ever said that."

To *William Cullen Bryant, Esq.*

St. David's, Sept. 12, 1871.

Dear and Venerable, — For it seems you grow old, and count the diminishing days, as a bankrupt his parting ducats. I never heard you say anything of the sort before, and have only thought of you as growing richer in every way. I don't in any way; but though well, considering, I find myself losing strength and good condition every year. That is why I move about less and less, sticking closer to my own bed and board, furnace and chimney-nook, — shelf for shoes, and pegs for coat and trousers.

I am very glad to hear from you, and that you will come and see us on your way home. Don't slip by us. Don't be miserly about time. Odysseus took a long time for his wanderings ; take a hint from the same, not to be in a hurry.

To Mrs. David Lane.

ST. DAVID'S, *Nov.* 25, 1871.

DEAR me! and dear you, yet more. If I *should* write to you " often," what would be the condition of us both? I very empty, and you with a great clatter in your ears. Think of a hopper, with very little grain in it, to keep shaking! It would be a very impolitic hopper.

I am laughing at myself, while I write this, for I am *not* an empty hopper, and if I could "find it in my heart to bestow all my tediousness upon you," you would laugh at me too. Ay, but in what sense would you laugh? That is the question. I laugh at myself, proudly, for calling myself empty ; and you, perhaps, would laugh at me piteously, on finding me so.

But a truce with this nonsense. Anybody will find enough to write who will write out what is within him. Did you ever read much of German letters, — those, for instance, of Perthes and his friends? They are full of religion, as our American letters, I think, are not. We seem to have been educated, especially we Unitarians, to great reserve on this subject. I remember Channing's preaching against so much reserve. It is partly, I believe, a reaction against *profession.* But there is another reason ; and that is, in religion's having become, under a more rational culture, so a part of our whole life and thought and being, that formally to express our feelings upon it seems to us unnecessary, and in bad taste, as if we were to say how much we love knowledge or literature, or how much we love our friends or our children. Much talk of this sort seems to bring a doubt, by implication, upon the very thing talked about. Channing talked perpetually about religion, — that is, everything ran into that, — but never about his own religious feelings.

Do get the life of Perthes, if you have never read it. That and " Palissy the Potter " are among the most interesting biographies I know.

It is grim November weather up here, and I like it. Everything in its place ; and we are having considerable rain, which is more in place, as winter is approaching, than anything else could be. Wife and I are bunged up with colds. No, *I* am ; that ugly epithet can't attach to the grace and delicacy of her conditions and proportions. But alas ! I am losing my old and boasted security against colds. I but went out one evening, to give a lecture at the Friendly Union,[1] and this is the way I

[1] The Sheffield Friendly Union is the name of an association for purposes of social entertainment and culture, which meets one evening in the week, during winter, at a hall in the village, to enjoy music, lectures, reading, dramas, or whatever diversion its managers can procure or its members offer. Dancing and cards are forbidden, but other games are played in the latter part of the evening ; and there is a small but good library, slowly enlarging, and much used and valued by the members. The subscription fee is small, and the meetings are seldom of less than one hundred or two hundred people, many coming three or four miles. The society was started in 1871, and Dr. Dewey took a great interest in it from the first. It was he who chose its name ; and while his health lasted, he was a frequent attendant, and always lectured or read a play of Shakespeare before it two or three times every winter.

pay for it. If there is any barrel in town bigger than my head, I should like to buy it, and get in.

I was sorry not to see Coquerel, and pleased to hear that he had the grace to be disappointed at not seeing me. But I don't *seek* people any more. Why, I don't think I should run in the mud to see Alexis [1] himself. And to a New York lady I suppose that is about the strongest thing I could say.

All send their love to you and yours.

Yours ever,
ORVILLE DEWEY.

To the Same.

ST. DAVID'S, *March* 7, 1872.

DEAR FRIEND — OF ALL MANKIND, — I see you have let them make you President of the Bellevue Local Visiting Association. Was there nobody else that could take that charge? Was it not enough for you to have the Forty-ninth Street Hospital to look after? But M. says, " Let her ; let her work." And she talks about " living while you live," and comes at me with such saws. Saws they may well be called, for they sever prudence from virtue, instead of making them a rounded whole. The fact is, nobody has any sense — I mean the perfect article — but me. For I say, what if " living while you live " comes to not living at all? Is *that* what you call working? And why not let other people work? Is Mrs. Lane to be made the queen bee of New York philanthropy, and to become such an enormous conglomeration of goodness

---

[1] The Grand Duke of Russia, whose visit to New York was the excitement of the day.

that she can't get out of her hospital hive to visit her friends, nor let them visit *her*, with any chance of seeing her? And is nobody worth caring for unless he has been knocked down in the street, and has got a broken leg or a fever?

I am quite serious, though you may not think so. I do not like your taking another hospital, or the visitation of it, in charge. It must devolve an immense deal of care and thinking upon somebody. There 's reason in all things, or ought to be. Your brains and eyes ought to be spared from overwork. We shall hear of you as blind or paralytic next.

   .   .   .   .

Tell your mother that we have to "stand to our colors " for the climate of New England nowadays, else they would be all blown away. It 's awful weather in New York too, I hope. I don't go out much. Really, if this March were not a march to spring, it would be a hard campaign. With love to all your house, I am, as affectionately and warmly as the weather will permit,

Yours,

ORVILLE DEWEY.

To Rev. Henry W. Bellows, D.D.

ST. DAVID'S, *Feb.* 21, 1873.

DEAR FRIEND, — I need not say we shall be rejoiced to see you. Don't be proud, but it is "real good " of you. If "a saint in crape is twice a saint in lawn," a friend in winter is twice a friend of any other season. "If I shall be away?" Only by being *beside myself* could I be away in winter. "Or have other guests." No, indeed, they don't fly like doves to our winter windows. But the white snowflakes do, and it will do your eyes good to see the driven and drifted snow. We have had a very quiet winter, and few drifts, but to-night, I see, is blowing them up. I should not wonder if they blocked the road and kept my letter back a day or two.

To the Same.

March 5, 1873.

. . . WE thought you might be stopped somewhere, and not to go at all would be the worst "go" that could be.   All Sunday we kept speaking about it, with a sort of feeling as if we were guilty of something ; so that I felt it necessary to calm the family distress by setting up a new and original view of the whole matter, to this effect : " Well, if he has been stopped over Sunday at the State Line, or Chatham Four Corners, it may be the most profitable Sunday he ever passed. What a time for calm meditation and patience ! — better things than preaching.   You know he lives in a throng ; this will be a blessed ' retreat,' as the Catholics call it.   He is stomach-full of prosperity ; perhaps he needed an alterative.   Introspection is a rare thing in our modern outward-bound life.   He is accustomed to preach to great admiring audiences ; to-day he will preach to his humble, non-admiring self."

Well, I am glad, — so ready, alas ! are we to escape from discipline, — but I *am* glad that you got through, though by running a gauntlet that we shivered to read of. But you did get through, and got home, having accomplished what you went for. Any way, you did *us* so much good that it paid, on the great scale of disinterested benevolence, for a great deal of trouble on your part.

> "Shall we be carried to the skies
> On flowery beds of ease?"

. . . .

With our love to the entire quaternity of you,
Yours ever,

ORVILLE DEWEY.

On his eightieth birthday my father was surprised and touched by the gift acknowledged in the next letter to the old friend through whose hands it was conveyed to him. It will be seen, that in the private letter accompanying this response, he was under the mistaken impression that Mr. Bryant was writing a history of the United States, while, in fact, he was merely editing one written by Mr. Gay.

To William Cullen Bryant, Esq.

SHEFFIELD, *March* 30, 1874.

MY DEAR SIR AND FRIEND, — Your letter, which came to me to-day, crowns the birthday tokens and expressions of regard which I have received from many. It takes me entirely by surprise, only exceeded by the gratification I feel at having such a generous gift from my friends in New York and elsewhere. I thank them, and more than thank them, and you, for being the medium of it. I am alike honored by both. Thanks is a little word, and dollars is called a vulgar one; but two thousand two hundred and sixty-two of the latter, and the sense I have of the former, make up, I feel, no vulgar amount.

I don't know how you will convey to my old parishioners and friends my sense of their good will and good esteem, but I pray you will do so as largely as you can; and to Dr. Osgood particularly for the care and trouble I cannot but suppose he has taken in this matter. I am sure it will please them to know, that on account of the increased expenses of living, and the failure of some stocks, this gift is especially convenient to me, and will help to smooth — for the steps now, perhaps, but few — my remaining path in life.

I am, as ever, with great regard,

Your friend,
ORVILLE DEWEY.

To the Same.

ST. DAVID'S, *March* 30, 1874.

DEAR BRYANT, — I send you enclosed my formal answer to your letter on behalf of my kind friends in New York and elsewhere, but I must have a little private word with you. . . . That speech of yours at the Cooper[1] was one of the best, if not the very best, of the little speeches that you have ever made. But good gracious! to think of your undertaking a Popular History of the United States! The only thing that troubles me for you is the taskwork of investigation. Supposing you to have the whole subject in your mind, nobody can write the story better than you can. Put fire into it, my dear Senior; or rather do what you can do, — for I have seen it, — so state things in your calm way as to put fire into others.

---

[1] A meeting at the Cooper Institute.

This is a great work that you have in hand ; everybody will read it, and will be instructed by it, I trust, in sound politics, and stirred to holy patriotism.

Ever yours, faithfully,
ORVILLE DEWEY.

To the Same.

ST. DAVID'S, *Aug.* 6, 1874.

WE have had a good deal of conference together, you and I, old friend, but I do not know that we ever discussed the subject of bores. You have raised questions about it, both for the next world and this, which, though I said nothing about them in my book, as you facetiously remark, it may surprise you to know are quite serious with me. Thus, if there is to be society in the next world, what can save it from the weariness of society in this, — save it, in other words, from bores? The spiritists say that Theodore Parker gives lectures there to delighted audiences. And, truth to say, I do not know of any other social occupation that would be so satisfactory as that of teaching or learning. What is all the highest conversation *here*, but that by which we help one another — teaching or being taught — to higher and juster thoughts? That would shake off the yoke of boredom under which so many groan now. If, instead of eternal surface-talk, we could strike down to reality, to something that interested our minds and hearts, fresh streams would flow over the arid waste of commonplace. Real thoughts would be a divining-rod. If, when a man calls upon me, he could teach me something upon which he knows more than I do, or I could do the same for him, neither of us would be bored.

Do I not talk like a book? But, to be serious, so much am I bored with general society, that I am inclined to say I had rather live as I do here in Sheffield. Is n't Cummington a blessed place for that? But alas! it don't save you from being bored with letters, — *vide*, for example, this, perhaps, which I am now writing.

But, O excellent man! though you never bored me in talk, you have lately bored into me; I will tell you how.

A month or two ago a book agent came to me, asking me to subscribe for "Bryant's Pictorial America." I was astonished, and said, "Do you mean to say that Mr. Bryant's name will appear on the titlepage of this work, and that it was written by him?" — "Certainly," was the reply; "not that he has written the whole, but much of it." I could n't believe that, and was declining to subscribe, when my wife — that woman has a great respect for you — called me aside and said, "I wish you would take this book." So I turned back and said, "My wife wants this book, and I will subscribe for it." Well, yesterday the first volume came to hand; and, turning to the titlepage, I found *edited* by W. C. B., which means not that you wrote the book, but seem to father it. · Next year a man will come along with "Bryant's Popular History of the United States of America," and the year after, for aught I know, with "Specimens of American Literature," by W. C. B. I do seriously beseech you, my friend, to look into this. These people take advantage of your good-nature; and ill-nature will spring up about it, if this kind of thing goes on. With love to J., and hoping to see you,

Yours ever,

ORVILLE DEWEY.

To the Same.

St. David's, *Sept.* 14, 1874.

Dear Friend, — It was very amiable in you to write to me on getting home ; and, not to be outdone, I am going to write to you ; and for the both sad and amusing story you repeated of Mr. G., I will give you a recital of the same mixed character.

I have been this evening to hear the Hampton Singers. Two of them, by the bye, are our guests, — for we offered to relieve the company of all expenses if they would come down here, — and very well behaved young men they are. The tunes they sing, remember, come from the tobacco and cotton fields of the South. I asked them how many they had. They said, two hundred, and that there were a great many more which were sung by the slaves of the old time. Is it not an extraordinary thing ? I do not believe that more than *ten* are ever heard from the farms of New England. I don't remember more than *five*. What a musical nature must these people have ! I imagine that no such musical development, no such number of songs, can be found among any other people in the world.

The chief interest with me in hearing them was thinking where they came from, what was the condition that gave birth to them. Their singing is both sad and amusing, but partakes more of aspiration than of dejection ; and it has not a particle of hard or revengeful feeling towards their masters. But here again, — what sort of a people it is ! The words of their songs are of the poorest ; not a soul among them has arisen to give us anything like the German folk-songs, or like Burns's. Still, their songs are a wonderful revelation from the house of bondage ; such sadness, such domestic tenderness, such feeling for one another, such hopes and hallelujahs lifted above this world, where there was no hope !

Heartily yours,

ORVILLE DEWEY.

To Rev. Henry W. Bellows, D.D.

ST. DAVID'S, *Nov.* 24, 1874.

DEAR FRIEND, — I have read and read again what you have written upon the Great Theme. What a subject for a *letter !* And yet the most we can say seems to avail no more than the least we can say. Some one, or more, of the old Asiatics — I forget who — says he "would have no *word used* to describe the Infinite Cause." I suppose no word can be found that is not subject to exceptions. The final words that I fall back upon are *righteousness* and *love*. Even the word *intelligence* is perhaps more questionable. If it implies anything like *attention* to one person and thing or another, anything like imagination, comparison, reasoning, we must pause upon the use of it. To say *knowledge* would perhaps be better, for there must be *something* that knows its own works and creatures. To suppose the cause of all things to be ignorant of all things seems like a contradiction in terms. It would be, in fact, to deny a cause ; to say that the universe is *what it is* without any cause. Even that awful supposition, the only alternative to theism, comes over the mind sometimes ; but if I were to accept it, "the very stones would cry out" against me.

Oh, my friend, I lie down in my bed every night think-ing of God ; and I say sometimes, is it not a false idea of greatness, to suppose the Infinite Greatness cannot regard *me* ? Worldly great men shrink from little things, from little people. But it is not so with the most truly great. They come down in art, in poetry, in eloquence, in true learning, to instruct and lift up the lowly and ignorant.

And again I say, when trying to reckon up the account with myself before I sink into unconsciousness, thinking of this bodily frame, with its million harmonious agencies, and the mind more wonderful still; or when I sit down in my daily walk, and sink into the bosom of nature, with light and life and beauty all around me, — surely the author of all this is good. It would be monstrous fatuity to question it, utter blindness not to see it.

And yet again, I say, there are *relations* between the finite and the Infinite, between my mind and the Infinite mind, between my weakness and the Infinite power. And why should conscious Omnipresence in our conception *localize* it? Presence is not limited to contact. I am present here in my room; I am present in the field where I sit down. Why, with the whole universe, should not the Infinite Being thus be present?

What a wonderful chapter is the twenty-third of Job! There are many things in that book which touch upon our modern experience. "Oh! that I knew where I might find him, that I might come near even to his seat. I go forward, but he is not there, and backward, but I cannot perceive him; on the left hand where he doth work, but I cannot behold him; for he hideth himself on the right hand that I cannot see him." But I come with undoubting faith to Job's conclusion: "But he knoweth the way that I take; when he hath tried me I shall come forth as gold." There *are* deep trials, at times, in the approach to God, in lifting the weak thoughts of our minds to the

Infinite One ; there are struggles and tears which none may ever witness ; but still I say, " O God, thou art my God, early will I seek thee," — ever will I seek thee. Let him who will, or must, walk out from this fair, bright, glowing world, thrilling all the world in us with joy, upon the cold and dreary waste of atheism ; I will not. I should turn rebel to all the great instincts within me, and all the great behests of nature and life around me, if I did. Ah ! the confounding, ever-troubling difficulty is not to believe, but to *feel* the great Presence all the day long. This is what I think of, and long have, with questioning and pain. What beings should we become — what to one another — under that living and loving sense of the all-good, the all-beautiful and divine within us and around us ! And, for ourselves, what a perfect joy it is to feel that, in this seemingly disturbed universe, all is order, all is right, all is well, all is the best possible !

Yours ever,

ORVILLE DEWEY.

From a Note-Book.

THE pain of erring, — the bitterest in the world, — is it not strange that it should be so bitter? Is it not strange that growth must be attained on such hard terms? Nay, but is it not simply applying the sharpest instrument to the cutting and carving of the finest and grandest form of things on earth, — a noble character?

The work is but begun on earth. Man is the only being in this world whose nature is not half developed, whose powers are in their infancy ; the ideal in whose constitution is not yet, and never on earth, realized. The animal arrives at animal perfection here, — becomes all that it was made to be. The beetle, the dragon-fly, the eagle, is as perfect as it can be. But man comes far short of the ideal that presided over his formation. Any way it would be unaccountable, not to say incredible, that God's highest work on earth should fail of its end, fail of realizing its ideal, fail of being what it was made for. But when the process, unlike that in animals, which is all facility and pleasure, is full of difficulty and pain, then for the unfinished work to be dropped would be, not as if a sculptor should go on blocking out marble statues only to throw them away half finished, but as if he should take the living human frame for his subject, and should cut and gash and torture it for years, only to fling it into the ditch.

To William Cullen Bryant, Esq.

ST. DAVID'S, *Dec.* 22, 1874.

THANK you, my friend, and three times over, for Allibone's volumes. I did want and never expected to have them. But I had no idea Allibone was such a big thing. All the bigger are my thanks. What an ocean of drowned authors it is, — only here and there one with masts up and the flags flying !

My little oracular, pro-Indians admonition was correctly printed, and the changes you made were good.

Do you know that to-day *sol stat?* I don't believe that you mind it in the city as we do in the country. To-day the glorious orb pauses and rests a little, to turn back and march up and along the mountain top, — about a mile and a half a month on the same, — and bring us summer. And there is cheer and comfort in that, though the proverb about the cold strengthening holds for a couple of months.

With our Merry Christmas to you all, I am, all days of the year,

Yours heartily,

ORVILLE DEWEY.

To Rev. Henry W. Bellows, D.D.

ST. DAVID'S, *May* 9, 1875.

MY DEAR FELLOW (of the Royal Society, I mean),— I have had it upon my mind these two or three weeks past to write to you; and I really believe that what most hindered me was that I had so many things to say. And yet, I solemnly declare that I cannot remember now what they were. They were things of evanescent meditation, phases of the Great Questions; but for a week or two I have been saying, I will not weary myself so much with them. So you have escaped this time. One thing, however, I do recall, though not of those questions; and that is, reading the Psalms through for my pillow-book. And it is with a kind of astonishment that I have read them. Did you ever look into them with the thought of comparing them with the old Hindoo and Persian or Mohammedan or Greek utterances of devotion? How cold and formal these are, compared with the earnestness, the entreaty, the tenderness of David and Asaph,— the swallowing up of their whole souls into love, trust, and thankfulness! What is this, whence came it, and what does it mean? This phenomenon in Judæa, how are you to explain it, without supposing a special inspiration breathed into the souls of men from the source of all spiritual life and light? The Jewish nature was not more keen than the Greek, or perhaps the Arabians, yet all their religious utterances are but apothegms in presence of the Jewish vitality and experience. I do not deny their grandeur and beauty; but the Bible brings me into another world of thought and feeling, — into a new creation. And when we take into the account the Gospels, we seem to be brought alike out of the old philosophy and the new, — out both from the old formalism and the vast inane and unknown, which the science of to-day conceives of, into new and living relations with the Infinite Love and Goodness. In this, for my part, I rest.

To the Same.

St. David's, July 24, 1875.

My Dear Friend, — Thank you for one of your good, long, thoughtful letters. My thoughts in these days run in other directions. I cannot tell you what they are; no language can; at least, I never used any that did. Almost all human experience has been described; but what are the thoughts and feelings of a man who says with himself as he walks along upon the familiar path, " A few more steps and I shall be gone; — what and where shall I be then?" No mortal speech can tell. Meditations come, you may imagine, at such a crisis in one's being, too vast, too trying for utterance. Wearied and weighed down by them, I sometimes say, " I will think no more about it; all my thinking will alter nothing that is to be; what can I do but lay myself on the bosom of that Infinite Goodness, in which, without doubting, I believe? What would I have other than what God appoints?"

Yet, after all, I am far from losing my interest in the world I am leaving. I am much struck with what you say about the press, — the money interest involved, and the direction which that interest is likely to give it. I wish there were a distinct education for editorship, as there is for preaching, or for the lawyer or physician. There is an article of Greg's in the last " Contemporary Review," following out his " Rocks Ahead," that it has distressed me to read. The great danger now is the rise of the lower and laboring classes against capital and intelligence. And nothing will save the world, but for the higher classes to rouse themselves to do their duty, — in politics, in education, and in consideration and care for the lower. Have you seen the pamphlet of Miss Octavia Hill, of England? That is the spirit, and one kind of work that is wanted. O women ! instead of clamoring for your rights, come up to this !

This is the most beautiful summer that I remember. I am glad to hear of your enjoying it, and of the bevy of young people around you. Such I see every day in the street and the grounds, as if Sheffield were the very paradise of the young and gay.

To William Cullen Bryant, Esq.

ST. DAVID'S, *Dec.* 30, 1875.

DEAR FRIEND, — . . . I am glad to have your opinion of Emerson's and Whittier's verse Collections, and especially your good opinion of Cranch's translation, for I am much interested in him. . . .

My own reading runs very much in another direction, among those who "reason of" the highest things. Especially I have been interested in what those old atheists, Lucretius and Omar Khayyam, say. Have you seen the " Rubaiyat " of the latter? And, by the bye, have you an English translation of Lucretius's " De Rerum Natura "? It must be a small volume, only six books; and if it is not too precious an edition, I pray you to lend and send it to me by mail.

What atheism was to the minds of these two men amazes me. Lucretius was an Epicurean in life, perhaps, as well as philosophy, but I want to understand *him* better. I want to see whether he anywhere laments over the desolation of his system. That a man of his power and genius should have accepted it calmly and indifferently, is what I cannot understand. As for Omar, he seems to turn it all into sport. " Don't think at all," is what he says; " drown all thought in wine." But he writes very deftly, and I cannot but think that his resort is something like the drunkard's, — to escape the great misery.

To Rev. Henry W. Bellows, D.D.

ST. DAVID'S, *Jan.* 11, 1876.

. . . IT is n't everybody that can turn within, and ask such questions as you do. But though I laughed at the exaggeration, I admire the tendency. I suppose nobody ever did much, or advanced far, without more or less of it. But your appreciation of others beats your depreciation of yourself. For me, I am so poor in fact and in my own opinion, that, — what do you suppose I am going to say? — that I utterly reject and cast away the kind things you say of me? No, I don't; that is, I *won't.* I am determined to make the most of them. For, to be serious, I have poured out my mind and heart into my preaching. I have written with tears in my eyes and thrills through my frame, and why shall I say, it is nothing? Nay, though I have never been famed as a preacher, I do believe that what I have preached has told upon the hearts of my hearers as deeply, perhaps, as what is commonly called eloquence. But when you speak of my work as "put beyond cavil and beyond forgetfulness," I cover my face with my hands, with confusion.

But enough of personalities, except to say that I think you exaggerate and fear too much the trials that old age, if it come, will bring upon you. Not to say that your temperament is more cheerful and hopeful than mine, you are embosomed in interests and friendships that will cling about you as long as you live. I am comparatively alone. . . .

But after all, the burden of old age lies not in such questions as these. It is a solemn crisis in our being, of which I cannot write now, and probably never shall.

> "Wait the great teacher, Death, and God adore."

That is all I can do, except reasonably to enjoy all the good I have and all the happiness I see. Of the latter, I count A.'s being "better," and of the former, your friendship as among the most prized and dear.

With utmost love to you all,

ORVILLE. DEWEY.

To William Cullen Bryant, Esq.

ST. DAVID'S, *March* 14, 1876.

MY DEAR FRIEND, — I have begun to look upon myself as an old man. I never did before. I have felt so young, so much at least as I always have done, that I could n't fairly take in the idea. The giftie has n't been gi'ed me to see myself as others see me. Even yet, when they get up to offer me the great chair, I can't understand it. But at length I have so far come into their views as seriously to ask myself what it is fit for an old man to do, or to undertake. And I have come to the conclusion that the best thing for me is to be quiet, to keep, at least, to my quiet and customary method of living,—in other words, to be at home. My wife is decidedly of that opinion for herself, and, by parity of reasoning, for me ; and I am inclined to think she is right.

This parity, however, does not apply to you. You are six months younger than I am, by calendar, and six years in activity; you go back and forth like Cicero to his country villas ; pray stop at my door some day, and let me see you.

You see where all this points. I decide not to go to New York at present, notwithstanding all the attractions which you hold out to me. I don't feel like leaving home while this blustering March is roaring about the house. And from the mild winter we have had, I expect it to grow more like a lion at the end.

With love to J. and Miss F.,

Your timid old friend,

ORVILLE DEWEY.

To Rev. Henry W. Bellows, D.D.

Aug. 7, 1876.

DEAR FRIEND, — I can't be quite still, though I have nothing to say but how good you must be, to see so much good in others ! That is what always strikes me

in your *oraisons funèbres*, and equally, the fine discrimi-
nation you always show. And both appear in your loving notice of my volume.[1] Well, I take it to heart, and
accept, though I cannot altogether understand it. Such
words, from such a person as you, are a great thing to
me. It is to me a great comfort to retire from the scene
with such a testimony, instead of a bare civil- dismissal,
which is all I was looking for from anybody.

Mr. Dewey was urged to the publication of this
last volume of sermons by several of his most
valued friends; and its warm acceptance by the
public justified their opinion, and gave him the
peculiar gratification of feeling that in his old age
and retirement his words could yet have power
and receive approbation.

Rev. J. W. Chadwick wrote a delightful review
of the book in the " Christian Register;" and,
supposing that the notice was editorial, my father
wrote to Mr. Mumford, then editor, as follows:

SHEFFIELD, *Nov.* 22, 1876.

MY DEAR SIR, — It is taking things too much *au
sérieux*, perhaps, to write a letter of special thanks for
your notice of my volume in last week's "Register."
If I ought to have passed it over as the ordinary editorial courtesy, I can only say that it did not seem to
me as such merely, but something heartier, — and finer,
by itself considered. I was glad to have praise from
such a pen. You will . better understand the pleasure

---

[1] The " Two Great Commandments."

that it gave me, when I tell you that I set about the publication of that volume with serious misgiving, feeling as if the world had had enough of me, and it would be fortunate for me to be *let off* without criticism. And now, you and Bellows and Martineau (in a private letter) come with your kind words, and turn the tables altogether in my favor.

I once wrote a review of Channing, and, on speaking with him about it, I found that he had n't read the praise part at all. His wife told me that he *never* read anything of that sort about himself. Well, he was half drowned with it; but for me, I think it is right to express my obligation to you, and the good regard with which I am,

Very truly yours,

ORVILLE DEWEY.

To Rev. Henry W. Bellows, D.D.

ST. DAVID'S, *Jan.* 16, 1877.

DEAR FRIEND, — A New Year's word from you should have had an answer before now, but I have had little to tell you. Unless I tell you of our remarkable snow season, snow upon snow, till it is one or two feet deep; or of the woodpeckers that come and hammer upon our trees as if they were driving a trade; or of our sunsets, which flood the south mountain with splendor, and flush the sky above with purple and vermilion, as if they said, "We are coming, we are coming to bring light and warmth and beauty with us." You can hardly understand, in your city confines, how lovely are these harbingers of spring. And see ! it is only two months off. And withal we are ploughing through the winter in great

. comfort and health.　No parties here, to be sure; no clubs, no oysters and champagne, but pleasant sitting around the evening fire, with loud reading, — Warner's "Mummies and Moslems" just now, very pleasantly written. . . . Have you seen Huidekoper's "Judaism in Rome"?　It has interested me very much.　The Jews, as a people, present the greatest of historic problems. A narrow strip of land, that "scowl upon the face of the world," — a small people, no learning, no art, no military power; yet, by the very ideas proceeding from it, — Christianity included, — has influenced the world more than Greece or Rome.　Huidekoper's book is very learned.　I am glad to see such a book from our ranks.　We have done too little elaborate work in learning or theology.　Your Ministers' Institute promises well for that.

To his Sister, Miss J. Dewey.

St. David's, March 26, 1877.

Your letter has come this afternoon, astonishing us with its date, and leading us to wonder where your whereabouts are now.　Such an *ignis fatuus* you have proved for the month past !　With plans· of goings and comings, with engagements and disengagements, you· have slipped by us entirely, so that the kind of assurance I have had that you would come and pass two or three weeks with us before going eastward has come utterly to nought.　You *should* have come; our chances of seeing one another are narrowing every year.　But we will not dwell gloomily upon it.　We may live three or four years longer, — people do; and I think I am more afraid of a longer than of a shorter term.

The "pain at heart," of which you speak at putting a wider space between us, is what I, too, have felt ; and your thoughts, taken literally, are pleasant, while spirit-ualized, they are our only resource. Yes, the heavenly spaces unite us, while the earthly separate. Oh ! could we *know* that we shall meet again when the earthly scene closes ! But what we do not know, we hope for, and I think the supports of that hope increase with me. *Development for every living creature*, up to the highest it can reach, is the law of its nature ; and why, according to that law, should not the poorest human creatures — the very troglodytes, the cave-dwellers — rise, till all that is infolded in their being should be brought forth? Where and how, is in the counsels and resources of infinite power and goodness. Where and how creatures should begin to exist would be as much mysterious to *us* as where and how they should go on.

To Rev. Henry W. Bellows, D.D.

St. David's, *April* 22, 1877.

Dear Hospitality, — I minded much what you said about my coming down in May, but I have been so dis-couraged about myself for six weeks past, that I have not wanted to write to you, — besieged by rheumatism from top to toe ; in my ankle, so that I could not walk, only limp about ; in my left arm, so that I could not lift it to my head, and, of course, a pretty uncomfortable housekeeper all that time. Nevertheless, I expect May to bring me out again, and do think sometimes that I may take C. with me, and run down for two or three days. . . . I am reading the Martineau book, skip-pingly. . . . It seems that Miss M. was not an atheist, after all. She believed in a First Cause, only denying that it is the God of theology, — which who does *not* deny? — denying, indeed, with Herbert Spencer, that it is knowable. But if they say that it is not knowable, how do they know but it is that which they deny?

Miss Martineau's passing out of this world in utter indifference as to what would become of her, seems to me altogether unnatural, on her ground or any other. Any good or glad hold on existence implies the desire for its continuance. She had no. hope nor wish for it, as well as no belief in it.

As to belief in it, or hope of it, why should not the law of development lead to such a feeling? The plant, having within it the power to produce flower and fruit, does not naturally die till it comes to that maturity. The horse or ox attains to its full strength and speed before its life is ended. Why should it not be so with man? His powers are not half, rather say not one-hundredth part, developed, when he arrives at that point which is called death. Development is impossible to him, unless he continues to exist, and to go onward. And why should not the same argument apply to what may trouble some people to think of, — that is, to the three hundred and fifty millions of China, or even the troglodytes, the cave-dwellers? To our weakness and ignorance, it may seem easier to sweep the planet clean every two or three generations. But of the realms and resources of Infinite Power, what can we know or judge?

Until this spring, my father's health had been exceptionally good, notwithstanding his allusions to increasing infirmities. Indeed, apart from his

brain trouble, he had always been so well that any
interruption to his physical vigor astonished and
rather dismayed him. His sleep was habitually
good, and his waking was like that of a child,
frolicsome in the return to life. He was never
merrier than early in the morning, and his toilet
was a very active one. He took an air-bath for
fifteen minutes, during which he briskly exercised
himself, — and this custom he thought of great
importance in hardening the body against cold.
Then, after washing, dressing, and shaving,
breakfast must come at once, — delay was not
conducive to peace in the household; and immediately after breakfast he sat down to his desk
for one, two, or three hours, as the case might be.
He was singularly tolerant of little interruptions,
although he did not like to have any one in his
room while he was writing, and when his morning's task was done, especially if he were satisfied
with it, he came out in excellent spirits, and ready
for outdoor exercise. He walked a great deal in
New York, but never without an errand. It was
very seldom, either in town or country, that he
walked for the walk's sake; but at St. David's
he spent an hour or two every day at hard work
either in the garden or at the wood-pile, and made
a daily visit in all weathers to the village and the
post-office.

, After his early dinner he invariably took a
nap; and after tea, went again to his desk for an
hour, and then came to the parlor for the even-

ing's amusement, whether reading, or music, or talk, or a game of whist, of which he was very fond; and in all these occupations his animation was so unfailing, his interest so cordial, that family and guests gladly followed his leadership.

But in this spring of 1877 the rheumatic attack of which he speaks was the beginning of a state of languor which in July became low bilious fever. He was not very ill; kept his bed only one day, and by the autumn recovered sufficiently to walk out; but from that time he was an invalid, and he never again left his home.

To Rev. Henry W. Bellows, D.D.

St. David's, *May* 4, 1877.

Dear Friend, and Friends, — I see that I cannot do it. You ought to be glad, not that I *cannot*, and indeed that would not be strictly true, but that I do not judge it best. I really think that I myself should be afraid of a man, that is, of a man-*visitor*, in his eighty-fourth year. But what decides me now is that my rheumatism still holds on to me, and does not seem inclined to let me go, or rather to let go of me. This weather, chilly and penetrating to the bones and marrow, is a clencher. I do not walk, but only creep about the house, and can't easily dress myself yet; all which shows where I ought to be. What a curious thing it is! I had n't a bit of rheumatism all winter till March came, and *never* had any before. Was n't it the Amalekites that were smitten "hip and thigh"? Well, I am an Amalekite, and no more expected to be knocked over so than they did.

I have read with extraordinary pleasure Frank Peabody's sermon on " Faith and Freedom." I saw it in the " Index." I don't know when I have read anything so fine, from any of our young men. . . . As to the limitations of free-will, even more marked than those of heredity and association are those imposed by the law of our nature. I am not free to think that two and two make five, or that a wicked action is good and right. But am I not free to *pursue* the worst as well as the best? But I am not fit to *discuss* anything.

To the Same.

Dec. 13, 1877.

YESTERDAY the mail brought me Furness's new book, " The Power of Spirit," and I have already read half of it. It seems to be the finishing up of what may be called his life-work, that is, the setting forth of the character of the Master. The book is very interesting, and not merely a repetition of what he has said before. To be sure, I cannot go along with him when he maintains that the power of Christ's spirit *naturally* produced those results which are called miracles. You know what Stetson said, — that if that were true, Channing ought to be able to cure a cut finger. But the earnestness, the eloquence, the spirit of faith pervading the book are very charming. Look into it, if you can get hold of it. The chapter on Faith in Christ is very admirable, and that on Easter is a very curious and adroit piece of criticism. I wish that Furness would not be so confident, considering the grounds he goes upon, and that he would not write so darkly upon the materialism of the age.

To the Same.

ST. DAVID'S, *Feb.* 1, 1878.

How I should like to take such a professional bout as you have had ! Now I wish you could sit down by my side and tell me all about it. I think preaching was always my greatest pleasure ; and in my dreams now I think I am oftenest going to preach. People try to sum up the good that life is to them. I think it lies most in activity. Bartol, and that grand soul, Clarke, discussed it much.

To the Same.

May 13, 1878.

DEAR FRIEND,— I am so much indebted to your good long letters, that I am ashamed to take my pen to reply. . . .

Your Sanitary Commission Report came to hand two days ago, and I began at once to read it, and finished it without stopping, greatly interested in all the details, and greatly pleased with the spirit. What a privilege to be allowed to take such a part in our great struggle ! I cannot write about it, nor anything else, as I want to. I don't know why it is, but I have a strange reluctance to touch my pen.

I see that the death of Miss Catherine Beecher is announced. There were fine things about her. What must she not have suffered, of late years ! But I am disposed to say of the release of every aged person, " Euthanasia."

16*th.* I will finish this and get it off to you before Sunday. You have a great deal to do before vacation. Let me enjoin it upon you to *have* a vacation when the time comes. Don't spend your strength and life too fast. Live to educate those fine boys. Thank you for sending us their picture. See what Furness does. That article on Immortality is as good as anything he ever wrote. Did you read the paper on the Radiometer in the last " Popular Science "? What a (not *world* merely) but universe do we live in ! I am not willing to go out of the world without knowing all I can know of these wonders that fill alike the heavens above and every inch of space beneath. What a glorious future will it be, if we may spend uncounted years in the study of them ! And, notwithstanding the weight of matter-of-fact that seems to lie against it, I think my hope of it increases. This blessed sense of what it is to *be*, — this sweetness of existence, — why should it be given us to be lost forever?

To the Same.

St. David's, *June* 16, 1878.

. . . One point in your letter strikes very deep into my experience, — that in which you speak of my " standing so long upon the verge." To stand as I do, within easy reach of such stupendous possibilities, — that of being translated to another sphere of existence, or of being cut off from existence altogether and forever, — does indeed fill me with awe, and make me wonder that I am *not* depressed or overwhelmed by it. Habit is a stream which flows on the same, no matter how the scenery changes. It seems as if routine wore away the very sense of the words we use. We speak often of immortality; the word slides easily over our lips; but do we consider what it means? Do you ever ask yourself whether, after having lived a hundred thousands or millions of years, you could still desire to go on for millions more? — whether a limited, conscious existence could bear it?

L—— read the foregoing, and said, " I don't see any need of considering matters so entirely out of our reach ; " but the question is, can we help it? Fearfully and wonderfully are we made, but in nothing, perhaps, more than this, — that we are put upon considering questions concerning God, immortality, the mystery of life, which *are* so entirely beyond our reach to comprehend.

To the Same.

ST. DAVID'S, *July* 19, 1879.

DEAR FRIEND, — After our long silence, if it was the duty of the ghost to speak first, I think it should have been me, who am twenty years nearer to being one than you are ; but it would be hardly becoming in a ghost to be as funny as you are about Henry and the hot weather. A change has come now, and the dear little fellow may put as many questions as he will. It is certainly a very extraordinary season. I remember nothing quite so remarkable.

. . . .

Have you Professor Brown's " Life of Choate " by you? If you have, do read what he says of Walter Scott, in vol. i., from p. 204 on. I often turn to Scott's pages now, in preference to almost anything else, as I should to the old masters in painting.

Good-by. Cold morning, — cold fingers, — cold everything, but my love for you and yours.

ORVILLE DEWEY.

To the Same.

ST. DAVID'S, *April* 14, 1880.

MY DEAREST YOUNG FRIEND, — For three or four years I have thought your mind was having a new birth, and now it is more evident than ever. Everybody will tell you that your Newport word is not only finer than mine, but finer, I think, than anything else that has been said of Channing. The first part was grand and admirable; the last, more than admirable, — unequalled, I think. . . .

Take care of yourself. Don't write too much. Your long, pleasant letter to me shows how ready you are to do it. May you live to enjoy the budding life around you. . . .

My writing tells you that I shan't last much longer. *Then* keep fresh the memory of

Your loving friend,

ORVILLE DEWEY.

To the Same.

June 15, 1880.

DEAR FRIEND, — To think of answering *such* a letter as yours of June 5th is too much for me, let alone the effort to do it. It seems absurd for me to have such a correspondent, and would be, if he were not of the dearest of friends. For its pith and keenness, I have read over this last letter two or three times. . . . I see that you won't come here in June. Don't try. That is, don't let my condition influence you. I shall probably, too probably, continue to live along for some time, as I have done. No pain, sound sleep, good digestion, — what must follow from all this, I dread to think of. Only the weakness in my limbs — in the branches, so to say — admonishes me that the tree may fall sooner than I expect.

Love to all,   O. D.

To his Sister, Miss J. Dewey.

St. David's, *Oct.* 13, 1880.

DEAREST SISTER, — Why do you tell me such " tells," when I don't believe a bit in them? However, I do make a reservation for my preaching ten years in New Bedford and ten in New York. *They* could furnish about the only " tells " in my life worth telling, if there were any-body to tell 'em. Nobody seems to understand what preaching is. George Curtis does his best two or three times a year. The preacher has to do it every Sunday.

I agree with you about Bryant's " Forest Hymn." I enjoy it more than anything he ever wrote, except the " Waterfowl."

Yours always,
ORVILLE DEWEY.

To Rev. Henry W. Bellows, D.D.

St. David's, *Dec.* 24, 1880.

DEAR FRIEND, — My wife must write you about the parcel of books which came to hand yesterday and was opened in the midst of us with due admiration, and with pleasure at the prospect it held out for the winter. My wife, I say; for she is the great reader, while I am, in comparison, like the owl, which the showman said kept up — you remember what sort of a thinking. But, comparisons apart, it is really interesting to see how much she reads ; how she keeps acquainted with what is going on in the world, especially in its philanthropic and religious work.

Then, in the old Bible books she is the greatest reader that I know. I wish you could hear her expatiate on David and Isaiah ; and she is in the right, too. They leave behind them, in a rude barbarism of religious ideas, Egypt and Greece. By the bye, is it not strange that the two great literatures of antiquity, the Hebrew and Grecian, should have appeared in territories not larger than Rhode Island? This is contrary to Buckle's view, who says, if I remember rightly, that the literature of genius naturally springs from a rich soil, from great wealth and leisure demanding intellectual entertainment.

To his Sister, Miss J. Dewey.

ST. DAVID'S, *April* 4, 1881.

DEAREST RUSHE, — . . . I am glad at what you are doing about the " Helps," [1] and especially at your taking in the " Bugle Notes." Of course it gives you trouble, but don't be anxious about it ; 't will all come out right. The book has met with great favor, whereat I am much pleased, as you must be.

Yes, Carlyle's " Reminiscences " must be admired ; but it will take all the sweets about his wife to neutralize his

---

[1] " Helps to Devout Living " is the name of a collection of beautiful and valuable passages, in prose and verse, compiled by Miss J. Dewey, in the second edition of which she included, at her brother's request, Mr. Wasson's " Bugle Notes," a poem which had been for years one of his peculiar favorites.

supreme care for himself, and careless disparagement of almost everybody else. Genius is said to be, in its very nature, loving and generous; it seems but the fit recognition of its own blessedness; was his so? I have been reading again "Adam Bede," and I think that the author is decidedly and unquestionably superior to all her contemporary novel-writers. One can forgive such a mind almost anything. But alas! for this one — . . . . It is an almost unpardonable violation of one of the great laws on which social virtue rests. . . .

Ever yours,
ORVILLE DEWEY.

To Rev. Henry W. Bellows, D.D.

ST. DAVID'S, *June* 30, 1881.

. . . . SINCE reading Freeman Clarke's book, I have been thinking of the steps of the world's religious progress. The Aryan idea, so far as we know anything of it, was probably to worship nature. The Greek idolatry was a step beyond that, substituting intelligent beings for it. Far higher was the Hebrew spiritualism, and worship of One Supreme, and far higher is Isaiah than Homer, David than Sophocles; and no Hebrew prophet ever said, "Offer a cock to Esculapius." So is Christianity far beyond Buddhism; and far beyond Sakya Muni, dim and obscure as he is, are the concrete realities of the life of Jesus. Whether anything further is to come, I tremble to ask; and yet I do ask it.

To the Same.

July 23, 1881.

DEAR, NAY, DEAREST FRIEND, — What shall I say, in what language express the sense of comfort and satisfaction which, first your sermon years ago,[1] and now your letter of yesterday, have given me? Ah! there is a spot in every human soul, I guess, where approbation is the sweetest drop that can fall. I will not imbitter it with a word of doubt or debate. . . .

Come here when you can. With love to all,

Ever yours,

O. D.

To the Same.

ST. DAVID'S, *Sept.* 23, 1881.

DEAR FRIEND, — I am waiting with what patience I can, to hear whether you have been to Meadville or not. . . . In that lovely but just picture which you draw of my wife, and praise her patience at the expense of mine, I doubt whether you fairly take into account the difference between the sexes, not only in their nature, but in their functions. We men take a forward, leading, decisive part in affairs, the women an acquiescent part. The consequence is that they are more yielding, gentler under defeat, than we. When I said, yesterday, " It costs men more to be patient, to be virtuous, than it costs you," — " Oh! oh !" they exclaimed. But it is true. . . .

Sept. 26.

WHAT a day is this ! A weeping nation, in all its thousand churches and million homes, participates in the

---

[1] See p. 358.

mournful solemnities at Cleveland. A great kindred nation takes part in our sorrow. Its queen, the Queen of England, sends her sympathy, deeper than words, to the mourning, queenly relict of our noble President. Never shall I, or my children to the fourth generation, probably, see such a day. Never was the whole world girdled in by one sentiment like this of to-day.

To the Same.

St. David's, *Jan.* 1, 1882.

. . . For a month or two I have been feeling as if the year would never end. But it has come, and here is the beginning of a new. And of what year of the world? Who knows anything about it? Do you? does anybody? What is, or can be, known of a human race on this globe more than 4,000 years ago — or 4,000,000? Oh! this dreadful ignorance! Fain would I go to another world, if it would clear up the problems of this.

.   .   .   .

All I can do is to fall upon the knees of my heart and say, " O God, let the vision of Thy glory never be hidden from my eyes in this world or any other, but forever grow brighter and brighter ! "

.   .   .   .

We have had some bad and some sad times here. M. must tell you about them.

Happy New Year to you all.

Orville Dewey.

It was now nearly five years that my father had trod the weary path of invalidism, slowly weaning him from the familiar life and ties he loved so well. The master's interest was as large, as keen as ever; friendship, patriotism, religion, were even dearer to him than when he was strong to work in their service; but the ready servants that had so long stood by him, — the ear, always open to each new word of hope and promise for humanity; the eye, that looked with eager pleasure on every noble work of man and on every natural object, seeing in all, manifestations of the Divine Goodness and Wisdom; the feet, that had carried him so often on errands of kindness; the hands, whose clasp had cheered many a sad heart, and whose hold upon the pen had sent strong and stirring words through the land,— these gradually resigned their functions, and the active but tired brain, which had held on so bravely, notwithstanding the injury it had received in early life, began to share in the general decline of the vital powers. There was no disease, no deflection of aim nor confusion of thought, but a gentle failure of faculties used up by near a century's wear and tear.

He was somewhat grieved and harassed by the spiritual problems which were always the chief occupation of his mind, and which he now perceived, without being able to grapple with them; and life, with such mental and physical limitations, became very weary to him. But his constitution was so sound, and his health so perfect, that he might have lingered yet a long time, but for his grief and disappointment in the unexpected death

of Dr. Bellows, Jan. 30, 1882. When that beloved friend, upon whose inspiring ministrations
he had counted to soothe his own last hours, was
called first, the shock perceptibly loosened his
feeble hold on life; and truly it seemed as if the
departing spirit did his last service of love by
helping to set free the elder friend whom he
could no longer comfort on earth.   He

" Allured to brighter worlds, and led the way ; "

nor was my father long in following him.   For a
few weeks there was little outward change in his
habits; he ate as usual the few morsels we could
induce him to taste; he slept several hours every
night, and, supported by faithful arms, he came
to the table for each meal till within four days
of his death.   But he grew visibly weaker, and
would sit long silent, his head bent on his breast.
We gathered together in those sad days, and read
aloud the precious series of Dr. Bellows's letters
to us all, but principally to him, — letters radiant
with beauty, vigor, wit, and affection; we read
them with thankfulness and with sorrow, with
laughter and with tears, and he joined in it all,
but grew too weary to listen, and never heard the
whole.   He was confined to his bed but three
days.   A slight indigestion, which yielded to
remedies, left him too weak to rally.   He was
delirious most of the time when awake, and was
soothed by anodynes; but though he knew us
all, he was too sick and restless for talk, trying

sometimes to smile in answer to his wife's caresses, but hardly noticing anything. At one o'clock in the morning of March 21st, his sad moans suddenly ceased, and he opened his sunken eyes wide, — so wide that even in the dim light we saw their clear blue, — looked forward for a moment with an earnest gaze, as if seeing something afar off, then closed them, and with one or two quiet breaths left pain and suffering behind, and entered into life.

For a few days his body lay at rest in his pleasant study, surrounded by the flowers he loved, and the place was a sweet domestic shrine. A grand serenity had returned to the brow, and all the features wore a look of peace and happiness unspeakably beautiful and comforting. Then, with a quiet attendance of friends and neighbors, it was borne to the grave in the shadow of his native hills.

In those last weeks he wrote still a few letters, almost illegible, and written a few lines at a time, as his strength permitted.

To Rev. John W. Chadwick.

SHEFFIELD, *Feb.* 2, 1882.

MY DEAR BROTHER CHADWICK, — A few lines are all that I can write, though many would hardly suffice to express the feeling of what I owe you for your kind letter, and the sympathy it expresses for the loss of my friend.

You will better understand 'what that is, when I tell you that for the last two or three years he has written me every week.

I have also to thank you for the many sermons you have directed to be sent to me. Through others, I know their extraordinary merit, though my brain is too weak for them.

Do you remember a brief interview I had with you and Mrs. Chadwick at the " Messiah " on the evening of the [Semi-] Centennial? It gave me so much pleasure that it sticks in my memory, and emboldens me to send my love to you both.

Ever yours truly,

ORVILLE DEWEY.

To his Sister, Miss J. Dewey.

ST. DAVID'S, *Feb.* 7, 1882.

DEAREST RUSHE, — Your precious, sweet little letter came in due time, and was all that a letter could be. I have not written a word since that came upon us which we so sorrow for, except a letter to his stricken partner, from whom we have a reply last evening, in which she says his resignation was marvellous; that he soon fell into a drowse from morphine, and said but little, but, being told there were letters from me, desired them to keep them carefully for him, — which, alas ! he was never to see.

Dear, I can write no more. I am all the time about the same. Give my love to Pamela.

Ever your loving brother,

ORVILLE DEWEY.

To Rev. John W. Chadwick.

SHEFFIELD, *Feb.* 26, 1882.

MY DEAR CHADWICK, — When Mary wrote to you, expressing the feelings of us all concerning the Memorial Sermon,[1] I thought it unnecessary to write myself, especially as I could but so poorly say what I wanted to say. But I feel that I *must* tell you what satisfaction it gave me, — more than I have elsewhere seen or expect to see. I feel, for myself, that I most mourn the loss of the holy fidelity of his friendship. All speak rightly of his incessant activity in every good work, and I knew much of what he did to build up a grand School of Theology at Cleveland.

You ask what is *my* outlook from the summit of my years. This reminds me of that wonderful burst of his eloquence, at the formation of our National Conference, against the admission to it, by Constitution, of the extremest Radicalism. I wanted to get up and shortly reply, — "You may say what you will, but I tell you that the movement of this body for twenty years to come will be in the Radical direction." In fact, I find it to be so in myself. I rely more upon my own thought and reason, my own mind and being, for my convictions than upon anything else. Again warmly thanking you for your grand sermon, I am,

Affectionately yours,
ORVILLE DEWEY.

---

[1] On Dr. Bellows.

I feel that I cannot close this memoir without
reprinting the beautiful tribute paid to my father
by Dr. Bellows, in his address at the fifty-fourth
anniversary of the founding of the Church of the
Messiah, in New York, in 1879. After comparing him with Dr. Channing, and describing the
fragile appearance of the latter, he said : —

" Dewey, reared in the country, among plain but not
common people, squarely built, and in the enjoyment of
what seemed robust health, had, when I first saw him,
at forty years of age, a massive dignity of person ; strong
features, a magnificent height of head, a carriage almost
royal ; a voice deep and solemn ; a face capable of the
utmost expression, and an action which the greatest
tragedian could not have much improved. These were
not arts and attainments, but native gifts of person and
temperament. An intellect of the first class had fallen
upon a spiritual nature tenderly alive to the sense of divine realities. His awe and reverence were native, and
they have proved indestructible. He did not so much seek
religion as religion sought him. . His nature was charac-
terized from early youth by a union of massive intellectual power with an almost feminine sensibility ; a poetic
imagination with a rare dramatic faculty of representa-.
tion. Diligent as a scholar, a careful thinker, accustomed to test his own impressions by patient meditation,
a reasoner of the most cautious kind ; capable of holding doubtful conclusions, however inviting, in suspense ;
devout and reverent by nature, — he had every qualification for a great preacher, in a time when the old founda-
tions were broken up and men's minds were demanding
guidance and support in the critical transition from the

days of pure authority to the days of personal conviction by rational evidence.

"Dewey has from the beginning been the most truly human of our preachers. Nobody has felt so fully the providential variety of mortal passions, exposures, the beauty and happiness of our earthly life, the lawfulness of our ordinary pursuits, the significance of home, of business, of pleasure, of society, of politics. He has made himself the attorney of human nature, defending and justifying it in all the hostile suits brought against it by imperfect sympathy, by theological acrimony, by false dogmas. Yet he never was for a moment the apologist of selfishness, vice, or folly; no stricter moralist than he is to be found; no worshipper of veracity more faithful; no wiser or more tender pleader of the claims of reverence and self-consecration! In fact, it was the richness of his reverence and the breadth of his religion that enabled him to throw the mantle of his sympathy over the whole of human life. He has accordingly, of all preachers in this country, been the one most approved by the few who may be called *whole men*, — men who rise above the prejudice of sect and the halfness of pietism, — lawyers and judges, statesmen and great merchants, and strong men of all professions. He could stir and awe and instruct the students of Cambridge, as no man I ever heard in that pulpit, not even Dr. Walker, — who satisfied conscience and intellect, but was not wholly fair either to passion or to sentiment, much less to the human body and the world. Of all religious men I have known, the broadest and most catholic is Dewey, — I say religious men, for it is easy to be broad and catholic, with indifference and apathy at the heart. Dewey has cared unspeakably for divine things, — thirsted for God, and dwelt in daily reverence and aspiration before him ; and out of his awe ·and his devotion he has looked with the tenderest eyes of sympathy, forbearance, and patience upon the world and the ways of men ; slow to rebuke utterly, always finding the soul of goodness in things evil, and never assuming any sanctimonious ways, or thinking himself better than his brethren.

" Dewey is undoubtedly the founder and most conspicuous example of what is best in the modern school of preaching. The characteristic feature is the effort to carry the inspiration, the correction, and the riches of Christian faith into the whole sphere of human life ; to make religion practical, without lowering its ideal ; to proclaim our present world and our mortal life as the field of its influence and realization, trusting that what best fits men to live and employ and enjoy their spiritual nature here, is what best prepares them for the future life. Dewey, like Franklin, who trained the lightning of the sky to respect the safety, and finally to run the errands of men on earth, brought religion from its remote home and domesticated it in the immediate present. He first successfully taught its application to the business of the market and the street, to the offices of home and the pleasures of society. We are so familiar with this method, now prevalent in the best pulpits of all Christian bodies, that we forget the originality and boldness of the hand that first turned the current of religion into the ordinary channel of life, and upon the working wheels of daily business. The glory of the achievement is lost in the magnificence of its success. Practical preaching, when it means, as it often does, a mere prosaic recommendation of ordinary duties, a sort of Poor Richard's prudential maxims, is 'a shallow and nearly useless thing. It is a kind of social and moral agriculture with the plough and the spade, but with little 'regard to the enrichment of the soil, or drainage from the depths or irrigation from the heights. The true, practical preaching is that which brings the celestial truths of our nature and our destiny, the powers of the world to come and the terrors and promises of our relationship to the Divine Being, to bear upon our present duties, to animate and elevate our daily life, to sanctify the secular, to redeem the common from its loss of wonder and praise, to make the familiar give up its superficial tameness, to awaken the sense of awe in those who have lost or never acquired the proper feeling of the spiritual mystery that envelops our ordinary life. This was Dewey's peculiar skill. *Poets* had already done it *for* poets, and in a sense neither strictly religious nor expected to be made practical. But for preachers to carry ' the vision and faculty divine ' of the poet into the pulpit, and with the authority of messengers of God, demand of men in their business and domestic service, their mechanical labors, their necessary tasks, to see God's spirit and feel God's laws everywhere touching, inspiring, and elevating their ordinary life and lot, was something new and glorious. Thus Dewey revitalized the doctrine of Retribution by bringing it from the realms of futurity down to the immediate bosoms of men ; and nothing more solemn, affecting, and true is to be found in all literature than his famous two sermons on Retribution, in the first volume of his published works. Spirituality, in the same manner, he called away from its ghostly churchyard haunts, and made it a cheerful angel of God's presence in the house and the shop, where the sense and feeling of God's holiness and love make every duty an act of worship, and every commonest experience an opportunity of divine service. Under the thoughtful, tender yet searching, rational but profoundly spiritual preaching of Dr. Dewey, — where men's souls found an honest and powerful interpreter, and nature, business, pleasure, domestic ties, received a fresh consecration, — who can wonder that thousands of men and women, hitherto dissatisfied, hungry, but with no appetite for 'the bread' called 'of life,' furnished at the ordinary churches, were, for the first time, made to realize the beauty of holiness and the power of the gospel of salvation?

"The *persuasiveness* of Dewey was another of his greatest characteristics. His yearning to convince, his longing to impart his own convictions, gave a candor and patient and sweet reasonableness to his preaching, which has, I think, never been equalled in any preacher of his measure of intellect, height of imagination, and reverence of soul. For he could never lower his ideals to please or propitiate. He was working for no immediate and transitory effects. He could use no arts that entangled, dazzled, or frightened; nothing but truth, and truth cautiously discriminated. His sermons were born of the most painful labors of his spirit; they were careful and finished works, written and rewritten, revised, corrected, improved, almost as if they had been poems addressed to the deliberate judgment of posterity. They possess that claim upon coming generations, and will, one day, rediscovered by a deeper and better spiritual taste, take their place among the noblest and most exquisite of the intellectual and spiritual products of this century. There are thousands of the best minds in this country that owe whatever interest they have in religion to Orville Dewey. The majesty of his manner, the dramatic power of his action, the poetic beauty of his illustrations, the logical clearness and fairness of his reasoning, the depth and grasp of his hold on all the facts, human and divine, material and spiritual, that belonged to the theme he treated, gave him a surpassing power and splendor, and an equal persuasiveness as a preacher. But what is most rare, his sermons, though they gained much by delivery, lose little in reading, for those who never heard them. They are admirably adapted to the pulpit, none more so ; but just as wonderfully suited to the library and to solitary perusal. I am not extravagant or alone in this opinion. I know that so competent a critic as James Martineau holds them in equal admiration.

"I shall make no excuse for dwelling so long upon Orville Dewey's genius as a preacher. No plainer duty exists than to commend his example to the study and imitation of our own preachers ; and no exaltation that the Church of the Messiah will ever attain can in any probability equal that which will always be given to it as the seat of Dr. Dewey's thirteen years' ministry in the city of New York. Of the tenderness, modesty, truthfulness, devotion, and spotless purity of his life and character, it is too soon to utter all that my heart and knowledge prompt me to say. But, when expression shall finally be allowed to the testimony which cannot very long be denied free utterance, it will fully appear that only a man whose soul was haunted by God's spirit from early youth to extreme old age could have produced the works that stand in his name. The man is greater than his works."

In the August following my father's death, an appropriate service was held in his memory at the old Congregational Church in his native village. It was the church of his childhood, from whose galleries he had looked down with childish pity upon the sad-browed communicants;[1] it was the church to which he had joined himself in the religious fervor of his youth; from it he had been thrust out as a heretic, and for years was not permitted to speak within its walls, the first time being in 1876, when the town celebrated the hundredth anniversary of the Resolution that had marked its Revolutionary ardor, and called upon him, as one of its most distinguished citizens, to preach upon the occasion; and now the old church opened wide its doors in affectionate respect to his memory, and his mourning townspeople met to honor the man they had learned to love, if not to follow.

It was a lovely summer day, full of calm and sunny sweetness. The earlier harvests had been gathered in, and the beautiful valley lay in perfect rest, —

> " Like a full heart, having prayed."

Taghkonic brooded above it in gentle majesty, and the scarce seen river wound its quiet course among the meadows. No touch of drought or decay had yet passed upon the luxuriant foliage; but the autumnal flowers were already glowing

---

[1] See p. 16.

in the fields and on the waysides, and, mingled with ferns and ripened grain, were heaped in rich profusion by the loving hands of young girls to adorn the church. It was Sunday, and people and friends came from far and near, till the building was filled; and in the pervading atmosphere of tender respect and sympathy, the warm-hearted words spoken from the pulpit seemed like the utterance of the common feeling. The choir sang, with much expression, one of my father's favorite hymns, —

" When, as returns this solemn day ; "

and the prayer, from Dr. Eddy, the pastor of the church, was a true uplifting of hearts to the Father of all. The fervent and touching discourse which followed, by Rev. Robert Collyer, minister of my father's old parish, the Church of the Messiah, in New York, recalled the early days of Dr. Dewey's life, and the influences from home and from nature that had borne upon his character, and described the man and his work in terms of warm and not indiscriminate eulogy. The speaker's brow lightened, and his cheek glowed with the strength of his own feeling, and among his listeners there was an answering thrill of gratitude and of aspiration.

Dr. Powers, an Episcopal clergyman, then read a short and graceful original poem, and some cordial and earnest words were said by the two Orthodox ministers present. Another hymn was sung by the whole congregation; and thus fitly closed the simple and reverent service, typical throughout of the kindly human brotherhood which, notwithstanding inevitable differences of opinion, binds together hearts that throb with one common need, that rest upon one Eternal Love and Wisdom.

So would my father have wished it. So may it be more and more!

University Press, Cambridge: John Wilson & Son.